UNMASKED!
THE RISE & FALL OF THE 1920s KU KLUX KLAN

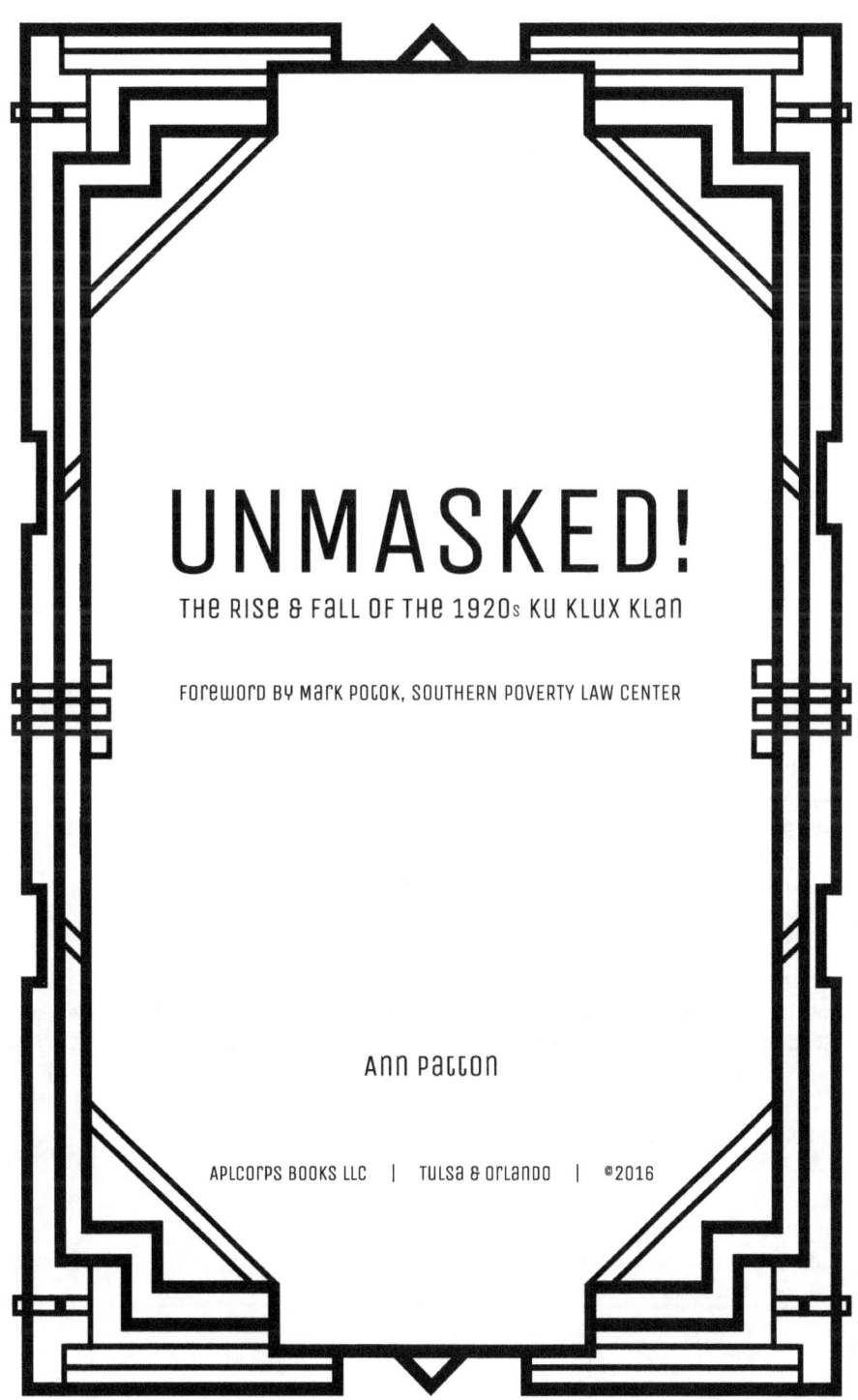

UNMASKED!

THE RISE & FALL OF THE 1920s KU KLUX KLAN

FOREWORD BY MARK POTOK, SOUTHERN POVERTY LAW CENTER

ANN PATTON

APLCORPS BOOKS LLC | TULSA & ORLANDO | ©2016

Published by **APLcorps Books LLC**
Tulsa, Oklahoma, and Orlando, Florida
http://annpatton.net

ISBN 978-0-9839131-5-3

Foreword by Mark Potok, Southern Poverty Law Center
Cover design by William Franklin
Book design by Carlos Moreno

This book is dedicated to the late Neal McNeill Jr., who suggested the story to the author, served as advisor during the research, and contributed invaluable insights during the writing.

Neal was a distinguished City Attorney for Tulsa, Oklahoma from 1980 to 1992.

Neal knew this story well because he was the son of Neal McNeill Sr., a pioneer Oklahoma attorney who opposed the Klan. The elder McNeill served on the state Supreme Court from 1919 to 1925, critical years in the story of the 1920s KKK.

Neal McNeill Jr. died in 2014.

"Human actions are not to be ridiculed,
feared, or hated, but rather to be understood."

(Translation of a Spinoza quote from the front matter of John Moffat Mecklin's
1924 book, *The Ku Klux Klan, A Study of the American Mind*.)

contents

Foreword

Anyone reading the newspapers these days can attest that hate, terror and political violence continue to bedevil our society. As Ann Patton's book about the 1920s Ku Klux Klan shows, the fight against the forces of darkness stretches back across generations.

There are important lessons in this true story of the "second era" Klan that emerged from the ashes of the Reconstruction Klan. A Jazz Age fraternal association, hidden behind masks and united around hatred of Catholics, Jews, black people and others seen as not "100 percent American," mushroomed from a small club into a political powerhouse with stunning reach. The Klan of the '20s used fear, propaganda, terror and a remarkably effective recruiting apparatus that are similar to the techniques used effectively by demagogues today.

People of good will, engaged and often exhausted in the fight against those forces of evil, may find that this instructive story can help replenish their faith in the eventual triumph of justice.

Here at the Southern Poverty Law Center (SPLC), we are dedicated to combating hate, intolerance, and discrimination through education and litigation. An important part of the work of the SPLC, which is a nonprofit public-interest organization based in

Montgomery, Alabama, is tracking the activities of hate groups such as the Ku Klux Klan. Over many years, we have worked to counter hate and its many manifestations. It is a tribute to our nation's strength that the Klan has been unmasked and that its illegal activities are no longer accepted in civilized society. But, as today's headlines prove, the battle continues.

We recognize, as the late civil rights leader Julian Bond once wrote, that there is a history of hate in America—*"not the natural discord that characterizes democracy but the wild, irrational, killing hate that has led men and women throughout our history to extremes of violence against others, simply because of their race, nationality, religion, or lifestyle."*

Those of us working to foster social justice recognize the importance of tracing the long roots of intolerance in our history. Toward that end, I commend this book to you. Ultimately, it is important that we try to understand the villains as well as the heroes in our history and in our midst, if we are to continue building a nation where equality and democracy are prized and preserved.

—Mark Potok
Editor-in-chief of the *Intelligence Report*, Southern Poverty Law Center

prologue

The beginning of the end for the Roaring Twenties' Ku Klux Klan came in the spring, in Indiana, in Madge Oberholtzer's bedroom.

It was 1925; St. Patrick's Day.

Outside, a blessed sun was returning to Indianapolis, warming all it touched. It had been a hard winter. Patchy snow still lingered in shadows, but overcast skies were moving out to a far horizon, above a city in the grip of a bizarre possession. Within, the sunshine cut a slant through lace curtains, tracing intricate patterns across the puzzled face of Madge's doctor.

He was examining the young woman gingerly, noting that she was in shock. Her back was arched in agony. Her body was like ice.

He proceeded methodically. Her face and body were covered with bruises and open wounds. Many were of a peculiar oval shape, about the size and shape of an egg, purplish bruises with jagged cut marks all around. On her right cheek was a dark dented wound, bruised and bloody. The same marks were on her arms, legs, and torso, deepest on her chest.

Her wounds were appalling, but there was something even worse, some other puzzling malady that the doctor could not identify. She lay groaning and delirious, veering toward death.

"Who did this to you, Madge?" he asked gently.

She would not answer.

Beyond the lace curtains, the spring sun rose and fell above a city at the center of an American phenomenon.

It was a time of strange happenings. Masked knights in white bedsheets and pointed hoods were cavorting through Indianapolis, around the Hoosier state, and throughout the country.

This new Knights of the Ku Klux Klan was a different creature from the first KKK that quickened and then faltered in the South after the Civil War, whose work was done through ghostly night-riding and grisly terror, battering blacks back into a kind of legalized slavery.

Roaring Twenties' Klansmen were marching all across America, in an invisible empire millions strong, gathering in Klaverns in every state in the union to a rallying cry of "100 percent Americanism."

Their goal was political power. They intended to take over the government.

Their first enemy was the Pope. They crusaded against the sins of "otherness"—by Catholics, Jews, aliens—and "immorality," by Klan standards.

Into the Klan's mysterious fraternal fold, they lured the best citizens and God-fearing Protestants, forming a militant army of native-born, white fundamentalists who operated in secret and above the law—the community vigilante policeman, judge, jury, and sometimes executioner.

For the privilege of pursuing their moral mission, 1920s Klansmen, Klanswomen, and Klankids poured millions of dollars into the pockets of the pyramid-scheme evangelists who were their leaders. They were acting out America's experiment with Fascism, in an era when many thought world and national order too precarious to trust to democracy.

Their center of power was Indiana, that most American of states.

Many thought the Hoosiers' dynamic young leader was the Moses—or the Mussolini—who would lead the Klan movement into the White House. He was a blond, boyish charmer. He was the Imperial Wizard of the North. His name was David Curtis Stephenson.

Trained on the Oklahoma frontier, Steve came to Indiana about 1920. His past was a mystery; his style elusive as quicksilver; his rise mercurial. At 30, he became a millionaire, several times over, on his cut of Klansmen's dues and the markup on the sale of sheets.

By 1925 he had sewed up the state, virtually owning the governor and officials across Indiana, from State House to school house. From his urbane mansion, his summer White House, his 98-foot yacht, and his gilded aero plane, Stephenson made and broke politicians with a nod.

They called his headquarters "Klanapolis."

Steve was on his way to becoming a veritable Hoosier Hitler, riding to national power on a wave of masked, marching Klansmen draped in white sheets.

In the raw spring of 1925, Stephenson could not have known that the Klan's fate—and his own—rested on other bedsheets, as the beginning of the end was being played out in the lace-curtained bedroom of an Indiana librarian, Madge Oberholtzer.

Madge's family had found her tossed on her bed, crumpled and pale, stark-white around her mouth. Her clothes, a black velvet dress and black shoes, were soiled and in disarray. Her coat had been dropped on the floor. She had no hat.

"I'm done for," she muttered to the family attorney as he knelt beside her bed.

"Who did this to you?" he demanded.

She would not answer, but he would not desist.

At length, she whispered: "Stephenson...."

"How did he make those marks on you?" the attorney asked.

She turned her face to the wall.

Slowly the story came out, from Madge and others. Its threads traced across the country and the years in intricate patterns of light and shadow.

"Let it go," Madge Oberholtzer said hoarsely. "Let him.... Don't do anything. He's a power.

"He'll crush you. He'll crush you.

"He is the law."

PART I

1
THE KOKOMO KONKLAVE

July 4, 1923
Kokomo, Indiana

Perhaps there was a speck on the horizon.

Perhaps not.

It was hard to be sure, with the waves of heat and dust rising toward the clear blue bowl of the sky.

Dust, raised by some 50,000 cars on dirt roads, hung over everything: the sycamore-dotted, summer-green meadow stretching to far horizons, the Independence Day flags and bunting, the white shrouded clusters of gossiping families and friends, the picnic lunches and hooded youngsters playing hide and seek.

The acrid scent of dust mingled with other odors: of 200,000 sweltering bodies in damply clinging white robes, of crackling home fried chicken, of cinnamon-sweet home baked apple pie.

Perhaps it was an illusion.

No. It was real. The speck was growing, slowly drifting nearer from the south, catching the gleam from the blazing afternoon sun.

"He's coming!" someone cried, pointing to the speck. "He's coming!"

With a cheer, the crowd savored delicious anticipation, as sweet as frozen cream on any long parched, small town, Fourth of July tongue.

Klansmen and their families had gathered on the Kokomo meadow, 200,000 strong, for a coronation of one known to them as The Old Man. This day, in their presence, he would become Grand Dragon of the Indiana Ku Klux Klan, elevating Hoosier Klankdom to the status of a full realm. For the occasion, they swarmed over the fields in numbers that would never be exceeded by any gathering, anywhere, in the history of the Ku Klux Klan.

The Old Man's Kokomo Klonklave was destined to become the stuff of legend.

Much earlier in the day, before dawn, a cub reporter named John Niblack had donned his linen duster and set out on the long gravel road from Indianapolis to Kokomo.

Niblack was running late. He hit the street, which was damp with early morning dew, and catapulted into his baby blue 1919 Model T coupe with a broken windshield wiper. The voice of his conscience—eerily like that of his *Indianapolis Times*' editor— screamed in unison with his tires: "Niblack! You slug a bed. You'll be scooped again."

Niblack was lithe and slight, a skeletal 130 pounds even when he was chock full of white mule, which was fairly often. A child of Indiana's farm country, he had learned early to make up for his size by speed and cunning. He was the epitome of the Hoosier idea: by hard work and mettle, a boy from the Indiana backwoods could rise to outsmart the most sophisticated city slicker.

South on Meridian Street, toward town. The elms, soldierly like the old fence rows on the farm, sped by as if he were fixed in space and they were marching at triple-time speed. Humankind was stirring within the closed-face, double-decked bungalows, and Niblack waved jauntily to a pajama-clad duffer stumbling down the steps to retrieve his morning *Indianapolis Star*.

The *Star* and the *News*: they were the big guys. But the *Indianapolis Times* was like Niblack, an undersized scrapper. He resisted the urge to call out, "Want a real newspaper? Read what I write in the *Times* tonight!"

Meridian Street was slick, paved with oil soaked wooden blocks, now damp with dew. He slowed prudently at a corner. Seeing no cross traffic, he gunned his coupe through the intersection, flipped the steering wheel to one side, and slammed on his brake. Like a crazed bug on ice, the little car spun out of control and into a whirl, spinning around dizzy fast—one, two, three, four complete circles. He had broken his all-time record!—before coming to a drunken halt, inches from a beat-walking cop.

Niblack took a deep drag on a cigarette, raised his hand to his forehead in a salute, and turned primly down Market Street, heading for another day on the job.

It was later in the morning when the family of little Bobby Coughlin headed for Melfala Park outside Kokomo. Bobby was nine, the son of one of Kokomo's few Catholic families. "We're going," his father said, in a rare display of reckless bravado. "This should be a day Bobby will never forget."

His mother was nervous. Already there were rumblings that his father could be fired. The Klan didn't want Catholics teaching school, whispered old Mrs. Crousore, their neighbor. The Coughlin family nightmares rose or fell with accounts of Klan atrocities around the country. If trouble was to come to Indiana, the Kokomo Klonklave could well bring it.

"We're going," Coughlin said. And they set out in the family Chevrolet, through a town awash with white sheets. Klansmen from three states had taken over Kokomo, arriving in throngs by private auto, special railway car, and horseback. It was already steamy hot, Bobby recalled later, "the kind of day when the heat shimmers off the tall green corn and even the bobwhites seek shade."

The human flood had flowed through the night. By daylight, Klan officials were posted every few yards, on foot or horseback. They tried valiantly to manage the traffic glut, which crept forward with a cacophony of police whistles and shouts. Flags and bunting draped cars, with signs: "America for Americans." "The Pope will sit in the White House when Hell freezes over."

Dust sifted over cars loaded for family outings with luggage and camping gear. Sweating Klansfellows and steaming, sheeted Klanwives fanned themselves and occasionally swatted the wriggling miniature Klankids in their little white hoods and robes.

Some, perhaps less ardent, abandoned the road and spread their picnic blankets on the grass and over the wooded fields in far-flung little knots of white.

It had been a rich, full day. First the Rev. Mr. Kern of Covington, Indiana, warmed up the crowd over the machinations of Catholics and foreigners. They sang "America," accompanied by the Alliance, Ohio, 50-piece boys' band. Then the New Castle, Indiana, band played "The Star Spangled Banner," and Kokomo pastor Everett Nixon invoked blessings on the day.

None other than Imperial Wizard Hiram Wesley Evans lectured

next, at some length. He spoke with fervor, as befitted the number one Klansman in the world, on the foreign peril lurking in America. "Klankraft in Indiana," he said, "is now completely organized, and the red-blooded citizens of this Realm...constitute an unconquerable power for the right, which will forge ahead brooking no interference from malingering disloyalists."

Evans was second billing on the program. He graciously conceded that the center of the Invisible Empire had moved from the South to Indiana. If he resented The Old Man's rapid rise to power, Evans gave no public hint. He exhorted the crowd to political action to rehabilitate America for Americans.

Then the luncheon, as the sun rose high in the sky. White shrouded shapes hunched over picnic cloths spread throughout the 185-acre park, owned by the Klan as a tax shelter. Many had brought their meals. For others, block-long cafeteria tables lined the banks of Wildcat Creek, where the faithful women of the Klan, as do women everywhere, doled out the provisions: six tons of beef, 800 pounds of ham, 55,000 buns, 5,000 cases of soda pop and near beer, 1,500 cakes, 2,500 pies, and enough other delights to fill a fair-sized train of boxcars. It was the sort of culinary orgy that only a people devoted to temperance could truly appreciate.

A shaky old duffer, wilting from the heat, stumbled beneath a golden raintree and crumpled into a heap. "Humph," whispered one Kokomo Klansman to another. "That's old Colonel Simmons. Pitiful what he's become."

The Old Man was late. Excitement mounted. Many in the crowd had never seen an aeroplane before. Even fewer had seen The Old Man, known to them by no other name. High-ranking Klansmen circulated, whispering: "The President summoned The Old Man last night to devise a means of repelling a Papal invasion. The Old Man has saved the country. But he will be here. He wants to see you."

When the drone of his aeroplane neared the crowd, somewhere

around 2 p.m., they could see that it was gilded, catching the sunlight and flinging it back, emblazoned with the letters "K.K.K." Now it neared and then, like a kitten teasing a mouse, seemed to depart. Was he leaving? Nearer again, then away; crowd tension rose to ever sweeter heights.

"We would circle around over the heads of the people," The Old Man's pilot, Court Asher, later recalled, "and they'd be looking up at us as if we came from another world....

"He'd be late on purpose.... He knew how to set a stage....

"I'd swing her down gradually, so that the folks could see the silver tip and the bright colors on the aeroplane. Then I'd land in a space that had been cleared in the field.

"The Old Man would be dressed in a purple gown. He'd drop a hood over his face just before we came down.... Sometimes...he'd raise his hood just a little, so that some of the crowd could get a glimpse of his face for just a few seconds....

"It was a great show, believe me."

The drama rose above mere show as the plane dipped downward, lower, lower. Many in the crowd could see the two men into the open cockpit as the fragile, double-winged plane tipped to one side and jerked as it plowed into the tops of a row of trees. The branches ripped at canvas wings, but the pilot steadied the plane and brought her down safely.

A bumpy landing on a cleared field. The great man emerged, agile, vigorous, not overly tall, but moving with remarkable precision and grace.

The specific events that followed are lost in legend. Bobby Coughlin, who grew up to write the most famous account of the day, recalled that The Old Man was dressed in a robe of purple silk with gold piping and occult symbols.

A small band of dignitaries drew near him and stopped respectfully. He stepped forward.

"Kigy," he said.

"Itsub," they replied, solemnly.

Fathers hoisted children above their hooded heads for better views, while armed policemen, sheriffs, and Klan guards cleared a path. Bowing stiffly to left, then to right, The Old Man led the group across the field, through the cheering crowd. Some say people fell at his feet as he passed; those bold enough kissed the hem of his garment.

Up the steps and on to the bunting-draped platform, a large open pavilion with a concrete floor, rising from a manicured green. Across the stage, past the *Times'* reporter John Niblack, who was seated at a little press table right behind the rostrum. His lighted cigarette was shelved above one ear.

The Old Man arrived at the podium and stood perfectly still, waiting for the cheering to subside. He waited, waited, waited.

Only when the countryside was dead silent, with every eye on him, did he lift his hand. It was no gentle motion. In the fascist-like Klan salute, he thrust his right hand into the air, stiff palmed, stiff elbowed, toward the horizon, with triumphant force, the command of a czar. With the other hand, The Old Man ripped aside his visor, revealing his face: surprisingly young. Surely no more than 30. It was the scrubbed, boyish face of a blond cherub, lively, fresh, rosy, with—something else; what was it? In the petulant, sensuous mouth, in the hint of dark fire in the eyes—a kind of animal cunning.

The crowd returned his imperious salute, as one body.

It was a delicious moment, well worth the wait.

"My worthy subjects, citizens of the Invisible Empire, Klansmen all—Greetings!"

The mass leaned forward to hear the word.

"It grieves me to be late. The President of the United States kept me unduly long counseling on vital matters of state. Only my plea that this is the time and place of my coronation obtained for me surcease from his prayers for guidance."

In a low buzz, the crowd thanked the President.

"Here in this uplifted hand, where all can see, I bear an official document addressed to the Grand Dragon, Hydras, Great Titans, Furies, Giants, Kleagles, King Kleagles, Exalted Cyclops, Terrors, and All Citizens of the Invisible Empire of the Realm of Indiana.... It is signed by his Lordship, Hiram Wesley Evans, Imperial Wizard, and duly attested.

"It continues me officially in my exalted capacity as Grand Dragon of the Invisible Empire for the Realm of Indiana. It so proclaims me by virtue of God's unchanging Grace. So be it!"

He paused, and thunderous cheers echoed across the meadow.

And then his speech, "Back to the Constitution," a testimony to 100-percent Americanism. He spoke of "straight Americanism," of the schools, the nation, the Bible, the flag. He exhorted them to eschew violence.

Legend holds that his speech was a show-stopper—not surprising, since The Old Man was an unparalleled orator who could go for hours, picking up fervor as he went, sometimes all day and all night. No one left while The Old Man spoke.

Some say women swooned, that grown men wept, that children wet their pants.

But the surviving text of his speech was even more remarkable than legend. The Old Man surveyed government like a quasi-Socialist civics professor and proposed far-reaching reforms, including curbs on imperialism and the military, to be harnessed into a peacetime army corps for public works; an end to the spoils system, the electoral college, and deficit spending; control of inflation before it wiped out the middle class and resulted in economic chaos and class war within half a century; and a fulltime government printer to make all documents open information.

"Where there is no vision, the people perish!" The Old Man cried.

Bobby Coughlin remembered that when the speech was through, the new Grand Dragon stepped back and "a coin came spinning through the air. Someone threw another. Soon people were throwing rings, money, watch charms, anything bright and valuable. At last, when the tribute slackened, he motioned to his retainers to sweep up the treasure."

Then he strode off to a nearby pavilion to consult with his attendant Kleagles, Cyclopes, and Titans, perhaps with the customary Klan greetings: "Kigy"—Klansman, I greet you—and "Itsub"—In the sacred, unfailing bond.

But Independence Day 1923 was not yet over. Still to come was the evening's entertainment, the Kokomo Klonklave Klavalkade, a memorable show of strength.

The little Catholic boy, Bobby Coughlin, watched in awe. Outsiders might make sport of the Klan, he said later, "but no one could have seen the parade that night without feelings of solemnity."

Thirty bands, but no music; only the drums, rolling a slow, deep tempo up Main Street, clear through the town. Three hundred mounted Klansmen. Fifty thousand faceless, hooded Klansmen and women on foot, whose measured footfalls merged with the thud of drums and the off-beat clatter of hooves to fill the night, overpowering. Flaming torches threw grotesque shadows.

An army was on the move.

The boy steeped in Catholic tradition surely noticed the striking similarity between the KKK Knights' flowing white robes and the traditional cassocks of their arch enemies, the priests.

Flag bearers, usually carrying two Klan flags and an American flag, preceded every Klan chapter, Coughlin remembered.

"The word would ripple down the rows of spectators lining the curbs, Here comes the flag! Hats off for the flag!' Near the place where I was standing with my parents one man was slow with his hat and had it knocked off his head. He started to protest, thought better of it, and held his hat in his hand during the rest of the parade.

"Finally the largest flag I have ever seen came by. It must have been at least 30 feet long, since it took a dozen or more men on each side to support it, and it stretched almost from curb to curb. It sagged in the center under a great weight of coins and bills. As it passed us, the bearers called out, 'Throw in! Give to the hospital!' And most of the spectators did."

Of course, the hospital: money for a new one, sorely needed in Kokomo to spare the faithful the indignity of care in the town's only existing hospital, which was operated by nuns. The collection that night was said to net $50,000. It never reached any hospital board.

The parade culminated outside town at Foster Park, with fireworks and the burning of the largest fiery cross in history, 60 feet tall. The lumber, burlap, and kerosene alone cost $2,000.

Now the Klansmen were spent, emotionally and physically.

Bobby Coughlin and his family sat on their front porch and watched their neighborhood Klanfamilies return home, most too tired to bother taking off their regalia or to maintain their usual pose of secrecy.

"Others carried little bundles of white; they were the ones who still made some pretense of secrecy about being members.

"One of the last home was old Mrs. Crousore, who lived a few doors away. Her white robe clung damply, and her hood was pushed back. As she climbed her steps and sank solidly into a rocking chair on her porch, we could hear her groan, 'Oh, my God, my feet hurt!'"

Like the dust, the spell of the bizarre day hung over John Niblack as he drove through the thick summer darkness, back to Indianapolis.

As the black road stretched ahead, blessedly cool after the overheated day, Niblack tried to make sense of it. It was like trying to get a bead on quicksilver; every time he tried to pin it down, it shifted again.

This story was not to Niblack's liking. He much preferred the precision of the courts. In this story, there were too many unanswered questions. Who was this strange young man with the cherub face and his even more peculiar band, thousands strong?

They seemed to have sprung from nowhere, fully grown, casting shifting shadows.

Why would grown-up Indiana men flit about in nightgowns and hoods, in broad daylight, while their sheeted womenfolk swooned at the feet of a gewgaw actor who seemed to have them all mesmerized?

Back in Indianapolis, Niblack told his editor that the whole affair was like a mild nightmare.

"Men in white sheets and masks, in pointed hoods, staring up at me," Niblack said, rubbing his eyes at the memory. "It was pretty hot, and a lot of the yokels out in front got up a pretty good sweat under their robes....

"Some of them may have been women, for all I know."

The cynic Niblack was not awed by legend. He saw no purple robes or shower of gifts. "This Grand Dragon mounted the stage whereon I sat and made a speech about the Little Red School House and the American Way of Living, and this and that and the other, which didn't amount to two whoops, as far as I could see. But everybody cheered."

Where's the guy from? the editor wanted to know.

"Who knows? They say from Texas—somewhere—maybe a

wealthy oil man."

"And this KKK? Were they like the old KKK, the one that rose up after the Civil War in the South?"

"Yes and no," Niblack said. "Seem to be after Catholics most of all now, plus foreigners and Jews. Seem all of a sudden to be everywhere, but I can't say for sure where it comes from, or the 'old man' either, for that matter. A lot of preachers are recruiting, I hear. Most of the sheriff's deputies are in it now, and they say the sheriff and the judges, too."

A silence. A tiny muscle began to twitch beneath the editor's left eye as he stared at Niblack's copy, seemingly indifferent.

The editor did not look up when he spoke, but his words snapped like a bone breaking.

"Find out."

2
A NEW RUGGED CROSS

April 27, 1913
Atlanta, Georgia

The 1920s' Knights of the Ku Klux Klan was born, as it was to die a decade later, with the brutal death of a young girl.

The first to die was Mary Phagan, 14.

Little Mary was a golden girl, with black-fringed eyes and dark red curls tied up in cabbage-rose ribbons.

Mary Phagan was found dead on April 27, 1913, her mutilated body dumped in the basement of the Atlanta, Georgia, pencil factory where she worked. Her lavender, lace-trimmed dress was tossed above her hips, ripped and blood-stained. She had been strangled with pencil box cord.

"he said he wood love me...while play with me," read a note scrawled on a scrap of an order blank.

The factory owner was Leo Frank, a frail bug-eyed Jew originally from New York.

Frank was alone in his office that Saturday when Mary tapped on his window and whispered, "I came to get my pay." Frank counted out her $1.20 for ten hours' work.

Within the hour, she was dead.

Despite his pleas of innocence, Frank was found guilty of the murder and sentenced to death. His sentence was protested by civil liberties groups, who contended the evidence against him was contradictory and biased.

On June 21, 1915, Governor Slaton commuted Frank's sentence to life in prison. Slaton would never be safe in Georgia again.

Public anger over the governor's action was fed by Tom Watson, an Atlanta publisher, embittered ex-Populist, and future U.S. senator.

Watson used his publications to urge an alternate route to justice. "Our Little Girl—ours by the Eternal God—has been pursued to a hideous death and bloody grave by this filthy perverted Jew of New York," Watson wrote. "When mobs are no longer possible, liberty will be dead.... RISE! PEOPLE OF GEORGIA!"

They rose. On August 16, 1915, twenty-five men, including a Methodist minister, abducted Leo Frank from a prison farm and lynched him.

The people of Georgia, and many other states, were jubilant. For years thereafter, any Peachtree tourist with a nickel could buy a drugstore postcard photo of Leo Frank dangling by his neck from a Georgia oak.

It would be half a century before Frank's name was cleared, in a posthumous pardon after a deathbed confession.

Leo Frank's lynch mob named themselves the Knights of Mary Phagan. Two months after the lynching, they climbed Stone Mountain outside Atlanta and burned a triumphant cross, visible throughout the city. Watching Atlantans, in large measure, approved.

The fiery Tom Watson applauded. It was time, he trumpeted in his *Jeffersonian*, for the Ku Klux Klan to ride again.

The battle cry of Tom Watson did not go unheeded. His challenge was shortly taken up by Atlanta's William Joseph Simmons, a boozy dreamer, erstwhile Methodist minister, garter salesman, insurance peddler, and organizer for fraternal lodges. Simmons had long hoped to revive the Klan that flourished in the South after the Civil War.

Simmons was an engaging, deep-voiced orator, born somewhere around 1880 in Alabama. He always looked as if he could mount the pulpit and preach a funeral at any given moment, equally eloquent for brother or stranger—notwithstanding the fact that the Methodist Church had booted him from the pulpit for incompetence.

On his chatty rounds through Atlanta's streets, Simmons cut a memorable figure: 6 feet 2 inches tall, lanky, clean-shaven, with flaming red hair, crinkled gray eyes, a prominent nose, thin lips perennially set in a straight-line semi-smile, good teeth, and a pointed chin. His gold pince-nez spectacles hung from a gold chain clipped to his right ear; and a gold watch chain was looped under his cutaway frock coat, swinging above his striped trousers. He was a walking bulletin board for lodge pins.

He liked horse racing, boxing, and booze.

Simmons was a professional joiner. His nights were filled with meetings. He had earned 23 degrees—in the Masons, the Odd Fellows, the Knights of Pythias, the Great Order of the Knight Templars, the Woodmen of the World, and a dozen others. His fellows called him Doc, after his rumored medical training, or

Colonel, because he led the Woodmen's drill team.

Colonel Simmons was an idealist. He believed in men's lodges. "I am a fraternalist," he said.

He knew a bit about the Klan: "From a child in dresses, I can remember how old Aunt Vinney, my black mammy, used to pacify us children late in the evening by telling us about the Kuklux," he recalled fondly.

And he was given, by his account, to visions. In fact, he had seen a vision about the Ku Klux Klan.

After a drink or two on a summer night, he had been visited by ghostriders. "On horseback in their white robes they rode across the wall in front of me. As the picture faded I got down on my knees and swore I would found a fraternal organization that would be a memorial to the Ku Klux Klan."

It was not until 1911 that Simmons got around to completing his grand plan, while recovering from an auto accident. He worked out the details finely, poetically, with alliteration. He fell in love with the eleventh letter of the alphabet, picked up the name of the old Klan, went one better to quadruple the K, and named his lodge the Knights of the Ku Klux Klan.

He invented secret codes, hand signals, passwords, a Klan Kalendar. He devised an intricate hierarchy, whose officials bore nonsensical names all beginning with the letter "K." Those Kludds, Klexters, and Kleagles would be guided by a constitution—Kloran—and meet in Klaverns, Klonklaves, Klonvokations, and Klonciliums.

"KIGY," they would say to each other. "AYAK?" "AKIA." And only they would know....

He was proudest of the secret rituals that he said were more elaborate, mysterious, and weird than any other fraternity. "It unfolds a spiritual philosophy that has to do with the very fundamentals of life and living, here and hereafter," he said.

So it was that on a dark Thanksgiving Day in 1915, Simmons

literally picked up a new rugged cross, padded with excelsior
and doused with kerosene, and lugged it atop Stone Mountain
to re-birth the Klan. The cross was an innovative twist; the
Reconstruction Klan didn't use them, but Scots had burned crosses
to summon their clans. It seemed to fit.

Colonel Simmons returned that night with 15 fellow believers,
following footsteps made a month earlier by the Leo Frank lynchers,
the Knights of Mary Phagan. Some were stepping on their own
earlier footprints.

It was pitch dark and freezing, Simmons later recounted,
with "icicles a foot long hanging on the rocks." (One cynic later
determined, however, that the temperature that night was 45
degrees.)

They carried flashlights. The mountain was a Confederate
monument, 650 feet tall, solid granite. The trail was steep and stony.
They slipped and stumbled in the wind.

"Down at the bottom of the mountain there's a spring of
sparkling cold water. I stopped at the spring and took some of the
water into my old army canteen....Then we struggled to the top....
Each pilgrim, when nearing the crest, gathered a granite boulder,
and on the summit of Stone Mountain the sixteen boulders were
built into an altar."

Simmons made a few remarks about purity and honor, arranging
on the altar the canteen, an American flag, an unsheathed sword,
and a Bible.

"Suddenly I struck a match and lighted the cross.... And while
it burned I administered the oath.... And thus on the mountain
top that night at the midnight hour while men braved the surging
blasts of wild wintry mountain winds and endured temperatures
far below freezing, bathed in the sacred glow of the fiery cross, the
Invisible Empire was called from its slumber of half a century to
take up a new task and fulfill a new mission for humanity's good...."

Simmons was an incurable romantic. Lacking even a charred piece of the true cross to commemorate that Thanksgiving beginning, he would soon be selling millions of his Klan followers "inspiration water from the Stone Mountain spring" for $10 a quart.

It was drawn from the Chattahoochee River.

Luck was with Colonel Simmons. His timing was right on target.

Only days after his freezing, cross-bearing trek up Stone Mountain, he busily set about promoting his new Knights of the Ku Klux Klan, Inc. He was precisely in time for the December 6, 1915, Atlanta opening of the blockbuster Klan film, "The Birth of A Nation."

In fact, he ran Klan ads—"The World's Greatest Secret, Social, Patriotic, Fraternal, Beneficiary Order.... Col. W.J. Simmons, Founder and Imperial Wizard"—right next to the "Birth of a Nation" advertisements in the Atlanta papers.

It was a stroke of genius. For "Birth of a Nation" was the film that would make the Reconstruction Klansmen national heroes in 1915.

Several years before, in 1906, a young North Carolina writer, Thomas Dixon, had published *The Clansman, An Historical Romance of the Ku Klux Klan.* Dixon's book, a syrupy romance, glorified the Reconstruction Klan as a crusading army of white knights saving the South and virtuous white maidens—symbolizing the South, of course—from Northern devils and leering, raping black savages. Later, Dixon adapted the story to the stage and acted, himself, as the lead Southern knight.

In 1914, movie director D.W. Griffith converted the book into the silent movie classic, "The Birth of a Nation," which revolutionized the film industry and mesmerized the country. At 3 1/2 hours, it was the longest movie yet made, by far; until then, movies were little more than nickelodeon clips. It incorporated techniques, camera work, and scope never dreamed of before. It played to the accompaniment of a 30-piece orchestra. It was viewed by an astounding 50 million, who cheered, cried, stomped, and ignored the scattered protests by black groups that the film made heroes of marauding mass murderers.

The *Atlanta Constitution* gave it a glowing review: "Never before, perhaps, has an Atlanta audience so freely given vent to its emotions.... Cheer after cheer burst forth from the audience It makes you actually forget decorum and forces a cry into your throat."

"Birth of a Nation" ultimately grossed somewhere upwards of $60 million. And it impressed on America a heroic vision of the Klan that was accepted as historical truth for decades.

After a private showing, President Woodrow Wilson was moved. "It is like history written with lightning," Wilson said, "and my only regret is that it is all so terribly true."

If "Birth of a Nation" was a sensation, it was also a not-to-be-missed opportunity. Simmons jumped on it. He was certain rival Klans would be springing up around the country; no time to waste. Right before the Atlanta opening, he dressed a group of his own fledgling knights in bedsheets and sent them careening down Peachtree Street, on horseback, firing rifle salutes. Public reaction seemed favorable, so he repeated the trick elsewhere.

But timing and hit and miss promotions weren't enough. Simmons, it turned out, wasn't much of a manager. Imperial Wizard, yes, but no financial wizard.

Under his leadership, the new KKK limped along for several years. True enough, his KKK was able to generate a little excitement during World War I, working as a kind of ad hoc secret service, hunting spies, hassling labor goons, and staging a few patriotic parades. Secrecy became increasingly necessary, befitting the urgency of the KKK's calling and the pervasiveness of the nation's enemy.

But by 1920 the Klan still had no more than 3,000 members in a dozen Klans in three klaverns, as the townships were called, scattered in Atlanta, Birmingham, Mobile.

Simmons thought he had done the important things. He had, for example, made up a catchy motto: "Non Silba Sed Anthar." When asked, he admitted he had improvised it from a couple of languages, "a bit of Latin, a little bit of Saxon." He said it meant "Not for self but for others."

And he had endowed the group with noble purposes: To promote "comprehensive Americanism;" to oppose unions, foreigners, Reds, and Jews; and to spawn brotherhood among those of "the highest class." He had laid out its goals in an "Imperial Proclamation," in a grand style that one weekly would later call "a verbal magnificence... that should perhaps be described as 'neo African.'"

He had contracted with a sheet company to make regulation hooded white uniforms.

He had sent out a clever membership recruiting letter: "... REAL MEN whose oaths are inviolate are needed (to join) the most powerful, secret, non-political organization in existence, one that has the Most Sublime Lineage in History, one that was 'Here Yesterday,' 'Here Today,' 'Here Forever.'"

He had targeted the audience pretty precisely. As his good friend Jonathan Frost, the former head of the Woodmen of the World, wrote of the new Klan, "Only native-born American citizens who believe in the tenets of the Christian religion and owe no allegiance of any degree or nature to any foreign Government, nation, political institution, sect, people, or person are eligible." Frost had learned well from his mentor, the fiery old Atlantan Tom Watson.

But, as one writer would later note, Simmons' retreaded KKK was short on PROGRAM. In fact, "in spite of his religious reverence for its predecessor and his passion for fraternalism, Simmons hadn't the slightest idea of what a revived Ku Klux Klan should DO."

Times were hard for Simmons, notwithstanding the fact that he was collecting membership dues, his just recompense as entrepreneur. "There were times," he recalled later, "when I walked the streets with my shoes worn through because I had no money." He mortgaged his house, if not his soul, for the Klan.

To make matters worse, after Simmons sent his good friend Jonathan Frost on a special mission to Birmingham, Frost absconded with the Alabama dues. Worst of all, Frost left in his wake ugly rumors that Simmons was the real thief who had stolen the whole idea from Frost.

Jonathan Frost thus became the first Judas in the history of Simmons' new Knights of the Ku Klux Klan, Inc. He would not be the last.

Carrying out the divine plan was not easy for Simmons. His fiery cross, as the weekly *Nation* later noted, was hidden under a bushel.

What he needed to supplement his glad hand and open palm was a strong marketing arm.

Again, luck was with him. In 1920 he found the perfect person; in fact, not just one but two. On June 7, 1920, Simmons hired Edward Young Clarke and Mrs. Elizabeth Tyler to manage public relations for the Knights of the Ku Klux Klan, Inc. The decision was destined to make the Klan.

Together, Bessie Tyler and Ed Clarke comprised a shoebox company called the Southern Publicity Association that trifled in the new science of public relations. Hard-sell advertising was into its first golden era in the 1920s, and Clarke and Tyler were ready to move to the cutting edge. They had done a series of do-gooder campaigns around town—Better Baby Parades, the Anti Saloon League promotion, that sort of thing.

Together, Bessie and Ed were a pair, in more than one way.

Ed Clarke was short, kinetic, perpetually coiled to spring, with bushy black hair and black-rimmed spectacles, coming to public relations from the school of newspaper journalism; married at the time.

Bessie Tyler was a blue-eyed, strawberry blonde bull of a woman, in build and will. In her mid 30s, she was gutsy beyond her time; married at 14 and widowed at 15, with a daughter. She was, one writer said, "chunky, buxom, and blowzy. Even a man who detested her was forced to call her 'an extraordinary woman.' She was untaught, but endowed with unusual mentality." She was sharp, in mind and tongue.

Picture the three of them, Clarke, Tyler, and Simmons—a study in contrasts, in black, white, and red—meeting to consummate the contract. Clarke's modest office was, as one observer recalled, above "the never-sleeping eye of an oculist's office" in Atlanta.

Clarke: black hair, intense eyes burning brightly behind black rimmed spectacles, pacing. He could pass for an intellectual in a short encounter.

Bessie Tyler: forceful, sturdy as a stone, in black patent leather pumps, black broadcloth cape, black scowl; she was not a woman to argue with.

And Simmons: brightening the room with his fiery hair, his visionary rhetoric, his gold pince-nez, his cutaway coat and striped pants. His outrageous collection of lodge mementos flashed when he waved a long, graceful hand to illustrate an important point.

Clarke's speech was staccato, like a machine gun. Simmons' words flowed like a river, sweeping a listener along involuntarily. Bessie Tyler spoke seldom—but when she did, the men listened.

Clarke and Tyler approached the Klan like a business, a serious business.

If you were selling Fuller Brushes, Colonel Simmons, how would you do it? Identify your territories and send salesmen—call them Kleagles, if you must—into each territory—ok, "province;" "realm"—on worthwhile promotional commissions. Give them maybe $4 of every $10 entrance fee—"klectoken"—they bring in. Install some tough regional managers—"King Kleagles"—and give them one dollar of every ten. That leaves you maybe half the cut, 5 of every 10.

Think of a pyramid: you're at the top, and beneath you spreads out this giant power pyramid of people, working for you, growing day by day. You're King Arthur, with a pyramid of Knights, each level feeding the one above it. This thing could be big—real big.

Now, what's the product you're selling here? What's the hottest thing going? Americanism, that's what. One hundred percent, not any of your watered down 80-90 percent Americans but pure, all the way 100-percenters. That means white, Protestant, Anglo Saxon—the man who worries that his daughter is hiding rouge and his son is stealing a smoke, that his wife may want to cut her hair and take a job.

That's our customer, and there are millions of him out there. He NEEDS the Klan; alone he is nothing. We're doing him a service; he is crying for a purpose, a mission, a calling, a crusade. Reform. Clean up these lawless towns. For our women. Protect them from the negras—God made them to be serfs. From the Pope—the Pope!—coming any day, to take over America: our churches, our schools, our government. Any day! Protect this country; the enemy is everywhere, ever resourceful. America needs these good folks, and they need us. We just need to give them a chance.

Tailor the spiel to the yokels. Are they worried about Catholics taking over the schools? Alien inspired strikers? Money grubbing Jew bankers? The "new negra?" The—ah—mongrelization of the race? Sin—bootleggers, prostitutes, loose women, card players?

Are they just plain bored, tired of a lonely life in the sticks? These backwater towns, these smoke-belching factories, these ritual-stripped Protestant churches are—let's face it—dreary. Bleak. Dull. We have the answer.

Now this is a big job, and we're bound to offend some of our standing clients—the Jews and Catholics—so this is a big commitment for us. But we've sized you up. We've investigated this thing—and you—from every angle. You're clearly a good man, clean living, a minister. We know you're heart and soul for the Klan, and we believe in your cause. We're willing to pay the price and go it with you. It will cost us a lot, but we'll risk it and take the job on the come—for 80 percent of the take.

In the end, Simmons bought it.

The new triumvirate dispatched 1,100 Kleagles—recruiters—across the country to "klux" the nation, with Tyler and "Imperial Kleagle" Clarke pocketing $4 of every $5 in the Imperial Treasury.

Even Bessie Tyler was pleased with the results. "The minute we said Ku Klux, editors from all over the United States began literally pressing us for publicity," she said.

In the following 16 months, 100,000 white Protestants paid $10 each to join, plus the $6 rental fee for the regulation regalia ($2 for costs, $3-$4 for Klan headquarters) and a host of taxes, special assessments, donations, and fees. The Atlanta trinity was well on its way toward a million-dollar gross.

They had hit upon, as one journalist put it, "a highly skilled combining of mystery and hocus pocus with very business-like methods.... Mr. Clarke's hustling agents sought out the poor, the romantic, the short-witted, the bored, the vindictive, the bigoted, and the ambitious, and sold them all their heart's desire." Following directions, the Kleagles pandered to every known regional fear, hatred, and prejudice, offering a scapegoat and simple solution for every pressing problem.

Their Kleagles sold 100 percent Americanism, on 40 percent commission.

Theirs was very much a macho appeal: It took guts to be a Klansman.

Colonel Simmons rose to the challenge. When he was introduced to a Georgia audience, he responded first with silence, then drew out a pistol from one pocket, a revolver from the other, and placed them on the table in front of him. Then he unbuckled his cartridge belt and arranged it between the two weapons, in a crescent shape. Then, still in silence, he pulled out a bowie knife and plunged it into the center of the table.

"Now let the Niggers, Catholics, Jews, and all others who disdain my imperial wizardry, come on!"

The Klan even took on the Boy Scouts, condemning them as un-American because they allowed Catholic and Jewish members. But, while they preached exclusivity, the cash-hungry Kleagles signed up anyone—from among the chosen people—with a $10 bill. A journalist later tried to find whether any white Protestant male applicant had been rejected; he found not a single case.

They began in the Old South, spread west, and in time moved northward to the Middle West, sweeping—"kluxing"—their way, ultimately, into every state in the union. The Klan was destined to become a big business; its founders, at least temporarily, would reap lavish wealth.

3
BIrth OF a salesman

1899
Houston, Texas

About the time Colonel Simmons was seeing visions of his
retread Ku Klux Klan, the fellow who would become the greatest
Kleagle of them all was coming of age on a distant, fresh frontier.

His name was David Curtis Stephenson. They called him Steve.

Most of his early years are lost in mist and myth. "It's nobody's
business who my folks are or where I come from," he often said. The
formation of his character and genius can be pieced together now
only from surviving shards.

When cornered in later years, Steve told the version of his story
contained in official government records:

Stephenson fixed his birth date as September 21, 1893, in
South Bend, Indiana; his father as Howard R. Stephenson, a Yale-

graduated lawyer with a lucrative practice, from a Massachusetts family of "considerable social standing;" his mother, Blanche Bennett Stephenson, as "a woman of breeding and training, a graduate of Bryn Mawr..., a genteel lady."

Both parents and his brother James died in 1920 or before, he said; and his sister, Clariece, was "a well educated woman of high ideals" who never married.

Their home was harmonious, Steve said. The parents were affectionate, slightly indulgent but never lax in discipline. The children were educated in a private school Steve said was maintained on the third floor of their home.

Steve said he entered the University of Michigan at age 16, graduated at 19, "read the law," and was admitted to the bar in Iowa, Illinois, and Indiana—after 14 months' World War I Army service overseas, including Belleau Woods, the scene of horrific and heroic deeds he sometimes recounted modestly.

But the idyllic tale in Steve's official history bears almost no resemblance to the story that others—his adversaries in later years—pieced together after they investigated his beginnings. They say his life began August 21, 1891, in Houston, Texas.

The humid heat pressed down on Houston like a skillet lid, without a hint of a breeze, as the Stephenson family moved north: father, mother, brother, sister, and young Steve, who could not have known where or why they were going.

He would have been 7, a tow-headed, round-faced, pink-cheeked charmer with clear eyes the color of winter skies—the kind of son every mother longs for, the kind of lad who evokes praise on the street from elderly women: such a clean young man!

They drove through Houston at the end of the gay Nineties, 1899; an overgrown village built on a flat swamp, landlocked 50 miles inward from the Gulf of Mexico. Through rising waves of summer heat, Steve watched the town pass by. Here was Steve's little Catholic school, down the street from the grand brick hotel where his father whisked the drummers—salesmen—back and forth from trains.

There was little hint of the city that would rise from the mud in later years. The ship channel that would later make the town was hardly a glint in the eyes of Houston's leaders, a shrewd core of men who knew, even then, that Houston was first and foremost a place to make money.

His father had made little of it there.

Some say his father's name was Arizonia Stephenson; others, that it was Andrew Monroe Stephenson. Some say he was a day man who subsisted on odd jobs. Or, more probably, a dray man, a wagon driver who met trains and carried deliveries and the drummers who would have been young Steve's heroes.

The streets held memories of drummers pitching their wares into his father's wagon, hawking them along the ride, drawing street corner crowds with flowery oratory and gaudy shows, lounging artfully in fine shops and ornate hotels. Decked out with flashing gems and silver tongues, they could not but dazzle a poor boy, teaching him that there was life beyond squalor, for those who seized it from others.

Houston would mark young Steve forever. He was never to be a rural man; instead, he would remain all his life a man of the towns. And whatever his other passing occupations, he would remain all his life, at base, a salesman.

Some went north by wagon. More went by train.

Steve, his brother Arizonia, and his sister Clara would have been awed by the fire-breathing engine and red plush and brass rail cars that clattered north on freshly laid rails linking Kansas with Texas. The ash-spewing train crossed Texas hills and prairies, over recently abandoned cattle trails, across the shifting pink sands of the River called Red, into the exploding frontier of a separate nation called Indian Territory.

They left the law behind.

Indian Territory was still largely lawless, a favorite hiding place for Texans pursued by the law. It was an American anachronism in an industrializing age. As America's advancing frontier pressed Indians farther and farther west, the government set aside the most useless of lands and forced the civilized tribes there.

The hissing train clanked into the nation set aside for the land-loving Chickasaws, in the south center of what would later become Oklahoma. Here, in the basin between the Canadian and Red Rivers, ancient seas had layered their secrets beneath soils, sands, and clays of black mulatto, white gold, and Indian paint red.

From the train, the country rolled out over wide valleys where remnants of bluestem—tall as buffalo bellies—still waved in raw prairie winds. A quick eye could catch wild turkey or deer in the brambled ravines and cross timbered hills of oak, hickory, bois d'arc, pecan.

Forced into Indian Territory, the Chickasaws tilled the soil with Negro slaves and white tenant farmers, thus peopling their new nation in red, black, and white, like the soil itself. But now the government was breaking up their nation's holdings into individual allotments. Grafters were developing land stealing into a high art. Just to the west, runs were opening up the unassigned lands to white homesteaders, and the infiltration into Indian Territory was no less a run. Non-Indians were beyond the local law. What non-Indian law as existed was largely vigilante. Outlaws flocked to the Territory. Women learned to draw the shades at night.

The northbound Santa Fe hissed and clattered into a region

convulsing with change, on rails linking time and space between alien worlds. Along the rails, overnight towns were springing up to greet the promise of this newly-minted, roughshod, mud-mired new frontier.

The little party of Stephensons veered to the left at Smith Paul's Valley, crossing the line where black gumbos and pale sands gave way to the ruddy Permian red bed clays of western Indian Territory. They traversed primeval sod so dense only four-team oxen could break it. The land rolled up to high plains and, in the distance, green blue vistas.

Just this side of the western boundary of Indian Territory, the Stephensons reached a marginal nub of human habitation called Beef Creek, on the lowlands beside the Washita River. And there they stopped. Who knows why?

It was the land of the big sky. Beneath it lived perhaps 100 souls, scratching out a living around the farming town nucleus, an early stage coach stop point on the Arbuckle trail.

In 1902 they renamed the town Maysville.

By one account, the Stephensons began their new life in that most humble of abodes, a dugout—really, no more than a hole in the ground. It was sometime later that Maysville gathered itself together to form a school. When Steve began schooling, his desk would have been at best a split log, set on pegs with the splintery split side up. His school record was that of "a normal boy with a very retentive mind."

Some say his family held high hopes for Steve, urging him to better himself. Some say the Stephensons did right well in the new land and came into money. History lists a Stephenson Browne Lumber Company in Maysville that might have belonged to the elder Stephensons; the Maysville Masons met upstairs.

Others say the family never rose above poverty, never owned land or the house in which they lived.

What shaped the boy into the man, if not the place and its people?

The people of his little world were, by and large, hardy folk in a harsh environment; the soft could not survive. They were town builders and tenant farmers, church founders and crooks, opportunists and optimists. Many were populists or Socialists. Many were transient, tumbling around the territories like wind-tossed cottonwood tufts. Some were dedicated to creating civilization; others, to exploiting the land and each other.

They were all Steve's teachers.

All together, they knit, as one national magazine wrote at the time, "...a social fabric [of] haphazard homespun [in a] territory peopled largely by land gamblers instead of home seekers.... They gambled, because the state has been from the first one vast roulette wheel played by adventurers from other states."

They were fiercely political. Many were, conversely, both agrarian rebels and Jacksonian Democrats, firm in their belief that "one's friends are patriots while one's opponents are enemies of the state," wrote one observer.

Steve would have been 16 on a glorious fall day, September 17, 1907, when the twin territories were joined to become Oklahoma, the 46th State. In Maysville, nearby Pauls Valley, and Purcell—and throughout the state—celebrating throngs clogged streets.

It was a new era, a time of boundless optimism.

The Stephenson boy had finished the eighth grade. Dashing his parents' hopes for his higher education, Steve left school, declared himself to be a man of the new state, and set forth to find his future. His real education was just beginning.

Steve began work, as best is known, with odd jobs that landed him in time as a printer's apprentice. Probably he worked first at the *Maysville News*, founded July 5, 1907, by T. D. Jones. His first mentor may have been John Cooper, a nearby farmer who bought into the paper. Cooper was an avowed Socialist.

Bent over the type bins, Steve stood no more than 5 1/2 feet tall. He would have been a chubby, rose-cheeked, clean-cut lad, with close-cropped blond hair. His thin-line eyebrows arched above steel blue eyes that were cool and clear as spring water but remarkably intense. Above his dimpled chin, his soft mouth pursed, in concentration, into a pink cupid's bow.

There was a rigorous precision to the job, in the midst of the hurly-burly, cluttered back shop of country papers where the battle was long since lost against the forces of ink and grime. The printer held a compositor stick in his left hand and, letter by letter, set each word, line, and galley of type.

After the hand-crank, hand-fed Washington, Army, or cylinder press had churned out the papers, Steve's first job began— redistributing the individual letters of type back into their cases, ready for flying fingers to set the next edition.

In time, Steve's fingers would set the type.

For several years he rattled around the small presses of the region as tramp printer, then printer, then editor, then publisher.

Sometimes he worked with his brother; sometimes alone. His brother, Arizonia, was fondly remembered by some but shared "a family failing of forgetting to pay his bills," said one acquaintance.

A printer's world is words, images, precision, speed. Thus, in the drafty board-on-batten or sheet-iron print shops, Steve could have fairly drowned in words.

An early winter twilight might well have found him hunched over swimming reams of words, near a central pot-bellied stove, beneath the dim light of a kerosene lamp—or, later, an electric bulb hanging low from the high ceiling.

Scrubbed and precise, Steve must have been at peculiar variance with the stained and cluttered print shop, a one-room pit of ancient type bins, mountains of newsprint, klatches of pamphlets, a hand-crank press, vats of ink, and other paraphernalia of the trade.

Some say he memorized the dictionary, and it would have been a logical step for a boy with a keen, retentive mind, eager to speed the work and escape into other pleasures. Others say he memorized the galleys of copy he proofed, learning in the process of worlds far beyond the small town confinement of his life.

There are those who say he saw then a future beyond his present and, in private moments, began to read aloud before a mirror, in unrelenting drill, training himself to go beyond the written word. He was teaching himself to become not only a writer but an orator.

Who knows what produces the drive, the overwhelming desire to rise above poverty and ignorance? This much is certain: a passion for power and achievement seized him early. The surviving scraps of his early writing throb with drive and life beyond the cold brittle pages of old newsprint.

He saw himself as more than he was.

He was not long for Maysville.

From Maysville, Steve's first move out would have been toward neighboring Pauls Valley or Purcell, small towns that were high toned—by frontier standards.

In such towns, Steve would have learned to play the newspaper game for sport. Most county towns had two or more newspapers whose editors loved nothing more than to exchange barbs, in barroom language.

Here he could learn the art of setting up an adversary to garner support in a brawl of words, never more artful than during the fiery political campaigns.

Turnover was rapid. Publishers scrambled to pay the rent, write, edit, set the type, print, tear down, and begin again.

Some newspapers had a new proprietor every time the bills came due.

True to the trade, Steve moved rapidly around the area, landing awhile in the nearby crossroads village of Byars ("a good moral town," population 800, "all white, as no colored people are allowed ")

The newspapers of the day carried a few chatty items about the Stephensons.

"D.C. Stephenson, late of Warner, Oklahoma, was in Purcell Wednesday and paid the *Register* a visit," wrote the *Purcell Register* July 13, 1911. "The young gentleman is the proprietor of the *Warner (Oklahoma) Times*, which paper he has leased to other parties, and he informs us that he has made all arrangements for starting a paper at Wayne [Oklahoma], the first issue to make its appearance on Friday, August 4th.

"Mr. Stephenson was with the *Washington (Oklahoma) Press* last summer and is a young man of much ability and energy. We doubt not that he will give the people of the good town of Wayne a first class paper, and we hope that he will receive a liberal support."

And again, from the *Pauls Valley Enterprise*, November 6, 1913:

"D.C. and A.M. Stephenson, formerly and for several years citizens of Maysville but now of Purcell, were greeting their old friends here Tuesday."

His world was centered around Purcell.

If Steve had found a proud town at Pauls Valley, he found it double at Purcell: in McClain County, 30 miles south of the state's capital Oklahoma City. Purcell had a covey of self consciously cultured social leaders who worked tirelessly to put all possible distance between themselves and the roughshod wilderness so fresh in their past.

A high class town. At Brown's Opera House, Thomas Dixon himself, author of *The Clansman*—soon to become a moving picture—appeared to play the title role in another of his plays.

Standout items in the Purcell press that year, though unsigned, have a Stephenson flair. Perhaps he wrote them; perhaps they trained him.

Steve was growing to manhood in a place intent on wresting civilization from the wilderness, less than a generation into organized law, still far from order. The vigilante Horse Thief Detective Association still rode in the new state.

White justice was swift and personal. It was no accident that Steve's home basin was called "Little Dixie." If King Cotton demanded black hands to pry him from claw-like bolls, white will vowed to keep those hands shackled. By an overwhelming vote, Oklahomans amended their constitution with a "grandfather clause" to disenfranchise black voters.

Steve would have been at or near Purcell, at age 20, when Main Street was lighted by a town celebration August 25, 1911.

Of the 3,600 souls in town, more than 3,000 crowded the broad main drag. Women hung from the windows of cars, cheering town fathers who seized a Negro named Pete Carter, lashed him to a telephone pole in the middle of Purcell's Main Street, heaped straw and wood at his feet, doused him with kerosene, and lighted the fire.

As he begged for mercy, they tortured him until he confessed to assaulting a white woman the night before. "I am the man," he muttered.

And then they burned him alive.

"Three thousand men, women, boys, and girls cheered while the devil was dying," reported the nearby Madill press.

"The mob seemed to have become frenzied as the fire

preparations were completed," wrote the *Vinita Weekly Chieftain*.

"Prominent citizens fought to hold the writhing form of the negro. Others fought to pour more oil on his body.

"His hideous shrieks rent the air and some of the coal oil found its way into his open mouth.

"'It's better that way,' remarked one of the mob. 'He'll burn quicker.'

"A sheet of flame enveloped his body and, screaming, he died."

The next morning two laborers shoveled up the ashes "where Pete Carter... died under the provisions of that unwritten white man's law which demands a life for the lost honor of a white woman...."

Although thousands viewed the lynching, "none recognized any of the leaders of the mob," and the county attorney said there was no chance of legal action against them.

So much to learn, so little time.

The area around Purcell was a hotbed of Socialists. "While we have no sympathy whatever for their vulgarities, we are always willing to accord them respectful...notice of their meetings as they request of us," snipped the Purcell Register.

Byars Socialists paraded the streets, "led by the red flag of anarchy."

"Boiled down, the Socialist doctrine is...that the negro is naturally the white man's equal but is kept in an inferior position by the system," sniffed a Purcell columnist who longed for the return of the old KKK to settle "the race question" once and for all.

Politically, Steve was a Democrat. They were a lively bunch, too. One day he might go over to Byars—"this live town" —for a Democratic rally, enlivened by a couple of fights and raiding a joint.

The next night he might go back, this time over to the Socialist

Hall, and deliver a rousing speech for the Socialists—for pay, but equally impassioned. "He was very eloquent and convincing in his talks and was considered very bright," an observer recalled.

There was passion at a Socialist meeting, where the poorest of the poor usually crowded into the one-room shack that served as school, church, and meeting hall. Steve would have made his way through the night, perhaps with the lively Socialist organizer Oscar Ameringer. Across the black prairie, stable and coal oil lanterns twinkled like lightning bugs, swinging on wagons or in hands of the faithful.

Inside, Ameringer recalled, "Sleeping babies were deposited on the platform....

"Young children from toddlers up crowded to the front school seats by twos and threes. Women with babies on their laps or at their breasts took the seats farther back in ones and twos. There was always at least one crying baby in the audience...."

They frequently held box socials.

"The young ladies of the block would bring boxes filled with sandwiches, cakes, pies, and other delicacies," he recalled.

"Advertising was done by giving 'general ring' calls over the party lines, which were free....

"We often arranged for horseback parades through the town proper.... A few thousand men riding through a town of perhaps not twice that many inhabitants looked...as though the social revolution was just around the corner...."

Steve drifted on—Oklahoma City, Ada, over into Texas and back again. Floating, he landed on his feet again in Oklahoma at Surphur, a particularly graceful little town growing up around "healing" sulphur springs.

Steve hit Sulphur about the time newspaper editor J.Y. Schenek lost a fight with a political adversary. Schenek, a paralytic, was sitting in a buggy with the wheels off. His enemy ambled over and riddled Schenek's body with the payload from a sawed off shotgun. In Little Dixie, newspapering and politics were serious business.

When his newspaper ran a contest to find the prettiest girl in Oklahoma, Steve pursued the winner, Miss Jeanette ("Nettie") Hamilton, across Little Dixie into the far southeastern corner of Oklahoma, to an up-and-coming little city named Hugo.

Their courtship was short but spirited. In 1915 Steve and Nettie made a trip back up the Washita River, to Tishomingo, the old capital of the Cherokee Nation.

And there they were wed.

Wedded bliss.

The new young couple, Steve and Nettie Stephenson, set up housekeeping in Madill, Oklahoma, in Little Dixie's cotton belt, where the Washita River meets the Red. He told people he was from Sulphur.

Madill was a town ripe for a young man on the make. With capital from some source—or, a detractor said, through trickery— Steve assumed control of the leading newspaper, the *Marshall County News-Democrat.*

It was a rich time. Now, at last, HIS name was on the masthead: "D.C. STEPHENSON, MGR. EDITOR." Right under "Official Organ of Marshall County."

He entered Madill April 9, 1915, like a civic-booster cyclone, launching a dizzying whirlwind of crusades. The hand was glad, the laugh affable, the cheeks pink with excitement, the steel-gray eyes brightened by zeal.

It was spring. Violets and dogwoods were in bloom, and the air was sweet with wild plum blossoms.

He was 23.

His surviving columns from Madill give the clearest picture of
the emerging Stephenson.

"It shall be the purpose of the *News Democrat*," Steve wrote
earnestly, "to pull for the very best interests of Madill and Marshall
County..., and at no time shall any matter enter the paper that
is intended to do personal injury to any individual. The present
management has no 'club' to break over your head, no brickbats to
throw, nor mud to sling, but proposes to sail on in the even tenor of
its own good way and try to please all the folks.

"It shall not assume the position of official dictation or Czar rule
of the city and its affairs, but will be busy most of the time running
its own affairs and will put forth an honest, through rugged, effort
to carry out these convictions."

He was well nigh-irresistible.

"*News Democrat* is no perfectionist," he wrote soon thereafter.

"It does not build the spasmodic sob nor spill the scalding tear
because all men are not Sir Galahads in quest of the Holy Grail and
all women angels with two pair of reversible wings and the aurora
borealis for a hatband. *News Democrat* would be lonesome in a world
like that.

"It does not expect to see religion without a cant, wealth without
a want, virtue without a vice, but it does hope to see an honest
umpire calling base decisions in the next game played between
Madill and Marietta."

Madill had possibilities. It was less cosmopolitan than Hugo,
less self-confident than Pauls Valley, less self-consciously cultured
than Purcell. Madill's tone was more southern, with an aura like

honeysuckle: sweet, meandering, and perennially persistent.

Ambling to work of a morning toward his little print shop on the north side of the town square, Steve would have cut cattycornered across by the latticed band stand.

He would have walked gingerly. Madill's square was bordered by watering troughs for horses whose droppings mingled in the streets with foot-deep sand, impassable when it rained. In serious downpours, he would have crossed Main Street in a boat.

A trip out of town promised even worse trouble. A 20-mile horseless carriage drive could take a day on "roads"—really, wagon ruts over the deep black gumbo—often ending with the indignity of hiring a horse to pull out the car. One did not so much drive on Madill roads as IN them.

Boosting and boasting Madill, Steve pressed for parks, for hard surface streets and sidewalks. He pushed the spring "swat a fly" campaign. He touted the new $2,000 Wurlitzer Orchestra Piano at the Colonial Theater and the new phone service: "every single—and married, for that matter—citizen of the city feels a particular pride in this service...."

He had barely hit town before he audaciously convened all Marshall County newspaper editors to form their own association, thrusting himself into leadership of a town he hardly knew.

"*News Democrat* has locked arms with the new elected...city officials," he wrote, "and will march up the road of progress fighting the battles of Madill with a high head and a light heart, bearing the knowledge that we have stood by the city, in its trying times, and have given the most favorable publicity.

"The new men elected, and those holding over, are a bunch of good fellows every man of them and *News Democrat* predicts a prosperous future for Madill. The retiring officials have, in the language of Timothy, fought a good fight, they have kept the faith, and deserve all manner of credit for the dutiful manner in which

43

they have stood by the city and watched her climb on the summit of success...."

Breaking for lunch, Steve might have paused to exchange town gossip with Indiana's fiery Socialist Eugene V. Debs, who maintained a Madill office across the square.

The gloomy Socialists might see the "electric light" town boosters like Steve as the enemies of the rural poor, particularly in Marshall County, where 80 percent of the farmers were landless tenants alien to the town's gentry. The festering rural poverty made Marshall the banner county of the Socialists' peak of power during Steve's tenure, in the state that briefly gained more dues-paying Socialists than any other.

Steve saw them all, town or farm alike, as potential customers.

In the halcyon days of summer, Steve wandered around the farmlands, pitching subscriptions, visiting Misses Rosa and Florence Cole while they were chopping corn, old John Buckholtz who was tearing down shocks to let the sheaves dry, J. F. Andrews who was plowing cotton.

"Mr. and Mrs. Andrews cordially invited me to stay for dinner with them, and it was a splendid one, too, both fried chicken and chicken and dumplings, hot biscuits, milk and many vegetables. Mrs. Andrews is a splendid housekeeper and ...the no-frill eggs she sells have an established reputation...."

Clearly, Steve was having the time of his life.

"*News Democrat* wonders if everybody enjoys their work as we do," he mused. "It is indeed a pleasure to perform our daily duty...."

Still in his green weeks at Madill, Steve cast his editorial net beyond Marshall County. He caught some big fish.

A crisis erupted on June 21, 1915, when the U.S. Supreme Court ruled Oklahoma's "grandfather clause" unconstitutional. Now white

Oklahomans could no longer require literacy tests of any man whose ancestor was not a qualified voter before 1866—the year of the 14th Amendment.

The U.S. court's decision overruled an opinion of the Oklahoma Supreme Court that had been written by one Bob Williams, now the state's governor. Steve praised Williams lavishly. "Long live Bob Williams!" Stephenson wrote.

There was more at issue than mere race. Blacks had voted Republican since Lincoln freed the slaves. Little Dixie, like Steve, was yellow-dog Democrat.

"Give us a special session of the Legislature, Governor Williams," Steve pleaded. "The people of Southern Oklahoma have come in a single voice and cried out for relief. Have something done to substitute our White Man's Law, the 'grandpa' clause."

The power of the pen was heady stuff.

"Great things have been accomplished by men who came from what might be considered the lower walks of life," Steve wrote. "Napoleon was once in the very dregs of humanity...."

"Fairness should be a man's closest friend, his honor, his life."

"If we were to 'fall for' all the bouquets that have been handed us on the last issue of *News Democrat*, our head would burst with personified egotism," he wrote modestly in August of 1915, five months into the job.

"*News Democrat* is not invincible. Compliments usually, when they are well meant, penetrate to our finer feeling.... We endeavor to avoid the lusterless and hackneyed, giving only the matter which will be of benefit.... Besides carrying advertising for all the representative firms of the city."

While Steve and his new bride were living blissfully in Madill, events elsewhere were moving swiftly to a conclusion that would profoundly affect Steve's future.

The Stephensons had been in Madill only weeks when Georgia Governor Slaton made the perilous decision not to hang Leo Frank for the murder of little Mary Phagan. Slaton's order of commutation was dated June 21, 1915—the same day the U.S. Supreme Court ruled Oklahoma's grandfather clause unconstitutional.

Steve reported both decisions prominently on the front page, giving priority placement to the Frank decision.

And again, on August 19, 1915, Steve reported that a party of 25 men had lynched Frank three days earlier. Hundreds were mobbing the scene to see Frank hanging from a Georgia oak. Steve gave the bigger play to Atlanta's mayor, who called the lynching a "just penalty for an unspeakable crime....

"When it comes to a woman's honor, there is no limit we will not go to avenge and protest," the mayor said.

The following week, Steve yielded to "great demand" to editorialize on the Frank lynching. He took on the "solemn duty... absolutely without prejudice or passion." Before he was done, he wrote three editorials on the subject. He wrestled editorially, first, with the question of Frank's guilt or innocence and, second, with the issue of mob law.

The first question was clouded by a second suspect in the case, a Negro janitor. At length, Steve concluded that both the Negro and Frank must have been guilty.

On the second question: "*News Democrat* does not believe in mob violence under any slightest doubt exists as to guilt," he wrote. "The lynching of Leo Frank is nothing short of a homicide.... Of course, ...there had been a crime—the most damnable in history..., a pure, sweet, innocent lamb of the upper fold was ravaged and raped by a beast too low to be called a brute, and then her tender little body was mutilated by the fiend....

"The men who killed Frank...were brave, loyal, true-born

Southern gentlemen, in whose veins flowed so much red blood that they could not stand by and see the law cheated (if it was) in a case of such gravity, so dastardly and inspired in hell in the minds of those who blotted out the life of little Mary Phagan....

"Those men who lynched Frank were not murderers.... 'These men were inspired by the kind of high devotion that has frequently made heroes,' ...to avenge the death of the innocent and unsophisticated little fairy who was murdered and ravaged...at the hands of one or two men—the negro and his co murderer, Leo Frank."

Steve's conclusion?

"If Leo Frank was guilty of the crime charged against him, and for which he died, he deserved the worst punishment conceivable to human mind. If he was not guilty, then he was entitled to his freedom and liberty—God alone can testify."

Steve could not then have known that Atlanta editor Tom Watson was at the same time drafting far less moderate commentaries, calling for the rebirth of the Ku Klux Klan, while the Knights of Mary Phagan were preparing for their march up Stone Mountain to burn a triumphant cross. Or that Colonel Simmons three months hence would follow their steps to resurrect the Klan. And none of them could know that, before his death in 1962, the black custodian would confess that he alone had killed Mary Phagan, that Leo Frank was innocent.

At the time those later events transpired, Steve would be preoccupied with other affairs.

4
JUS' SAILIN' 'LONG,
DOIN' THE BEST WE CAN

August 1915
Madill, Oklahoma

The merciless August Oklahoma sun beat down on a teeming
crowd that milled around the new Madill courthouse, downing
lemonade, ice cream, and watermelons by the wagonload.

Steve had trumpeted the event for weeks: "Three of the biggest
days ever celebrated in Madill," to feature "Best speakers in the
entire country."

It was a rally of the leading Madill fraternity, the Woodmen of
the World. Speakers included the cream of the region's political
crop—state senators, Supreme Court justices—and a young
newspaper editor named D.C. Stephenson, representing the newly
formed Oklahoma Press Association.

All would come with "a message of fellowship, impressing the necessity for harmony," instilling " the spirit of brotherly love," Steve promised.

But the crowd knew better than to expect sweetness and light. Steve was engaged in what he must have believed to be the fight of his life.

The new clerk of the Supreme Court, a fellow named William M. Franklin, had challenged Gov. Bob Williams' right to curtail the clerk's budget by some $1,800. For unknown reasons, Steve took the tiff personally. Rushing to the governor's defense, Steve threw himself into the center of the fray.

After Steve editorialized on behalf of his beloved governor, an angry Franklin sputtered that the *News-Democrat* was "a dirty, lying sheet, edited by an ignorant, blown up egoist."

Steve dutifully published Franklin's comments and then had no choice but to rise, reluctantly, to oratory to defend his governor.

Stephenson would have mounted the lattice bandstand modestly, with youthful vigor. True to his pattern, he was most apt to begin with silence that commanded the attention of the raucous crowd. When every eye was on him, he would begin.

"We have been advised, 'an editor who has no opinions has no business running a newspaper, and if he has opinions he had better keep them to himself,'" he began, pausing for the crowd's chuckle. "But still this game is fascinating....

"Let me make one thing perfectly clear. *News Democrat* bears no ill will, no hatred, no enemy. It owns nor controls anything.... No desire exists on its part to monopolize anything—jus' sailing 'long, doin' the best we can, trying to please all the folks, and taking care of our own affairs—wishing everyone all that is good."

He reached for a glass of lemonade nearby, drank it down, and surveyed the crowd intently.

"Fairness should be a man's closest friend; his honor, his life.

And so, I seize this opportunity to go on record as endorsing every official act of the great Governor of Oklahoma!

"Long live Bob Williams!" he shouted, and a burst of applause rose from the crowd.

Steve's voice rose even higher. "I swear by the throne of Heaven, before which I shall one day appear..., that my conduct throughout this entire controversy has been governed only by the convictions I have uttered as to the perfect honesty of our governor."

He bowed his head. "I have done that only which I believe to be my duty, as a citizen of this great state." A murmur of agreement rose from the crowd.

Raising a fist to heaven, Steve concluded with an impassioned shout: "When I go to that celestial beyond, I do not want the bleeding spirit of Bob Williams to approach me in the presence of an angry God and say, 'Why were you meek and gentle to my character butcher down at Madill?"

He dropped his hands to his sides, in humility, and received the welcome applause.

It was vintage Stephenson.

And what did the selfless young editor receive for his fearless stands? Martyrdom.

"GUNMAN THREATENS EDITOR," he wrote August 5.

"Late Sunday evening, as the editor was sitting in the office, a big, burly, hyena-looking burglar appearing individual came in and asked who wrote that dam stuff in last week's paper....

"*News Democrat* grabbed his favorite weapon (a stool) and ordered the fiend to leave the office. Several heated and uncomplimentary words escaped the lips of *News Democrat*, a thing that seldom happens, and the big ruffian said, 'If any more of that rot comes out, you'll get yours,' at the same time patting himself over his pistol pocket.

"Certainly," Steve wrote, "we will get ours, and no man, regardless of...reputation as a desperate character, can so intimidate us as to arouse a fear sufficient to cause us to refrain from expressing an honest sentiment as we see it, while holding a fear of God and respect for men.

"Bluffs are alright, but threats from men such as above described mean little to the experienced. During our newspaper career, we have been threatened 999 times and injured none, have had 500 fights and been whipped 499 and are ready to lose one more if necessity requires.

"No, cowardly threats will not effect the editorial policy of *News Democrat* so long as the present incumbent wields the quill."

Steve had been wielding his quill at Madill nearly six months when he wrote that, at the *News-Democrat*, "...truth is diligently sought..., and we are commanded, sometimes at the point of a gun, to suppress the facts....

"All big men who actually accomplish something...are subject to criticism from the opposing political forces....

"We have been threatened, have been assaulted, and have been offered bribes. But God forbid that, while we keep the sacred memory of our loved and loving Mother, our fear of God, and respect for men, that we ever weaken either to bribery, threats, or the ironical hand of justice meted out by a tribunal purporting to be a medium of justice.

"Passion cannot reason, envy cannot prophesy, malice knows no honor, and men of criminal career, either in state matters or as private citizens, should not expect to be obeyed when they have committed error and are so adjudged by the great commonality of constituency.

"So let it be that *News Democrat* will continue with open hands and a fearless publication of facts regardless of the victim or the victor."

And then, as suddenly as he came, Steve was gone.

One account, by an enemy, holds that Steve was fired from the Madill newspaper "as the proprietors realized that Stephenson was not capable of properly editing the paper."

In fact, however, the *Marshall County News-Democrat* was lively and informative during Steve's tenure. By community standards, he was a moderate, at least in print, on "the race question." Unlike other contemporary editors, Steve published no Madill editorials calling for the mob lynchings that some of his peers inflamed.

The Madill paper, on September 16, 1915, noted merely that the *Marshall County News-Democrat* had changed hands again and "The young men who have heretofore been running the paper will be retained in its employ." But by the next issue, both Steve and his name had disappeared.

Life was not so simple now for Steve—for Nettie was with child.

According to a contemporary, he persuaded his young wife to move back with her parents while he went looking for work. He found it, the account goes, in Ada, then Sulphur, as a linotype operator.

He surfaced next at Cushing, in northern Oklahoma, in the spring of 1916, at the height of the oil boom. It was a time like none other, inevitably marking all who lived through it.

In the Cushing field, Steve came into a world where only the bold survived; where fortunes were made or lost in a wink; where black gold spewed from the earth faster than it could be sold, with incalculable waste.

At Cushing, they were all Steve's teachers: the daring, the sooner, the boomer, the grafter, the wildcatter. He couldn't have chosen a better place and time than Cushing, 1916, to learn from those who were not constrained from exploiting each other or the Mother Earth.

Cushing had little reason to hope, or even exist, before 1912. But it was a time when faith abounded. Across the globe, a unsinkable ship named the Titanic was sailing into open sea.

In March of 1912 in the Cushing field, after a year of dry holes, a wildcatter named Tom Slick hit pay dirt.

The rush was on. Cushing mushroomed into the fabled frenzies of an oil boom.

By the time Steve ventured into the Cushing field, the countryside was awash in derricks, tent encampments, board-on-batten cities, sheet metal shops, tarpaper shacks, and false-front hotels, bars, and bordellos.

The niceties of social intercourse that Steve had learned at Purcell and Pauls Valley were of little benefit in the Cushing field.

Cushing's main drag was appropriately named Broadway. It was as wide as any other six roads. They threw up buildings alongside it, up three steps to tether horses, above a sea of mud called a street. "It was commonplace," one settler recalled later "to see ten or twelve horses hitched to a wagon, up to their stomachs in mud, the wagon wheels out of sight and the vehicle sliding along the mud....

"It was a thrilling place for a young man to be. You couldn't tell day from night. Everything was wide open."

Roustabouts are not, by nature, gentle men. On Steve's rounds through the teeming streets, the packed gambling houses, the steamy brothels, he learned humility. A man with a sledge hammer—who that morning might have blown a well with nitroglycerin—was not a man to cross.

The flow from the earth, once summoned, would not be stemmed, and markets were teetering on glut. Prudent Cushing-ites were throwing up storage tanks, casting out pipelines, nailing down refineries.

Steve's newspaper in Cushing was modest. Over the way was the *Cushing Citizen*, staid, long-lived, secure in its spanking clean new quarters, anchored by its powerful new, 3,200-pound Mergenthaler linotype. Steve, on the other hand, was hired to edit a fledgling little weekly called the *Cushing Independent*, whose principal job appeared to be glorifying local Sheriff J. H. Townsend.

Sheriff Townsend was "a manly man," Steve wrote, who could take on odds of 1000 to 1 and beat them, "unflinching, undaunted, courageous, and true." Perhaps it was a coincidence that the *Cushing Independent* was owned by Henry Townsend.

"SHERIFF TOWNSEND CLEANS UP CRIMINAL ELEMENT," Steve reported on June 23, 1916. "County Enforcement Officer Leads Bunch of Stern and Determined Men in Campaign That Sweeps Clean All Known Law Violation in City of Cushing."

The good sheriff began the sweep at 9:30 a.m. By noon, when Steve interviewed him, vice was on the run. "I am resolved to clean up this town," Townsend said. "The 'free and easy' elements...have served their time in Payne County...."

Steve was big on law and order, no question about it.

Steve also crusaded earnestly for roads and bridges. He offered "liberal prizes" for the Cushing merchants with the best Fourth of July decorations. And he took out after the Socialists:

"Socialism would pull every man down that is up, and keep every poor man that is down from ever rising, and the worker would be a hopeless wage slave...."

Steve hit Cushing somewhere in early 1916. As late as the end of June, the *Cushing Independent* was a weekly. But progress blossomed quickly. Without comment, the masthead was switched to a daily on

July 7: "A Live Daily Newspaper, Daily Except Saturday."

"Fundamentally," Steve wrote in the July 7 issue, "vision is required for the big developments of civilization. Dessect [sic] any step of progress in whatever line of business, you will find that it was nurtured in the see-ahead brain of an ambitious man...."

He called for a system of hard-surfaced, transcontinental roads, concluding: "Cushing will do her part. The 'vision' is here, and the men to back it."

And then, as swiftly as he came, Steve was gone.

In later years, after enemies decided to investigate D. C. Stephenson's beginnings, they told this story:

Nettie Stephenson bore a daughter, Florence Katherine Stephenson, in Oklahoma City while Steve was at Cushing.

"When word and an appeal for money to help defray expenses reached Stephenson from the hospital where she was confined, he sent word that he was unable to get to the state capital.... It has been charged that while operating the Cushing newspaper, that Stephenson posed as a single man and held intimate relations with a young girl who had great faith in him. The appearance of Mrs. Stephenson and the baby, in Cushing, created quite a stir...."

Steve split the scene, they said.

"According to Mr. Townsend, D.C. collected about $800 and when he left for parts unknown he neglected to leave the money or an accounting...."

His adversaries said he moved north, working briefly as a linotype operator in the town of Miami in far northeast Oklahoma.

Then he drifted into Iowa, to a little town called Story City.

Shortly thereafter, in the spring of 1917, the World War erupted. On April 23, 1917, Steve joined the National Guard at Boone, Iowa. He was assigned to the Iowa infantry, Company B, 127th MG Battalion.

He began his military career with characteristic energy. On August 5, shortly before his 26th birthday, Steve was made a corporal.

November 26 he was called to active service and promoted again, this time to second lieutenant. He was assigned to Company D, 36th Infantry, and transferred to Officers Training Camp at Fort Snelling, Minnesota.

Clearly he showed promise

For countless young men like Steve, the military has provided a future: perhaps education that leads out of poverty into a profession. Or training in the fundamentals of The Military Machine: discipline, strategic planning, mobilization, and organization. By some accounts, Steve recouped all that and more.

He came away, moreover, with a spine-tingling series of stories of heroic deeds overseas, in the fierce fighting in Belleau Woods. But his investigators contended he never left the states. After the war, he was honorably discharged February 4, 1919, at Camp Devens, Massachusetts.

Steve surfaced next at Akron, Ohio, where he married again on January 7, 1920, to Violet Mary Carroll, a girl he met while he was a salesman for a linotype company. They say she was beautiful. His first wife, Nettie, had divorced him during the war.

In Akron he raised money to start a newspaper.

Now Violet was with child. The union produced a son, David James Stephenson. But around the time the son was born, as quickly as Steve had appeared, he moved on again.

His trail is muddy here. Violet divorced him February 28, 1924, and said he tricked her mother out of money.

Somewhere in these years he landed at Davenport, Iowa, working as a newspaper proofreader and linotype operator. A contemporary recalled that Steve "had acquired a considerable amount of learning through reading copy.

"He was blessed with an abundance of native intelligence, but cursed with a colossal ego....

"After the paper had gone to bed each night at Davenport, he would invite the other boys of the composing room to his quarters, where he would discourse learnedly on such subjects as biology, politics, human traits, chemistry and so on, cautiously holding himself within subjects in which his audiences were unversed.

"Few men ever were able to cover a larger slice of educational bread with a stingier smattering of information than the great Steve. One night at the close of one of those panel discussions—in which D.C. was the entire panel—a member of the group patted the oracle on his shoulder and called him 'The Old Man.'"

Steve fairly loved the new name, his contemporary reported. It stuck.

Soon it became a privilege to know him well enough to use Steve's new nickname. Only those of his inner circle, who were able to "listen to his words of wisdom and bask in the reflected glory of his personality," were close enough to call Steve "The Old Man."

By 1920 he had surfaced again, this time in Indiana. He had a fresh slate, a chance to make his mark in an up-and-coming state. From whatever source, he had a nest egg. And he had a new identity.

The Old Man was 28, and his future was before him. The boy was a man now, fully formed. This stop would be for keeps.

Steve set up his new headquarters in the Vendrome Hotel of Evansville, where the Ohio River makes a lucky horseshoe bend into Indiana. He dealt in stocks and coal, in partnership with

Evansville's L.G. Julian.

As he told the story in later years: "In 1919 I was engaged in business in the city of Evansville, and was a legal resident of the city, having returned to Evansville upon being discharged from the United States Army at the expiration of the world war.

"I became interested in the welfare of former service men, and at one time started to organize the discharged soldiers of Indiana with whom I had served in the 36th Infantry.

"This activity inevitably led to politics. I became interested in the local ticket, in Evansville, and only incidentally in the state and national issues, during the 1920 election."

Evansville was under control of a Democrat boss named Big Ben Bosse, mayor since 1913, who saw that Steve could be an asset to his organization. The mayor took Steve under his wing.

All was not peaceful with Bosse, nor with Evansville. From the roustabout-ruled riverfront to the train depot where the Red Special ran, the rollicking town had been rocked by scandals almost since its founding in the early 1800s. Among its claims to fame was a rip-roaring red light district where prostitutes and gamblers operated openly, with police protection.

When Steve landed there, Evansville was in the throes of the "Red Scare" that swept the country in 1919 and 1920. The war had ended too soon, some said, leaving Americans tumescent with unreleased passion against an enemy. They found new enemies at home.

Mayor Bosse personified the spirit, calling himself the "100 percent American" mayor of a "100 percent American city." He defined the term with heavy-handed curbs on Germans, "aliens," and labor unrest among the city's pottery and furniture workers.

It was a city tailor made to become the first northern outpost in Indiana for the new Ku Klux Klan.

Steve said later that Mayor Bosse was the first to point out to him the political potential of the Klan, possibly as an aid toward Bosse's goal of becoming governor. About the same time Atlanta had dispatched a Kleagle named Joe Huffington to sell the Klan in Evansville.

Steve recalled that he was pressed by "reliable men..., prominent citizens of Evansville," to join the KKK to achieve goals that were "entirely political." They assured him that the group was "not engaged in propagating hate against racial and religious groups." They said it was "sponsoring a program through politics which was designed to place in public office a class of men upon whose integrity the better citizens could depend."

With those assurances, Steve joined Evansville's Indiana Klan Number 1, which was chartered August 13, 1921, by Indiana's affable Secretary of State, Ed Jackson, over some public opposition. But after the local election in 1921, Steve dropped out.

Huffington was not making much of the local Klan, in Steve's view. The fellows were primarily focused on raiding bootleggers and hassling couples parked on country roads. To make matters worse, Huffington was always in hot water with Atlanta.

Steve turned his attention to his own affairs. In the spring of 1922 his thirst for politics lured him into the race for Congress as a "wet" Democrat. When he saw his support was faltering, Steve tried to withdraw from the race, but he was too late to erase his name off the ballot. The Anti Saloon League sank him, and he came up as a "dry" Republican. He was trounced by William E. Wilson, who won both the primary and the First District congressional seat.

For Steve, the defeat brought a sobering lesson. Never again would he engage in a battle without consolidating his power base.

In 1922, the Evansville-Atlanta dispute came to a head, and Simmons dispatched a representative named Mahoney to

Evansville to straighten things out. The locals asked Stephenson, the great debater, to have it out with Mahoney.

Steve demurred. He had his own affairs to attend to.

But at length he agreed, on their petition that he should help revive the group for the 1922 elections to "rebuild its voting power and throw the organization's political strength behind a slate of candidates in which the local community was interested," Steve later recalled.

Steve's performance so satisfied his fellows that they asked him to carry the message to a meeting in Chicago with Imperial Kleagle Ed Clarke. Steve demurred but, when pressed, agreed. He had assumed leadership of Indiana's first Ku Klux Klan.

Steve's meeting with Clarke was a grand success.

The Old Man impressed Clarke—so much so that the Imperial Kleagle offered Steve a job. He could become a Kleagle in his own right, making good money in his spare time by spreading the news about the KKK among his friends—on 40 percent commission.

Steve demurred. He was a business man, a busy man. But, after appropriate hesitation, The Old Man agreed.

5
THE TEXAS TOOTHPULLER

1921
Atlanta, Georgia

Meanwhile, back at Klan Central in Atlanta, Colonel William Joseph Simmons had his hands full.

Those hands were as memorable as they were busy, given to grand and airy gestures, mesmerizing interviewers who by 1921 were flocking to his Imperial desk before a mammoth American flag.

"His hands are graceful," wrote one journalist. "The fingers are long and tapered. They might be those of a pianist. The fingers move independent of each other, not clumsily all together."

As he entertained reporters with his visions for the Kuklux, Simmons' hands played a sort of mid-air, invisible grand piano. It was seductive, irresistible. Interviewers concluded that he was a true believer.

"When he grasps your hand," another wrote, "you feel that he has to hold himself back to keep from crushing it, so vigorous is his grip."

His reach was sweeping, but it had exceeded his vigorous grasp. His empire was growing, klavern by klavern, into an invisible, national octopus.

By September of 1921, Simmons had earned more than $200,000 from the Klan—although he modestly contended he accepted no more than $100 a week.

By numbers he publicized, the Klan had 650,000 native-born, white, Protestant, Gentile members—equal to $6.5 million gross in membership fees alone, at "$10 per bonehead," as one periodical sputtered. More conservative estimates placed the membership in the 100,000 range in 1921.

The Klan crossed Mason and Dixon's line in the winter of '20-'21 and broadened its crusade into international waters, thriving on its favorite rumor that the Pope was coming—any day—to take over America. One hundred percent Americans must mobilize; the war was not over; it had only begun.

Reversing the path of Union soldiers in the Civil War, the Klan was marching relentlessly northward, then westward. Klan membership, Simmons announced, was about half North and half South, extending into 38 states.

Ed Clarke had a plan for the KKK to cross the oceans, a sort of Klan International scheme—in the right populations, of course, of Anglo Saxon, Germanic, and Scandinavian descent. He managed to organize branches in Alaska and the Canal Zone, with scattered pockets in Hawaii, New Zealand, Shanghai, Lithuania, Czechoslovakia, England, Cuba, and Mexico. But the only measurable success was in Germany, where in the mid 1920s some 300 Germans organized but quickly floundered on internal strife.

Perhaps it was just as well, since Clarke stayed busy picking the fruits of his success in the United States. Sometimes the newly established klaverns were puzzled; now they were organized, but what should they be doing? The answer from Atlanta became standard: Clean up your town.

By the close of 1921, the Imperial command announced that local chapters had given more than $1 million to charities. "The pursuit of charity has become a paramount issue with members of the Ku Klux Klan," Simmons said, "and whenever the organization is active, assistance will be rendered to the needy."

Colonel Simmons was beginning to grow into the lifestyle that befitted his Imperial Wizardness.

The Klan was moving uptown. The business could no longer be contained in its executive offices, occupying the entire third floor of Atlanta's Haynes Building. Its sea of stenographers and clerks spilled over into half a dozen rooms in another building.

Spreading the word required larger quarters, centralization. For about $1 million, the KKK purchased an entire block on Atlanta's prestigious Peachtree Road, to be converted into Imperial Headquarters. A $65,000 Georgian mansion, white pillared, became the Imperial Palace. Landscaping included an artificial lake and $30,000 in new marble and plastic statuary.

The Klan set up its own propaganda publishing house. In time, it would publish or control 150 publications.

On May 6, 1921, the Klan presented Simmons with gifts, including a $1,000 monthly salary, $25,000 back pay for his first five years' struggle, and a sedan. In silk purple robes, a crown, and a death mask, he posed for reporters at the largest gift, a $40,000 house he named Klan Krest.

But all this pomp had a price. Like Simmons' fingers, the

tentacles of his far flung, invisible octopus empire were beginning to move independently of one another, beyond his grand, airy control.

By happenstance, he had devised a military-style, secret hierarchy whose lower reaches were given to spasms of independent anarchy and twitches of mayhem. All he had in mind was a warmly spiritual fraternity. He was as surprised as anybody at its growth. He had accidentally created an unmanageable monster.

Simmons' headaches were mounting. First there was the problem of imitators, then the problem of critics among what he considered to be dangerous elements such as the NAACP and the Catholics. Newspapers and periodicals took out after the Klan.

To make matters worse, there was an ugly rumor about Ed Clarke and Bessie Tyler. And from the field, out in the hinterland Klans, embarrassing reports kept popping up about over-zealousness among some of the boys. The crowning straw on Simmons' beleaguered head came from none other than the United States Congress.

Some of his imitators simply declared themselves to be Klansmen, without paying the dues. There was a price to be paid for the order's secrecy; if others got into mischief, the Klan was blamed. Some militant groups organized like the Klan but actually used its tactics to fight Simmons' knights; the Imperial Palace had to set up its own protective secret service, headed by a tough New York strike breaker named Fred Savage. Still other imitators set up rival groups, such as the 19-year-old in North Carolina who organized a Junior KKK, appointed himself "Exalted Dragon," and collected 25 cents apiece from his friends.

By 1921 the Klan was a hot item for the press, producing a barrage of publicity that was a bit unseemly for a secret fraternity.

The Catholic and Jewish press, with some Protestant groups,

denounced the Klan as "perhaps the most serious menace now threatening the national unity and religious harmony for which all the moral forces of this country are striving." Wrote the *Michigan Catholic*: "They have blasphemously adopted the Cross as their ensign and under the banner of this sacred symbol would deny to Jews the rights of our common humanity." The KKK, said a New York Jewish rabbi, arose from the belief of many Americans "that there is no crime quite as grave as that of difference, or otherness."

In the summer of 1921, Catholic Klan fighters established the American Unity League, to reawaken "true American principles," with its own journal named *Tolerance*.

The National Association for the Advancement of Colored People stooped to quoting Simmons' own words: "We don't bar niggers; they bar themselves. Let them change their color." The NAACP recalled that Clarke had publicly urged sterilization of black male babies so the race would disappear in the United States. "If America wishes to avert racial clashes..., it will take immediate action to stamp out, not only the farcical organization of Imperial Wizard Simmons but the spirit which makes so un-American an organization possible."

Even more stinging were reports from a growing segment of the popular press. It was a golden era for newspapers and magazines, and reporters dipped their pens into deep wells of acid sarcasm that seemed to have been lying untapped for years, just waiting for the Klan.

"All the balderdash in which native-born Americans have indulged in recent years seems to have coagulated in this cesspool of the Ku Klux Klan, to be ladled out by its Kludds, its Klokards and its Kleagles, as a poison which the feeble-minded cannot distinguish from anything but normal loyalty," fumed *The New Republic*.

"It all sounds as tho Tom Sawyer and Huck Finn had got together and devised the whole thing...," wrote *Current Opinion*.

On July 28, 1921, after a KKK organizer hit Kansas, scrappy Emporia editor William Allen White began a series of anti-Klan editorials, in the style that won White national acclaim:

"For a self-constituted body of moral idiots who would substitute the findings of the Ku Klux Klan for the processes of law, to better conditions, would be a most un-American outrage which every good citizen should resent," White wrote.

The blockbuster blow came from the daily *New York World*, which on September 6, 1921, began a two-week, screaming-headline series of articles condemning the Klan. The stories were syndicated and carried in papers around the country.

The *World*'s sensationalized—and not totally accurate—accounts came from disgruntled Klansmen and alleged Klan victims. *The World* claimed the Imperial Palace cleared $5 million in 5 years, that its leaders lived in grotesque excess, and that the Klan had 500,000 members active in every state except Montana, Utah, and New Hampshire.

The World printed lurid details of 152 Klan "outrages," nationwide, including 4 murders, 41 floggings, 27 tar-and-feather parties, 1 branding with acid, 1 mutilation, 5 kidnappings, 43 individuals ordered to leave town, and 14 raids of masked men with threatening placards. When the editors received crudely illustrated death threat letters signed by "the Ku Klux Klan," the World printed those, too.

"Ku Kluxism as conceived, incorporated, propagated, and practiced has become a menace to the peace and security of every section of the United States," *World* editors wrote. "Its evil and vicious possibilities are boundless.... Irresponsible men without the sanction of the law have announced aims at variance with the law and by lawless acts of terror have proceeded to their enforcement. Such a rule within a rule cannot continue if legitimate government is to stand unmocked...."

The World called for a congressional investigation into the Klan.

The World also alleged that Ed Clarke and Bessie Tyler had a more than platonic relationship. Ed and Bessie had been arrested, in their nightclothes, for drunk and disorderly behavior at an Atlanta house of ill repute. Clarke panicked at the *World* stories and resigned—to protect Mrs. Tyler's honor, he said. Mrs. Tyler was not grateful. She blistered Clarke in the press, calling him "weak-kneed." He meekly withdrew his resignation, while his wife proceeded to divorce court.

In Klan lore, Clarke and Tyler thus earned the distinction of producing the first sex scandal in the 1920s Klan. It would not be the last.

Clarke's panic turned out to be premature, in terms of Klan health. The series set people around the country talking about the Invisible Empire, and with the free publicity came a blizzard of new members. Klan headquarters couldn't process them fast enough, even with added staff. The *World* and syndication papers had printed an exhibit of a KKK membership blank; eager Klan applicants filled it in and sent it to Simmons with $10 bills.

When rumors surfaced that Congress was serious about a Klan investigation, the staff at the Imperial Palace panicked again. But in the crisis, it was Colonel Simmons himself who rose imperially to the occasion, with unforgettable flair.

Let the Jews, the niggers, the Catholics—even the Congress of the United States—come after him. He was ready.

He spent $2,000 to send telegrams to every member of the House urging them to proceed with their investigation, forthwith. He welcomed the hearings, which began in October of 1921.

Simmons testified for two days, and it was by all accounts a show stopper. He arrived looking like an affable uncle in his maroon Prince Albert coat, high white collar, and generously knotted tie. He posed for photographers with an innocent semi-smile, "as full of sentiment as plum is juice," one reporter said.

"Those were exciting times in Washington," an observer

remembered later. "Government detectives, Klan detectives, and newspaper reporters scurrying all over the place."

"I am a sick man," Simmons announced at the outset of his testimony. He respectfully asked the House committee's pardon if he succumbed to a coughing spell, brought on by laryngitis.

He then launched into an hours-long monologue covering the history of the Klan and its good works. He parried deftly, deflecting criticisms with aplomb, defending the Klan's honor, refuting all charges of violence and mismanagement. "Our mask and robe, I say before God, are as innocent as the breath of an angel," he said, in his flowing river, sonorous voice.

It was a tour de force, ending with a hoarsely whispered "Christ on the cross speech" to his adversaries: "…You do not know what you are doing. You are ignorant of our principles as were those who were ignorant of the character and work of the Christ. I cannot better express myself than by saying to you who are persecutors of the Klan and myself, 'Father, forgive you, for you know not what you do.' Mr. Chairman, I am done."

With those words, Colonel Simmons crumpled to the floor in a dead faint.

"We got hold of the hot end of a poker," one of the committee members muttered. Congress took no action.

KKK membership exploded. Applications poured in, sometimes 3,500 in a single day. With them, the money flowed in, too, faster than headquarters could open the mail—as much as $35,000 a day in new members klectokens alone. The Imperial Palace and its sheet factory were humming, 24 hours a day. By 1922, Simmons' Invisible Empire had risen from 100,000 to more than 1 million members.

"It wasn't until the newspapers began to attack the Klan that it really grew," Simmons would later recall. "Certain newspapers also aided us by inducing Congress to investigate us. The result was that Congress gave us the best advertising we ever got.

"Congress made us."

Some of Ed Clarke's best young men went west. His field hands found a gold mine in the fertile fields of Texas. On April Fool's Day, 1921, a band of Klansmen in the Lone Star State hit on an innovative variation of the old Texas practice of branding cattle.

Rumor had it that a black bellhop at the Dallas Adolphus Hotel, Alex Johnson, was making a little money on the side as a panderer, arranging for prostitutes for guests.

Members of Dallas Klan No. 66 were righteously irked by the rumor. Fired by passion for community reform, they decided to teach Johnson a lesson that would make him an example for other wrong doers.

At the appointed hour, a group of knights assembled, waylaid Johnson, dragged him from the hotel, and carted him to a secluded spot. There they gave him a good flogging and burned the Triple K brand across his forehead with acid. Then they dumped him back at the hotel, bearing a permanent mark of the beast, the initials KKK.

Although Johnson's assailants were well known, historians do not report prosecution of the vigilante mob.

Their leader, by most accounts, was the head of the Dallas KKK, Exalted Cyclops Hiram Wesley Evans, an amiable Dallas dentist who was increasingly obsessed with his Klan activities and growing obligations to his fellows. The Klan was taking over his life; in time, he would return the favor.

Early prospecting for Klan proselytes showed that Texas had promise, from the day in September 1920 that Klansman Z. R. Upchurch alighted from a train at Houston's Southern Pacific depot to survey the territory. Upchurch was a consummate Kleagle. He ambled around Houston, talking to men about the Klan, and nearly all eagerly signed membership applications.

By the first week in October, Upchurch had a hundred converts. It was a big state; he would need at least 20 men to work it. He wired Clarke that he had hit pay dirt.

When the big annual Confederate Veterans parade wound through the streets of Houston on October 9, in its midst was Colonel Simmons, with the grandson of the Reconstruction Klan's revered leader, Nathan Bedford Forrest. The KKK name was emblazoned on the side of their automobile. Behind them in the parade, hooded and robed Klansmen carried banners: "We were here yesterday, 1866; We are here today, 1920; We will be here forever."

Texans were far enough south to be reared on tales of the Reconstruction Ku Klux Klan, which had a good name in those parts. And they were far enough west to be steeped in vigilante frontier tradition. Stampeded to missionary zeal by the high-pressure pitch of cash-hungry Kleagles, Texans managed to create a Klan revival that combined reform and direct action into the worst of both worlds.

Fiery crosses flared on both sides of the Red River, first in Texas, then north into Oklahoma. The Klan traveled through contiguous territories, "like its great prototype, the boll weevil," one journalist wrote.

Law and order was still a stranger in many Southwestern communities, newly emerging from the frontier into the twentieth century, still lively with vice and bootlegging as well as more subtle sins that needed correction. The Klan gave ragamuffin and leading citizen alike a white horse to ride while cleaning up their towns. In time a KKK powerhouse half a million strong extended in all directions from the Red River, growing hottest in Texas, Oklahoma, Arkansas, and Louisiana. That broad, deep Southwestern basin of Klandom would set records for 1920s' outrages.

In Texas the Invisible Empire spread outward from Houston, north and west, like a white ink blot. By 1922 Texas had about 200,000 members, requiring division into five provinces.

In terms of history, although perhaps not in terms of his Lone Star influence at the time, the most significant provincial leader was the Texas tooth puller and part time brander, Hiram Wesley Evans. He was promoted to Grand Titan, head of Texas Province 2 centered in Dallas.

H.W. Evans liked to refer to himself as "the most average man in America." He looked the part: He could have been a used car salesman or the proprietor of a hardware store in any small town in the country. He was maybe 5 feet 7 inches tall, of average build, on the roly-poly side. He had dark hair and a squarish face that looked like it hurt a bit when the occasion forced him to smile, like an anti-social accountant forced by the missus to a party.

In his ordinary business suit, Evans seemed curiously out of place in the flamboyant, purple silk and spangles world of the 1920s Ku Klux Klan hierarchy. In photos of its leading citizens, Evans looks a little fuzzy, as if he should be taking the photo rather than appearing in it, or perhaps holding the coats of the stars. A reader's eye moves to his face last, if at all.

Given a chance to make a speech, however, Evans was transformed, hooded or not. Clearly, the Klan made him a bigger man than he was. He became a leader of men. His knights liked him for his practicality and frankness, but they positively loved him for his barn-burning speeches. One of his followers said that when Evans got charged up, he could convince the Klansmen Jesus wasn't Jewish.

Klan history abounds with Evans' written proclamations over the years, but little is documented of his actual words. Perhaps they were not memorable; perhaps they lost their verve when they cooled on a black and white page.

After he ascended to a plateau that made his philosophy worth recording, he uttered words assembled or laundered by speech writers. Some journalists were grateful to accept assistants' rewrites of even interviews with Evans because the man found it impossible to be succinct. One reporter wrote that Evans had "a tendency toward oratorical prolixity," reminding one of "a rough and ready evangelist," who began most of his statements with "Brother, I'll say to you...."

Like Colonel Simmons, Evans was born in Alabama. Before the war he migrated to Texas, where he engaged in the practice of dentistry, with considerable success. His credentials were open to some question, however. There were persistent rumors that he was actually qualified to work only on animals. A variation of that rumor was that his only training was obtained by U.S. Mail.

The April Fool's Day branding by Evans' Klan was not the first or the last violent incident laid at the door of the Texas KKK. The brutal 2 ½-year record opened February 4, 1921, when hooded Houston Klansmen whipped a lawyer named B.I. Hobbs, thrust him into a vat of boiling tar, and coated his body with feathers. His crime: he had the "wrong kind" of clients, mostly blacks and chronic violators of the law.

From that beginning, the list grew rapidly in Texas and throughout the Southwest, drearily repetitious. In 1921, as the Klan marched across the South into the Southwest, the number of lynchings markedly increased, in areas where both the KKK and the lynch tree tradition was strongest.

In Texas alone, 21 lynchings were reported between 1921 and mid 1923. By the end of the bloody spring of 1922, Lone Star Klansmen were credited with 500 tar/feather/lash parties, plus sundry other threats, assaults, and homicides.

Even more crippling to communities than the violence, wrote one journalist, was the terror, "the implied threat of the mask." Yet, the KKK's veil of secrecy rendered it "perfectly ungatable by either the public or the government."

At tiny Tehana in the piney woods of east Texas, knights seized a young white woman from a hotel porch. She was taken into the country, undressed, tarred, and feathered, to cure her of what they contended was bigamy. Before they returned her to town, they cut her hair.

In Beaumont, after they treated a physician to the whip, tar, and feather for allegedly performing abortions, Klansmen sent the local newspaper a boastful, 4,000-word essay on their work, complete with a poem. "The eyes of the unknown had seen and observed the wrong to be redressed," they wrote. "Dr. Paul stood convicted before God and man... The law of the Klan is JUSTICE."

A mother in Lufkin, Texas, appealed to the American Civil Liberties Union by letter:

"My 19-year-old boy, Sherwood Vinson, received a letter through our mail ordering him to leave and advise his bootlegger friends to go with him. I took the letter to the grand jury and ask the jury to tell my boy if he was violating the law but they done nothing so far as I could tell. Later they caught the boy on the streets of Lufkin with a pistol in the hand of one of them, put him in a car, went to the woods, tarred and feathered him, brought him back to the streets of Lufkin, set him out, and our Sheriff paid no attention.... The boy says he knows the men that done the work. I have lived here sixty-four years, not educated, but want right, want the laws executed, and tried to get the grand jury to do so. We can get the bunch if we can get the law handed out honest...."

By late 1921 the *Houston Chronicle* summed up the summer:

"Texas Klansmen have beaten and blackened more people in the last six months than all the other states combined....

"Boys, you'd better disband. You'd better take your sheets, your banners, your masks, your regalia, and make one fine bonfire.... Your methods are hopelessly wrong. Every tradition of social progress is against them. They are opposed to every principle on which this Government is founded. They are out of keeping with civilized life."

But the pattern, now becoming well established over the country, held true: the more the press attacked the Klan, the more men flocked for memberships. The boys didn't disband; rather, they continued to multiply.

In Dallas and Waco, anti-Klan forces hit on a new lash curb trick: for each citizen whipped or abused, they treated a randomly selected Klansman to the same indignity.

The burgeoning Klan carried a virus of violence that spread on the wind, in a scatter pattern with no apparent rationale. Like smallpox, media reports of bizarre outrages attributed, rightly or wrongly, to the Klan broke out in disparate pockets around the country—the Southwest, the deep South; California and Oregon; New York and New Jersey; the Little Egypt fringe of southern Illinois.

The genie was loose again.

Now the man who summoned it from its slumber was awash in problems and paperwork. As reports of Klan violence continued to mount around the Imperial Palace, the Imperial Wizard first denied them, then decried them, then ceremoniously revoked charters of some errant Klans. Like his membership, Colonel Simmons' troubles continued to grow.

Despite overwhelming financial rewards, success was not painless for the unrelenting Bessie Tyler or Imperial Kleagle Ed Clarke, either.

Clarke sustained a hard blow when one of his most valuable employees in the Propagation Department, Z.R. Upchurch, the

Kleagle who first kluxed Texas, resigned in disgust. With three Goblins, Upchurch sued Clarke and Tyler in 1921. In court testimony, the four regional sales managers fired various morals volleys at Ed and Bessie, including their purported bawdy house pajama party in 1919. They revealed that Clarke had been charged, without conviction, of mishandling church funds in 1910.

The press made much of the titillating Clarke-Tyler rumors, but even more damaging was the widespread belief that Bessie Tyler was the actual head of the Klan. In Chicago, 18,000 Klansmen reportedly resigned in protest.

Clearly, there was more than enough fat in the fire, as the Klan rounded out the corpulent year of 1921. Colonel Simmons proposed a solution: he wanted an administrative assistant, someone who could handle the bureaucratic paperwork.

Ed Clarke had just the man for the job, a fellow who would also appease the Texans pressuring for stronger Atlanta representation. Clarke's man was reportedly a bit bland but had potential as a good mechanic. They could put him in charge of the 13 states chartered so far. Like Simmons, he was a native Alabaman; they should get along well.

They all agreed, and the Imperial family adopted a new member, the Dallas dentist named Hiram Wesley Evans.

6
onward, christian klansmen

Spring
Evansville, Indiana

Onward, Christian Klansman,
Marching as to war,
With the cross of Jesus
Going on before....

The minister was just warming up. His rumpled suit showed dark veins of perspiration.

But already the sultry summer air, sweet with honeysuckle, was falling heavily on some members of his congregation. There was no breeze through the open windows or elsewhere, despite the demure tic-tock of women's handheld cardboard fans that touted the town mortician.

Here and there among the pews, a half-dozen chins were slipping suspiciously near the vests and overall bibs of some of the faithful. Eyes were heavy on another eight or so; perhaps they were in silent prayer.

One elderly stalwart on the front row, in cabbage rose hat and heat-defying black silk, slumbered brazenly, her undertaker's fan discarded from her gloved hand, her head tipped backward toward heaven, snoring fitfully.

A child still in short pants had escaped the once-watchful eye of his dozing father and sprawled in the center aisle.

Suddenly, with a crack like a pistol shot, the back door opened.

The cabbage roses jerked to attention. The fans froze halfway between tick and tock. The lowered chins popped up and to the rear in a single motion. The father swatted involuntarily in the direction of the aisle child, who vacated the walkway just in time to avoid being trampled by a brisk, military-style procession of ghostly figures.

Silently they came, perhaps twenty of them, two abreast, robed in white, taller than belief in their hoods that draped over their shoulders and shielded their faces. They might have been from another world, but for the shoes—some scuffed, some shined, some field-muddied—betraying individual humanity as they padded against the wooden floor, in unison, to center front.

With flourish, the leader placed a small packet in the minister's hand. "In the interest of the work you are doing in the church, we present you with this sum of money," the Klansman said.

The masked band nodded, then turned smartly. And silently they departed, softly closing the door.

The minister's eyes misted over as he opened the packet and counted its dollar bills: twenty-five of them.

Sometimes during this oft-repeated performance, the packet contained a note, too, perhaps declaring that "The All-Seeing Eye has looked on your work and found it good. Like you, we fear none but God."

The local press, carefully alerted, was sure to carry an item about the visit, like the first one reported in Indiana in March of 1922 at Evansville's Central Methodist Church.

In April the knights knelt in prayer at Muncie's First Methodist before they gave the Rev. J. C. Fred some $30. "Klan Prays, Then Pays," the local press reported.

The grateful minister, probably impoverished, might well call on his choir to sing "Onward, Christian Soldiers" after the visitation.

Or he might exclaim, as did the Reverend Doctor E.J. Bulgin in Indianapolis, "In the early days of Christianity, the children of God had to hide their faces, too." The entire congregation rose to applaud.

The clique of visitors, friend to the godly but relentless enemy of the errant, had given the minister joy and his flock fodder for endless tale-telling, good for at least several months of free advertising for the Indiana Ku Klux Klan.

David Curtis Stephenson was on the move.

With almost maniacal energy, he set out to klux Indiana. If he wanted to clean up on Indiana's Ku Klux Klan, the newly hired Kleagle first had to clean up the KKK's image.

It was no small order for The Old Man.

Indiana, now generations from the frontier, was not Indian Territory. Hoosiers were more easily touched by the symbol of a burning cross than a burning lynch tree.

He had to take a group sold on hate in the South and Southwest, where news kept floating up about KKK brutalities, and convert it into one that Indianans would buy. He welcomed the challenge.

He was a charmer, this 30-year-old, ruddy faced Kleagle with the powerful personality, indefatigable energy, soaring ambition, gift for the flamboyant phrase, and overwhelming lust for the good life.

Of a morning, he would park his old Dodge slantwise at the curb and amble down Main Street in any one of the dusty Indiana country towns, into a feed store where old men gathered to bemoan the price of hogs and corn. He might beg a cup of water in the steaming summer heat and, striking up a conversation, linger long enough to preach the gospel of the Klan.

Then on across the rolling cornfields. In his wake trailed a growing army of disciples, taking up the cause with burning zeal.

Something about him said they could trust him. People struggled to describe it. "Men trust another man who is tangibly there," someone said of him.

Among children, he became childlike, sometimes dropping to the floor to crawl with giggling babies. "The little ones adore him," young mothers said, smiling at the memory of him nuzzling into the necks of the babes, with mock bites and playful kisses.

Among women, his taste ran toward dazzling beauties. There seemed no shortage of them in his fast-paced life.

Standing only 5 feet 6 inches tall, The Old Man nonetheless stood out in a crowd. Always impeccably dressed, he posed with the poise of a dancer. Wherever he was became center stage.

Somehow he cloaked himself in an artful aura of mystery that grew even stronger when he discarded it momentarily to become "just folks" in an Indiana farmhouse or village. Whether on street corner or formal gathering, he seemed to ascend to a platform when he spoke, with a smile. The mouth was sensuous; the tongue, golden.

"He moves with an air of regal serenity..., erect..., rather like a soldier on parade," someone said. "He is so neat and clean that he virtually shines. There isn't a single hair out of place, his trousers are sharply creased, and his shirt is starched and smooth. The immediate impression is of someone who...has an aversion for being soiled."

He was "given to flashes of spiritual beauty," said a friend.

His blond hair and cherub face gave him a boyish look. His clear gray eyes were penetrating, "like they could look into your soul," another remembered.

Those eyes! They were a window into his soul, as clear as an eastern Oklahoma spring bubbling from the earth.

It was sometime later that a leery journalist noted, "strangely enough, the eyes do not sparkle. They observe, study, impress one with expediency, as their owner 'sells himself' to his prospect. Beneath what is intended as disarming frankness, stratagem obviously lurks."

Oh, the moon is fair tonight along the Wabash,
From the fields there comes the breath of new mown hay;
Through the sycamores the candle lights are gleaming....

First he had to know the territory. Steve became a relentless student of the Indiana psyche, circa 1922.

Indiana: that most American of states, a microcosm of all we hold most dear. Schooled on Indiana writers' works, generations of children have embraced their ideal of America.

When the frost was on the pumpkin and the fodder in the shock, folksy Indianans produced the nation's largest crops of corn and books; never mind the snobs who thought the books were corn, too. Dreamy, canny Indianans wrote stories and poems for the people, and best sellers, too.

Blest Indiana! In thy soil
Are found the sure rewards of toil,
Where honest poverty and worth
May make a Paradise on earth....

Indiana's idyllic charm, wrote Theodore Dreiser, surely sprang from some mystic magnet fields in her soil and her light.

Steve wandered, purposefully...across her glacier-shaved industrial north, peopled from New England before the Civil War by English, Scotch Irish, Germans; now a hotbed of jazz, aliens, and Catholics.

...Across her ripe midlands, a hub of transportation and commerce, with some of the best rails and roads in these United States, where the world's best automobiles were hand-crafted— the likes of the Apperson and the Studebaker, and none of those assembly line tin cans turned out by Henry Ford, either.

...Across her dreamy southern hills, caves, and crannies, haven for artists and writers, settled from Kentucky and Tennessee into peaceful hamlets and bucolic farms.

Indiana. A more advanced society than Indian Territory, by far. Three million Hoosier souls, all told, with no more than a tenth of them Catholics. No more than one in a hundred was Jewish; not enough blacks to count. Times were no worse than usual, the farmer's lot was no worse than elsewhere, and 300,000 homes had electric lights.

Indiana men, grown tall on corn to dominate the basketball courts, were gentle folk. Politics was every man's passion; some said as strong a love as basketball. It was no accident that Indiana produced a bumper crop of vice presidents.

Menfolks were well domesticated, by and large, perhaps kept humble on a land where no man could rise higher than the omnipresent Portland silos.

Every farmhouse had a bathtub and an encyclopedia, wrote Hoosier Meredith Nicholson, and folksiness had been a religion at least since poet James Whitcomb Riley, "apostle of sweetness and light, came down the historic National Road...with 'The Old Swimmin' Hole' and 'Leven More Poems' in his pocket."

Back home in Indiana, Steve surveyed the state from stem to stern, from Gary, Indiana, to the River City of Evansville, and he found—trouble. With a capital T.

Beneath the stately sycamores, he saw not candle lights gleaming but the glow of headlights, as a sinful couple parked beside a babbling brook. And down the way—a dance hall, players of cards, purveyors of immorality, desecrators of the Sabbath, bootleggers of booze, young boys stealing a smoke, young girls rouging their knees, swarthy foreigners pouring off teeming Ellis Island boats every single day, speaking strange and heathen tongues, bringing alien customs and ways, fanning out on every train and possible method of conveyance, streaming out in an inundating flood across our beloved land, conspiring to take it over and destroy our American Way of Life forever.

There was no time to waste, if American was to be saved for Americans. There was hope! But only if 100-percent Americans banded together, in a holy war, to preserve our great land before the forces of darkness overpowered us!

He journeyed on a holy mission, and his converts flocked to the cause. He had found a way, as somebody said, to put uplift on a paying basis.

If 100-percent Americanism was selling in Indiana—and it was—Steve sold it well.

As he was selling memberships in HIS Klan, the Klan of the North, Stephenson pushed promotion, too. Indiana newspapers abounded with stories of white-hooded visitations: food baskets for the poor, donations for the churches, funeral wreaths for the bereaved. Always the masked band came suddenly, seeming to appear and disappear from the very air, with military dispatch, silently—but with appropriate tips to the press.

Before the 1922 corn sprouted, he had a string of junior Kleagles, each sharing with him their cut of the Klan's entrance and regalia fees. Hoosier KKK membership rose to nearly 3,000.

Before the corn reached knee high, he was named King Kleagle, in charge of all of Indiana sales, with an army of field salesmen engaged in an all-out statewide membership drive. He imported the hardest of the nation's hardcore salesmen, fresh from the Florida land scams. Membership rose to 5,000.

Before the tassels flowered, he had hit on an idea of giving free memberships to every Protestant preacher in Indiana, and dispatched them out on the lecture circuit as the KKK speakers' bureau. Overnight membership swelled above 40,000.

And before the green corn ripened, he was bringing in one fine harvest.

Before the frost was on the pumpkin and the fodder in the shock, he was a wealthy man.

Steve virtually took over the Indiana Protestant pulpit. His Klergy was told to speak in open meetings of unity among all Protestant churches, to save the anti-Catholic and anti-Jewish venom for closed sessions. By the very nature of their calling, they enjoyed high credibility among their flocks.

Some even had pictures to prove the truth of the Catholic menace in America.

The Klan circulated pictures of an Episcopal cathedral under construction in Washington, claiming it was being built for the Pope's new Vatican. The old stories about Catholics hiding a gun under the church every time a baby was born—to prepare for the revolution—were embellished by "escaped nuns and priests" who verified, in lurid detail, the fundamentalists' fantasies about convent life, complete with photos of the little leather bags used to take the newborn babes to convent furnaces.

The takeover might well start with the public schools and local governments, so the faithful were urged to trounce any Catholic attempts to teach in public schools, run for school boards or local offices.

One horror story was summarized in an old favorite, a false oath supposedly adopted on initiation by Knights of Columbus:

"I do further promise...that I will...wage relentless war, secretly and openly, against all heretics, Protestants, and Masons...and that I will hang, burn, waste, boil, flay, strangle, and bury alive those infamous heretics...rip up the stomachs and wombs of their women, and crash their infants' heads against the walls in order to annihilate their inexecreble race."

Indianans were told that the Pope well might be eyeing the Hoosier state for the base of his takeover. It might not be clear to an outsider, wrote one native, "just why...the Pope should select Indiana as the object of his wicked desires...; but to the Hoosier it is clear enough. Indiana is the most desirable spot on earth, and any potentate might reasonably covet it."

When your minister tells you the Pope is coming—any day!—to take over America, what's a patriot to do?

"He may even be on the next train," cried a Klan lecturer at North Manchester, a college town in northern Indiana. "He may! He may!

"Be warned! Prepare! America for Americans! Search everywhere for hidden enemies, vipers at the heart's blood of our sacred Republic! Watch the trains!"

Eternally vigilant, somewhere around 1,500 of the faithful— precise numbers are lost in apocrypha—dutifully met the next northbound train into the North Manchester station. And there he was: the Pope! cleverly disguised as a mild mannered traveling man.

(Damned devious, these Romanists. As one Kleagle told a South

Bend audience: "Now let me make one thing straight. It ain't you Irish Catholics we're opposed to. It's them ROMAN Catholics we're against.")

If legend is to be believed, they tried to drag the little fellow from the train, ignoring his frantic protestations that he was not the Pope.

He believed he was to be lynched, and it was perhaps not beyond the realm of possibility, since mere mortals chosen to be knights errant must carry out their missions, no matter how burdensome.

Only when he dragged out his luggage and displayed his wares did they believe that he was not the Pope at all, merely a corset salesman.

Tedious legal curbs on search and seizure initially hampered Klansmen in their crusade to clean up lawless towns. Steve would have recalled that before statehood, Indian Territory had maneuvered around the nuisance by enacting a law empowering a volunteer constable force, called by name the Horse Thief Detective Association. The vigilantes were given extraordinary powers during emergencies, on the theory that a frontier man who stole another's horse struck at the very core of life.

Imagine Steve's delight when he discovered that Indiana also had such a law, created by the Legislature in 1865 during the post-Civil War emergency. And, glory be, when he began to sell the Klan, Steve discovered the law was still on the books.

Steve reactivated the Indiana Horse Thief Detective Association and made it the legalized, law-and-order arm of the Hoosier KKK. It was a stroke of pure genius.

The act created a vigilante force, organized them along military lines, and gave them remarkable powers. They could bear arms. They could discipline members by whatever method was needed "to enforce obedience." They could search and seize anyone suspected of a felony, even without a warrant. And they could call on the established law enforcement personnel for any help they needed.

What now was the emergency that justified such a force? The need to clean up those lawless towns.

First, there was the sin den auto, which had become, in the view of many, a traveling bedroom, a rolling house of prostitution. The fast life epitomized by automobiles was, in a larger sense, zipping by too fast for many, especially in small town America. They saw traditional values being undermined and dealt powerless to halt the careening, out of control changes reshaping the world. Doctors speculated, in all seriousness, that driving at automobile speeds would cause insanity. The traditional American was becoming a minority in his own land. In Indiana and elsewhere, he pinned an all-encompassing label on his fears: sin and lawlessness.

Second, there was the overpowering problem of booze.

Carrie Nation had flung her last hatchet a decade earlier and, despite the valiant efforts of the Anti-Saloon League, demon rum was flowing freely. Prohibition had failed to deliver its promised reform of human nature; indeed, more booze was being consumed after Prohibition than before, in Indiana and elsewhere.

The national Volstead Act, intended to implement Prohibition, was the most ignored law in the land. Indiana enacted her own version, the "smell law," that made it a crime to be caught with an empty bottle that even smelled of alcohol. Zealots still complained that sinners were going free because traditional powers of search and seizure were curbed by concern for the rights of the accused.

Chaffing worst under the restrictions were sheriffs and police. It was no accident, then, that law enforcers flocked to join Steve's Horse Thief Detectives. Thousands of policemen and sheriffs joined, augmenting their badges with Detectives' extraordinary power to stop, search, and seize. In time, the sheriff of Indianapolis'

Marion County would be elected to head 17 companies of Detectives, which included most of his deputies as well as hundreds of volunteers eager to play legalized cops and robbers.

Within two years, law enforcement personnel would head vigilante forces in at least 49 of Indiana's counties, where as many as 20,000 Klansmen busied themselves at community reform as commissioned and armed "horse thief detectives."

Indianapolis courts ruled in favor of the volunteer constables, adding to their invincibility.

Knights gave monthly reports to their Klans on the affiliates' activities. In addition to more mundane duties such as directing traffic at Klan doings, the knighted detectives reported on raids that shattered gambling dens, quieted stills, routed liquor violators, and broke up roadside petting parties. Before the association was two years old, the group claimed credit for more than 3,000 liquor cases prosecuted in Indiana courts.

As the group and its enthusiasm grew, so did its scope. There were reports of armed men breaking into private homes on Sunday afternoons searching for suspected card players. Cars were searched so frequently that automobile associations quit sending out-of-state visitors through Indiana.

At its height of power, Steve's Horse Thief Detectives were credited with barn burnings, still raiding, floggings, and even running protection rackets.

Before he was through, Steve's Klan, the Horse Thief Detective Association, and the state's law enforcement forces were irrevocably intertwined into a paramilitary structure that paralleled his takeover of the Protestant church.

Things were going very, very well for the boy from Maysville, Oklahoma.

"I did not sell the Klan in Indiana on hatreds," The Old Man said later. "That is not my way."

And it was not, traditionally, the Indiana way. Steve didn't buy Atlanta's contention that direct action—a code name for extra legal activity and violence—built Hoosier membership.

"I sold the Klan on Americanism, on reform. There are two ways of accomplishing this, by the ballot and by direct action. I am a law-abiding citizen; naturally I abhor direct action. I sold the Klan as a political instrument for reform on a program wholly constructive."

Even taken with a grain or two of salt, Steve's recollection contained truth. HIS Klan, the Indiana Klan, was the least brutal in the nation. And by far the most successful at the game of politics.

If one law was good, more might be better. Whether for legislative or other ends, the Oklahoma-trained Old Man clearly needed to tap into the life blood of Indianans, politics. He needed control at its heart, in the ballot box.

Some contend the Indiana Klan would have turned to politics, with or without Stephenson, in the same way churches set up basketball teams. But by that move, the Klan took a giant step away from other, benign fraternities and secret societies, into the province of government. It set up an inevitable clash with the press and other assertive guardians of the public nature of public policy, who would not—could not—tolerate a secret government.

Stephenson had the manpower to mobilize for political power, but how to shape it? Again, he turned to the Klan-style military model, marrying it to the political "block club" model and creating what he called his "Military Machine." It was, by most accounts, pure Stephenson.

He began with the 1922 Indiana elections.

The machine's work, as he laid it out, included:

"...to get the vote out; to distribute slates; to distribute literature supporting the candidacy of individuals endorsed by the Klan; for the purpose of reporting upon the probable strength of candidates supported by the Klan; and to do any and everything that would be done by a normal, political organization in an effort to elect a slate."

It functioned thusly: A command from the general—perhaps a word that a certain state politician was friendly to the Klan and worthy of support—was transmitted to the state leader, who sent word to colonels in each congressional district, who passed it down to the county majors; thence to ward captains, then to precinct lieutenants and lesser sub-precinct officials. In the most organized cities, the machine was organized down to the block level; in rural areas, to the road level. An army at rest, of course, tends toward mischief, atrophy, or worse, but The Old Man had mission aplenty for his troops: community reform, as a means toward political power—reversing the more traditional pattern of amassing power to achieve reform.

He armed his troops well: with the ballot, a secret service spy network, an intricate operating structure, and actual firearms accommodating state commissions issued to thousands.

Like a good mechanic, Stephenson knew that the machine must not get rusty from disuse.

"The military coordinating machinery is the most important and should be the most highly operative part of your organization," he explained in a detailed mandate. "The Military Machine should be kept busy and should be given sufficient opportunity to develop its strength and harden its muscles for the battle which so rapidly approaches."

If there was no good news to transmit, bad news would have to do. Here he capitalized on two available raw materials, the telephone and the untapped womanpower of often isolated Klan housewives. He organized what he called "poison squads" and combined them with both The Military Machine and his own spy network that he called the "G-1 system."

Steve organized the ladies into their own Klan affiliate named "the Queens of the Golden Mask." The heart of the G-1 system consisted of two Stephenson spies in every Klavern in the state, a system so effective it was adopted by the national Klan and later used against Steve himself. "Like a circle," he would later say of the Klan espionage system, "every spy watching a spy."

Through The Military Machine, the Queens, the Horse Thief Detective Association, his political connections, the G-1 system, his Klergy, and regular Klan circles, he collected information. Further, he sent out flurries of questionnaires to politicians, assembling extensive dossiers of data. He ordered all Klaverns to submit to him written reports on all voting age citizens in their communities who were "undesirable"—pimps, prostitutes, Reds, agitators, Catholics, Jews, bootleggers, foreigners; the list went on and on. In addition, he ordered the Klaverns to submit detailed data on every official and office holder, down to and including school board members and firemen, including name, address, nationality, political affiliation, religion, and Klan support or opposition.

Thus armed with tubsful of mix and match data, he had "the goods" on virtually every politician, and many private citizens, throughout the state. He could—perhaps did—favor a bootlegger for the right return, in goods or service, and flay a recalcitrant or erring politician, up to and including battery at the ballot box.

If that wasn't enough, he could turn the little women—bless 'em—loose. The right rumor, perhaps some clue to a character flaw of a politician, could zip through the telephones of the "poison squad" within 24 hours, picking up steam as it traveled throughout the state.

And ultimately, he could direct the distribution of specially marked "scratch sheets," sample ballots clearly showing which candidates were or were not acceptable to the Klan and The Old Man.

Sometimes orders weren't carried out as well as he might have hoped; but he had a remedy. As King Kleagle, Stephenson had the Klan power of a czar, able to appoint or discharge Klan officials at will.

Within months, the general controlled an army. His words reverberated down through the hierarchy, through lesser generals and majors, through captains and field sergeants, to foot soldiers on all fronts. Shortly—some said in four hours, some said in only 30 minutes—his troops would be carrying out his orders. The enemy was routed, the evil curbed; the adversary could be, rightly or wrongly, as good as dead.

Soon rumors of The Old Man's power began to circulate, while fiery crosses burned on hillsides around the state. The rumors picked up substance and speed from their own weight and motion, like a snowball rolling down a steep hill, moving on Steve's faceless, numberless army.

Before 1922 was out, those in the know contended Indiana Klansmen numbered more than 100,000. But their real strength lay in their secrecy and innumerability.

The Stephenson threshing machine moved briskly through Indiana political fields. As early as 1922, it routed the foremost Hoosier statesman, the popular Albert J. Beveridge, a progressive Republican who made the fatal error of crossing the Klan in public. Klan-favored Samuel M. Ralston, a Democrat, won the November 7 election and took his seat in the Senate chambers. Steve had elected a United States senator.

The machine was, initially, avowedly nonpartisan. But soon Stephenson and his Klan so absorbed the Indiana Republican party that they became one body, in action indistinguishable one from the other. He had, as one writer put it, "Tammanized Indiana."

When he consummated his KKK marriage with the Hoosier church, law enforcement, and the GOP, Stephenson could say, with justifiable pride: "God help the man who issues a proclamation of war against the Ku Klux Klan."

7
FIERY DOUBLE CROSS

Thanksgiving 1922
Atlanta, Georgia

Colonel Simmons had plans, big plans.

He was, after all, head of what some in 1922 were calling America's most successful big business. "There was so much money in sight that we could lay almost any sort of plans," The Imperial Wizard recalled later.

He had figured a way to bring in $58 million. He saw a great Klan university, KKK hospitals, a network of 50,000 volunteers who would help the federal government police America. He had in mind to clean up America, "from the top of the Capitol dome at Washington to the Atlantic and Pacific oceans."

It never occurred to him that, with stakes that high, others might be making plans, too.

The key to cleaning up on the Klan was an intricate system of "degrees." For appropriate sums of money, a proud Klansman could move up a KKK ladder in giant "K" steps. Only the most select members would be invited to apply for the fourth and ultimate degree, which Simmons called "K-kwad." And significant "K-wads" of dough would be produced by the scheme; the fourth "K-kwad" degree alone should produce $24 million, Simmons calculated.

And what to do with the money? First he wanted a university. Six miles out from Atlanta was a fine piece of rolling, wooded ground, the site of the Civil War battle of Peachtree Creek—sacred ground to Georgians. A perfect site for his Klan college. Simmons bought it, Civil War trench and all. As step one, he erected a frame convention hall straddling the creek, which gave him a fitting site for grand oratory such as:

"On this very spot, beneath this woodland glade, you stand on the bosom of one of the nation's famous battle fields. From this brook, winding its way to the sea, with the rippling melody of its ancient spring, the wounded and the dying slaked their thirst and soothed their painful wounds.... Here we meet in convention with naught but brotherly love...."

Similarly, he dreamed of grand hospitals where the wounded and dying could slake their thirst, or whatever, in short- and long-term Klan care.

The key to cleaning up the country was his trusted aide, Fred Savage, head of the Imperial Palace guard. Savage had been brought into the Imperial family as "Imperial Night Hawk" by Ed Clarke, fresh from the New York shipyards where Savage had been a strike breaker. Some called him "sleazy," but Simmons found Savage trustworthy enough to give him a force of 50 Klan cops. The Wizard had in mind to give him 50,000.

Even for Simmons, it was a grand plan. He envisioned a national, secret, "secret service" of volunteer Klansmen, each unknown to the public or even to each other, who would spy on public officials, private citizens, each other—anyone.

He laid it out for a reporter later:

"My plan was to have the Klan agents make their reports secretly concerning law violators, immorality, law evasion, non-Americanism, etc., to a Klan secret service headquarters in every state. These state headquarters would have made regular reports to the head of the secret service at 'The Palace.' Savage...would have sifted out these reports and...turned his reports over to the (U.S. government) secret service...to help that department enforce the law."

It was a logical extension of a lodge that was moving toward becoming a secret, vigilante government. It was, furthermore, not entirely an original idea, since the federal government had sponsored Simmons and his fledgling Georgia and Alabama Klans during World War I for similar pursuits. Simmons had served as a sort of junior G Man in the "Citizens Bureau of Investigation" and organized a KKK double-secret service to ferret out those suspected of "Un-Americanism, etc." That's when the Klan became clandestine; Simmons learned it at Uncle Sam's knee.

Colonel Simmons was delayed in carrying out his grand plans, however, by a new series of troubles that popped up at the Imperial Palace and around his Klankdom.

First, there was a bothersome business from Texas. Simmons had to dispatch his new administrative assistant, Hiram Wesley Evans, back home to Dallas to try to straighten things out.

Klan leadership didn't bat an eye over routine kinds of direct action, harassing blacks to keep them from voting, that sort of thing. But, Evans argued, the Dallas Klan had gone a bit far in castrating a light-skinned black doctor whom they accused of consorting with white women.

"Come off it," countered H.C. McCall, the Houston Grand Titan. "That kind of stuff went on when you were here in charge of things."

McCall, particularly, remembered when Evans had agreed that the "2 percent of the rough stuff" was essential for Klan health.

Wasn't it true that Klansmen received training in Atlanta in methods to administer whippings and other discipline without leaving visible or life-threatening injuries? And that, as Ed Clarke would admit in Tulsa in mid 1922, the early Klan had solicited men "looking for a little rough stuff" to build membership?

It was also well known that some Klans, particularly in the Southwest, had adopted a quasi-regulation whipping strap. It was leather, 3 feet long and 4 inches wide, with the handle wrapped in heavy-duty automotive tape. It had seven to ten slits, each about 6 inches long, in the end to cut the back of a victim. Only high-class Klansmen could use the prestige whip.

Increasingly, from the spring of 1922, the Texas Klan would turn toward political action, rather than "direct action," to clean up the state. But since some in Texas thought they had sent Evans to Atlanta to straighten out the Imperial Palace, rather than the other way around, they didn't take too kindly to Evans' visit.

A second problem arose as the Imperial Empire kept reading embarrassing reports in the press about Ed Clarke and Bessie Tyler.

In one of the more curious political alliances of modern times, Clarke was flirting with Marcus Garvey, the militant separatist who was urging his fellow blacks to move back to Africa. Observers speculated that Garvey wanted the Klan to succeed so blacks would give up on America. Clarke's motives were not revealed—perhaps he saw Garvey's plan as an alternative to sterilizing black babies—but reports of Clarke's meeting with Garvey angered many Klansmen.

Even worse was the persistent rumor that the Klan was, in truth, being run by a feminine hand: the heavy handed Elizabeth Tyler. One news magazine called her "the Ku Klux Empress."

"In this woman beats the real heart of Ku Klux today, as it did yesterday and will tomorrow. If there are fools in the K.K.K. Mrs. Tyler is not one of them. She knew better than any one else what Ku Kluxism was leading to, but she was and is willing to chance the consequences. She has a positive genius for executive direction. Her courage is a thing to admire...."

It was enough to weary a wizard. And the good colonel was not well. In June 1922, at urging of both his wife and Clarke, Colonel Simmons took a six-month vacation. He left Clarke in charge. There were rumors that Simmons' health problem related to something he had been taking to slake his thirst.

More cutting was a suit filed in July by fired Imperial Kligrapp (Secretary) Louis Wade, who alleged that Clarke "has gained complete control of (Simmons) and has either kept him drunk or has taken advantage of his drunken condition" to allow Clarke to pocket Klan funds.

Embattled, Clarke turned more and more to the two aides he had brought to Atlanta, Guard Chief Fred Savage and the Dallas dentist Hiram Wesley Evans. Clarke put Evans in charge of the secretariat, replacing the fired Imperial Kligrapp. Evans, particularly, was showing a practical head for strategy and management and, when the situation demanded, for intrigue and manipulation.

But those troubles were minor compared to one that exploded, throughout weeks of nationwide press hysteria, from the dark swamps of Louisiana near the little Morehouse Parish cotton center of Mer Rouge.

On August 24, 1922, masked men carrying shotguns blocked traffic weaving through the night toward Mer Rouge, returning from a baseball game and "good roads boosting" barbecue in nearby Bastrop.

"That's the man we want," shouted one of the men, pointing to a planter's son, Watt Daniel. The black-robed and masked men grabbed Daniel—tore him from the arms of his 3-year-old daughter, his wife would later testify. They blind folded and hog tied him and threw him into the back of a Ford truck.

A woman screamed: "Watt—Watt—Watt!"

With Daniels they also seized Daniels' friend Tom Richards, a garage mechanic; their fathers; and another man. All were similarly packaged, and the loaded truck headed out through the moss-shrouded forest into the night.

Mer Rouge townspeople who returned home that night to summon help found the telephone lines cut into Bastrop, a nearby center of KKK activity since 1921. Earlier in the day, Bastrop's Captain J.K. Skipworth—"Cap'n Skip," a Klan leader who still wore his Confederate veteran's pin firmly attached to the velvet collar of his gray coat—had ordered the telephone operator to block all messages between the two towns, but she refused.

The Klan had brought serious trouble between the two towns, historic rivals. Mer Rouge was as violently anti-Klan as Bastrop was pro-Klan, led by Cap'n Skip and Dr. B. M. McKoin. Doc McKoin lived in Mer Rouge, which he considered a sin den, full of gambling, drinking, and Negro concubines.

Morehouse Parish became "perpetual Halloween," as one reporter wrote:

"It must have provided a real thrill to go scooting through the shadowy roads in somebody else's flivver, to meet in lonely dingles in the pine woods and flog other men, to bounce down the fifteen foot declivity where the ridge ends and swoop at twenty-five miles an hour...through phantasmal Lafourche swamp with its banshee live oaks waving their snaky tresses in the moonlight."

The Klan's efforts to "clean up the town" followed a logical pattern established in the South and Southwest. Discipline began with suspected lawbreakers: first blacks, then whites; first men, then women, then children; first for reform, then for control, then for grudges, ultimately even for speaking ill of the Klan. When the final stage was reached, the town could well be said to be in the grip of a reign of terror.

Townspeople generally reacted in one of three ways: succumbing in fearful silence, retaliating by open warfare, or—if the legal system was not Klan-controlled—by legal wars.

In Watt Daniels' case, he was alleged to be guilty of the first-level offense, perhaps making a little whiskey, and more importantly of the ultimate offense, for he brazenly opposed the Klan. In Tom Richards' case, he was guilty by association; he was Daniels' friend. "The boys had been talking too much;" they "knew too much." Daniels recently stumbled on to a Klan gathering in the woods, drew a gun when he was threatened, and defiantly ridiculed the ritual.

On that steamy night in August, the Ford truck stopped at a clearing in the woods.

The elder Daniels and another man were tied to a tree and whipped with a leather strap. Young Watt Daniels, rope tied, managed to break loose and tried to defend his father, then 70 years old. In the fray, Watt ripped a mask from one of the floggers and called out the man's name to Richards.

Later that night, three men were released, but Watt Daniel and Tom Richards were taken deeper into the woods. They were never again seen alive.

The next day in Bastrop, Cap'n Skip threw up a protective shield against retaliation. Klansmen checked the mails and telephone calls, stopped and searched cars. Days later, after an appeal from Mrs. Daniels, Louisiana's governor called for federal help. A long search ensued, while Klan nightriding continued unabated. The ringleaders were common knowledge, but prosecution was impossible without either Daniels and Richards or their bodies. The national press swooped down on the parish for weeks while federal troops clawed their way through alligator-infested swamps, bayous, and lakes.

One night three months after the disappearance, Lake LaFourche exploded. The mysterious dynamite blast, perhaps set to destroy evidence, delivered up the torsos of two hideously mangled bodies. By scraps of clothing, they were identified as young Daniels and Richards.

Medical examiners pieced together a grisly story. Daniels and Richards had been flogged and tortured, each arm broken in three places in what one witness later testified was "scientific butchery." They were tied spread-eagle to the cleated wheels of a large road grading tractor that was rolled downhill, splintering every bone in their still-living bodies. Then mutilated and hacked apart, their pulped corpses were dumped in the lake.

Now justice was on trial in Morehouse Parish. The grand jury investigations, trials, and appeals stretched over months, avidly reported by the national press which openly proclaimed the Klan guilty. Charges, counter charges, accusations, and alibis mounted.

No convictions were ever obtained. The most significant findings came from two successive Klan-dominated grand juries, who reported that Morehouse Parish needed a new jail and repairs on the courthouse roof.

The press circus over Mer Rouge, Clarke, Tyler, and other nuisances were troubling enough for Colonel Simmons, returning from his vacation in the fall of 1922. But something even more basic was gnawing at him.

He had never really been elected Imperial Wizard.

True enough, his Invisible Empire was based on a military-style dictatorship—necessary to avoid the weaknesses of democracy, as the Klansman's Manual said:

"The military form of government must and will be preserved for the sake of true, patriotic Americanism, because it is the only form of government that gives any guarantee of success. Both experience and history demonstrate the fallacy and futility of a so-called democratic form of government for any such movement as the Knights of the Ku Klux Klan. We must avoid the fate of other organizations that have split on the rock of democracy."

But Colonel Simmons was, after all, a romantic, and he wanted to be elected to rule.

He had another plan. He would gather Klan leaders into a grand, nationwide convention in his new meeting hall on the Peachtree Creek battlefield, so they could officially elect him Imperial Wizard.

His staff concurred. Thus, on the seventh birthday of his Klan, Thanksgiving of 1922, Colonel William Joseph Simmons officially convened the first Imperial Klonvokation in the history of the Knights of the Ku Klux Klan, Inc.

It was a crowning touch.

They summoned him from slumber, in the dead of the night before Colonel Simmons' big day.

Who?

Oh. Fred—Fred Savage, his chief of the Palace Guard, and that bright blond Kleagle from Indiana, Stephenson.

Simmons rose and let them in.

What time? Three o'clock?

He had been out late drinking with the boys. Now he struggled up from sleep, trying to grasp their news.

Trouble? What trouble? Everything was going great.

The first national Imperial Klonvokation of the Knights of the

Ku Klux Klan, Inc., had begun perfectly. One thousand delegates gathered in Simmons' new auditorium astride Peachtree Creek. He had thoughtfully fenced off the actual battlefield.

Klansmen were everywhere in Atlanta. Entire floors of the best hotels were reserved for them. They alighted in full regalia from railway cars and marched to their hotels, with flags and banners, to the beat of blaring bands.

The Indiana bunch was the most chic. Each wore a bright red silk scarf around his neck, tied like a cowboy's bandanna. It was a fine touch, worthy of their up-and-coming leader, the Stephenson boy who called himself The Old Man.

Simmons posed for photographers in a variety of garbs. He looked regal, his eyes fastened on some mystic, distant truth.

And there were the festive candid shots. He was eager to see the one where he and Evans lined up with the Indiana boys, Stephenson and Joe Huffington, looking like a merry barbershop quartet. Judge Chuck Orbison kneeled down in the foreground, and Simmons leaned over playfully and tweaked his ear.

The actual sessions, of course, were closed to the press. Fred Savage had trained a special crew of Klan cops and ushers, and they did their job commendably.

Simmons was identified in fitting style: "He who traversed The Realm of the Unknown, wrested The Solemn Secret from The Grasp of Night and became Imperial Master of The Great Lost Mystery." He couldn't have written it better himself. Maybe he did.

"All I could think of doing was praying," Simmons recalled later.

"Klansmen!" he said. "Let every man kneel while we pray."

Tears streamed freely down faces throughout the crowd as they prayed and sang "Onward, Christian Soldiers." Six men were converted on the spot.

He began the Klonvokation with a rousing speech:

"Doubtless the angels themselves, as they peer over the

battlefield of the eternal city, hold a kind of envy of you, in your position and the work you have to do.... If that work is well done there will be joy in the presence of the angels on high....

"The white men of the American nation were awaiting the proclamation of the principles of the Ku Klux Klan. On all sides the sons of the white man's breed were feeling the tremendous pressure that threatened to crush out the Anglo Saxon civilization. They saw the peril but there was no relief in sight.... The original sixteen members of the Klan lifted the fiery cross, announced the everlasting principles of white supremacy...."

They loved it. How could things be better?

What was he going to do about the election? D.C. Stephenson asked, seating himself near Simmons' hotel bed.

"Nothing," said Simmons, still fighting sleep. He would simply be confirmed, moving the KKK from its provisional status into the next phase, with an official Constitution and Imperial Wizard.

"Well, Colonel," said Fred Savage, "we just dropped around to tell you that, whatever happens on the convention floor tomorrow, there will be armed men stationed round on the floor to protect your honor."

"Protect my honor! What do you mean?"

"Why, there is a certain crowd of men here who say if you are nominated for the office of Imperial Wizard tomorrow they will get up on the floor and attack your character. And we've just come to tell you that the first man who insults your name will be killed by a sharpshooter right on the spot as he speaks. There'll be enough of us with firearms to take care of the whole convention, if necessary."

The envious angels were about to witness a blood bath. Simmons nearly collapsed at the thought.

Colonel Simmons had, as a journalist later noted, a deep aversion to murder close to him.

There is another version of this story, different from the one told by Simmons. In the second version, Savage and Stephenson blackmailed Colonel Simmons with compromising photographs.

In both versions, however, his visitors offered him the same way to avoid the "bloody shambles": Why not agree to let his low-key assistant, Hiram Wesley Evans, be elected Imperial Wizard? Simmons could take a new—and greater—position as Emperor. That way, he would still be in charge. It would require a minor change in the Constitution, but they could work that up quickly for adoption at the same meeting.

Ultimately, the befuddled Simmons agreed.

"I prayed for divine guidance," Simmons said. "I didn't want any killing in the hall."

By coincidence, the bloodless coup in Atlanta was occurring at the same point in time that an unexplained dynamite blast at Mer Rouge was delivering up the fragments of what had once been Watt Daniels and Tom Richards.

It was some days after the Klonvokation adjourned that Simmons realized what had happened, when he found Evans sitting in Simmons' office, at Simmons' desk. Evans did not rise when the kindly colonel entered his office.

"Colonel Simmons, I'm going to put you on a great white throne in this palace," Evans said. "I am planning to make a throne room for you where you can meet all visitors. You stick to me."

But, Simmons recalled later, Evans "never got around to making the throne room." When he read the Constitution, Simmons realized he had been stripped of all authority.

Too late, he learned that before the election Evans convened a group of "insurgents" who conspired to take over Simmons' Klan.

The group came largely from the militant Southwestern Klans. It included Fred Savage, H.C. McCall of Texas, H.C. Ramsey of Louisiana, Ed DeBarr of Oklahoma, J. C. Comer of Arkansas, and Nathan Bedford Forrest, Jr., of Atlanta.

They were dissatisfied with Simmons' woolgathering and Clarke's greed. Both had to go.

But how? They sent word to the private Pullman car of D.C. Stephenson, the rising star in the North. He seemed a cunning sort

Indiana Klansman Walter Bossert came, too, a darkly handsome, quiet chap. Stephenson was an outsider in the group, and they eyed him suspiciously, but his ideas made sense.

The pragmatic politician in Stephenson faced off with the practical politician in Evans, and they recognized kindred spirits. Evans saw that Stephenson shared his vision of the Klan as a movement, not a lodge. Even more than Evans, Stephenson saw the power that a Klan political machine could carry and what it could mean to his own future. The two led the discussion.

Evans said if necessary he would have the Texas delegation attack Simmons from the floor. Stephenson demurred: The Klan was valuable property and shouldn't be damaged in an open fight. There was a better way. He had a plan. Evans liked it.

The group reached consensus, and Stephenson and Savage spent the night making the rounds of the delegates, confiding that Simmons wanted the greater job of Emperor, with Evans as his assistant.

When they had the votes, they called on Colonel Simmons.

By 10 a.m., when the election occurred, everything went smoothly. By the close of the day, the new Imperial Wizard and Constitution had been peacefully approved, and the first national KKK Imperial Klonvokation adjourned. The Thanksgiving Eve massacre was done, with the Imperial turkey's consent.

Within weeks, the new Imperial Wizard, Hiram Wesley Evans, was proving himself to be a whiz. He canceled Clarke's contract, won approval to banish both Clarke and Simmons from the Klan, and was moving the Klan along the same path taken by his native Texans, into politics. Klansmen would later testify that Evans planned for the Klan to take over, first, the U.S. Congress, then the U.S. government. He even moved Klan headquarters to Washington.

Ed Clarke was weakened in his counter fight by, first, the departure of Mrs. Tyler to marry a wealthy Atlantan—she would die within a year, of unknown cause—and, second, by nagging legal problems. In quick succession Clarke was charged with—but never convicted of—mail fraud and violation of the white slave act. After his ouster, he turned his energies to fighting the Klan, as did Colonel Simmons. Together with other disgruntled Klansmen, they managed to say worse things about the Klan than its earlier enemies could have conceived.

Simmons was not well, but he managed quite a fight, even without his white throne. Evans learned, after the fact, that Simmons had providentially copyrighted the Klan's rituals, charter, regalia, and titles in his own name.

"I owned the Ku Klux Klan, like I own my hat or my car," Simmons said later, wistfully. Now his beloved baby was in the hands of "aliens" who were leading it where he promised the angels it would not go, into politics. "I tried to tell Klansmen what had happened to the Klan, but I couldn't get a hearing."

He wrote a book to tell "the truth," but Evans ordered any Klansman who read it banished from the Empire. Simmons tried to make the speaker's circuit, but they wouldn't let him speak. His enemies spread rumors about him.

At a northern rally in Ohio, D.C. Stephenson hired a shaky old drunk to sit on the stage, trying for hours to drink a glass of water or light a cigar before 30,000 Klansmen. Meanwhile, Stephenson's aides wandered through the crowd, whispering: "Too bad about that old man, isn't it? Why that's old 'Colonel' Simmons. Drunk as a Lord. We tried to keep him in his private car out in the railroad yards, but he insisted on coming. Too bad. What a shell of a man."

Discredited and embittered, Simmons—once "as full of sentiment as plum is juice"—went to court. The battles lasted for months, providing lively Klan scandals for the press; one reporter termed the whole affair a "fiery double cross."

At one point conciliation seemed possible, in an out-of-court settlement hammered out by a 15-man Kloncillium chaired by Stephenson "with elegant parliamentarianism." But the compromise fell apart when Simmons tried to start a women's Klan and Evans blocked it.

The dreamy Atlanta preacher with the pleasant face, who abhorred nearby murder, had met—and been bested by—the practical Dallas dentist with the square face and the pragmatic Indiana salesman with the round face.

Simmons settled for a lump sum $90,000 payment which he poured into creating an ill-fated, rival fraternity, the "Knights of the Flaming Sword." More successful was his continuing role as an irritating gnat buzzing around Evans' newly crowned Imperial head.

The one-night coup had been too easy. What it set up was a three-way, internecine war between Evans, Simmons, and the newest Klan powerhouse, D.C. Stephenson. In time, it would become only a two-way battle.

The biggest winner at Atlanta's 1922 Thanksgiving Klonvokation was David Curtis Stephenson.

The Old Man came to Atlanta a mere Kleagle of one state, and that far from the centers of Klan power. He returned to Indiana with three prize plums he snatched from Evans in exchange for his part in the coup:

Steve was named Imperial Klaliff, putting him first in line of succession for Evans' Imperial Wizard job.

He was placed in charge of "kluxing" all 23 Northeastern states, centered in Indiana and Ohio, the entire northern tier of the Invisible Empire.

Perhaps most important, he was given a free hand in Indiana to build the power base he needed—for future plans that were still taking shape in his mind.

Steve got exactly what he wanted. He was now a recognized force for reckoning. He had in hand the tools to forge the Klan of the North into a political power to rival, perhaps surpass, Evans' Klan. Now he was clearly the number one Klansman in the North.

Immense hordes were waiting to be kluxed, vast wealth to be plucked. As his private pullman car clattered and swayed homeward toward Indiana, Stephenson had reason to believe that things were going his way. The coming year, 1923, should be a great one for The Old Man.

8
Gentleman from Indiana

1923
Indianapolis, Indiana

A phone rang, one of eight on the desk of the busy young executive. He sighed, as an apology to his guest, and answered brusquely.

"Of course, put him through."

He listened intently.

In the silence, his guest, an Indiana reporter, surveyed the office: the Central States Coal Company, according to the sign on the frosted glass outer door. Entrance to the inner chamber had been gained at some length, after machine-gun questions from an attractive receptionist and an extended period of heel cooling in the outer office. While the journalist waited, various inner doors opened, discharging slouch-hatted men who scrutinized the visitor silently.

UNMASKED! Ann Patton

Suspended from the casing of the inner sanctum door was a sign: "The Bearers of Evil Tidings Shall be Slain."

The inner office was pleasant enough. An American flag drooped beside a small bronze bust of Napoleon on the burnished roll-top desk. The carefully dressed, affable young man on the swivel chair moved the way he spoke: decisively, energetically, incisively. His battery of books was dominated by psychology texts.

"NO!" he suddenly shouted into the phone. "I certainly won't do that!"

Another listening silence. The guest examined the book that had been offered to him. The young man—who called himself The Old Man—said he wrote it himself, the first of a ten-volume series on psychology. It was titled "Master Salesmanship." He should know.

The executive rose from his chair. "You tell Jim Watson that I don't want Harry New to do that!" A pause.

The reporter made a mental note; the names were political magic. His curiosity piqued, he wondered who was on the other end of that phone.

The Old Man nodded slightly. "Thank you, sir. And please give my regards to Mrs. Coolidge as well."

The soul of courtesy, The Old Man smiled sweetly, while he gently replaced the receiver on his fake telephone.

If Steve could make an impression with his dummy telephone—connected by a foot pedal to a receptionist, so he could signal when to have it ring—he could make an even greater mark with his Invisible Empire.

By 1923, Steve's realm had amassed enough real or perceived strength to make politicians very, very nervous.

When a reporter tried to razz a congressman about the Klan, the politician answered grimly:

"That's nothing to joke about, even in whispers. That stuff runs like quicksilver. You can never tell when somebody is going to pick up a word, and where it will end.

"There are thousands of those fellows in my district. But I don't know they are there. Nobody will be able to prove to me they are there. And if I don't know they are in my district, I'm not called upon to express an opinion about them. That's what I'm doing. That's the only thing to do. And don't you risk queering my game by any such jokes!"

By 1923 Steve's Klan had perfected the art of "The Whispers."

If rumors spread in undertones were not enough, he augmented them with a Klergy-based lecture squad so adept that they provided 80 percent of the KKK's national lecturers. And the major share of the national field men were born and bred Hoosiers.

In public, their spiels were apple pie.

"Such speeches as I have heard," one journalist reported, "...follow the lines of...better government, better citizenship, patriotism and religion in general, and 'native, white, Protestant supremacy.' They have been fine, spirited, balanced, eloquent, but without any attempt to stir prejudice or appeal to hatred except what comes from the subject itself. They are as good, or as bad, as the Klan movement at its best."

If whispered or shouted words were not enough, written words might do even more.

By 1923 The Old Man finally realized his lifelong dream: he founded his own newspaper, *The Fiery Cross.* In due time, he would have a circulation of 400,000.

By the spring of 1923 Steve had moved his office, first to Columbus, Ohio, then to Indianapolis—the city that would soon be known as "Klanapolis," in his honor.

He had chosen the Hoosier capital city as his center of operations after the Evansville Klan was divided by Steve's fight with his first

KKK enemy, organizer Joe Huffington. Atlanta offered Steve a choice of California or Indianapolis. He chose Indianapolis.

He could have done far worse. It was, in more ways than one, a crossroads of America—and such a well planned city, too, smack dab in the middle of Indiana by forefathers' design, laid out like Washington, D.C., in a series of boulevards fanning out from the hub of monument circle, with its towering soldiers and sailors monument, as tall as the Statue of Liberty.

A spring morning of 1923 might well find The Old Man on his way to the office, circling around what Indianans called "the monument," in his chauffeur-driven, closed-car Cadillac, cruising along streets with solid names like Meridian, New York, and Market.

The car would weave a bit, to miss construction. Indianapolis was in the throes of another building boom. Everywhere you looked, the city was thrusting up neo-Greco-Roman columns and citadels, pillars and porticos. Ornate and elegant, the buildings gave downtown a solemn, solid, Wall Street feel, securely corner-stoned in milky Indiana limestone.

This was a city, like Stephenson, here to stay.

At the corner of Washington and Pennsylvania, D. C. Stephenson alighted and marched into his Kresge Building suite of offices. In his felt fedora and pin-striped suit, puffing a fat cigar, he looked like the most sober of bankers.

Like Indianapolis' monument circle, The Old Man was the hub of a building boom, solidly corner-stoned on Indianans' natural inland isolationist tendencies, their tradition as joiners, and their love for the fundamentalist church, for law and order, for politics, for outdoor festivals, for family.

By May of 1923 there were a reported 150,000 Klansmen in

Indianapolis' Marion County. Klan recruiters were active in every sector of the state. Membership—and Steve's revenues from dues and sheet sales—were pouring in. He was gearing up to start his own factory to manufacture robes and hoods.

Always the family man, Stephenson appealed to the womenfolk, giving them their own Klan—The Queens of the Golden Mask—that was far more than just another ladies' auxiliary. They often became more impassioned KKK members than their men; one writer compared them to the women revolutionaries in Dickens' *A Tale of Two Cities*.

And he didn't neglect the little ones, who came to outings dressed in diminutive white gowns and hoods, even when they were too young to belong to the boys' Junior Klan or the girls' Tri K.

Stephenson might look like a banker, but he worked like a demon—14 hour days, for weeks at a stretch. Once he acquired his own aeroplane and pilot, he could make three to five cities in a day.

He worked like a man pursued, "fighting with our backs against the wall," for a cause he said was "America's last stand for her high ideals and patriotism, and for the wonderful principles handed down by our forefathers."

There was no time to waste, by him or his Knights, for their nation was under siege. Overwhelmed by waves of foreigners, the traditional American was becoming a minority stranger in his own land, inundated by the "religious, social, and political foundations of those of alien origin.... To ignore the problems of your race and country is to defraud posterity willfully," he declared.

They bought it, in droves, these Hoosier Klansmen who were, on the average, decent fellows who bought the contention that "The Ku Klux Klan is as American as chewing gum."

One contemporary writer described a typical Indiana Knight:

"He is not a terrorist with hate as his motto. He does not whip negroes, stage tar parties or write anonymous threats. He does not break down the machinery of regular law enforcement with informal extra-legal methods. On the contrary, the unbiased verdict in Indiana seems to be that he has been, all things considered, a real factor for the betterment of municipal rule.

"Most of the time he is pursuing the favorite vocation of all Hoosiers, which is, of course, politics; but he has found time to assist the regular officers in cleaning up some bad situations, and in some instances has gone in and cleaned a town himself. He has done that in a strictly legal fashion."

Well, perhaps. Other writers were less kind.

The typical Indiana Kluxer, wrote another, was a gentle and romantic man, slightly stooped and balding on top, garbed in iron gray, who gave little or no outward sign that "...his soul is tormented by tremendous and ghastly visions of the perils that threaten the very existence of true religion and unpolluted Anglo Saxon blood....

"In the voice of the organizer he hears a clarion call to knightly and selfless service..., and for the trifling consideration of ten dollars..., he is made...a knight errant vowed to the succor of the oppressed, the destruction of ogres and magicians, the defense of the faith. Bursting with noble ideals and lofty aspirations, he accepts the nomination....

"What is important is that the man walks through a cloud of unseen presences, terrible and repulsive."

And when the inevitable disillusionment sets in, he discovers that he is merely human, "neither royal, noble nor holy. So, under his white robe and pointed hood, he becomes not a Chevalier Bayard but a thug."

Nineteen twenty three was to be Steve's best year in the Klan.

As the lush green days of spring melted into a golden summer, he could claim an Indiana membership of 300,000 to 400,000—easily one in ten of the total population.

Before 1923 was out, Steve could boast that the Indiana Klan was the largest in the nation, both in terms of percentages and actual members. By Stephenson's estimate, the Hoosier state had as many Klansmen as cars—around a half million of each.

The automobile estimate came from the Indiana Chamber of Commerce, which noted that many of them were made in Indiana, too. It was no accident that auto racing, memorialized in the "Indianapolis 500," became a tradition in Indianapolis.

The Klan estimate, if accurate, gave the state the distinction of having in the Klavern, so to speak, one of every six of its total 3 million residents. Since the total population included many who were too young or too poor, the wrong color, the wrong religion, the wrong nationality to belong to the exclusive order, a far greater percentage of those eligible were counted among Klan members.

On the political side, 1923 started more modestly. The Indiana General Assembly convened in January with perhaps 50-60 Klansmen among its membership.

Steve was working to perfect his Military Machine, based on his test run in the fall 1922 election, when Klan-backed Sam Ralston was elected to the U.S. Senate. Ralston was a Democrat, aging but still popular, as was the reigning Democratic boss Tom Taggart.

There was some shifting going on at the top of the Republican heap.

On November 7, 1922, the Republicans' venerable Albert Beveridge had bested U.S. Senator Harry S. New. Then Democrat Sam Ralston had beat Beveridge, with Klan help. New bounced back to power when his friend President Harding named him U.S. Postmaster General. New was no friend to Steve, ever.

Party regulars elected Lawrence Lyons their state GOP chair. In the State House was Republican Governor Warren T. McCray; in Indianapolis' City Hall, Mayor Samuel "Lew" Shank.

The KKK was to become significant in all their lives, but none would be more affected than James Eli Watson, a veteran U.S. Senator from Rushville.

Senator Jim Watson undoubtedly led the Republican list. He had also won the Klan's heart in 1922, when Texans elected an avowed Klansman, Earle B. Mayfield, to the U.S. Senate. Senate opponents launched a fight to keep Mayfield from being seated, but Mayfield was seated—with help from Jim Watson who was said to have "kept quiet at all the right times."

Governor McCray tiptoed through a demand in January 1923 that he investigate charges that the Portland, Indiana, national guard had been taken over by Klansmen. McCray's report said no, though the evidence said yes.

These hazy indications of Klan influence were quickly overshadowed by the news that GOP Chair Lyons was a Klan member. Lyons resigned quickly from the KKK, denouncing the Klan as "unAmerican," but the controversy was to follow him the rest of his life. Stephenson's *Fiery Cross* blasted Lyons as a traitor, "born in hell and inspired by Satan."

It was only the beginning of trouble. Soon Lyons would be forced from the GOP state chair and, even worse, linked with the state's biggest political scandal in years, as Governor McCray was accused of defrauding the state of million of dollars.

With the Republican Party thus in turmoil and Indiana awash in months of headlines painting politicians as untrustworthy, Stephenson leaped into the fray. In one of the most adroit political maneuvers of modern times, The Old Man succeeded in turning the situation to his advantage. He capitalized on the public suspicion of incumbents, painted the Klan as the only savior that could restore integrity to public service, and began to elbow his way into the inner circles of Republican power.

On April 13, 1923, the *Indianapolis Times* published a telegram mysteriously intercepted on its way from Columbus to Secretary of State Ed Jackson, concerning the replacement of Lyons as Indiana GOP chair:

"PERMIT NO SELECTION TO BE MADE AND PERMIT NO ONE TO BE NAMED TO SUCCEED LYONS UNTIL I HAVE HAD AN OPPORTUNITY TO CONFER WITH YOU."

Who could issue such an imperious command to the secretary of state?

It was signed simply, "THE OLD MAN."

Within a month, after party skirmishes, a La Grange Republican named Clyde Walb assumed the chair of the state Republican Party. The following day the party vice chair, Mrs. Daisy Barr, resigned; she was head of the Stephenson-financed Queens of the Golden Mask. Walb was apparently not Steve's choice, and observers speculated that Indiana was ridding itself of Klan influence.

But, within the public view now, a new shadow had arisen, a potential kingmaker known only as The Old Man.

The newest rumors said Stephenson had decided to create his own king, that he had selected the compliant secretary of state, Ed Jackson, to become governor in the 1924 elections, and was pledging the Klan's faceless, numberless army to the fight.

Opposition was inevitable, as Steve's power rose. He would have recalled, from his newspapering days on the Oklahoma frontier, that the public loves a good fight.

So when the Indiana opposition began, he capitalized on— welcomed, encouraged, and sometimes even covertly consorted with—his adversaries. Some even said he created some of them.

United against common enemies, his empire's energies were focused, and he could show himself and the Klan as martyrs.

Steve picked up foes early on within labor unions, which represented a cross-section of ethnic and religious groups, and within the powerful Indiana American Legion. "The Ku Klux Klan is not recommended by this office as an American civilizing influence," sniffed Earl Moss, Indiana Legion official.

As early as 1921, Catholics began to fight back, although too slowly and less aggressively than suited some.

The Catholic-based American Unity League, formed in Chicago in 1921, was perhaps the most active anti-Klan organization. The League came to Indianapolis in May of 1923 and published its own newspaper, *Tolerance*, which rivaled Stephenson's *Fiery Cross* for shrill diatribes against its enemies.

Steve would have remembered that a good scrap between two rival newspaper editors was a sure-fire builder of readership. With the right adversary, the fight was great sport, too. He could not have created a better foe than the *Tolerance* publisher, "Mad Pat" O'Donnell, the most militant of the Klan's Catholic adversaries.

O'Donnell soundly reasoned that the only way to expose a secret order was with openness. So the names of Klan members were regularly published in *Tolerance*, under an attention grabbing headline: "Is Your Neighbor a Kluxer?"

O'Donnell got the names wherever he could—even, reportedly, if they must be stolen. The lists were not always accurate; a spate of lawsuits arose. He published thousands of names reputed to be Indiana Klansmen. In some instances, they were names of those contacted to join, rather than actual members.

An Indianan incorrectly identified as a Klansman might well be placed between the proverbial rock and hard spot. A politician, for example, had the most to gain by keeping his membership nebulous, so those who were in believed he was in, and those who were out believed he was out. Depending on the place and the day, a denial—or an admission—of membership could mean political death.

Perhaps the most curious story of the fight between "Mad Pat" O'Donnell and the Klan was told by a former Klansman who adopted the pseudonym of Edgar A. Booth and wrote a rambling, anti Catholic, anonymous expose on Stephenson in the late 1920s. It was named The Mad Mullah.

"Booth" contended that the two people who gained the most from the fight were Stephenson and O'Donnell, that they were secret cohorts who worked together behind the scenes to egg on their respective masses to fever pitched battles.

"The Catholics who were fighting the Klan…, stoning Klan parades and Klan meetings…, did much to swell the ranks of the Klan and add to Stephenson's…wealth and power," Booth argued.

"Some of the atrocities committed against Klansmen, such as hurling of bricks though plate glass windows of merchants believed to be Klansmen, were engineered by Stephenson, while in cahoots with certain Catholic leaders…."

Booth claimed O'Donnell was paying $1 a name for Klan rosters. He said Stephenson and O'Donnell broke their alliance in September of 1923, when O'Donnell printed a special edition of Tolerance containing the names of 14,000 purported Indianapolis Klansmen. But Steve "scooped" him and printed the identical list first in the *Fiery Cross*, which sold for a nickel, compared to the $1 charge for *Tolerance*.

"Stephenson and O'Donnell were deadly enemies from that day on," Booth said.

As discord rose in Indiana, Klan headquarters were robbed or burned on a fairly regular basis—which Booth, with or without evidence, attributed to the religious war.

There is little record of Indiana violence initiated by Steve's Klan. The *Indiana Catholic and Record* reported an exception on June 29, 1923: The Reverend Ulysses S. Johnson, pastor of an unnamed church in an unnamed town, reportedly burned down his own church, trying to make it appear the work of anti-Klan forces. He was charged with arson, as the story goes, but the Klan successfully applied pressure to keep the case from being prosecuted.

A year later the same newspaper reported that the parsonage of the Catholic priest in the little Indiana town of North Judson was bombed, seriously injuring his housekeeper.

Economic, political, and social assaults, however, were the order of the day for the Catholic minority throughout much of Indiana. Many Catholics reported receiving repeated anonymous telephone threats, vitriolic letters, and other harassments.

Boycotts ruined or crippled many a business. As businessmen in a town were organized into the Klan, "...one would begin to notice in some of the downtown store windows the appearance of placards bearing the seeming innocent letters 'TWK,'" one recalled. "It meant Trade With Klansmen. A shopper would thus be notified that he could spend his dollars inside with the comfortable assurance that the proprietor was a Klansmen and that he himself would not be abetting the Jews or Catholics in uprooting Hoosier culture.

"The technique worked brilliantly. It would not be unfair to say that merchants who were eligible scrambled to get into the Klan in order to display their placards. The Ku Klux Klan had come to town; no individual or group was to be unaffected."

Sometimes the job took only a rumor that a business, even a giant corporation, had one Catholic or Jewish employee. Catholics, distinctly in the minority, could produce little effect with counter boycotts.

With reports of Klan violence elsewhere, a cloud of fear settled down too quickly for the Catholic Church and tolerance groups to conduct more than a feeble defense. When *Tolerance* mistakenly printed the names of six South Bend men alleged to be Klansmen, the town Chamber of Commerce convened a meeting to try to iron out the problem. After listening to Protestant ministers rant about "that rotten rag," *Tolerance*, Notre Dame's Father John W. Cavanaugh responded:

"Reverend clergy, you are six months too late. For six months, that libelous and cowardly magazine of the Klan, *The Fiery Cross*, has circulated among you without let or hindrance. For six months, this sheet has been before your eyes and before the eyes of your congregations. And not once have you said anything to prevent the spread of that spirit of hatred of Catholics which fills the pages of *The Fiery Cross*."

In 1923 the Klan went to court to restrain *Tolerance* from printing Klansmen's names—and the Klan won.

When the Unity League pressed for an Indianapolis ordinance prohibiting masks except on Halloween, more than a thousand League members attended the City Council meeting. But the Klan won, six to two.

When O'Donnell jabbed at the Klan's softest spot, its secrecy, Stephenson threw the fight into the open. "Klansmen Raise Your Visors!" trumpeted Steve's *Fiery Cross* on April 13, 1923. To prevent his knights from being discredited, he ordered them "to limit the use of your full regalia to your naturalization work with, and on, your own premises, and to attendance at funerals in a body of not less than twenty-five."

Step by step, Steve backed the American Unity League and Mad Pat O'Donnell into an Indiana corner. Within a year, he had them soundly defeated; by the subsequent year, O'Donnell had retreated to Ohio, where he was "still running wild," according to *The Fiery Cross*, and trying to make the League a paying proposition.

Steve was riding high—too high to remain a child of Atlanta. The KKK constitution provided that when a state became well organized, it could become more autonomous, with its own Grand Dragon leader. It was time, Steve said, for Indiana to become a full fledged realm of the Invisible Empire.

The day was selected, July 4, 1923; the place, Kokomo; and the Grand Dragon, The Old Man.

Before the grand Kokomo Klonklave passed into history, Steve filed his financial report with Imperial Wizard Hiram Wesley Evans. For the quarter ending in July 1923, Stephenson sent a whopping $641,475 to the Imperial Treasury. By comparison, Indiana had spent $159,786 on Klan operations, he said.

Evans sent Steve glowing thanks for his "magnificent record," along with a congratulatory $5,000 check.

Steve sent it back.

PART II

9
Press Oppression

1923
Indianapolis, Indiana

"Hey, kid, how would you like to be naturalized tomorrow night?"

From the glowering deputy court clerk, the question shot like a challenge to John Niblack, the new courthouse reporter.

Niblack, fresh from covering the Klan's Kokomo Klonklave, decided to play for time. He raised a crooked eyebrow and pondered the question.

"What do you mean, 'naturalized?'"

The deputy leaned against the railing and grinned. Behind him, the hulking fort of the courthouse loomed, its limestone bulk shining softly in the bright morning light.

"Well, you know, you pay $10 and you get naturalized. We're

going to have a meeting out at Bridgeport in a grove."

Niblack measured the challenge and the challenger. Was this a trap, or an opening, finally, into courthouse circles? "I suppose you're talking about the Ku Klux Klan."

"Yeh, that's about it."

"Well." Niblack took out a cigarette, tapped it on the rail, and considered his answer. "Well. I don't have to be naturalized. I was born down by Vincennes, Indiana. And I am an American citizen. And I have no reason to be naturalized, let alone paying $10."

The clerk scowled. "You ought to join. Everybody else is joining."

"Well." Niblack lighted the cigarette, then perched it above his left ear. "Well. Tell me, friend, what is it with you fellows in the Klan? What do you stand for?"

The clerk rubbed his chin. "We're against the Negroes, the Catholics, the Jews, and the foreigners."

Niblack took a deep drag. "Let me put it this way. Now there are about ten million Negroes and there are about three million Jews in the United States, and God knows how many foreigners, and there are quite a few million Catholics. What are you going to do about this thing?"

The clerk opened his mouth to speak, but Niblack would not yield. "We have three alternatives. We can run them all out of the country, or second we can kill them, or third we can live with them. You can see it is impossible to run all of them out of the country; it's going to be impossible to kill them all; and therefore the only alternative we have is to live with them. So what I want to know is— why don't we live in peace and quiet and harmony, because there's nothing else to do."

"Niblack, you talk silly."

"Maybe I am silly, but I'm not going to join. I don't believe in it. I think it's unAmerican."

And with that, the new cub reporter crushed his cigarette

underfoot, nodded jauntily, and marched up the courthouse steps to work.

By luck, John Niblack had gone to work for the Indianapolis newspaper that agreed with him.

The stronger the Klan grew in Indiana, the more silence spread over the pages of most Hoosier newspapers.

But not the *Indianapolis Times*, which had been taken over in 1922 by the Scripps Howard chain. Like Niblack, the *Times* was a scrappy underdog in competition with the town's two established giants, the *News* and the *Star*. The more the knights' power grew, the more the *Times* took after them, like a yelping puppy dogging at their heels.

The *Times* was after fresh young reporters to liven up the news. They hired Niblack fresh out of school, for $25 a week, gave him a desk with an ancient Oliver typewriter, and dispatched him to conquer the courthouse.

It was a tough beat, and he was still a rookie, a kid from the country, but he had not wasted his 24 years. Nibby might still have hay in his hair, but he was no bumpkin.

In many ways, his life typified southern Indiana. He expected no coddling from life. His mother died in childbirth when he was three. John and his twin sister were reared by grandparents on a Knox County farm outside Vincennes.

He worked from the time he was in grade school. Hard work was a family tradition, at least since 1779 when his sternly principled, predestination Presbyterian people first came from Massachusetts and North Carolina to the free soil of southwestern Indiana: three parts Dixie to one part New Englander.

He worked like a man for a boy's pay, threshing wheat, slaughtering hogs, laying rail, growing through what he would later call the ages of man, from "an innocent predawn" yearling to "a caveman hunter, stalking the...unsuspecting sparrow and killing in cold blood," to the preteen "gangster—a member of a gang—prone to horseplay..., vandalism and fighting."

He mastered the maple fork slingshot and, later, the pencil-straight furrow, plowed with his eye fixed unblinking on the horizon.

On the basketball court, clay lot or schoolhouse, he learned to outwit giants, dodging artfully when they tried to slam dunk him into the red hot gym stove.

He learned to hop a rolling freight and ditch it, when booted off, without a scratch; to steal a chicken by feeling it up stealthily, then strangling it without a squawk; to plant his foot on a wild rabbit's head and rip it off for open fire roasting, without a pang of conscience; and—in a sunbaked summer working Kansas wheat—to bum the boxcars without companion, food, or money.

Niblack went forth into the world of Prohibition with a warning from his father, a leader in the church and the Anti-Saloon League, to eschew nicotine, whiskey, wild women, and gambling. Sometimes, on a rough morning, young John wished he had abided by at least part of that counsel.

He lived by his wits, well-honed. In time he grew taller, maybe 5 feet 8, but never filled out. As he stretched upward, he carried with him wild wisdom and scars of his youth. A bloody schoolyard brawl permanently wrinkled one eyebrow, lending a perpetual quasi-wink to his well-boned, boyish face that always looked on the verge of a wry grin.

He was clean and keen, with the eager look of a scrubbed, land visiting sailor. Given time, he would make a patrician old man.

John Niblack rose to manhood during a stint as a country school teacher, worked his way into Purdue, then Indiana University, interrupted by the Navy during the war that robbed America of her innocence.

Times were hard. When he graduated from Indiana U—cum laude, with a Phi Beta Kappa key in English and history and experience on the college newspaper, Niblack counted himself lucky to find a job. Tom Adams, the crusty editor of the *Vincennes Commercial Appeal*, hired John as a reporter as a family favor, because Niblack's grandfather helped Adams start the paper in the 1880s.

Within weeks, an even better break came along, with the *Times*. Nibby packed all his belongings in his little blue coupe with the broken windshield wiper and headed east, to Indianapolis.

The courthouse processed the county's dregs, who in return left their grime and odor on the place.

Poorly maintained by political hacks called custodians, the old courthouse was a haven for cockroaches, rats, and winos. The courts reeked of decadent humanity and, after occasional treatments of poison, decaying rats that crawled within its walls to die.

Niblack, in the throes of first love of his job, found it a place filled with wonders.

"So you're the new *Times* reporter, huh?" snorted Judge James A. Collins on Niblack's first day. "Well, you'd better stay out of my Criminal Court!"

Collins had a red mustache and a black disposition. Rumor was that he was a Klansman. He had just sentenced Kilgallen, the *Times* city editor, to 10 days in jail for reporting that offended His Honor. Kilgallen, father of columnist Dorothy Kilgallen, had been spooked into leaving the country, literally; he headed south to Mexico City.

Clearly the runts—John Niblack and the *Indianapolis Times*— would have to be scrappy and quick, to avoid being trounced by the big guys.

Things might have been tense in Indianapolis, in the era of the Klan, but they were surely better elsewhere. Probably—but not in Muncie.

The Klan came in 1921 to help Muncie get rid of a corrupt mayor. Some 50 miles northeast of Indianapolis, Muncie was a flourishing Klan town. The Muncie Klan, Delaware (county) #4, was one of the strongest in Indiana. But the town was also a center of stubborn resistance to Steve's program to control the Indiana press.

Members of Delaware Klan #4 lived in a colorful spot. Muncie, recounted Morton Harrison, a writer of the day, was home of "the notorious Chicken Blood Gang," confidence men whose game was persuading farmers from distant states to come to Muncie to back the challengers in fake prize fights.

"The farmer came expecting to win some easy money (and) the fights were staged with the cash in a neutral corner of the ring. At the appointed signal, the farmer's fighter went down with blood spurting from his mouth. The fighter achieved this remarkable effect by biting on a rubber sac of chicken blood concealed in his mouth. A doctor then pronounced the fighter dead and the farmer usually put three states behind him before he paused for breath."

The Muncie KKK was a lively bunch. A Muncie group was among 3,000 KKK members who went to Russiaville for a big initiation, parade, and cross burning three weeks before Stephenson's July 4, 1923, coronation at nearby Kokomo. The *Kokomo Tribune* reported that one Dr. H.V. Logan, of Russiaville, admitted he had stabbed two Klansmen during the parade. It sounded like another of the cases Stephenson loved to tout, in which the Klan's enemies were responsible for violence.

Dr. Logan's story was another matter, however. "Dr. Logan said he was returning home with his wife and daughter and was waiting for the parade to pass through the business district when a woman marcher, wearing a white robe, waved a tiny flag under his nose and demanded that he salute it. The physician said he stepped back and the woman called, 'Come and get him, Muncie No. 4!' He defended himself with his pocket knife against three men, Dr. Logan added, but a fourth knocked him unconscious."

Muncie was home to one of Indiana's most vociferous anti-Klan publishers, George Dale, editor of the weekly *Muncie Post Democrat*. The Klan's fight with Dale became a national cause for a while and was said to have helped intimidate other publishers throughout the state. State and national newsmen cheered—or cowered—while Dale took on the Klan and a fiery Klan judge of the Delaware circuit court, Clarence W. Dearth, a rousing KKK orator. Dale paid dearly for the fight, but so did Dearth and Stephenson's Klan empire.

Dale took on the Klan as early as 1922, with vigor. "Muncie," he wrote on June 8, 1923, "is now in a state of civil war. An armed, masked and secret organization has taken over the government.... They are above the law and can insult, assault and even murder, if the victim does not belong to their traitorous organization.... The law-abiding citizenship of Muncie has been aroused to the highest pitch and the law will be upheld and anarchy overthrown if it becomes necessary to wade knee deep in blood...."

Well, maybe it wasn't really that bad in Muncie, but Dale had reason for excess. He had been attacked by Klansmen:

"Two automobiles filled with black-hooded Klansmen assaulted me and my son one dark night within fifty feet of my home.... There was some shooting and the valiant Klansmen departed with a wounded comrade, leaving me with a black eye [and] a badly lacerated ear.... My son was badly beaten by the butt of a revolver in the hands of one of the robed assassins."

The rumors circulating among Hoosier newsmen were even worse. They said the knights intended to kidnap Dale and take him to a hospital "where an illegal operation would be performed." It was also said that Dale's shot killed the Klansman, "but the death was hushed up" to avoid linking the Klan with local authorities.

Dale said Klan harassment mounted; he received anonymous threats; a bullet was fired through his front window, narrowly missing his daughter. In early 1923, the publisher was arrested for illegal possession of liquor. He wrote in his paper that he was framed and that Judge Dearth was a Klansman, as were the prosecutor, sheriff, jury commissioners, grand jury, and most of the police department.

Judge Dearth retaliated by sentencing Dale to 90 days in jail and fining him $500 for contempt of court. When Dale was found guilty on the contempt charge, he reprinted his allegations—and Dearth gave him a second dose of the same punishment.

Dale appealed to the Indiana Supreme Court and lost—because, said the court, "the truth is no defense."

The case dragged on for years, and Dale became a "freedom of the press" cause for the national press. He sunk some $15,000 cash into the fight, lost his home in the process, and in time was "penniless."

Dale was not, however, beaten. He published an anonymous letter charging that Dearth and the Muncie mayor were responsible for recent homicides because they allowed lawless conditions to exist. Further, the letter said, Dearth illegally controlled jury selections to predetermine trial outcomes. Dearth ordered the letter suppressed and charged Dale with criminal libel. Dale had to flee to Ohio, where he directed the continued publication of the *Post Democrat* by long distance.

While Dale was out of the state, the Indiana House of Representatives, on petition of 250 Muncie citizens, voted to impeach Judge Dearth, the first such Hoosier action in nearly 100 years. He was charged on six counts, including illegally hand-picking juries; for example, he selected 12 women members of the Women's Christian Temperance Union to decide a prohibition case.

Dearth was then tried in the Senate, where he was acquitted

by a narrow vote in an upper chamber dominated by Klansmen. Nonetheless, the Senate trial was a publicity disaster for Dearth, a bonanza for Dale. Dearth had caused police to arrest 35 newsboys for selling Dale's newspaper, and the boys testified before national newsmen.

The climax of the trial, wrote journalist Harrison, was testimony from 14-year-old newsboy John Ranes, who said he was arrested for selling copies of the *Post Democrat* and taken before Judge Dearth. The judge took the boy's papers.

"Was any writ or any paper of any kind read to you?" asked the prosecutor.

"No," the boy answered.

"Did the judge say anything?"

"He told me to get out and if I sold any more papers he would put me on probation."

"What did you do then?"

"I went out and got some more papers and sold them till another policeman chased me up an alley and put his hand on his revolver and told me to stop. He took me over to the courtroom and smacked me. The judge said nothing more, but sent for my father."

At that point, the usually stoic newsmen burst into applause.

Klan intimidation of Dale was not unique in Indiana in the 1920s. Boycotts, threats to advertisers and against newsmen—and a reverse kind of intimidation, bribes—were reported at scattered sites through the state. If the Klan intended to use its harassment of Dale to intimidate other Hoosier newsmen, it worked.

Oh, the moon is fair tonight along the Wabash,
From the fields there comes the breath of new mown hay;
Through the sycamores the candle lights are gleaming....

As the Ku Klux Klan took hold of the Hoosier state in 1923, the idyllic ballad of moonlight on the Wabash, written by Indiana's Theodore Dreiser and his brother Paul, was sung sadly by a stream of reporters, former home state boys now dispatched back home to Indiana to see what had possessed their home towns.

They hardly recognized the territory.

"The once brilliant moon is now a pale and diabetic blur," one wrote. "The odor from the countryside is not of Alsace but of the smoking embers of some dance hall or other den of iniquity, touched off by the enemies of triumphant righteousness, and the light that gleams through the stately sycamores is not from candles but from the blazing new emblem of the Imperial Commonwealth of Indiana—the Fiery Cross."

How could Indiana be the heart of what one reporter called "the enlightened suzerainty of the Ku Klux Klan?'

"In Indiana, sir!" sputtered one of the more eloquent native sons, writer Meredith Nicholson. In Indiana, where "the spirit of the good folks" had "lived in peace and amity with their Catholic neighbors, sent a mighty phalanx across the Ohio to free the black man and neighbored happily with the son and daughters of Israel."

Now, Nicholson moaned, "Where Apollo once led the Nine, on bracing nights when the frost was on the pumpkin and the fodder in the shock, unfamiliar shapes—sheeted and hooded—moved with slow step in sinister silence. Here, verily, was a thing alien to an Indiana rich in political and cultural tradition and accomplishment...."

"Texas and Oklahoma might run amuck and bend the neck to false gods, but not Indiana, whose people have rejoiced in a reputation for seeing life steadily and seeing it whole, with an encyclopedia and a bath tub in every farm house."

Indiana had become, another said, possessed by fear and more slogans than chiggers. The most pervasive slogan: "Hush!"

Between 1921 and 1925, when the Klan power was building and peaking, most Indiana newspapers were passively supportive, reprinting glowing Klan puffery about parades, outings, mass initiations, and other galas—alongside other routine news of church socials.

Reporters such as John Niblack analyzed it later. Indiana newsmen "were scared," Niblack said. "Dale's case made all the papers. Everybody knew about that."

"There weren't any big expose stories at all" while the Klan was powerful, another reporter said. The Indiana press "...covered Klan rallies, and stories like that, but as far as getting in their inner-workings, they never touched it at all.... There was a lot of intolerance, and everybody was scared. And it took a lot of courage to go out and fight the Klan. You could get beat up."

At first the Klan seemed like a blip on the Indiana scene; some newsmen accepted it as harmless, others as useful for reform, still others as best contained by benign neglect. Its political power popped up suddenly, taking newsmen by surprise.

The rise of the 1920s Klan, in Indiana and elsewhere, placed newsmen in a most unenviable position. Some rose in remarkable heroism; others folded in fear; in both reactions, they wrote a unique chapter in journalistic history. The Klan put newsmen to one of their most severe and complex tests in modern times; journalism emerged from the fight with mixed scores but, as a profession, wiser.

Despite its failings and inconsistent successes, over the longer term the press proved the most pervasive and persistent adversary to Stephenson and the Indiana Klan. The fight, when it was joined, was memorable. It was an inevitable clash, arising from at least two basic causes.

First, they were natural competitors. Both knights and newsmen viewed themselves as anointed to pursue holy causes and crusades for reform. Their respective calls to service bear eerie likeness.

When Steve was at Madill, he printed the journalists' call:

"I AM THE NEWSPAPER.
Born of the deep, daily need of a nation –
I am the voice of Now, Monarch of the Things that Are....
I am the consort of Kings—the partner of Capital—the brother of Toil.
The inspiration of the Hopeless—the right arm of the Needy—
the champion of the Oppressed—the conscience of the Criminal....
I speak and the world stops to listen.
I say the word and battle flames the horizon.
I counsel peace and the war lords obey.
I am greater than any individual—more powerful than any group.
I am the Dynamic Force of Public Opinion....
I am the Newspaper!"

And then, after Steve moved into the Klan, his *Fiery Cross* printed the credo of the Klan; perhaps written by his hand:

"I AM THE KU KLUX KLAN.
I am a Searchlight on a high tower.
I run my relentless eye to and fro throughout the land;
my piercing glance penetrates the brooding places of Iniquity.
I plant my eyes and ears in the whispering corridors of crime.
Wherever men gather furtively together, there am I, an austere and
invisible Presence.
I am the Recording Angel's proxy.... I am the Ku Klux Klan!"

Second, the press and the Klan were not only competing for the same territory, they were natural enemies. The Klan was founded on secrecy; its innumerability gave it even more strength than its actual numbers. The press was founded on open public policy, which it must have for its very life; without openness, there would be nothing to report. Some newsmen were concerned about other issues—bigotry, violence, corruption. But whether he agreed with Klan philosophy or not, no newsmen worth a shake of salt could swallow a secret society that meddled into government.

The newsman's knotty problem was that the Klan also threatened the economic base of newspaper survival. Newspapers could not publish without advertisers and subscribers—and the powerful Klan in Indiana, as well as elsewhere, threatened uncooperative newsmen with loss of both advertisers and subscribers, as well as loss of social acceptance in their home communities. Occasionally, the threats included physical violence. Thus, a secret Klan that meddled in government threatened the base of press canons and survival, yet most newsmen could not attack it without threatening their personal and publications' survival.

As if that dilemma was not difficult enough, the problem was compounded because publicity helped the Klan grow. The national press attacks on the Klan were providing ample proof. National newsmen had been attacking the Klan with unprecedented vigor since 1921. In fact, many newsmen had long since given up any pretense to journalistic standards of fairness or objectivity. They declared the Klan the enemy and unleashed every possible journalistic weapon to annihilate it—but the more they fought it, the more the Klan grew, in almost direct proportion to national press attacks. Out of town attacks against the Klan just confirmed the belief of many "common people" that the "eastern press" was run by intellectuals, infidels, and worse—and that the KKK was worthy of support.

The press had another tool beyond attack, however, and another responsibility beyond ensuring its own journalistic and economic survival. Its most basic reason for existence was to provide accurate information to readers. Analysis of the 1920s press Klan fight shows, in the clearer vision of hindsight, that accurate information about what the Klan was doing—the truth, simply stated—was the most effective weapon the press could wield against the Klan. One editor sent a reporter to cover every Klan meeting and printed, calmly, everything that went on; the results were not immediate, but over time Klavern membership fell from thousands to tens.

The chief lesson to journalism from its historic 1920s fight against the Klan was that, as one researcher summarized it, "drawn as a sword, the pen proved a poor weapon. But used as a writing medium it again demonstrated its power as the mightiest instrument in human society."

The press/Klan clash proved another fundamental journalistic point. The closer to home the information was published, the more effective it was. But of 50 or so local, general circulation newspapers in Indiana in the early 1920s, all but a handful were passively or weakly supportive of Klan activities—or silent—in the important years of 1921-1924. Indiana produced a classic case study in the information vacuum when the general circulation press is silenced by intimidation or other means.

The vacuum could have been filled by other sources of information. There were four main alternate press options: anti-Klan organizations, local Klans, towns with strong anti-Klan factions, and stronger big city newspapers. Most were silenced.

Tolerance, the feisty publication speaking for some anti-Klan groups, had challenged the Klan's secrecy but actually spawned Klan support by its shrillness and illegal methods. Courts had ruled in favor of the Klan. By the mid-1920s, *Tolerance* was beaten in Indiana and had largely withdrawn from the state.

As more and more insurgents became disillusioned, local Klan publications could have criticized abuses of power. But Indiana's

Fiery Cross was controlled first by Stephenson and then by Evans. Evans systematically suppressed local Klan publications, including Indiana's, so the Klan would speak with one voice—his.

Even the often marginal small town papers could have spoken out—and a few did, in communities with strong anti-Klan factions. But their voices were weak. Even in communities such as South Bend, with its large Catholic population, the local press was more likely to criticize the Klan only at a safe distance, printing negative stories about distant outrages but ignoring the home town problems.

And the powerful big city newspapers had their own problems. Indianapolis was a case in point. Its establishment newspaper was the *Indianapolis Star*, a morning newspaper, whose pages were filled with chatty news of social goings on, the latest issue of automobiles, the terrific land deals available in Florida (which rated a special weekly section, filled with Florida land dealers' advertisements), and folksy columns of religious inspiration. The evening *Indianapolis News* was owned by the Fairbanks family, which was prominent in state Republican politics. Both the state giants, the *Star* and the *News*, were less than vigorous in their pursuit of the Klan issue while the Klan was growing or strongest. Niblack contended that some of their reporters were Klansmen and that at least one was bribed by Stephenson. Despite their size, neither newspaper was immune to Klan pressure. For example, the *News* lost 1,500 subscribers after it printed a story that riled the Klan.

The role of adversary fell, thus, to Indianapolis' third major newspaper, the *Indianapolis Times*—the paper where John Niblack worked. Perhaps it was in part because the *Times* was a smaller scrapper fighting for its slice of the Indiana subscriber pie; perhaps because its economic base could be more secure with its outside ownership by Scripps Howard. For whatever reasons, as the light of other information options grew dimmer and dimmer, the *Times* grew bolder and bolder, standing with George Dale and a very few other newsmen in opposition to the Klan in its powerful years.

By the end of 1923, Stephenson and the Klan, together or in opposition to each other, were largely in control of many Hoosier newspapers.

Now the printing press could be added to Steve's other array of Indiana power tools:

- the Protestant church;
- much of the legal system, through the vigilante Horse Thief Detective Association and established law enforcement and court systems;
- a large still-loyal army of Klansmen and women;
- a growing slice of the Republican party and many Democrats.

The Old Man's goal was to consolidate that power by taking over the Indiana ballot box, absorbing the balance of the Republican party and sweeping to control of the state executive and legislative branches, as well as local legal and policy-making bodies throughout Indiana. And beyond....

10
KKK Bar B Q

May 19, 1923
Valpariso, Indiana

The Old Man had plans, big plans.

Like old Colonel Simmons before him, D.C. Stephenson wanted a Klan university. It could be a beacon for 100 percent Americanism, in a land darkened by the Romanist, the unGodly, the unassimilated alien. It could help the KKK don a cloak of respectability and add a bracing breath of class to the booming brotherhood. It could focus fund raising and shelter taxes. It could be a monument to the movement—and perhaps to its Indiana leader, The Old Man.

So Steve, who had darkened no university door except in the shadows of his own fantasies, set out to establish one—which might well be known as KKK U.

It was only the latest in a series of plans taking shape in Steve's mind. Those who knew him best discerned that he was building a four-step political ladder:

Step one: take over the Indiana Republican party.

Step two: carry the state's 1924 elections.

Step three: U.S. Senator in 1926.

Step four: President in 1928.

He planned to make Ed Jackson, the Klan-friendly Indiana Secretary of State, the Hoosier governor in 1924; and Jackson was his Presidential backup.

The ladder rested on his Klan army and his control of the Republican Party, the fundamentalist church, the Horse Thief Detective Association and law enforcement systems, and the press.

It was a preposterous plan—but so were his accomplishments already. He completed the first step in mere months.

Beneath that plan was the shadow of something darker.

"Once in a great while," recalled the former Klansman Edgar A. Booth, "when drinking very heavily, he would talk revolution. He would pride himself that he was to lead this revolution."

Drinking? Ah, yes. The Old Man—the leader of the movement to clean up those lawless towns and scour them free of bathtub gin, the close compatriot of the Anti-Saloon League—was developing a bit of a drinking problem. The rank and file, of course, still believed their leader was "dry."

"The Old Man ran rather well on alcohol," one writer noted later.

"When drinking—but not too heavily—his brain was most active," Booth recalled, "and was always setting traps for his enemies, and planning those things which would get men he could use into his power when he felt, or knew, that he could not use them otherwise."

Booth believed Stephenson—the darling of the anti-Red crowd—was at heart still the boy who had espoused Socialist causes in Oklahoma, albeit for pay. He had grown up in poverty, rescued only by the Kleagle bounty. "As he grew to manhood, his thoughts were socialistic—he was embittered against those who had accumulated wealth" and did not lose that bitterness when he became among the wealthiest, Booth contended.

"Always he was possessed with the obsession that he was to become a leader among men; to gain power was his object, and to overthrow the existing mode of society was his coveted dream."

Booth recalled a night in Columbus when Stephenson was drinking heavily and began to "curse capital and talk revolution. I remonstrated until he grew abusive and then left him." In the sober light of the next day, Stephenson asked Booth repeatedly what he had said the night before. "I told him I paid no attention to 'his drunken mouthings'..., and he seemed much relieved."

If Stephenson hated wealth, he was nonetheless making the most of his. He had quickly acquired a habit of living rather well.

The private railway car gave way to the gilded aeroplane, which could carry him to three or more states in a single day.

He maintained what he called "the summer White House" at Buckeye Lake, east of his office in Columbus, Ohio. He also had a yacht on Lake Huron, the site of frequent high-level parties and strategy sessions among Klansmen and politicians. It was no ordinary little boat. It was a 98-foot, twin screw, mahogany and teak yacht, ocean-ready, which he named Reomas II. The boat had one bad problem: it was accident-prone: it caught fire twice and blew up once.

Booth wrote that one of the festive occasions aboard the yacht, in the summer of 1923, included a blue ribbon roster of guests: Evans; sculptor Gutzon Borglum and other members of Evans' Imperial Kloncillium; Indiana Senator James E. Watson; Ohio Governor Victor Donahey; Indiana Secretary of State Ed Jackson, later to be governor; John Duvall, later to become Indianapolis mayor; state senators from Ohio and Indiana; "some members of Congress and a few judges from Ohio, Indiana, Michigan, and Illinois." Plus their wives, and others.

Another trip was planned aboard the yacht, to include Evans, Borglum and other Kloncillium members, Senator Watson and other members of Congress. Stephenson planned to travel upstream and end up in Maine for a hunting trip. But the trip was abruptly canceled, because he didn't trust the group to be together when armed.

By July 1923, at the time of his Kokomo Klonklave coronation, Stephenson had moved from Evansville to Indianapolis. He acquired an imposing mansion in Irvington, a quiet, fashionable suburb of Indianapolis, in the shadow of a fine little school named Butler College.

The neighborhood dated back to 1873 and was one of the city's first planned neighborhoods, named after the writer Washington Irving. By the 1920s its gently curving, tree-shaded streets and homey two-story bungalows were a haven for writers and artists who banded together in "The Irvington Group."

Irvington was a real neighborhood, with dozens of social and intellectual groups, summer ice cream socials and croquet in the spacious parks, friendly churches, its own beloved college where the life of the mind could be explored and individuality was prized—a place of quiet, self confident, upper-middle-class.

Irvington was as good a place as mid America could offer, the stuff of Norman Rockwell paintings. It was what they had strived to become, those Oklahoma frontier climbers in Purcell, Pauls Valley, Hugo, and Madill, from Steve's past.

It was the sort of place where a bookish boy, battered by frontier poverty and squalor, who preferred to believe that his father had been a patrician Massachusetts lawyer, might figuratively stand with his nose against a window, watching a warm family gathering around a flickering fire, yearning to belong.

A stone's throw from Butler College was one house that stood out from the rest. A good address: 5432 University Avenue. You couldn't miss it, on an autumn stroll out from Butler, along the freeze-heaved sidewalks under the golden raintrees and sycamores.

The house was imposing—well, actually ostentatious: larger than the rest, two-storied with a dormered third floor and full basement, bay-windowed, and fronted by a magnificent portico with four tapered Roman columns supporting a lavish decked roof. It was well-placed on a good lot, carefully landscaped; with appropriate outbuildings, a garage and servants' quarters—but it was the columns that set it off from the rest. Walking down the street, Irvington might lull you into a soft intellectual purr; but when you came to that house, pow! You had to stop and look.

It was the kind of house that a poor boy from Beef Creek, newly rich, could buy and, in its acquisition, brush a perfectly manicured thumb lightly across his nose, with his eye fixed unswerving on the middle class intelligencia. The gesture was not lost on Irvington and Indianapolis. Years later, some in Indiana would say, "We could forgive him everything except—he was a newcomer, an outsider; maybe we're too clannish, but we could forgive him everything except that house."

What would soon be known as the Stephenson Mansion had been home to the girls of the Butler College Kappa Kappa Gamma sorority, whose spirits still danced through the place after Stephenson acquired and lavishly remodeled it into a carbon copy of the Klan's Atlanta Imperial Palace.

Driving by one night during the remodeling, he nodded to the house. "There," he told those in the car, "is the Imperial Palace of the North."

Soon his house was arrayed in Rudolph Valentinian splendor.

It was surrounded by his fleet of limousines and a pack of trained guard dogs. It was livened by elegant entertainment, lavish parties, sophisticated society meetings, and stealthy midnight strategy sessions. And it was peopled by his entourage of bodyguards, Klansmen, spies, aspiring politicians, climbing society matrons, international businessmen, dazzling women—all the best that money could buy (Among his personal staff: housekeeper Blanche and bodyguard Howard Bennett—whose names he later gave as his "parents, Blanche Bennett and Howard Stephenson.").

It was an appropriate setting for the man at center stage. As host of, perhaps, a community fund benefit, he was flawlessly dressed like a banker, classic black tie and shoes, not too much white cuff showing, blond hair cropped short and combed to the right and back like a school boy any mother could be proud of. The cherub face with its dimpled chin looked scrubbed, rosy, healthy; the outstretched hand was forthright but not too eager; the conversation was sparkling, not too filled with allusions to the classics to lose its folksy charm.

"Yes," he would concede with a knowing semi-smile, "I'm one of those 100-percent Americans you hear so much about." To the right people, the self-deprecating smile saved the preposterous line. It was the equivalent of a wink that said: I know that you know that I know....

But there was a darker side. It arose later in the nights, after society's upper crust had driven back into Indianapolis, when the early-to-bed-and-rise Irvington middle class would start from sleep at the sound of gunfire or other noises, less identifiable.

No matter how rowdy the second parties were, no policemen ever came around to check.

"I am the embodiment of Napoleon," he told guests one night. "Drink 'er down."

Stephenson was 32—an age when, a psychiatrist would later note, megalomania often begins to exhibit symptoms. And he was living in an age when revolution was shaking the world. A dictator was rising to power in Rome, leading black-shirted fanatics. The idea of white hoods and a Mussolini in America took hold of Stephenson.

He began meeting more and more often with his plant on Evans' Imperial Kloncillium, the sculptor Gutzon Borglum, often in the sculptor's home at Stamford, Connecticut, sometimes with a Dr. Edward Rumely who had been an object of spy investigations by the government during the War.

Gutzon Borglum himself was a man of no small dreams. He carved the bust of Lincoln that rested in the nation's capitol. Since 1916 Borglum had been carving a mammoth panorama of the Confederate Army into Stone Mountain outside Atlanta, an artistic and engineering colossus costing millions that he undertook when backers had only $250. Literally climbing the same stairs trod by Colonel Simmons when he revived the Klan atop Stone Mountain, Borglum was carving Lee's head. Lee was to be joined by Stonewall Jackson, Jefferson Davis, and a supporting line of mounted cavalry headed by Nathan Bedford Forrest. Evans' financial support of that project was a source of great irritation to Stephenson.

By 1927 Borglum would be carving the faces of four Presidents, a mile wide, into South Dakota's Mount Rushmore.

By any definition a bold man, Borglum was a supporter of Wisconsin Senator Robert LaFollette but won at least two Presidents, Harding and Coolidge, to support of his mountain-moving projects.

Borglum was a balding, stocky, stubby-fingered man, educated in Europe, who rose to political influence in the American Northwest through the agrarian revolt. He saw the Klan as an instrument of a pro-farmer, anti-tariff, Anglo Saxon progressive fight, expressing "the minds of the villagers and agrarians," opposing foreign ideologies and eastern alienism.

Revolution makes strange bedfellows. They were an incongruous combination, the blunt-handed agrarian sculptor Gutzon Borglum and the Republican velvet-gloved salesman D.C. Stephenson. They never agreed on the tariff, but ex-Klansman Booth contended they agreed to launch a revolutionary takeover of America.

The plot, as Booth described it, was intricate and convoluted. They planned to mobilize their Klan and agrarian machines to win enough votes for LaFollette (who knew nothing of the plan) to deadlock the 1924 Presidential election and throw the decision into Congress.

Democrats and Republicans would fight it out in Congress. The longer they wrestled with the dilemma, the better; a prolonged period of uncertainty and unrest would drive the country into a depression and perhaps widespread civil unrest, helping to foster the revolution. The country would cry for a Mussolini to rise from the turmoil and save America; to restore order and to make the trains run on time, so to speak.

When Congress chose either a Republican or Democrat, Booth said, Stephenson would "arise in his brilliant oratory, charge that capital had cheated LaFollette out of the Presidency; that Wall Street had bought out Congress." Stephenson would "stir the radicals and sway the bolshevists," and the country would arise and demand that Stephenson be President.

It was a mad scheme. Should it fail, he had others. "His plans were many and varied," Booth wrote. "His brain never ceased working; always some scheme brewing, (planning) revolution and... ways in which he himself could start a revolution in this country," working to create chaos under the guise of creating order, working to set man against man and North against South, working to touch off civil warfare from which he could emerge all powerful."

Stephenson had reason to foresee a Klan takeover of America. Around the United States, the KKK's power was mounting at a dizzying rate in 1923.

Back home in Oklahoma, for example, things were humming. Steve must have wondered if he left too soon.

The climate was ripe there. In oil-drenched Tulsa, for instance, *The Tulsa Tribune* pleaded as early as 1920 for an end to rampant lawlessness and immorality. In one of the bloodiest race riots in American history a year later, whites burned Tulsa's "Little Africa" to the ground. Uncounted truckloads of black bodies were floated down the muddy Arkansas River. The Klan used the riot as a recruiting ploy, and by mid-1921 white hoods began to bob up around the Sooner state. Before Oklahomans were through, they would rack up the greatest volume of KKK violence in the nation, in the name of law, order, and reform of personal misconduct.

Oklahoma whippings rose to one a day, in a hundred locations around the state. Many Oklahomans, weary of lawlessness that continued to rule the 15-year-old state, welcomed the Klan.

But opposition began to rise in the face of outrages such as the March 1922 kidnapping of Tulsa Negro John K. Smitherman, who was routed to a hillside outside town, accused of encouraging blacks to register to vote, and lashed with a blacksnake whip. One of the men spat in Smitherman's face, then whipped out a knife and cut off Smitherman's ear. Beating him all the while, they tried to make him eat his ear.

Oklahoma's rollicking political history took a new turn in 1922, with the campaign of Democrat Jack Walton for governor. Walton's supporters included Socialists, anti Klan forces, and Steve's former Cushing employer, Sheriff Henry Townsend.

Walton campaigned with a jazz band and, victorious, threw the biggest barbecue in Oklahoma history as his inaugural bash in January of 1923. By this time, one of ten eligible Oklahoma males had joined the Klan, making it second only to business as organized power throughout the state.

Governor Walton bore little resemblance to candidate Walton. From day one, his administration careened out of control. He shed his liberal supporters and began to court the Klan, secretly buying a lifetime KKK membership. Perhaps to shore up his political base— or perhaps because he was outraged by hundreds of reports of Klan violence—in July 1923 Walton declared war on the Ku Klux Klan.

By August he had Tulsa under martial law, and the streets were crawling with guardsmen. He installed a censor in *The Tulsa Tribune* newsroom. At Madill, Steve's old haunt, Walton announced he was banning all Klan parades in Oklahoma. By September, he had the entire state under martial law. By October, the state was on the brink of civil war.

Which was worse, the Klan or Jack Walton? "Neither Klan Nor King," newspapers trumpeted throughout the state. When the state legislature tried to impeach him, Walton sent his army to halt the "Klan legislature," with orders to shoot to kill. Citizens then called an election by initiative petition, to empower the legislature to meet without the governor's call. Walton ordered his guard to halt the election, dispatching them to ballot boxes around Oklahoma, again with orders to shoot to kill. But guardsmen disregarded his order, and 10,000 local volunteers watched over ballot boxes to protect the vote that Walton lost, 209,452 to 70,638.

The end was near. In October 1923, after only 10 months in office, "Jack the Klan Fighter" was impeached by the Oklahoma legislature.

Triumphant Oklahoma Klansmen were gleeful. Oklahoma membership soared about 100,000. They cheered their victory in November, in the neighboring state of Texas, where they joined

75,000 Lone Star Klansmen in a victory bash at Hiram Wesley Evans' "homecoming" celebration at the Texas state fairground.

Around the country, membership and political successes were booming. By the spring of 1923, the Klan was emerging as the leading political force in Denver, where Klan Mayor Ben Stapleton was unifying the KKK, the Republican Party, and the police force into a power monolith. In Oregon, the Klan took credit for passage of an anti-Catholic compulsory public school bill, by initiative petition and popular vote.

Every day brought new evidence that Steve's vision of a Klan takeover of America could come true.

Back in Indiana, Steve's university search was also going very well. By luck, there was a college in the offing, a fine little school off the tip of Lake Michigan, at Valpariso, Indiana—near enough to South Bend to show a thing or two to Notre Dame. Valpariso University was foundering in red ink, a victim of changing times and a short but disastrous spell of mismanagement. Steve determined to buy it.

Valpariso U dated back to 1873 and was widely respected for doing what it did very well. It was the antithesis of exclusivity; open admission was at the base of its policy It was called "The Poor Man's Harvard," where any boy or girl could go on a shoestring and obtain a solid education in the basics, with emphasis on every day commercial or industrial job skills. Never mind your fancy theories or degrees.

"Learned men theorize; educated men practice," its founders believed. Good old Valpo U: "Where Theory Squares With Practice."

Extraordinary as it was, the university was no more remarkable than the town of its location. Peaceful Valpariso, Indiana—with its tree-shaded streets named for Jefferson and Franklin, its green lawns, its scores of churches, its friendly houses—seemed an unlikely field for Klan seedlings to take root, let alone flower.

Valpariso's early Unitarian and abolitionist settlers packed up their liberal theories and carted them along when they moved west from New England, establishing a beacon of enlightenment on the prairie. But by 1923, many among the town's 10,000 residents had grown prosperous, more comfortable with conservative than liberal thought.

Many "leading citizens" of Valpariso joined the Klan, as one historian reported. They were the community's "solid, bourgeois doctors and lawyers, businessmen and boosters" whose economic energy, like that of their town, came from the university.

"Valpariso is Main Street softened by an additional generation or two of settlement," one writer wrote. "What could happen there might happen anywhere in the Middle West."

What happened there, in preparation for Stephenson's move on Valpariso University, was the biggest KKK barbecue in history.

It was also the first mass meeting of Klansmen without their hoods, after Steve and Hiram Evans ordered Klansmen to unmask, to appease that rotten, rabid Catholic rag, *Tolerance*.

And unmask they did, somewhere between 10,000 and 100,000 of them—the numbers always varied between crowd counters of the press and the Klan—on Saturday, May 19, at the great Valpariso KKK Bar-B-Q.

The event gave journalists their first, tantalizing glimpse of the faces beneath the bedsheets.

The day began with robed Klansmen streaming, with the May sunlight, into the fairgrounds. They were adorned with badges and banners, but there was little else to prove they were worthy of the reputation "which has aroused greater hysteria among its opponents—and produced more gray hairs among politicians—than any similar phenomenon since the collapse of the Know Nothing party nearly 70 years ago," one reporter wrote.

The farmers came in cars, with families: "bronzed, homely, good-natured persons who might have been selected at random from the farming populations of Indiana, Ohio, Illinois, Kansas, or Nebraska." The reporter could not imagine a group less compatible with the KKK savageries reported in the South and Southwest. Nor could he imagine that such people would take seriously "the mummery they had come to witness."

The city folk came by rail, with very different faces. The reporter judged them to be "an inferior type (from) the less successful strata of the white collar class. They might have been small storekeepers, corporation employees, clerks, and clingers to the edges of the professions."

He searched for some common thread.

"The one generalization which could be applied, I believe, to the Valpariso celebrants was that they had social or personal grievances. This was a parade of America gone a little sour....

"Behind the fringe of shrewd promoters, 'salesmen of hate,' politicians, addicts of hocus-pocus, skylarkers, and bootleggers who had earned the Klan a deserved odium, is a residue of earnest and aimless discontent....

"Socially it is a natural result of a period of unrest, uncertainty, and hard times, such as always goes with a great war. Well directed it might merge in an intelligent progressive movement. When selfishly exploited, as the Ku Klux Klan and its predecessors have exploited it, it may become fantastic, bigoted, and repellent...."

The reporter predicted that the naive, earnest members would be consumed in the Klan's "...secret conclaves controlled by hoary knaves versed in political intrigue.... Honest men in such places have the peculiar advantage that flies have in a spider's web: the privilege of losing their legs, of buzzing without flying, and being eaten at leisure by big-bellied spiders."

Probably the Klan families had a better time than the dour gentlemen of the press.

The Fiery Cross had gaily heralded the event months ahead, in full pages of bold type: "All roads lead to Valpariso (for the) Ku Klux Klan and the Women's Organization Home Coming and May Festival." A hundred thousand Klansmen were expected for an all day, all night diversion of "dazzling diversified delights," including tight rope walking "100 feet in the air," fireworks and parades, 200 horsemen, "wild bronco busting," "imported Texas cowboys,"—and "A Big Barbecue."

They had themselves quite a day. As befitted a gathering of knights, the event included a jousting tournament, complete with "gaily caparisoned horses, flying banners, martial music, marching ranks of robed and hooded knights." The revelers crowned a Queen of the Golden Mask and thrilled to the spectacle of a tightrope walker, 300 feet high—in hood and robe—carrying both Old Glory and a fiery cross.

A highlight of the day was Stephenson's arrival. He circled slowly down from the heavens, late—to lengthen the sweet suspense.

Sometimes at such events, his pilot Court Asher recalled later, "The Old Man used to wear a little paper tablet on his wrist, like a watch. He'd raise his hood just a little and write a few words, a message of some sort, to the crowd, tear off the sheet of paper, hand it to one of the officials, and we'd fly away again.... The official would read the message of greeting to the crowd, and the folks who were taking the whole thing seriously would open their mouths and act as if they had received a message from Heaven...."

When darkness gathered, so did the 100-percent faithful

families, for the most moving moment: the spiritual and symbolic cross burning. Its precise symbolism and spirituality was a bit elusive. It might spew fumes of burning kerosene and rags. It might be lighted by electric bulbs, in lieu of burlap and balsam; or perhaps a hundred torch bearing Klansmen might align themselves in cross shaped formation on a darkened hillside.

But, in whatever format, its flickering light and tantalizing shadows brought poignant and pensive moments to ritual starved Protestants.

Their religious devotion to the burning cross was described in a briskly selling, pro-Klan novel named *Harold the Klansman*, published by the Western Baptist Publishing Company. After the hero foils the demonic Catholic priests, Harold and his wife Ruth engage in some stirring dialogue in the fitful light of a burning cross.

"Isn't the cross beautiful and inspiring?" Ruth asks.

"Yes," Harold replies....

At the festive July 4 Kokomo Klonklave, when David Stephenson was "sanctified," as he called it, as Indiana Grand Dragon, he had discussed a Klan takeover of Old Valpo with Imperial Wizard Hiram Wesley Evans. They reached apparent consensus, and Stephenson dispatched *Fiery Cross* editor Milt Elrod to Valpariso to negotiate. By August, things were humming; 500 Indiana Klansmen came to Indianapolis to join in the talks.

University leaders were increasingly desperate, having failed to reach agreement with any other groups, including the Elks and the Moose. The university president by this time was ready to make a pact with the devil himself, if need be, to save the school.

Trustees agreed that a Klan takeover would be "one step better than death." They accepted the Klan offer.

"Klan to Perpetuate Valpo," Elrod announced in the August 24 *Fiery Cross*. The Klan was putting up $1.35 million in cash to ensure that the college would become "a monument to American ideals and principles," and remain open to anyone, "regardless of race or creed," he said. The announcement was a godsend to editors of national magazines and newspapers.

It was heartening to know that the school would remain open to all, one wrote. "Maybe the negroes, Jews, and Catholics are invited for laboratory purposes." Perhaps a forthcoming "Kollege Katalog" would describe "a nice kurrikulum in lynching, tarring-and-feathering, plain and fancy regulation of other people's business, horsewhipping...."

Perhaps, said the *New York World*, Klan U would add such courses as "Reasons for Anglo Saxon Supremacy" and "The Melting Temperature of Tar as a Medium for Affixing Feathers."

"Alma Mater, K.K.K.," mused *The New Republic*, "On the campus all is quiet save for a group of Phi Beta Ku Klux Kappa men who are hanging the dean over in a far corner near Mob Hall. The intramurals—the Running Gauntlet, the Standing Tar and Feather—are over. Alumni have completed their annual lighting of the flaming cross. The quiet campus gleams beneath an Indiana moon. Over the tree tops glows the fire of some lynching party late coming home," softly chanting Valpariso's new Alma Mater:

"My country Ku Klux Klan,
Down with the Vatican,
of thee I sing
Land where the mob is boss,
Land of the rope and toss,
On every flaming cross
Let freedom swing."

But the theory was not to square with the purchase. When Elrod rushed in to tell Steve of his successful negotiations, The Old Man blandly asked, "How do you propose to raise the money?"

Hiram Evans—perhaps miffed at Steve's Kokomo grandstanding, perhaps sensing in Stephenson either a dangerous rival or an uncontrollable radical—welshed on the deal. The national Klan refused to put up one cent toward the purchase.

After a two week silence, Elrod lamely announced that an attorney found a prohibiting clause in Valpariso's charter. A former Klansman later wrote that the attorney had been handsomely paid for unearthing a face saving clause.

The deal was dead. Stephenson had no university.

The endeavor was, as one historian wrote, "a vain foray into the world of higher education by an organization sadly in need of some." Maybe it was best, wrote one editor, since higher education would probably have lowered Klan membership.

The whole Klan affair, said Valpariso trustees, was "an erroneous humor of fabrication." The university was saved by town boosters and ultimately taken over by Lutherans in 1925.

His dream of a Klan U soured, Stephenson was in a fury. Even worse was the national ridicule. He muzzled Elrod, raged at Evans, and clamped down on *The Fiery Cross*.

And then, on September 28, 1923, less than three months after his triumphant Kokomo Klonklave coronation, the Indiana Grand Dragon took the ultimate step: he abruptly resigned all his offices in the national Ku Klux Klan.

UNMASKED! Ann Patton

11
Uncivil War

Autumn, 1923
Indianapolis, Indiana

It was nearly a month before Indiana Klansmen knew that Stephenson had resigned from the national Klan.

And it was nearly a year before it made any difference.

Steve proceeded to operate the Indiana Klan without significant change. The stories varied on whether he had resigned from the national KKK entirely, or only from his offices therein, or everything, or nothing.

The "strain and burden of multiplied battles" had forced the "Captain of Captains" to "resign all of his executive offices," The *Fiery Cross* reported on October 12, 1923. The problem, hinted editor Milton Elrod, was one of health, sacrificed in tireless work of this "personification of the true ideals and fighting spirit of the Klan" to bring peace to the order. His retirement (at age 32) would free him from dreary organizational details so he could provide "more guidance, more inspiration, more speeches, (and) new ideas" for the Klan.

In late 1923, Imperial Wizard Hiram Wesley Evans appointed a lackey, Willis H. Mullan, to the post of Indiana Grand Dragon. But he had little influence, and for some time operations continued largely as they had before.

Stephenson's resignation itself remained mysterious. "His innermost thoughts were never fathomed," wrote Klansman Edgar A. Booth. "Always there lurked in the deep recesses of The Mad Mullah's brain a thought, a plan of which no one knew but Stephenson.... His intrigues were many and varied. (He) was an enigma to his closest associates."

Steve's first serious loss was his newspaper. Milt Elrod, stinging from his rebuke in the abortive take over of Valpariso University and chafing under Steve's reins on *The Fiery Cross*, took some credit for The Old Man's resignation. Elrod quickly shifted his loyalty— and the editorial policies of *The Fiery Cross*—from Stephenson to Evans. Evans, clamping down on all independent Klan newspapers, moved the National Propagation Department from Columbus to Indianapolis and put Elrod in charge.

Stephenson had laid out his on-the-record reasons after a hot Columbus meeting with Evans on September 27: "...because I cannot with any element of decency or self respect continue to be a party to such small bickering.... I am endeavoring to defend the good name of the organization in this section of the country by ridding it of political mountebanks and shysters..., [while the Klan is being] prostituted and cheated in a manner which to a fourth grade school boy would seem either dishonest or silly or incompetent."

Even before the Valpariso rug was pulled out from under him, The Old Man had become riled at Evans' May 1923 secret strategy meeting in the New Willard Hotel in Washington, D.C. Steve went with Gutzon Borglum, the sculptor who was one of six members of Evans' inner circle Kloncilium. Steve was disgusted with Evans' leadership; he found Evans and his Southern cohorts small minded, missing the big picture of political possibilities that Stephenson saw ahead, and unwilling to take the bold and systematic political steps Stephenson believed necessary.

But there was more, much more. For Steve's part, the national Klan had become an embarrassment, racked by daily press dispatches of corruption, internecine courtroom brawls, and violence. Tales were circulating freely through the Empire of enemies within the Klan who, on the eve of damaging disclosures, mysteriously disappeared or died from food poisoning, ambush, or unaccountable suicide. Some of the reports were in states surrounding Indiana, within Steve's 23 state kingdom; but few or none were reported within the Hoosier state itself.

While things were—by Klan standards—peaceful and orderly within the Indiana realm, here came Atlanta representatives to stir up Steve's klaverns, recommending to the brethren that "a few beatings and some tar and feathers" would help "arouse interest and increase the membership." It was not the Indiana way and Stephenson, ever the pragmatist, disapproved.

Perhaps it was only coincidence, perhaps not, that Stephenson resigned on the same day Evans' staffer Phil Fox stormed into the office of Colonel Simmons' attorney, William S. Coburn, and shot Coburn to death.

The stories that circulated were as ugly as the deed. They said Coburn was near a victory for Colonel Simmons in court battles between the two Imperial Wizards and that Coburn was about to unleash damning testimony against Evans. They said that Fox was plied with liquor for two weeks before the shooting and egged on from high places; that he had felled Coburn with the first shot but had not halted his attack until every chamber of the revolver was emptied on Coburn.

The bloodless coup at Simmons' Thanksgiving 1922 Klonvokation had turned into a bloodletting and was threatening a bloodbath after all.

Simmons claimed he received regular death threats, that Fox had said both Simmons and his attorney Coburn were "marked for death.

"The next afternoon he (Fox) walked into the office of Captain Coburn and shot him dead, in cold blood, without giving him a chance for a fight," Simmons said.

"That murder was too much for me. I didn't want to fight men who could kill that way."

Simmons settled for a lump sum $90,000 payment which he poured into creating an ill fated, rival fraternity, the "Knights of the Flaming Sword."

Simmons and the discredited Edward Young Clarke were weak players in the Klan wars that rose in 1923. By the end of that year, Evans had washed their influence from his organization.

The dominant clash was between two raging bulls: Stephenson, the czar of the North; and Evans, the tyrant from the South.

From Evans' perspective, Stephenson was clearly becoming too powerful. His grandstanding at the July 4 Kokomo Klonklave, which relegated Evans to a mere bit part, was only one case in point. Steve's sweeping political ambitions were becoming common knowledge in Klan higher circles; he would not accept second billing in any arena.

Booth quotes a blunt message from an anonymous Klansman (apparently Steve), sent through a palace spy to a Klan leader called "Blank."

"I wrote a letter, put it in a safety deposit box and gave the key to a certain party with certain instructions.... If I should disappear, or anything should happen to me—I think you know what I mean—

nothing can save Blank.... Remember this—no matter how it happens, where it happens, or who does it, Blank must pay! And you can convey that to Evans and the rest of them! Now, for yourself, and I mean it every bit as earnestly as I mean the message for Blank. If you ever put your foot inside this office again while I'm here, I'll drag you outside and drop you down an elevator shaft!"

A second bone of contention was the women's organization. Stephenson had established his Queens of the Golden Mask. The banished Colonel Simmons had created his own, The Kamelia. And Evans had his own WKKK—Women of the Ku Klux Klan. Within the triangle of women's organizations, power struggles were raging that equaled those within the men's ranks.

The Evans-Stephenson war was probably inevitable. Both intended to control America from its grassroots to its White House. Both were heady with power, hankering for more. The square-faced Texas dentist/Imperial Wizard might be less brilliant but he was no less cunning or ruthless than the cherub-faced Hoosier salesman/ Dragon. Only one could be king; that kind of power was in finite supply.

The monetary spoils, however, seemed infinite.

During the brief time Steve held Klan office, the national Klan raised more than $80 million, he testified later—including $4.5 million raised in Indiana alone, of which $2.5 million was turned over to the Imperial Treasury.

No one will ever know where it all went, in Indiana, Atlanta, or elsewhere. Most historians believe Ed Clarke and Bessie Tyler pocketed perhaps $800,000 in clear profits. By comparison to the others, Colonel Simmons came out a pauper. In the clearer light of retrospect, compared to those who followed him, the cheery charlatan colonel Simmons was shown to be the most idealistic and least greedy of the Klan leaders; his reward was poverty and scorn.

In his latter days of hanging uselessly around the Imperial Palace, Simmons became agitated because Evans' spies were watching his every move. He complained to Evans. Simmons recalled that Evans listened quietly, then laughed and said "Don't worry. Let's go get the money, Colonel."

In the spring of 1923, the only records available show that the Indiana Klan had only $50,000 in its bank account. In the same general period, Dun and Bradstreet reported Stephenson's personal worth just short of a million dollars. That figure was probably conservative. Most scholars estimate that Stephenson made from $2 to $5 million or more in roughly three years, between 1922 and 1925; most of it rolled in during 1923 and 1924.

Sources can be only hazily traced. Certainly, for Stephenson and the national Klan, the base source was Klansmen themselves. Numbers and the precise splits of profits vary. Generally, a newly nationalized Klansman had to fork over at least $10-$16 for the initiation fee ("Klectoken") and $6 to $6.50 for the regulation robe. As the field salesman, Kleagle Stephenson would have received perhaps $4 of every $10; as regional sales manager over first Indiana and then 23 states, perhaps a $1.50 cut. The Imperial triumvirate took in about $4.50 of each $10 Klectoken.

The robe sales were even more profitable for the national Klan: Atlanta's Gates City Manufacturing Company, a Klan subsidiary, turned them out for about $2 apiece, producing a profit of two-thirds or more. They were not sold but only rented to Klansmen, so a resigning Klansman's robe could be recycled at a 100-percent profit to another 100-percent American.

Clearly, the markup from the sale of sheets was the cream of the business. Stephenson's own regalia factory turned them out for only $1.50 per—and with far better quality, his supporters said—but Evans stopped Steve's side business.

That initial take was multiplied by thousands and millions of members. Membership estimates range wildly—again, no one will ever know for sure. The most consistent estimates are that by 1923, the national Klan had at least 2.5 million members; other estimates place its stronger 1924 membership as high as 4-6 million. Indiana probably had one-quarter to one-half million members. For consistency, if nothing else, most historians end up with estimates around 5 million for the national Klan, around 500,000 in Indiana.

The Klan was a middle-class movement, in part, because the lowest classes couldn't afford it.

The Klectoken and robe charges were not the whole story. Klansmen also paid any number of regular and special taxes, local and national assessments, levies, charitable and building funds— although the charity or building might or might not ever see the funds. One writer estimates the national Klan's revenues from just one tax at $5.4 million for just one year, 1924. He estimated that the national Klan grossed at least $10.5 million between 1920 and 1922, before Simmons, Clarke, and Tyler were banished. It was only the beginning.

No question, the stakes were high enough to be worth fighting for.

And what was the Imperial Palace doing with all that money?

Living in style, if critics are to be believed. A $25,000 jeweled crown was made for Mrs. Robby Gill Comer, the "Imperial Commander" of Evans' Women of the KKK. Booth says $2,000 platinum watches were distributed at klonvokations the way teenaged girls gave out party favors. Klansmen "gave" Evans his own yacht. They also footed the bill when, during an emergency that arose because Mrs. Evans didn't have the right slippers to match a frock, Evans dispatched a palace detective to hot-foot it from

Washington to New York to buy her a pair of shoes.

Booth recalled a parade when Evans rode with his entourage in a ostentatious automobile. At some distance ahead, exhaustion overtook an elderly Klanswoman who had marched 5 miles.

The gray-haired woman fell, too sick to rise, and was carried to one side of the parade by fellow marchers who could not revive her. They flagged down Evans' car and asked that the old woman be allowed to ride.

"The Klansmen were waved back as though they had committed a crime against high society," Booth recalled. "And the old gray-haired lady lay at the hot curb, sick, faint, and helpless, until a conveyance could be gotten through the crowd."

Even as he resigned from the national KKK, Stephenson—a pragmatic politician—knew that a Klan war would be a serious handicap during the important election year of 1924.

Thus, on October 12, 1923—the same day *The Fiery Cross* mourned Stephenson's health problem that required his resignation—Stephenson sent a hot telegram to Evans urging a truce:

"I have been very much grieved to learn that you were in Indianapolis, engaged in a campaign to assassinate my character, and to know that this was your process of disposing of anyone who stood in the way...," Steve wrote.

"It is apt to be necessary for me to resort to the first law of the land, self-defense. If you insist on going further with your attack on my personal integrity, I shall be compelled to write a page in the history of these days which will be a final answer to the vulgar cowardly lies which are now being directed at me and which all honorable men will resent—with a decision which will rock the foul cesspools of hate and jealousy which now flood the dollar grabbers in Atlanta.

"I am constrained to the opinion that a lot of us would muster
a great deal more respect for your opinion if you would keep your
promise to refund to me all that I have advanced to support your
foul doctrines.... I assume you know I control papers in both Indiana
and Ohio, and I am just a little inclined to the opinion that you are
not unaware of my courage to use two papers to vindicate myself....

"Pull off your character vultures...."

Both sides wanted to win the 1924 elections. The war subsided, in
an uneasy truce.

David Curtis Stephenson began the big year of 1924 by getting
married for a third time, followed almost immediately by divorce.
He seemed to be developing a pattern with women.

The Indiana Klan year also began on a high note. Imperial
Wizard Evans came to Indianapolis' Cadle Tabernacle for a
powerhouse appearance; 4,000 had to be turned away. He spoke
on the need for federal aid to education and advocated creation of a
federal Department of Education.

But the fragile truce between Stephenson and the Evans/Bossert
faction quickly shattered into war.

The truth of the charges and counter charges can never be
known; all sides were tricking others with too many elaborate
character assassination rumors to sift fiction from fact.

The Indiana Klan splintered. Stephenson still commanded the
lion's share, at least 200,000 members. About 25,000 others were
Evans/Bossert loyalists. Another 15,000 to 18,000 were classified
as independents, in various stages of revolution against both Steve
and Evans; they fell into several groups, called Knights of the
North, Independent Klans of America, and Knights of American
Protestantism.

Evans sued the Independent Klans to prohibit their use of the

Klan name. The case dragged on for years, exposing an endless stream of embarrassing reports of malfeasance and chicanery.

As if that wasn't enough, a local Klan centered at Muncie, Delaware #4, formed its own investigating committee in March of 1924. Headed by two Klansmen, Samuel Bemenderfer and Orion Norcross, the committee looked into Klan operations in five states. They found that Protestant, patriotic Americans were victims of "a gigantic swindle." Outraged, they reported their findings to Evans, who told them to go along and mind their own business.

Stephenson's response was swift. He tried to put Bemenderfer into what was reported to be "a compromising position with a woman" and to bar him from access to any state Klans. The Muncie Klan, always an energetic group, rose in arms and threatened secession.

Meanwhile, Stephenson was preoccupied with politics.

He circulated an unsigned missive promising of "a civic Messiah who would be born in the manger of the Hoosier Ballot Box." Indiana Senator Sam Ralston was ill, and it was no secret that Stephenson hoped to replace Ralston if—when—he died.

In April, Steve published a high-toned article in the national magazine *McClure's*, named "Roosevelt's Unfinished Program." He assumed the mantle of Teddy Roosevelt, urging citizens to love the law and calling for "a strong man" to continue Roosevelt's programs. He stopped short of proclaiming himself the strong man, but he sent reprints to businessmen throughout Indiana and asked for funds. He ended the letter with a classic salesman's pitch: "An early and prompt response will be most valuable."

Some things were proceeding right on schedule. Others were not going so well.

On April 9, a month before the 1924 Republican primary, the *Indianapolis News* reported that one of Stephenson's bodyguards, Earl Gentry, tried to arrest Evansville Klan leader Joe Huffington on nebulous charges. Stephenson's troubles with Huffington dated back to 1922, when Stephenson wrested Klan control from Huffington, now firmly in the Evans camp. The Old Man's trick arrest backfired, and hundreds of robed Klansmen paraded through Evansville to show support for Huffington.

Within days, both Stephenson and Gentry were stripped of their commissions as Horse Thief Detectives. It was only the beginning.

Three days after Huffington's aborted "arrest," his home Klan in Evansville suspended Stephenson from the KKK and ordered him to stand for a Klan trial for "various major offenses."

Life around Stephenson had not been particularly slow for years, but now he began to move with dizzying speed. While he focused on politics, he was caught in the constant crossfire of Klan warfare.

Enraged, Steve sent out a letter that was hot enough to blister the hair off a dog. Titled "The Old Man's Answer to Hate Vendors," he advocated civil war against "Southern Rule."

Among other things, Stephenson contended Evans and his crew donated $100,000 toward Gutzon Borglum's Stone Mountain sculpture, "...a monument in Atlanta, Georgia, to the memory of the rebels who once tried to destroy America; yet they refused to give a single dollar for Valpariso University to help educate the patriots of the North.... They are spending Hoosier money like Nero drunk and make no account to any one in Indiana.... They have lied repeatedly and attempted to cover it with additional falsehood...."

"The men in Atlanta... have sowed hate and lived in fatted luxury, while honor weeps in a hovel. They have poured out poison vitriol by secret whisperings when they dare not face me in the open... because I would not be a supine instrument in nefarious murder plots.... While they committed murder and conspired to commit murder I voiced a vigorous protest against it...."

And more:

"They have bribed jurors and stained the judicial ermine.... They have accepted bribes from bootleggers on promises of immunity from prosecution. They have abused women and hired delinquent girls to indulge in evil things...."

As for Evans?

"The present national head is an ignorant, uneducated, uncouth individual who picks his nose at the table and eats peas with his knife. He has neither courage nor culture. He cannot talk intelligently and he cannot keep a coherent conversation going on any subject for five minutes.... The only thing he has ever been known to do was to launch an attack upon the character and integrity of men eminent in talent and virtue."

Stephenson exhorted Indiana Klansmen to fight as never before for their "... wonderful program.... Divine Providence guides us; we shall succeed. The unborn babes of the coming generation, posterity itself, cries out and commands us to go onward and upward to the goal honor has set and justice commands we attain.... The truth shall make us free."

On May 12, he convened his own personal Klonvokation. It may have been Steve's finest hour in the Klan.

Four hundred delegates attended, from every Indiana county but one. Stephenson told the Klansmen he was "fed up with control by Atlanta." It was time for Indiana Klansmen to demand independence, he charged, issuing a rousing challenge to his delegates:

"There's been a lot of talk going around, and there's going to be a lot more. And the fiery cross is going to burn at every crossroad in Indiana, as long as there is a white man left in the state....

"Either the Klan is a damnable mockery and ought to be disbanded, or it represents the militant will of the Master. I'll appeal to the ministers of Indiana to do the praying for the Ku Klux Klan, and I'll do the scrapping for it.... God help the man who issues a proclamation of war against the Klan in Indiana now!

"We are going to klux Indiana as she has never been kluxed before!"

After the meeting, the group secretary sent a telegram to the *New York Times* announcing that the Indiana Klansmen "with 91 of 92 counties represented" took "full control of their own organization," in line with American democratic principles, and elected Steve as their own Grand Dragon.

The Klan, of course, was not organized by democratic principle, since its forefathers recognized democracy as a failed theory. Under Klan law, only the Imperial Wizard could appoint a grand dragon. Nonetheless, in fact if not in Klan law, Indiana now had two grand dragons.

Evans retaliated in a rising series of minor and major skirmishes. *The Fiery Cross* denounced Steve. "Nobody can keep a jackass from braying," Joe Huffington said of Steve's letter.

May 16 Steve retaliated by filing four lawsuits for libel and slander against Evans, Bossert, and other Klansmen, seeking $200,000 in damages.

May 19 Evans named Bossert Indiana Grand Dragon. His appointment was clearly designed to recapture insurgents, since Bossert was widely esteemed.

Bossert, 40, was "tall and heavy without being fat, showing almost unimpaired the physique which twenty years ago made him fullback and pitcher for the University of Indiana," wrote one admiring reporter. "He has a calm, clean-cut face, a shock of black hair touched with gray, piercing black eyes, and a manner that, while slow to kindle, strikes fire often and has a remarkable charm when once aroused."

Walter Bossert was marked by culture, an idealist who was into Klan politics for reform rather than pushing Klan "reform" merely to gain political power, the reporter said. A lawyer, Bossert preferred to spend his days humbly raising police dogs and Belgian chickens on his farm near Liberty, Indiana.

Bossert was known, wrote the former Klansman Edgar A. Booth, as "The White Man of the Klan"—high praise indeed from the hooded knights:

"Good looking, clean cut, and sincere; highly educated and cultured..., Bossert had a program for the Klan—also, he had a code of honor. Double-crossing, double-dealing or the betrayal of friends was not found in his idea of things.... Highly intelligent, he talked of the needs of America, and all through his talk never once did he exhibit the extreme prejudice which filled the talk of so many other members of the Imperial Kloncillium."

Bossert intended to clean up the KKK from the inside, Booth said.

Bossert once quit the Klan, on principle. Steve convinced him to rejoin in 1923.

Bossert and Evans planned their own Indianapolis parade May 24. The event was less than satisfying. At the last minute, Indianapolis police changed the line of march, so regalia-clad knights marched through empty streets, while crowds thronged sidewalks where no march occurred. Worse, firemen were called to a rash of false alarms, requiring them to charge repeatedly through parade lines, destroying marchers' decorum. The Old Man's power was still intact.

On at least two occasions, the rival Grand Dragons sparred directly.

When Republican leaders met at Newcastle that spring, to reorganize party machinery, Stephenson said something—unknown—that angered Bossert. The former football player grabbed Stephenson by the collar and tried to punch out his cherubic lights, but he was restrained by bystanders. Thereafter, Bossert was said to fear for his life in any meeting of Steve's supporters.

For his part, Stephenson was never without his two hulking bodyguards, Earl Klinck and Earl Gentry. The reporter John Niblack said the trio reminded him of the Three Musketeers. Marion County prosecutor William H. Remy "always thought that Stephenson believed he was a reincarnation of D'Artagnan, who always went around with his two allies, Athos and Porthos," Niblack wrote. "He had a way of snapping his fingers and saying, 'Come on, boys, let's go,' then wheeling around and marching briskly away with Klinck and Gentry at his heels, which reminded Remy of D'Artagnan, who had a similar habit."

Niblack reported another confrontation. "One evening the two Grand Dragons met in the lobby of the Lincoln Hotel, and the two Earls pinned Bossert's arms while Dragon Stephenson administered a sound thrashing to his reluctant dragon rival. It was not the only fight that the 'Old Man' won with the aid of his gladiators."

Stephenson was growing stronger by the moment. In the dangerous game of Klan tit for tat, Steve moved into the lead—but Evans wasn't through yet.

12
warwick on the wabash

Spring 1924
Indianapolis, Indiana

Both the rival Indiana Grand Dragons, Walter Bossert and D.C.
Stephenson, knew the May 1924 primary was worthy of a truce—at
least in public. Both threw their Klan machines behind Ed Jackson
for governor.

The battle lines in the Republican primary were therefore drawn
between the Klan bloc and the anti-Klan Republican candidate for
governor, Lew Shank. Shank was Indianapolis' mayor, and he was
openly hostile to the Klan, calling the KKK "the most important
issue since Lincoln's day."

The existing governor, Republican Warren T. McCray, was not a
contender. The kindly McCray, a millionaire farmer much beloved
by his many friends, was entangled in a web of his own weaving. In
the fall of 1923, McCray had been indicted on 13 counts of using the

mails to defraud.

John Niblack, who covered McCray's trials for the *Indianapolis Times*, said McCray was caught short by the abrupt post-War farm deflation. He tried to cover the shortfall by a paper blizzard of fraudulent notes to himself, forging friends' signatures, and thoughtfully allocating state funds to the lending institutions. He wasn't sure how much he owed when the web snared him—perhaps $2 million.

McCray's troubles posed a critical problem for Stephenson. To make matters worse, the national Teapot Dome scandal was boiling throughout the country at the same time. For months, the press issued daily blasts calling Republican officials crooks—at precisely the time Steve was trying to marry his Klan machine with the Republican party and gearing up for the primary fight.

The Old Man's first attempt to save the situation did not become known until much later. Niblack later wrote the story. On November 30, 1923, the day McCray was indicted, the governor was visited by the Honorable Ed Jackson, then Indiana Secretary of State. Jackson offered the besieged governor a gift from Stephenson: $10,000 in cash and a guarantee of "absolute protection" from conviction on criminal charges.

"I have control of the county clerk's office, the two jury commissioners and the courts. I have the money. We have done it before and can do it now," Stephenson told the governor through Jackson.

"You can take your money back to your office, Ed. I am astounded," Governor McCray said when the money was shoved across his desk at the State House. "My fortune I struggled so hard to accumulate and to preserve, and my good name, may be in ruins, but I will never surrender my integrity. Take your money and get out."

After an agonizing string of court appearances and mounting

disclosures, Governor McCray was convicted. He resigned in disgrace April 29, 1924, one week before the primary election. He was fined $10,000 and sent to prison for 10 years, where he became editor of the prison monthly newspaper, *Good Words*. It was the first time a governor had been taken from office to serve a prison sentence on a felony charge.

In an added twist, McCray's new son-in-law was the Marion County prosecutor and, honorably, relinquished jurisdiction over the grand jury that indicted the governor. At the indictments, the son-in-law immediately resigned. Stephenson's $10,000 "gift" included an offered deal that the governor would name a Klan attorney, James A. McDonald, as replacement prosecutor. The governor instead appointed the chief deputy, over Steve's vigorous protests.

The new Marion County prosecutor was a hardcore enemy of the Klan, William H. Remy—a name Stephenson would soon know very, very well.

If he couldn't save Governor McCray from himself, how could Steve save the Republican Party? It was impossible—but he did it.

As one political analyst later wrote, Stephenson convinced the public that "...the (Republican) McCray scandal was proof of corruption in high places (and that) the Stephenson Klan, the great purifying Klan, working within the Republican Party, would set things straight. Hoosiers accepted the story. Stephenson's handpicked slate was viewed as the vehicle that would make the sacred Klan ideology the law of the land.... The imprisoned ex-governor became a symbol for all that a revitalized Republican Party would combat."

Thus geared-up, Stephenson steered his Klan/Republican machine toward the all-important May 1924 primary election.

He had picked his candidates throughout Indiana, from the State House down through local towns and school boards. There was really only one issue: the Klan. But his biggest fight was to get Ed Jackson nominated for governor. He had to win big. Under Indiana law, Jackson would have to get a clear majority in a crowded field of candidates; otherwise the nomination would be thrown to the wolves at the state Republican convention, where Indianapolis Mayor Shank controlled a giant bloc of Marion County delegates. Experts didn't give Jackson a chance for a majority.

Stephenson threw everything into the primary. Three weeks before the election he sent Klansmen 250,000 letters, in two waves, pushing Jackson as "...a clean upright Christian gentleman [of] patriotic devotion....

"It matters not whether we are Republicans or Democrats.... We all have the same common heart throb of sympathetic devotion to our state.... The bootlegger and the criminal, the political 'mountebank' and the skeptic have resorted to every resource of treachery, falsehood, and double dealing to defeat our program. But God still reigns in Heaven—we cannot fail."

Voters streaming to the polls May 6 included thousands of Democrats who asked for Republican ballots—after a Monday night "agreement" that Democratic Klansmen would vote for Jackson. The results? Jackson drew just under 225,000 votes, more than twice those of his closest Republican opponent, anti-Klan Lew Shank; more, in fact, than all his five opponents combined, and not far below the entire number of Democrats who voted for the eight candidates in the Democratic primary.

Stephenson had created a Jackson landslide.

The national press and politicians woke with a start the morning after the election, rubbing their eyes in disbelief and horror. The impossible was possible: The Klan had control of the Republican Party and maybe the state—in Indiana, a state well known to be a political laboratory.

"It is the best state in the Union for trying out a new political idea," a Klansman told one visiting journalist. "If we can get away with it here, we're all set to go."

Before the Republican state convention May 21, Steve had to turn his attention to a troubling soft spot in his Indiana realm: South Bend. The northern city was infested with Notre Dame Catholics, and a cancer of anti-Klan sentiment was eating into the guts of knights there.

South Bend was the town that produced both the thriving St. Joseph Valley Klan, headed by an Exalted Cyclops named Hugh Emmons, and an uncontrollable attorney general candidate, Arthur Gilliom. The town also produced the episode of the most serious mass violence in the history of the Indiana Ku Klux Klan.

Gilliom sneaked through Steve's net in the May 6, 1924, primary. Before the May 21 Republican state convention, Steve had to find a way to prevent Gilliom from getting the party nomination for attorney general.

What to do? One Klansman volunteered to float over Notre Dame in a helium balloon and bomb the school, but the idea was shelved. Instead, Steve called a klonklave at South Bend, on May 17 in Island Park.

Before the rally, knots of Klansmen began arriving on trains and private cars, directed by hooded and robed Klansmen stationed at street corners.

Soon other cars swerved through the intersections, loaded with Notre Dame students.

Some scuffling ensued. In the process, the Klan sentries were disrobed, exposing them so completely that they fled to hide in nearby businesses.

The students then took over the sentries' jobs of welcoming the Klan to the city.

Here for the Klan parade? This way, please: down a side street, up an alley. In time, all over town, Klansmen were emerging from dark corners, stripped of their regalia, shorn of their dignity, and considerably worse for the wear.

In the midst of the chaotic welcoming party, sirens sounded through the streets. With two squads of motorcycles flanking his Cadillac, The Old Man arrived.

Klansmen took refuge in their downtown headquarters. When they bravely lowered an electrically-lighted cross from the windows, students charged the building. A South Bend Baptist minister, who was also a KKK official, whipped out his revolver and held them at bay while a truce was called. The students called off the dogs, and Steve called off the parade.

Two thousand Klansmen gathered at Island Park for the klonklave. But a new threat emerged—this time from the heavens, which opened and unleashed a thunderstorm that drenched the knights, the remaining scraps of their regalia, their festivities, and their spirits.

Two days later, Klansmen lowered the electric cross from the downtown headquarters again; and again the students charged the building. This time the knights came out in force, armed with rocks and bottles. In the ensuing riot, the Klan had the edge on armaments, but the students had the edge on youth. The balance tipped when South Bend police sided with Notre Dame students. At least one cop furnished the boys with white potatoes to help them trounce the white knights.

It took a personal appeal from the Notre Dame president to call off the students.

The Republican state convention May 21 went better for Steve. He
was in the thick of it, and he got almost everything he wanted. His
one big loss: he failed to prevent the attorney general's nomination
from going to his bitter enemy, Arthur Gilliom from South
Bend. But Steve was credited with swinging the decisions on the
lieutenant governor and most other candidates.

Stephenson emerged, overnight, as one of Indiana's leading
political bosses

Things didn't slow down in June. In the midst of Steve's frenetic
work toward November's Indiana general election came the national
Republican and Democratic conventions.

The national Republicans met June 10, 1924, and nominated
Coolidge for reelection. Bossert arrived early, followed by Evans
with a 60-member entourage. They had two goals. First, they
wanted Indiana Senator Jim Watson nominated for vice president.
Evans never forgot that Watson was a "friend in need" who helped
Evans in the Washington fight to keep Texas Klansman Senator
Earl B. Mayfield seated. And second, they wanted to keep any
meaningful anti-Klan plank out of the platform.

Evans succeeded on the second goal but failed in the first. Any
chance Watson might have had at the vice presidential nomination
was dashed by a mysterious announcement by Klan publicist Milt
Elrod that Watson had Klan support. It touched off a storm at the
convention. "Are they trying to kill me politically?" Watson cried. "I
don't belong to the KKK. If they have issued a statement naming me,
they have done it for the express purpose of injuring me." The Klan
was a particular problem for Watson, whose actions marked him
as its friend. For politicians, the Klan required very fancy footwork
along the top of political fences.

Former Klansman Booth said The Old Man took the Klan's

Watson announcement personally. Booth said he saw Stephenson shortly thereafter. Steve had just received a letter from Watson.

Stephenson, nervously puffing on a cigar, waved the letter. "My God, Booth, look at that! Look at that! Where are the men of Washington's day! Are we to be placed in the category of ingrates?" He tossed the letter to Booth. "Read it. Are the thirty pieces of silver still changing hands? Have we no longer men with us? God give us men!"

"He puffed furiously on his cigar as I read the letter," Booth recalled. It said that the senator "was not only willing but glad to do all he could for Stephenson and the Klan, but that he wished to remain under cover."

"God give us men," Steve said again. "Men who will not stoop to the acts of a mongrel! And Booth, just as sure as you are sitting in this office, Doc Evans had a hand in that. I know his rotten tactics. He is trying to force Watson out in the open. He's trying to force the Senator's hand with me! He's trying to make Watson be good. He had Milt do that just as sure as the sun will set tonight. Evans and his clique will stop at nothing. They have already half of Congress scared to death. But I'll whip 'em, damn 'em! I'll whip the dirty dollar grabbers and profaners of womanhood."

Before he left, Booth recalled, Stephenson grew even angrier, "bewailed the fact that he had resigned, and declared Evans was profaning that which Stephenson built."

Nonetheless, Stephenson was in his element at the Republican national convention. He brought his yacht and entertained celebrities lavishly. When the convention adjourned, he moved the yacht to Toledo—where it inexplicably exploded, injuring two men badly. Stephenson blamed Evans and filed a $100,000 lawsuit against him for the damage.

Whether or not the Klan blew up Steve's yacht, they blew up the Democratic national convention, which began June 24, 1924, in New York's Madison Square Garden. The convention dissolved into chaos over a platform plank condemning the Klan specifically by name. Repeatedly, fist fights broke out on the floor, and near riots occurred as the endless debates raged on and on.

Eventually the KKK won the issue by the narrowest possible margin—4/5th of one vote—543 3/20th to 542 7/20th.

Then the convention deadlocked over its presidential nominee. Catholics supported Al Smith; the Klan, William McAdoo; neither side would yield. Compromise candidates rose and fell; Indiana Senator Sam Ralston, despite his ill health, was in the running for a while.

What had been planned as a short convention stretched on and on, and the delegates were running out of money. "Gentlemen," one delegate said, "either we move to a more modest hotel or a more liberal candidate." Finally, on a record 103rd ballot, they agreed on a colorless nominee, John W. Davis from West Virginia. By his choice and the convention debacle, the Democrats handed the election to Coolidge, who maintained a studied neutrality on the Klan issue. In effect, the Klan won.

The Klan's blowup at the Democratic convention had a bizarre side note. The Klansman/sculptor Gutzom Borglum refused to support McAdoo, thus breaking the final thread of the fragile network backing Borglum's colossal Stone Mountain sculpture. The Confederate memorial association fired him. Borglum responded by blowing up the mountainside, erasing all remnants of his unfinished work. The committee dispatched a posse after Borglum. After a careening cops and robber chase through the night, Borglum escaped into North Carolina, vowing never to return to Georgia.

Political pundits gave Steve credit—or blame—for much of the Klan's success.

Steve's political machine was well-grounded on solid organization that functioned, one political analyst wrote, "with military precision..., unique [in] its rapid creation and its bipartisan appeal."

Stephenson could have created a third party. Instead he chose a much more effective but far more delicate course of taking over the existing Republican Party and convincing Democrats to vote his way, too. "Almost overnight he put together an apparatus that caused thousands to cast off political loyalties of a lifetime and vote according to his bidding. His kind of machine was unparalleled in our experience...."

And he did it in the midst of what became a fight to the death with the national Klan.

National journalist Stanley Frost wrote in mid 1924: "I am convinced ...that [the Indiana Klan machine] is—while it lasts—the most effective political organization the country has ever seen, not excepting Tammany.... It has better leadership..., evangelistic enthusiasm..., [and] plays politics with a crusading spirit which is willing to make greater sacrifices and work harder than any organization has done in recent times....

"It makes its members desert their usual party affiliations, split tickets, and put the Klan ahead of any other consideration to an extent never before known in American politics."

While Stephenson was honing his political threshing machine, Klan seedlings were thriving in Indiana's fertile fields.

What was it like in the Hoosier hustings, where the Klan seeds—

sown by Simmons, Clarke, Tyler, Evans, Stephenson, and others—were sprouting around the state?

In the Indiana hinterlands, there were still cross burnings almost nightly, booming boycotts of businesses without the magic TWK—Trade With Klansmen—window signs, and political pressures against newspapers and others who did not bend to the Invisible Empire's stern will. There were, more rarely, moments of violence.

There were good times. The Junior KKK basketball teams were racking up good seasons, allowing the Klan to capitalize on the Hoosier passion for basketball and politics simultaneously. There were galas galore. *The Fiery Cross* continued to rhapsodize over each parade and all day outing as "the biggest in history."

And for some, there was a terrible silence.

The silence of the summer of 1924 was deafening for one Evansville boy, Bill Wilson. He was the son of the man (with the same name, William E. Wilson) who beat Steve in Evansville's 1922 congressional election.

Now Congressman Wilson was up for reelection. Young Bill, 18, was home from college for the summer; he wrote about it later, in an article he called "That Long, Hot Summer in Indiana."

The Wilsons couldn't wait to get home. They drove back together, Bill from Harvard, his parents from Washington, zipping along at 38 miles an hour in the family Hudson. As they crossed the state line, they all sang "Back Home Again in Indiana."

Bill couldn't wait to see his best friend, Link Patterson. But on the Patterson's porch, Bill noticed something strange.

"He looked the same..., but he was not the old Link Patterson. Nor were his parents the same." They were restrained, formal. "I remember especially how they watched me, as if they were waiting to accuse me of something that they knew about but I did not."

They left, abruptly, shortly after Bill came. "I'm sorry, Bill," Link said, "but Mom and Dad and I have to be somewhere at eight o'clock." Bill went home, disappointed and puzzled.

He drove with his father to the congressman's downtown office.

"As we approached a large vacant lot," Bill recalled, "we saw that a crowd was gathered under floodlights, and a fiddlers' contest was in progress on a platform in the blue haze of a pit barbecue. My father said, 'That's probably where the Pattersons are tonight. The Agora Bible Class is raising money to build a tabernacle on that lot.'"

"But the Pattersons aren't Baptists," Bill said.

"They aren't all Baptists," his father said, in a rare display of anger that left Bill even more confused.

Somewhat later his father said, without preface, "Bill, I'm not going to be re elected in the fall.... A lot of people have turned against me, a lot of good, honest, but misguided people like your friends the Pattersons." The problem, his father said, was not anything he had done. "It's what I have refused to do."

"What?"

"Join the Ku Klux Klan.... I was told to join the Klan, or else. I refused, of course, and now they're out to beat me if they have to steal votes to do it.... This summer is going to be an ugly business, son.... we've come a long way in this country, but apparently we still haven't freed men and women of their suspicion of each other, their prejudices, their intolerance. I think that is going to be the big battle of this century. My little fight here in Indiana is just a preliminary skirmish and my practical political sense tells me I'm going to lose it. I'm not a crusader by nature, but, by God, I'm not going to budge one inch from where I stand!"

If Stephenson had won the 1922 election, he would have earned a senator's salary of $7,500 a year for two years—rather than the millions he earned in that time in the Klan, Bill Wilson said. But his father's 1924 re-election campaign was a grudge fight for The Old Man. Stephenson was supporting Congressman Wilson's Republican opponent, Harry Rowbottom.

Bill took a summer job at a service station, where he was taunted by the other workers.

"Are you a crossback, kid?" another worker asked him.

"A what?" Bill said.

"Catholic."

"No. Why?"

"We don't want no crossbacks or kikes around here."

At least he knew where the workers stood. It was not so elsewhere.

"On the subject of the Ku Klux Klan, a strange silence prevailed everywhere that summer, and you could not be sure whether your friends were members of the Invisible Empire or not.... In the main, the politicians too were silent.... The opponents of the Klan, such as my father, found themselves boxing with shadows."

Summer waned on; hot; the kind of weather, one writer noted, that seemed designed in some "conspiracy to make corn grow."

Bill found a girl and "for awhile we thought we were in love.... Almost every time I took her out, my car was trailed by the Horse Thief Detective Association.... I finally got used to it."

One night he eluded the trailing car and parked with his girl on a country road. "A farmer pulled up beside us and said, "If you kids know what is good for you, you'll move along. The Kluxers are patrolling this road tonight, and God knows what they'll do to you if they catch you here."

Wilson knew what they would do. "They entered homes without search warrants and flogged errant husbands and wives. They tarred and feathered drunks. They raided stills and burned barns. They caught couples in parked cars and tried to blackmail the girls, or worse. On occasion, they branded the three KKK's on the bodies of people who were particularly offensive to them. Over in Illinois, there had ever been a couple of murders. I took my girl home."

Bill saw crosses burned on hillsides where his father spoke, but he and his family were never harmed.

"But there was always the threat of violence around us in the hot and humid air of those breathless months." The phone would ring. Bill would try to grab it first, but his father would answer, listen quietly for a minute, then hang up, saying, "Wrong number." Bill answered enough of them to know. They would begin, "Hi, nigger lover," and then proceed through unrepeatable diatribes.

And there the petty annoyances—the air let out of the Hudson's tires, the "KKK" soaped on window screens. "It was like a perpetual Halloween in midsummer."

As the weeks wore on, the Klan grew more bold. Klantauguas—lectures on Klan principles—were common at club meetings. While an airplane circled overhead dragging a 20 foot cross, 3,000 robed knights gathered for an all day outing at Boonville, "where Abe Lincoln used to come afoot from his father's cabin on Little Pigeon Creek. A recalcitrant Indiana preacher in northern Indiana was dragged across the state line and branded.

"The Klan licensed bootleggers, and the Horse Thief Detective Association raided those who did not pay.... By mid August, they were parading in Evansville. I stood one steaming August noonday at the corner of Seventh and Main and watched them march past, men on horseback, men in cars, men on foot, women, children, all in robes, all hooded, some carrying flaming crosses on long poles, silent except for the hum of motors and the clop of hooves and the soft shuffle of shoes on the half molten asphalt. Afterward, the newspapers said there were more than five thousand of them. I wondered whether the Pattersons or my girl's family were among them. I wondered how many of them were our neighbors on Chandler Avenue."

Sometimes during the summer when they were alone, his father would shake his head in dismay and say, "I never would have believed that a thing like this could happen in Indiana. Hoosiers have always been so generous, friendly, and kind. A poison has got into their blood."

On his way to the train back to Harvard, Bill went by to tell the Pattersons goodbye. It was awkward. As he was leaving, Mr. Patterson pushed Link aside, moved close to Bill's face, and held up three fingers—the three Ks. "Tell your father," he whispered. "It's not too late."

Harry Rowbottom won the 1924 election, as Congressman Wilson had predicted, and was reelected again in 1926 and 1928. In 1931, he went to prison for accepting a bribe.

Bill Wilson's father called him at Harvard to tell him of his 1924 defeat. "Next time, son," he said. "Next time."

There would be no next time for Congressman Wilson, but Bill said his father's voice on the phone, "strong and clear..., gave me the confidence and courage I needed. I knew that as long as there were men like him in Indiana, the Ku Klux Klan too would pass."

13
DAVID BECOMES GOLIATH

June 9, 1924
Columbus, Ohio

With the 1924 primary under his belt, Steve turned his attention to his toughest challenge yet, the fall general elections—after he resolved a minor unpleasantness with the Evansville Klan.

A Klan trial was a somber affair, as sober and rigidly structured as a civil trial.

First, notices were issued from the accused's home klavern— Evansville, in Steve's case. Then witnesses were called, with sworn testimony taken and transcribed. The actual trial was held by a Tribunal.

Testimony in the case of the KKK versus D.C. Stephenson began June 9, 1924, first at the Columbus Deschler Hotel in a room registered under the name of C.G. Meeker. Then the somber band, meeting as the Klokann of Evansville Klan No. 1, moved June 12 to the Lincoln Hotel in Indianapolis, to a room registered in the name of Joe Huffington. June 16 they convened again for testimony at No. 1 Edgar Street, Evansville.

The Klokann considered the transcripts, exhibits, and other evidence against Stephenson, as presented by a prosecutor. Then they voted unanimously to suspend him from the Klan and submitted his case to trial before "The Tribunal" at Evansville, which began June 23. Steve was, in effect, "indicted" on six charges: one for slandering the Klan, one for leading a Klan revolt, and four on morals charges.

Stephenson sent an attorney but refused to attend any of the sessions.

Had he attended, he might have been hard pressed to deny speaking ill of the Imperial Wizard or leading a revolt against him. But as to the morals charges—Was he falsely accused? He never dignified them with denial or other comment. They were serious charges, particularly for the leader of a body whose program was based on moral uplift.

Witnesses charged that The Old Man was often drunk; that he was arrested in a Columbus drunken brawl January 5, 1924, and jailed for 24 hours. They accused him of attempting a drunken assault on "a virtuous young lady of Evansville, Indiana," one of his employees, on July 15, 1923. And they said he was arrested and fined after a deputy sheriff found him in an "indecent" position with a young woman in a car parked "on a prominent public highway" near Columbus June 10, 1923.

Witnesses included a Columbus policeman who said he answered a trouble call at the Deschler Hotel on January 5, 1924, and found three men. He identified one as D.C. Stephenson, "as drunk as any man I ever saw..., standing by the bed with a death grip on the foot of the bed.... A large mirror in the room was broken, some chairs smashed, and the room presented evidence of a wild party.

"I was informed that they had sent for a manicurist (with whom) Stephenson tried to have intercourse..., and that upon her refusal to permit it, he had thrown her from the room, and when a bell boy, at her request, had gone back into the room to get her tray, Stephenson had struck him several times."

A young woman testified that she was the hotel manicurist summoned by Stephenson, who tried to get her to drink with him. "Well, I had finished manicuring one hand, and then he got up to get a drink of whiskey and when I told him that I didn't want any, he came over to me and grabbed me. He said that he would give me a hundred dollars if I would allow him to have intercourse with me. Of course, he was more rude than I care to be in expressing it....

"I told him that I was not in the habit of being insulted by any one like that, and he said, 'You little, you will, or I'll kill you.' And then he went over to his grip, I thought to get a gun. Then, while he was doing that, I went out the door that led to the hall outside....

"The two other men who were in the other room came out; and I was crying and they said, 'Don't pay any attention to him; he is a good fellow; he is drunk; he is all right when he is sober.'"

Later, the manicurist said, a doctor friend of Stephenson's tried to pay her $50 to sign a statement that one of the other men in the room, not Stephenson, had attacked her. He said he needed the statement because "'Stephenson was a dandy fellow.'... I told this doctor that he could tell Stephenson, the less he said about it or asked me to say about that affair, the better off he would be."

Another witness said she was working for Stephenson at his Buckeye Lake, Ohio, office and living in a cottage there July 15, 1923, when "he came to my room about 3:30 o'clock, a.m.; he was clothed in his underwear; he was intoxicated.... I jumped from the bed. He tried to kiss me; put his arm around me and told me it seemed everyone in the office had gone back on him but myself. He tried to force me on the bed. I refused to do this and threatened to scream if he went any further. He then released me and left the room."

Charles M. Hoff, a deputy sheriff from Franklin County, Ohio, said he was patrolling roads the night of June 10, 1923, and found Stephenson parked in a Cadillac with a woman. "They were both in the back part of the car. The young lady had her clothes up above where you could see part of her body was exposed. The man had his clothes unbuttoned, his trousers unbuttoned, his coat off, and in his shirt sleeves.

"I asked them what was going on, and he says, 'Why, there is nothing going on.' I says, 'By the looks of things, it looks like there has been something going on.'"

An accompanying special deputy reported generally the same story as Deputy Sheriff Hoff. "Well, we pulled the door open, throwed the flashlight in.... Mr. Hoff says, 'What are you doing there with your pants unbuttoned," and he reached around and grabbed the girl's hand and says, 'My God, would you insult this girl?' He says, 'Do you see that ring, diamond ring?... I'm going to marry this girl....' Hoff says, 'I don't care if you are married now.' He said, 'You have violated the law; you didn't have no headlight or tail light.' 'Why,' he says, 'I am a special deputy myself.' Hoff said, 'Let me see your card.' He pulled his card out. He says, 'It don't make any difference...if you have got a card... You have violated the law by being parked without any lights...'"

Stephenson said he was "well acquainted with the sheriff" and would get Hoff fired, the special deputy testified. Hoff said Stephenson pleaded guilty to parking without lights and paid a $17.50 fine.

The prosecutor presented other witnesses and exhibits, including Stephenson's recent letter to Indiana Klansmen, "The Old Man's Answer to Hate Vendors," intended to show that Steve had damaged the Klan by his actions.

On July 10, 1924, the Tribunal issued its judgment: guilty on all charges.

The punishment: "Banishment forever and complete ostracism in any and all things by each and every member of this order."

The man who built the Indiana Klan—and, in large measure, the successful political programs and practices of the national Klan—was expelled.

But there was little immediate effect. Evans and Bossert were drilling significant caverns into his power base, but from an external view—the vantage point of the press, public, and politicians—the structure looked stronger than ever. For months more, he would continue to dominate the Indiana Klan, and his political power mounted every day. He said he resigned from the Klan; the Evans/Bossert faction said he was banished; no matter—his eye was on the November Indiana elections and beyond.

Mounting with his political power, however, were evil rumors and signs of some fissures of stress.

They said the charming man with the glad hand was running a protection racket with bootleggers he had identified in his political data base. The racket was: pay The Old Man now or pay more dearly later to Stephenson's Horse Thief Detectives, Stephenson's moral reform armies, Stephenson's Klergy, and Stephenson's sheriffs, policemen, judges, and jailers.

They said the boyish Old Man had a web of underworld connections—and another more insidious web that ensnared most Indiana politicians in his bribes, threats, and double deals.

They said behind his cherub face and lively eyes was a mind veering into madness.

"If ever a man was susceptible to the Klan trick of 'hanging a woman around his neck,' it was Stephenson," a historian wrote later.

"He had a more than common fondness for booze and women," said another.

He was oversexed, said another, bluntly.

The Old Man railed in retaliatory rage. Stephenson said he was a victim of Evans' "campaign of slander against me in which every conceivable form of vulgar and libelous statement was circulated through the State of Indiana in whispering campaigns and...anonymous literature." He accused Evans of propagating hate, quoting the Imperial Wizard as saying "You gotta give 'em something to hate to keep 'em stirred up."

But, in truth or slander, more and more people whispered that, going home from his flights of crowd mesmerizing rhetoric and baby-tickling folksy politicking, Steve and his cohorts followed a bawdy path through roadhouses, hotel rooms, and speakeasies.

And when he arrived home! The worst whispers were about bacchanalian revels in his Irvington mansion.

They said the Imperial Palace of the North, where the maidens of the Kappa Kappa Gamma sorority once frolicked, was now filled with other maids.

Perhaps his pilot, Court Asher, could not be considered a credible witness, since Asher's long-term profession—bootlegger—placed him outside the law for much of his life. But Asher's stories seemed too bizarre to be untrue. The reporter John Niblack later wrote down a few of them. Asher said Steve was "mighty impetuous and wild as to women when drunk."

One of The Old Man's favorite Irvington orgies, Asher said, was "when he played Satyr to a bunch of naked wood nymphs.... They would all strip naked and the Old Man would take a whip and lash the girls as they all whirled around the room, to see who could stand pain the longest. The survivor would then be rewarded with a handsome gift of money, and get to grace the great man's bed the rest of the night."

As if the rumors were not enough, the Klan sent investigators to find out more—back into Stephenson's past, into Oklahoma, as far back as his beginnings, which the investigators said were in Texas. They found his two early ex wives, both abandoned, then granted divorces on grounds that Stephenson had been brutal and cruel.

The investigator said his second wife, Violet Mary Carroll, had charged him with "excessive drinking, associating with other women, and having tricked her mother out of a good deal of money." And further that he physically abused her, left marks and bruises, gave her a black eye, "took off my dress and scratched me," pulled her hair, and gave her "some trouble."

As Stephenson immersed himself in preparation for the November 1924 elections, there were some signs that the stress fissures were widening.

The reporter John Niblack tried to interview Stephenson twice. The first was in a Kokomo hotel, immediately after Steve's triumphant July 4, 1923, Kokomo Klonklave.

"Passing quite a few guards, I was admitted to the august presence," Niblack wrote later. "And I asked him some questions, such as: What did he intend to do with the Catholics, Negroes and Jews? Did he intend to kill them, run them out, or live with them? What is the ultimate object of the Klan? And how much money did he make out of it?

"The last question brought rain, and when I got to that point, he said, 'Just a minute, young man, just stop right there. You are a part of a national conspiracy to upset this Klan. I have been propounded this very same set of questions at least thirty different times in thirty different States.'

"I said, 'Well, I don't know anything about that. I made the list up myself yesterday before I came up here.'

"He said, 'I can see you are just a bigot, you are not for us, you are against us. So just get out of here.'" And Niblack did.

Niblack's second aborted interview was at Stephenson's Kresge Building office in downtown Indianapolis, probably about the summer of 1924. Niblack went with Walter Snead, the *Indianapolis Times*' City Hall reporter.

"We...were admitted rather soon because Stephenson was publicity conscious. We went into his room and he was sitting at a big desk facing the old Indiana Trust Building.

"All of a sudden, he jumped up and came around the desk and said, 'Get to one side! Don't stand there in front of that big window. There are people lying over there in the point of the Indiana Trust Building with high powered rifles, just trying to shoot me, and they might shoot you by mistake.'

"Needless to say, Snead and I both jumped to one side pretty quickly," Niblack said. "That was about all there was to the interview, though we talked a little bit more, and then I went over to the Indiana Trust Building and walked up the six floors and made an investigation."

The Indiana Trust Building was triangular in shape, Niblack recalled, and in the front office on the point, facing Stephenson's office, on the sixth floor were offices of Klan attorneys Arthur R. Robinson, later to be "Stephenson's Senator," and Frank Symmes. Other attorneys, some of whom worked for the Klan, occupied the other upper offices at the point.

"I went into each room of each office at the point, and saw no riflemen. I concluded that Stephenson must have been having hallucinations," Niblack recalled.

"In fact, after I knew him pretty well, I decided he was a slight mental case, which by no means dimmed his brilliance of thought or action. He certainly had a lot of the two main symptoms of dementia praecox, illusions of grandeur and delusions of persecution."

Stephenson may well have been growing paranoid—but other

paranoids, led by Imperial Wizard Evans, were, in truth, really after him.

As Indiana's 1924 fall elections drew near, the *Indianapolis Times* pulled out all the stops.

They moved their editorials to the front page, printing them in type normally reserved for the second coming of Christ:

"STOP THE KLAN!
The Ku Klux Klan must get out of Indiana politics.
It can parade and kavort and Klonklave as much as it wants to,
but it must quit tampering with the government.
Indiana is not Russia.... Indiana wants no... Hoosier Lenin, oath-bound to a masked and hooded soviet sitting in secret session in the Kremlin of the Invisible Empire.
Our nation was conceived in Liberty and dedicated to the principle that all men are created equal.
The Klan was conceived in secrecy and bigotry and dedicated to the principle that all men are NOT created equal.
Thereby the Klan strikes at the very vitals of our national life....
Let's stop the Klan while the stopping is good.
A vote for Jackson is a vote for the Klan.
A vote for McCulloch is a vote against the Klan."

These pesky problems—Evans, Bossert, the *Times*—kept getting in the way of The Old Man's moves.

But move he did—moving out, into the world beyond the Klan, establishing himself as a spokesman on sweeping national issues. November 1, less than a week before the election, he made a rare speech to the general public, a booming oratory at Rushville. The occasion was National Defense Day. Steve spoke out boldly against presidential candidate Robert LaFollette and against government ownership of railroads. He closed in vintage Stephenson style:

"If the candidacy of some individual were the only thing in jeopardy in the election of November 4, there would be little cause for debate. But the American people have been challenged by an alien force which threatens to rend asunder our sane structure of government and industry. It threatens to throw America into the red panic of the mob.

"I appeal to you, therefore, to stand firm under the protecting wing of the American eagle, guided by the militant patriotism symbolized in the red, white and blue of the American flag. The blue for loyalty, the red in recognition of the blood our fathers spilled upon a dozen battlefields for the liberty of the world, the white emblematic of purity.

"Guided by this inspiration, let us rededicate ourselves to our country and underwrite the guaranty of the founding fathers of the Republic whose promise to posterity is set forth in the eloquent language of the Declaration of Independence, setting up a government with the solemn pledge to mankind that a good citizen shall be protected in his property rights, and shall be rewarded in proportion with his ability to serve."

Who could disagree? Thus wrapped in the flag, under the protecting wings of the American eagle, Stephenson sent copies of the speech to a long list of patriots who might want to help gird him to fight the red panic of the mob and the alien force—ever more threatening for being wispily defined.

He was moving from identification with the Klan, but it still caused him no little trouble as Klan-related troubles continued to mount within and without Indiana. In the days before the election, the papers were filled with irritating dispatches of Klan problems.

In Indiana, there was trouble with the Klan ladies and with KKK mimicking anti-Klan forces. Beyond Indiana, there was trouble to the right of him, in the snow-softened valley near Niles, Ohio; and even worse trouble to the left of him, in a place known as "Bloody Herrin," Illinois.

The women! They were a powerful force, and opening the Klan to them was one of Steve's more masterful moves, if only because it doubled his prospect pool. But as they took on more and more autonomy, the women became more and more trouble. Some insisted on looking for noble purposes such as building hospitals, rather than being content to snipe at Catholics endlessly. Others were constantly carping, fighting each other, wrestling in the mire of interpersonal power plays and disgruntled insurgency. The women of the Klan, in short, were behaving more and more like their men.

The anti-Klan adversaries were sometimes useful, sometimes a nuisance. Among groups that emerged: the MMM, the Militant Minute Men of Indiana; and the LLL, a national group of blacks who called themselves the Liberal Loyalists of Lincoln. As the Klan rose to power in the Indiana Republican Party, blacks increasingly deserted the GOP that they had backed since Lincoln freed the slaves. They rallied to fight Ed Jackson's candidacy.

At rallies, the LLL burned its own fiery "L."

Over in Ohio, Steve's second favorite stronghold, things were cooking between Klan and anti-Klan forces in the industrial Mahoning Valley near Youngstown. Miscellaneous melees had erupted there over recent months. The Klan planned to show its strength at a parade scheduled at the nearby little town of Niles, Ohio—an anti-Klan hotbed of foreigners and aliens. The anti-Klan forces countered by calling their own parade at the same time on the same route. When the Niles mayor issued a permit for the Klan but not the anti-Klan parade, a bomb exploded by his house.

On November 1, the same day Steve delivered his rousing Rushville speech and only three days before the Indiana election, hooded Klansmen poured into Niles in flag-draped cars. They met an armed army of anti-Klan guerrilla fighters, the Knights of the Flaming Circle—some hooded, all with bright orange six-inch circles over their hearts. The Circle knights were street fighters, and a riot broke out that was one of the most brutal in Midwest history, wounding more than a dozen. It was finally quelled by the National Guard—after some delay, since many of the Guard troops were Klansmen who had to drive back to their home towns, strip off their Klan regalia, and don their Guard uniforms before reporting for duty.

It was even worse over at "Bloody Herrin," across the state line from Evansville in a lower pocket of southern Illinois known as Little Egypt. The area was home to "real people, congenial and hospitable," as Will Rogers said. "But instead of being like a lot of committees, fussing and arguing, calling each other names, they just shoot it out if it's necessary."

In 1922, twenty strikebreakers were killed and their bodies mutilated in a labor dispute at the little town of Herrin. The Herrin Massacre was followed by years of war between gangsters and the reforming Ku Klux Klan, which killed fifty people in two years. The press rocked with frequent reports of each series of killings and the antics of a fanatical gunslinging prohibition agent, S. Glenn Young. A Klansman, Young was expelled from the KKK September 13, 1924. He took on both the bootleggers and the sheriffs until he and a deputy killed each other January 24, 1925, in a frontier-style shoot-out.

And there were embarrassing troubles beyond Steve's empire that tarnished the Klan's image.

In Kansas, the feisty Emporia editor William Allen White filed for governor so he could "laugh the Klan out of Kansas." By the end of 1924 he had largely succeeded.

In Georgia, the prestigious Nathan Bedford Forrest Klan Number One had withdrawn from the KKK, citing misuse of power by the Imperial Palace.

In Oklahoma and Oregon, the Klan's peak of power had passed. Even in Texas, that stronghold where as many as 200,000 had joined the Klan, the KKK was floundering. Members were demanding democracy, at the very moment when they were fighting for their political lives in the governor's race.

It was not a pretty fight. A former Texas governor, "Farmer Jim" Ferguson, was taking on the Klan which had defeated him in 1922 when Klansman Earle Mayfield was elected to the U.S. Senate. Now, in 1924, Ferguson wanted to be governor, although he was constrained from running because he had been impeached in 1917. What to do? Ferguson vowed a fight to the death with the Klan and ran his wife, Miriam Amanda Ferguson—"Ma" Ferguson.

Ma and Pa Ferguson ran a spirited race. He called her KKK opponent the "great grand gizzard" and dubbed the knights "longhorn Texas Koo Koos." When someone lent Ma a sunbonnet for a campaign photo, they hit on the campaign slogan "A Bonnet or a Hood?"

In November 1924 Ma Ferguson won the Texas governor's chair, by a vote of more than 4 to 3. The Klan was washed up in Texas. "It was all over," a former Klansman sadly recalled.

The national press played it all out to the hilt, just as Stephenson was pressing his last minute election push.

But what did newsmen know? The mighty *New York Times*, for

example, had already given last rites to the Indiana Republican Party:

"...Hoosier Republicans are driven almost frantic with the troubles besetting them on all sides as election day is drawing near.... This year they are fighting with their backs to the wall....

"The hooded brotherhood is beginning to disintegrate to such an extent that its continued existence may depend upon the [election] outcome.... Only a miracle can save the Republican State ticket, and... the miracle is not likely to occur....

"The Democrats have circulated photographs of Klan records to prove that his (Ed Jackson's) name appears on the rosters of the masked fraternity. He is bidding openly for Klan support..., and the Klan is openly supporting him....

"The result of all this has been to array against the Republican candidates...at least 75 percent of the Negro vote...approximately 80,000 in the state—a considerable factor in a total vote which four years ago was 1,263,000 for the Presidential candidates of all parties.... There is a Jewish vote of 50,000 to 60,000 [and a] Catholic vote [of about] 137,000."

Tough odds. But then Stephenson set his military machine on the roll.

He flooded the mails with his "Bulletins" to Klan members, full of timely information on candidates. If the Klan wasn't mentioned, the readers could assume the candidate was a knight. In the governor's race, for example, Stephenson wrote:

"Republican: ED JACKSON,... Secretary of State.... He is a self made man and has always been a thorough gentleman, capable attorney and honest public official...."

"Democrat: DR. CARLETON B. McCULLOUCH,... He is antagonistic toward the Knights of the Ku Klux Klan; has openly and publicly denounced the Klan and otherwise stated publicly that if elected governor of Indiana he will exert his best efforts and energies toward the end of eliminating the [KKK] of Indiana...."

The Stephenson army papered the state with Klan information sheets called "scratch sheets." They were dummy ballots, with each candidate's religion helpfully added and the name of each unacceptable candidate scratched through with a large "X." Right before the election, Stephenson's machine members rolled them the size of cigarettes, jammed them between the jaws of clothespins, and tossed them from passing cars on to nearly every front porch in Indiana.

Some machine members managed to get hold of Protestant Sunday School papers and stuff them with information sheets before they were distributed.

On election day, the ever helpful machine provided voter services on an unprecedented scale, driving voters to the polls, minding the little ones while mamas voted, and working around the clock to get out their votes.

It worked with the precision of a—machine.

The night before the election, the *Indianapolis Times* put out the big, black type again, bold enough to be read from across the street.

"CHOOSE SECRECY, SUSPICION, HATE, RACIAL BITTERNESS, RELIGIOUS INTOLERANCE, NEIGHBOR AGAINST NEIGHBOR, OLD FRIENDSHIPS BROKEN, INVISIBLE EMPIRE, THE MASK OR GOVERNMENT OF THE PEOPLE, FOR THE PEOPLE, AND BY THE PEOPLE, DEMOCRACY. PEACE.

"WHICH?"

The *Times* might as well have saved its ink.

The results: Jackson, 654,784; McCulloch, 572,303. Jackson had topped Steve's predicted 80,000 winning margin by roughly 2,000 votes.

Jackson was the new governor, but the biggest winner was David Curtis Stephenson.

Two significant adversaries slipped by Steve's opposition: The anti-Klan Marion County prosecutor, Bill Remy; and the equally hidebound anti-Klan South Bender, Arthur Gilliom, who would now be state attorney general. With those notable exceptions, Stephenson had reason to celebrate. Throughout Indiana, city by city, county by county, from schoolhouse to statehouse, his slate won the state.

The national press howled in dismay. In Indianapolis, the *Times* made a solemn pledge. As governor, Jackson surely would be "courageous enough to shake off the influence of the Ku Klux Klan," the *Times* wrote. If not?

"We repeat again that the Klan MUST get out of Indiana politics. *The Times*...pledges itself to continue its fight against the domination of the state government by any secret organization or empire... If the Klan should begin to exercise its influence in the state house, the *Times* will fight it to the last ditch."

Marion County Prosecutor Bill Remy later recalled one of the most remarkable events of the era. Steve had unsuccessfully fought Remy's appointment, even to the point of trying to bribe Gov. McCray, and Remy had campaigned for reelection on a virulent anti-Klan platform. Shortly after the election, Remy was invited to a formal dinner for the winners.

After a congratulatory address by Stephenson, Marion County Sheriff Omer Hawkins rose. "Well," he said, "I guess we all know why we're here, and I'll start off. I realize that I owe my nomination and election to The Old Man. I now pledge that I will make no official appointment, nor do any official act, which does not meet with the approval of D.C. Stephenson."

One by one, the sheriff's pledge was repeated by the winning officials—until it came Remy's turn.

Bill Remy was a slight fellow, looking far younger than his 34 years. They called him "the boy prosecutor." But he rose to his full height, took a deep breath, and said, "I have had a good dinner and enjoyed meeting you chaps. I hope we can give Marion County a good administration." And, in silence, he sat down.

Could it have been coincidence that, shortly thereafter, Remy discovered that most of the funding for his prosecutor's office was cut off?

As always, Stephenson met one victory with plans for the next. Indiana's frail Democratic senator was not long for the world, The Old Man confided to a few listeners during the post-election glow.

"Sam Ralston is going to die. Governor Jackson will offer me the appointment as United States Senator from Indiana. I will turn it down and the Governor will name Arthur Robinson for the place. As for me, I want no public office. Some day, perhaps in 1928, I'd like to be Republican national committeeman from Indiana and maybe national chairman.

"After that—well, the hands of the gods will direct."

UNMASKED!   Ann Patton

14
THE DRAGON MEETS A LADY

January 12, 1925
Indianapolis, Indiana

They marched with studied slowness, waiting, watching,
waiting, inching forward for another wait.

The line stretched far into the vestibule, back beyond the massive
doors and dark paneled walls that stretched higher than the eye,
with its demurely lowered lash, could see. Gleaming black wingtips,
topped with spats, marched and milled beside satin slippers with
their gold-trimmed straps that wrapped up silk-hosed ankles, all
well-heeled and mostly shapely. With remarkable restraint, the
slow parade of footwear padded softly on the hard waxed floors.

Within, there seemed a million lights, sparkling from slowly
circling, mirrored chandeliers. White satin, silk, and sequins
gleamed against black sheens of tie, tuxedo, tails. Pearl, diamond,
gold, and silver nestled into crisp starched cuff and shirtfront; at

perfumed bosom, wrist, and earlobe; and out along a thousand fingers, arched in delicate sophistication. Beneath the pleasant din of small talk and the muted violins, there was a faint purr of rustling feather boas, taffeta, and tulle.

In the center, at the apex of the fashionable parade, Governor Ed Jackson, just inaugurated, welcomed dignitaries to his celebration ball; at his right, the focus: David Curtis Stephenson.

"See Steve." It was the word now, in the slow receiving line at the governor's inaugural ball, in the street, in the City Hall, and in the Indiana General Assembly, just convened over at the State House. Do you need a bill introduced, or killed; a politician made or ruined; a business undertaken or destroyed?

See Steve; he can do it.

If you need to curry favor with George Coffin—over there by the palm-banked bar, the reigning boss of Indianapolis' GOP, whispering with Clyde Walb, the chairman of the state Republican Party, both Stephenson men to the core—or find a loophole in the sheriff's law; to run for office or continue running rum: See Steve.

Unlike the governor's receiving line, the General Assembly was moving along at a rapid clip. Both houses were packed with Klansmen. Stephenson controlled the executive branch, the Republican Party, and, most said, the Senate. The House was dominated by Evans' Klansmen, but Steve's man was elected Speaker.

The Klan had an agenda for the Americanization of Indiana. The Bossert/Evans agenda included a "bone dry bill" that would give Indiana the most drastic prohibition law in America, a "religious garb bill" to prohibit nuns from teaching in public schools, a "flag bill" to require schools to fly the American flag, and a "Bible bill" to require the Holy Book to be read in public schools.

The Republicans had an agenda, including an old-fashioned gerrymandering bill to redistribute power in their direction; it was called the "ripper bill."

And Stephenson had an agenda, including a rider on the ripper bill to give him control of the Indiana Highway Commission with its $15 million annual budget. He was after patronage, contracts, power. In return for $227,000 he gave Ed Jackson's campaign, Steve had a written contract which, he said later, pledged "that I was to get it back by getting the coal contract from the State, by control of the Highway Commission, and of the State Purchasing Department." Steve also wanted control of the State Board of Education, in part because The Old Man had decided to move into the nutrition field. He had written a new book, "One Hundred Years of Health," that pushed what he called a miracle food product. He wanted the book—and education courses pushing the product—required in all public schools.

Stephenson's agenda was fashioned to consolidate and expand his power, through wheeling-dealing maneuvers that he performed with dizzying finesse. He was charming, he was ruthless, he was the consummate salesman turned politician.

And he was in his element, whether in the halls of the legislature or the halls of Indianapolis' most fashionable Athletic Club, beside his governor at the January 12, 1925, inaugural ball.

Slowly, through the line, moved a young woman with another agenda. She seemed curiously out of place among the sequins and tulle. She was, if her friends are to be believed, shy and unsophisticated, a gentle girl not given to or even overly impressed with the glisten and glitz world of politics.

The young woman was not overly tall, standing perhaps 5 feet 4. She was not overly thin, weighing perhaps 140 pounds; and not

overly young: 28. She was no dazzling beauty; her nose was a bit
heavy, her eyes darkly sad and reserved. She tied her prematurely
graying, chestnut hair back simply in a velvet ribbon. Dark curls
framed and spilled over the forehead of a face that could have been
the model for the cameo of Liberty on the nation's coins.

Her name was Madge Oberholtzer.

Madge was bright and determined. You could see it in the tilt of
the head, the set of the jaw, the slight upward thrust of the square
chin, the firm, straight gaze of the pensive dark eyes. She was
an honor graduate of Butler University, in her neighborhood of
Irvington, where she had been a Pi Beta Phi girl.

She was the only daughter of a postal clerk, from an old Indiana
family of more refinement than financial worth. Madge was a good
daughter, deferential to authority but not obsequious to ignorance.
"The Drift," the Butler Yearbook, described her in 1917: "Madge is a
timid creature with a baby voice, who allows professional gruffness
to frighten her into speechlessness, but once outside the depressing
influence of the class room walls she waxes adjectivorous and
verbiforous and is able to hold at bay the most fluent masculine
word artist on campus."

She was also curiously out of place in the age of the flapper. She
"valued her virtue" above all else, her friends said. There was not
a hint of scandal ever attached to her name, they said; her closest
intimates said her private life was "exemplary in every way." Some
said she had been in love with a young man once, but he "had to go
to war."

"Madge Oberholtzer: ...pleasant in friendship, faithful in duty, of
fine Christian character," the Butler Alumni Quarterly wrote of her
later.

After her 1918 graduation from Butler, Madge taught in the
public school at Hagerstown, Indiana. Now she was living at
home again, working at the State House, running a little education

program called the Young People's Reading Circle. She was
managing librarian, distributing books from an office in the
Lemcke Building. Madge was considered quite a success. She made
a good salary, drove a little Model T coupe, and was on her way to
independence that was remarkable for a 1920s' girl. But her program
was in trouble; there was a bill floating around to kill it. Thus, as
she took her place among the satins and sequins of the inaugural
ball receiving line, with her simple velvet ribbon and cameo face,
she carried her own agenda to save her program and her job.

Miss Oberholtzer: Mr. Stephenson. The cameo face met the
cherub face. Perhaps she reminded him of someone else, some
tantalizing unattainable girl from his childhood. Perhaps she
represented the quiet class of Irvington he had not acquired.
Certainly she was a breed apart from the nymphs who usually
caught Steve's fancy. Whatever: For reasons known only to him, he
asked her to dance. For reasons known only to her, she accepted.

Oh—she was his neighbor? He at 5432 University, Irvington; she
at 5802. What a coincidence. Well, wasn't it a small world?

Was it mere coincidence that the banquet placecards, which
Madge had helped arrange, seated her at Steve's table?

For reasons known only to him, he asked her out. And for
reasons known only to her, she declined.

See Steve. But it was not easy to do. The crush of the General
Assembly business, in addition to his Klan affairs and business
dealings, made him a busy man.

It was a session like none other in history, a drama played out
against the backdrop of a state where crosses still burned almost
nightly and thousands marched through the streets with robe and
hood, silently, with arms crossed and feet padding along to the
solemn beat of drums.

Steve could decide the fate of some bills by a nod of his head. Inexplicably, he killed most of the Klan agenda's bills—the only significant Klan legislation to survive was the bone dry bill. He succeeded in getting a bill passed to require teaching nutrition in public schools. The big test was the ripper bill—riding with it the Republican gerrymandering and his control of the Highway Commission.

Things were going along pretty well on the ripper bill until February 24, when the Senate suddenly came up missing a large slice of its membership. Without a quorum, the Senate could not vote on the ripper bill. It was a curious development, more curious because the missing members were all Democrats, recalled John Niblack, who covered the legislative session for the *Indianapolis Times*.

Niblack said another Senator explained that all the absentees were ill, "from eating fish taken from the polluted streams of this state."

Republicans suspected that something was indeed fishy when the absences stretched into a second day. With due references to the penalties for willfully breaking a quorum, the Republicans dispatched the chief door keeper, one Jerome Brown, to find the Democrats, bring them back, and restore the Senate quorum.

He found them, Niblack wrote later, "in Dayton, Ohio, at the Gibbons Hotel, where the faithful Jerome, fully earning his $6 a day salary...read his arrest warrants, only to be laughed at, as he plaintively informed the Senate by telephone." Thereupon, the absentee quorum proceeded to get rip-roaring drunk.

Into the crisis rode The Old Man, who hotfooted it to Dayton to rescue the quorum. He went, strangely enough, with his rival Indiana Grand Dragon, Walter Bossert. Even more bizarre was his plan: to kidnap two Democratic senators, with their consent, and return them to Indiana for arrest. The kidnapping was aborted by other Democrats but nonetheless agreement emerged. The ripper bill was dead, and the senators returned February 26, rolling across the state line singing "Back Home in Indiana." When the senators reconvened, Niblack said, they all joined in singing "Blest Be the Tie That Binds."

Now Stephenson could add to his list of accomplishments that he had saved the government of Indiana.

But ultimately, he grew bored; having gained a large measure of control over the state legislature, he discovered it was of only short term use. Later he evaluated his Klansmen in the 1925 House: "Those fellows didn't amount to anything. Representative in the Legislature is no good, only for sixty days, and when you get through with him is mere chaff. Very few of them you can ever put over on the public twice."

In the midst of the legislative fray, he killed a minor bill that would have abolished the Young People's Reading Circle. He had saved Madge Oberholtzer's job and her program. The gallant knight asked her out again, to dinner at one of Indianapolis' finest hotels. She accepted, for that and a couple of other dates, including a high-toned party at his mansion. The killing of the bill and the minor dates both passed unnoticed in the storm of the General Assembly session, fraught with far more significant happenings.

Some semblance of peace was restored to Indiana by March 11, when the General Assembly adjourned after 62 of the stormiest days in its history.

Steve had not only saved the Reading Circle, he had virtually saved the state. He had climbed another mountain—following without a letup on the heels of an action packed three years or so since he came to Evansville and cast his lot with the Indiana Ku Klux Klan. His past had been rich, filled with heady success; as to his future—he modestly demurred. God would direct what lay ahead.

The Old Man deserved, by any standard, a little time off for some rest and recreation, on the following weekend that would include a Sunday, March 15, the Ides of March.

A few days after the Indiana General Assembly closed, an *Indianapolis News* reporter, Harold Feightner, was crossing monument circle in downtown Indianapolis when he heard some news that made him freeze, even on the balmy spring day.

Like the streets that fan out from the towering soldiers and sailors monument across the city and state, the events of March 1925 would reverberate throughout the lives of all involved.

Like Feightner, they would remember distinctly the precise moment when they first heard the news.

"I was crossing..., coming across the monument in downtown Indianapolis," Feightner recalled years later. "I was going to work. In those days we got to work at seven o'clock on the *Indianapolis News*, and Walter Bossert hailed me from across the street and told me the story of Stephenson and Madge Oberholtzer, how they had brought her back and thrown her on the bed....

"And I went in and Mr. Hodges (*News* editor) said, 'Well, you've got nothing else to do but that for awhile.'"

Asa Smith was an attorney for the Oberholtzer family. He remembered that his wife, nicknamed Tweedy, "was down getting breakfast, and I was getting ready to shave, and the phone rang. And Tweedy called me and said, 'You're wanted on the phone.'

"And I said, 'Who in the hell would be calling me at such an hour as this?'

"And she said, 'Mrs. Oberholtzer.'

"Well, I came down and got some of the soap off and then Mrs.

Oberholtzer told me, she said, 'I'm in the coat room. I don't want Mr. Oberholtzer to hear this.' His arthritis, you know. But she said, 'Last night a Mr. Stephenson called Madge and just had to see her at once. It was very important in connection with her job.' And (Madge) said, 'Well, I'll see him in the morning.' 'No, he has to see you tonight. He's leaving town tonight. And he'll send an escort for you.' ...She said that Madge left with this escort without any hat.... And she said, 'I went sound asleep but I just woke up a few minutes ago. This was at six o'clock, a little after, and I looked in Madge's room and the bed was vacant and she hasn't been back.'

"And I said, 'Now you just leave everything to me, Mrs. Oberholtzer.' So I went down to my office. And in the meantime, here came a telegram from Madge from Hammond (Indiana): 'We are driving through to Chicago. Will be home on night train.' Well, that would mean crossing the state line, you know....

"So I got ahold of (Mrs.) Oberholtzer and (Madge's best friend) Ermina Moore.... We...went over to Stephenson's mansion and I sat there with a gun where I could shoot if anybody..., you know. And they knocked on the door until a man...came to the door and said, 'Why, no, Mr. Stephenson is not around here.' As a matter of fact he had just driven in and had Madge up in the loft of the garage." In the darkness, Smith saw the car pull to the garage.

"Well, then the next morning Klinck, that was one of the parties with Stephenson, brought her home carrying her. And she said,... 'I'm dying.'

"...And she said to me later, 'Let him.... Don't do anything. He's a power. He'll crush you. He'll crush you. He'll crush you,' Madge said to me...."

The story was still in pieces, frustratingly fragmented for all who heard it.

The *Indianapolis Times* reporter John Niblack heard it some days later, when "William Lowell Toms, who was the *Times* reporter at the State House where Madge was employed..., got wind that the 'Old Man' was in serious trouble about some woman. 'Tubby,' as he was called, and I were jointly assigned to the case...."

The puzzle was most painful for Madge's mother.

Matilda Oberholtzer was a time-worn version of Madge, a short woman with dark, graying hair, a quiet but lined face, and nervous hands. Her husband George was not well, plagued with arthritis. Mrs. Oberholtzer worried over him on Sunday afternoon, March 15, 1925, while she took a series of telephone messages for Madge, who spent the afternoon and evening with some young friends.

Madge returned shortly before 10 p.m.

Mr. Stephenson had called, leaving his phone number: Irvington 0492. It was important to Madge that she call right away.

Madge returned the call, and left with the escort Stephenson sent. And did not return.

Her mother remembered later that she stood by the window and watched Madge and the escort walk away in the glow of a street lamp. Matilda recalled that she had an overpowering urge to call out to Madge, "Come back!"

After she whispered her call for help to Asa Smith Monday morning, Mrs. Oberholtzer received Madge's telegram: "We are driving through to Chicago. Will be home on night train."

Matilda Oberholtzer met the Monday night train, but Madge was not on it.

There was no question now. Something terrible was wrong.

With Asa Smith and Madge's friend, Ermina Moore, Matilda Oberholtzer went to Stephenson's house, some three blocks away in Irvington.

Mrs. Oberholtzer would later hear that Stephenson's car had just reached his garage when they knocked on his door; that Stephenson said, 'There is someone at the front door of the house,' and sent his driver, Shorty, to see who it was. Shorty returned and said, "It was Miss Oberholtzer's mother."

A neighbor later reported waking that night, Monday night, to the sound of a horrifying scream from Stephenson's garage.

Tuesday morning the Oberholtzer's roomer, Eunice Schultz, was in the kitchen preparing lunch when she heard a terrible groaning at the front door. She went into the dining room and saw a large man, someone she did not know, carrying Madge into the house and up the stairs. He returned in a great hurry, trying to keep his face averted from Mrs. Schultz.

"Is Madge hurt?" she asked.

Yes, he said. An automobile accident. Probably no bones broken.

"I will get a doctor quickly."

"Yes."

"Who are you?"

"My name is Johnson. From Kokomo. I must hurry."

As he ran out the door, Mrs. Schultz caught a glimpse of his face. She later identified him as one of Stephenson's bodyguards, Earl Klinck.

She hurried up the stairs to see Madge. From behind the closed door to the girl's bedroom, Mrs. Schultz could hear Madge moaning. She found her crumpled on the bed, her black velvet dress, coat, and black shoes in disarray. She had no hat.

From head to toe, she was bloodied and bruised, marked by strange egg-shaped wounds.

"Oh, dear mother," she moaned. She could barely speak. "Oh, Mrs. Schultz, I am dying."

The Oberholtzer family's doctor, John Kingsbury, arrived shortly, expecting to find Madge suffering from injuries in a car accident, as Mrs. Schultz said when she called him. What he found were wounds of a very different sort.

The wounds Mrs. Schultz had seen, on her face and limbs, were not the worst.

Dr. Kingsbury found a bruise on her left hip and buttock the size of a dinner plate. Her left breast was the worst wound, torn so deeply that it was nearly gone. Something had ripped her, from head to toe. And there was something else, some puzzle he could not crack....

15
Irvington 0492

March 1925
Irvington

Over the years, Asa Smith had become more than a family
attorney for the Oberholtzers. Through their mutual friend, Ermina
Moore, the Smiths and the Oberholtzers had become friends.

Smith came immediately when he learned that Madge had been
returned home. "Her mother showed me her chest," Smith recalled
later. "It is almost impossible to describe. It was simply solid black
and blue and purple..., bloody."

Smith and Ermina Moore visited her every day, carefully noting
the fragments of her story which Smith began to compile into a
draft written statement. It would be needed if she did not survive.

"My name," the statement read, "is Madge Oberholtzer. I am a
resident of Marion County....

"I first met D.C. Stephenson at the banquet given for the Governor at the Athletic Club early in January, 1925. At that time I was impressed with Stephenson's power and influence.

"At that time, he seemed to take a great liking to me and danced several dances with me. During the dances he said he liked me very much.

"This was while the Legislature was in session. Then we drove back home and he acted toward me in a gentlemanly manner, although he said to me, I thought jokingly, "Are you afraid of me?' He said, too, that I should not be so aloof from him and said, 'I always get what I want.'

"After the banquet, he asked me for a date several times, but I gave him no definite answer. He later insisted that I take dinner with him at the Washington Hotel and I consented."

Stephenson picked her up in his Cadillac, Madge recalled, and they dined together at the Washington Hotel, then and on one other occasion. Once she went to a party at his house "with several prominent people, when both gentlemen and ladies were present."

On one of those occasions, "he said to me, 'I would never hurt you even if you asked me to, and you know that,' and I believed him. I was at first attracted by his apparent influence and power with State officials and his general political influence and because of his respectful attitude and conduct toward me. I believed that he was my friend.

"The two evenings I took dinner with Stephenson at the Washington Hotel, he drove me home and was very nice to me. Whenever we met during these times, he was so especially nice to me, and once, when he overheard me talking about wishing to kill a bill in the Legislature, providing for the abolishment of my office —that of business manager of the Teachers and Young Peoples Reading Circle—he said to me that I should have come to him and that he would use his influence to kill it. And the bill was killed."

She did not see him again until Sunday, March 15, when she returned home about 10 p.m. and took his messages from her mother.

"I called Irvington 0492 and Stephenson answered and said to me to come down if I could to his home, that he wished to see me about something very important to me; that he was leaving for Chicago and had to see me before he left."

He said he was too busy to leave but would send someone to pick her up. "I recognized Stephenson's voice," she said. Soon a "Mr. Gentry, whom I had never seen before" came and walked with her the three blocks from her house to Stephenson's.

"When we arrived there we went inside. I saw Stephenson and that he had been drinking." A young man named Shorty, Steve's driver, came in.

"Soon as I got inside the house I was very much afraid, as I first learned then there was no other woman about, and that Stephenson's housekeeper was away or at least not in evidence."

They took her to the kitchen and tried to get her to drink, as another man, Earl Klinck, came in.

"I said I wanted no drink but Stephenson and the others forced me to drink. I was afraid not to do so, and I drank three small glasses of the drink." She became dazed and ill. She vomited.

"I want you to go to Chicago with me," Stephenson said.

"I was very much terrified and did not know what to do. I said to him that I wanted to go home.

"He said, 'No, you cannot go home. Oh yes! You are going with me to Chicago. I love you more than any woman I have ever known.'

She tried to call home, got no answer, then tried to call again but "they would not let me. These men were all about me."

They took her to Stephenson's room, where he opened a dresser drawer filled with guns. Each of the men selected a gun, Stephenson taking a pearl-handled revolver that he had Shorty load. They were going to drive to Chicago, he said. She protested, and he had Gentry call Indianapolis' Washington Hotel and reserve a drawing room for two on the midnight, northbound Monon train.

"They all took me to the automobile at the rear of Stephenson's yard and we started the trip. I thought we were bound for Chicago but did not know. I begged of them to drive past my home so I could get my hat, and once inside my home I thought I would be safe from them. They drove me to Union Station in the machine, where they had to get a ticket. I did not get out of the automobile all the way."

Before they left the house, Stephenson told Klinck to get in touch with the Marion County prosecutor's investigator, Clyde Worley, to "tell him we are going to Chicago on a business deal to make money for all of us." Clyde Worley could see that they were not harassed by law enforcement officers. Klinck stayed at the house.

"Stephenson and Gentry sat in the car all the time with me until we got onto the train. We stopped at the Washington Hotel on the way down. Shorty got out and went into the hotel and came back. They would not let me out. I was dazed and terrified that my life would be taken and did not know what to do. Stephenson would not let me get out of the car and I was afraid he would kill me.

"He said he was the law in Indiana. He also said to Gentry, 'I think I am pretty smart to have gotten her.'"

They got on the train. "I think only the colored porter saw us. They took me at once into the compartment.

"I cannot remember clearly everything that happened after that." She remembered that Gentry got into the top berth of the compartment.

"Stephenson took hold of the bottom of my dress and pulled it up over my head. I tried to fight but was weak and unsteady. Stephenson took hold of my two hands and held them. I had not the strength to move. What I had drunk was affecting me.

"Stephenson took all my clothes off and pushed me into the lower

berth. After the train had started, Stephenson got in with me and
attacked me. He held me so I could not move. I did not know and I do
not remember all that happened.

"He chewed me all over my body, bit my neck and face, chewing
my tongue, chewed my breasts until they bled, my back, my legs, my
ankles, and mutilated me all over my body."

Madge passed out. Early in the morning she heard a buzz and
the porter calling them to get off at Hammond, in far northwest
Indiana. A stop there, rather than crossing the state line into
Chicago, would avoid any possibility that a kidnapping charge could
become a federal offense.

"Gentry shook me and said it was time to get up, that we were to
get off at Hammond. At this time I was becoming more conscious
and Stephenson was flourishing his revolver.

"I said to him to shoot me. He held the revolver against my side,
but I did not flinch. I said to him again to kill me, but he put the gun
in his grip."

Gentry and Stephenson helped her dress and took her off the
train at Hammond.

"I remember seeing the conductor. I was able to walk to the
Indiana Hotel. I remember begging Stephenson and saying to him to
wire my mother during the night, and he said he had or would, I am
not clear about that. At the Indiana Hotel, Stephenson registered for
himself and wife. I tried to see under what name but failed to do so."

It was about 6:30 a.m. on Monday. She saw two black bellhops
and two black girls in the lobby. Stephenson and Gentry took her up
to their rooms, Stephenson and Madge in 416, Gentry in 417.

Madge had come without a purse or money. "I kept begging
Stephenson and saying to him to send my mother a telegram." She
secured a telegram blank, and Stephenson made her write out the
message he dictated, which Gentry dispatched.

"Stephenson lay down on the bed and slept. Gentry put hot

towels and witch hazel on my head and bathed my body to relieve my suffering." She recalled that they were in room 416 with Stephenson while Gentry was bathing her wounds.

"Stephenson said he was sorry, and that he was three degrees less than a brute.

"I said to him, 'You are worse than that.'"

Breakfast was served in the room, as Shorty came in, having driven up from Indianapolis. Stephenson ate heartily: grapefruit, coffee, sausage, and buttered toast. She drank only coffee.

"I said to Stephenson to give me some money, that I had to buy a hat. Shorty gave me $15 at Stephenson's direction and took me out in the car.... Shorty waited for me while I went into a store close to the hotel to get a hat."

She bought a small black silk hat for $12.50, then asked Shorty to drive her to a drugstore so she could buy some rouge.

"We drove to a drugstore near the Indiana Hotel and I purchased a box of bichloride of mercury tables. I put these in my coat pocket. Then we went back to the hotel."

The clerk sold her the tablets without objection, she recalled. "He was tall and slender, about the age and build of my brother, with black hair."

She asked Stephenson to let her go into Gentry's room to rest, but he refused: "Oh, you are not going there. You are going to lie right down here by me."

When he was asleep, she went into Gentry's room, alone. "I laid out eighteen of the bichloride of mercury tablets and at once took six of them. I only took six because they burnt me so. This was about 10 a.m. Monday, I think."

She intended, she said, to die. Earlier in the morning, while Gentry was out sending the telegram and Stephenson was asleep, she had started to kill herself with Stephenson's revolver. "Then I decided to try and get poison and take it in order to save my mother from disgrace. I knew it would take longer with the mercury tablets to kill me."

After swallowing the tablets, she became sick and lay down on the bed. At about 4 p.m. Shorty came into the room, saw she was ill, and asked her what was wrong.

"I replied, 'Nothing.'

"He said, 'Where is your pain?'

"I said it was all over

"He said I could not have pain without cause.

"I said to him, 'Can you keep a secret?'

He said, 'Yes.' He said to me he had never mistreated a girl in his life.

I said, "I believe you can," and then I said to him that I had taken poison, and said to him not to tell Stephenson. I was very ill and almost delirious at this time. I had vomited almost all day."

Shorty turned pale, left, and returned quickly with Stephenson and Gentry, who were agitated.

"Stephenson said, 'What have you done?'

"I said, 'I asked Shorty not to tell.'"

Steve ordered a quart of milk and made her drink it. She told him she had taken six bichloride of mercury tablets, that the proof was in the cuspidor. He saw that it was half full of clotted blood and some of the tablets. He emptied it into the bathtub.

"I said to Stephenson, 'What are you going to do?'

"And he said, 'We will take you to a hospital here and you can register as my wife. Your stomach will have to be pumped out,'" She could tell the hospital staff that she had gotten the mercury by mistake, thinking the tablets were aspirin, he said.

"I refused to do this as his wife.

"Stephenson said, 'We will take you home.'

"I said I would not go home. Either I would stay right there, and for them to leave me there and go about their own business, or to let me register at another hotel under my own name.

"Stephenson said, 'We will do nothing of the kind. We will take you home.'"

The best way out, Stephenson said, was "for us to drive to Crown Point and for us to get married." Gentry agreed with him. Under Indiana law at that time, a wife could not testify against her husband.

"I refused. Stephenson snapped his fingers and said to Shorty, 'Pack the grips.' Stephenson helped me downstairs. I did not care what happened to me."

As they were leaving Hammond, she asked Shorty to call her mother He answered, 'If I do that, she will be right up here.'

"And I said, 'Nothing could be sweeter.'"

Stephenson said that he had already called Mrs. Oberholtzer and that she said it would be all right if Madge didn't come home that night.

"I don't know much about what happened after that. My mind was in a daze. I was in terrible agony."

They put her in the back seat of the car and started for home. The trip would cover 250 miles on bad roads and would take hours. Stephenson had Shorty remove the license plates and told him if they were stopped to say the plates had been stolen.

"All the way to Indianapolis, I suffered great pain and agony and screamed for a doctor." She begged for medicine to ease the pain, for them to leave her along the road so someone else could help her. "I said to him that I felt he was more cruel than he had been the night before.

"He said he would stop at the next town before we got there but never did. Just before reaching a town he would say to Shorty, 'Drive fast but don't get pinched.'

"I vomited in the car all over the back seat and grips. Stephenson did not try to make me comfortable in any way. He said he thought

I was dying, and at one time he said to Gentry, 'This takes guts to do this, Gentry. She is dying.'

"I heard him say also that he had been in a worse mess than this before and got out of it. Stephenson and Gentry drank liquor during the entire trip. I remember Stephenson having said that he had power and saying he made $250,000. He said that his word was law."

They drove into Indianapolis and straight to Stephenson's house, late that night

"When we reached Stephenson's garage he said, 'There is someone at the front of the house.' ...Stephenson said to Shorty to go and see who was at the front door.

"Shorty came back and said, 'It's her mother.'

"I remember Stephenson said to me, 'You will stay right here until you marry me.'"

Someone carried her to the loft above the garage. "Stephenson did nothing to relieve my pain.... I was left in the garage." She remembered nothing else through the night.

Klinck shook her to waken her the next day, late Tuesday morning. "You have to go home," he said.

"I asked him where Stephenson was and he said he did not know. I remember Stephenson had told me to tell everyone that I had been in an automobile accident, and he said, 'You must forget this, what is done has been done. I am the law and the power.' He said to me several times that his word was the law."

Klinck intended to call a taxi to take her home, but she persuaded him to take her in Stephenson's Cadillac. "He put my clothes on me and then carried me down to the car and put me in the back seat and drove the car to my home.... I was suffering and in such agony.... I said for him to drive up the driveway. He did and then carried me into the house and upstairs and into my bed. It was about noon Tuesday when we got into the house...."

UNMASKED! Ann Patton

16
From Mayhem to Murder

March 1925
Irvington

When Madge came home Tuesday morning, her parents had gone downtown to see a detective.

Then her mother went home, but George Oberholtzer stayed downtown. "I then went to Union Station and watched all the afternoon trains to see if my daughter would come in on any of them. I stayed there until I was satisfied all the afternoon trains were in—I judge around four o'clock—and then I went home."

He was undone by the news Dr. Kingsbury gave him. "I judge it was an hour before I could control myself, then I saw my daughter only a few minutes. She was in bed in her room...and she said, 'I am going to die.'

"I tried to encourage her and she said, 'No use, Daddy, I am not going to get well.'"

The sight of her wounds overwhelmed him. He could not stay with her long.

Over the next few days, as they talked again, the story slowly came out. "She called me to her bed and asked me to sit down on the edge of the bed and took hold of my hand and wanted me to stroke her forehead, and she said, 'Daddy, that was the longest trip from Hammond.' She said, 'I was so sick I thought I would die every minute, and I begged and begged them to get me a doctor and they refused that, and I begged them to throw me out at the side of the road that somebody might pick me up.'

"And I asked her then why she had not cried for help, and she said, 'They stopped at the Washington Hotel a while; Stephenson had Shorty, the chauffeur, to call Claude Worley to look after protecting them on their trip.'

"And I said, 'Why didn't you make an outcry?'

"She said, 'Why Daddy, I had no show. Stephenson was on one side and Gentry on the other, both with guns in my side, telling me if I made a noise they would shoot me through. She said, 'I had no show, he told me his word was law.' And she said, 'Daddy, if you can't get the federal authorities, I don't—'"

George Oberholtzer had never seen Madge ill before. She had a light case of flu about two weeks earlier, "about the only illness she had had in her life." She was "rugged and strong.... I don't think there was ever a more healthy looking girl than Madge...."

As soon as he knew Madge's story, Dr. Kingsbury began the known treatments for mercury poisoning. It was a formidable challenge.

Bichloride of mercury is among the most deadly of poisons, a powerful disinfectant. Women of Madge's sisterhood sometimes used it, greatly weakened, as a cleaning douche, as a prophylactic;

it was thought to deter syphilis. In a stronger solution, they used it to induce abortions. Perhaps it was more than chance, then, that made Madge turn to bichloride of mercury to rid herself of the shame of Stephenson's attack. There was a symmetry to her choice: the mercurial Stephenson, slippery as quicksilver; the cleansing bichloride of mercury, stripping her of all remnants of his touch.

But any use of bichloride of mercury carried grave risks. Taken internally, as much as two or three grains could cause death. It corrodes the stomach and bowels, literally eating its victim alive, from the inside out.

It is quickly absorbed into human tissue. Death usually occurs within hours, at most a few days, from as little as two to three grains—unless immediate medical treatment is obtained.

The first life-or-death question is: How much poison has been absorbed? The first key to survival is early treatment to reduce the amount of poison absorbed into tissue.

If the victim lives longer than five days, the poison attacks the kidneys and throws the patient into acute nephritis.

But it was in Madge's favor that she had lived this long. In a patient surviving 12 days, the dead kidney tissue begins to be absorbed and replaced with new tissue. Patients sometimes survive if they can make it to that stage. Each day of life after the twelfth day brightens the chance of survival—if, and only if, no other complications arise.

As the days passed toward the close of March, Madge went into the acute nephritis stage. Dr. Kingsbury could treat her for nephritis; but from the moment he first saw her, he knew it might be too late to arrest the spread and absorption of the poison. He administered the known antidote, a continuous internal flow of alkaline solution to try to counteract the poison. But what corrosive work it had done, and whether that damage was reversible, he could not yet say. She was tremendously ill—but she was still alive. Each day brought fresh hope of her survival.

George Oberholtzer retained Asa Smith "to bring suit or whatever was necessary."

The day after Madge was returned home, Smith got word that Stephenson was about to fly to New York, with an alibi that he had been there all the time and could not have been with Madge.

"I had a legal assistant who grabbed his hat and said, 'Let's go over to Stephenson's office.' And we went right over and walked in and said, 'We want to see Mr. Stephenson.' And sure enough out he came and we told him we were going to sue him. Actually we didn't have any suit planned but that's the way we opened the conversation. But we had him fixed, so he couldn't say he was in New York."

After Smith's visit one evening, a week after she returned home, "I said good bye to her and she said good bye with a voice of great anguish. And the next day when I saw her she said to me, 'When I said good-bye last night I thought it was good-bye.'"

Soon Dr. Kingsbury began to detect that something else was wrong. The wounds were healing, at least externally. He added it all up: the shock, the lack of food or rest, the lack of early treatment, the corrosive tissue damage from the poison, the nephritis. Now the kidneys should be trying to repair the damage. Something else was going on. He called in a battery of specialists, the best in the state, and ordered frequent blood tests. He had Madge's only sibling, a brother working outside Indianapolis, stand by for a possible blood transfusion.

The "something else" was staphylococcus infection, slowly and silently growing beneath the healing surface of Madge's left breast; and beneath her breast, into her lung; and into her blood stream, into her kidneys fighting to reestablish life.

Staphylococci: the most common of germs. They are routinely found in the mouth, and infection can easily follow a human bite.

On the critical twelfth day of Madge's illness, March 28, Dr. Kingsbury ordered a blood test to evaluate her progress. It should show whether the tissue damaged by the poison was regenerating or deteriorating. If the tissue was continuing to die, so would she.

The test results were conclusive. Madge was not getting well. In fact, the rate of deterioration had speeded up. She was getting worse, rapidly.

Early in the evening on March 28, Dr. Kingsbury spoke to Madge, alone. "I told her that she had no chance of recovery, that she was going to die, she had no chance to get well....

"She said, 'That is all right, Doctor, I am ready to die.'

"I said, 'Now I want you to understand it.'

"She said, 'I understand you, Doctor, I believe you, and I am ready to die.... I want to die.'"

Asa Smith and Ermina Moore had completed drafting Madge's story in writing, opening it with these words: "I, Madge Oberholtzer, being in full possession of my mental faculties and conscious that I am about to die, make as my dying declaration the following statements...."

After Dr. Kingsbury had told Madge she could not recover, the group gathered beside her bed: the doctor, Ermina Moore, Asa Smith, and Smith's law associate George Dean, with the draft declaration.

"I read very slowly and very distinctly," Smith said later, "every word, every sentence and every paragraph and every page. At the end of every sentence I stopped and asked her if she affirmed or denied it and whether it was true or not and she interrupted several times in the midst of sentences to say, 'Yes, that is right.' [Or] she would stop me and say, 'No, that is not right,' if I said a certain person had done this; 'No, he didn't.'

"...While I read it to her I made corrections with a fountain pen... in her language."

When Smith finished reading, the doctor propped her up; they took a magazine and laid it against the pillow.

Smith said, "Madge, here is the place to sign.... If it is true you may sign it, if you desire to do so, and if it is not true you will not sign it."

"I will sign it," Madge said, taking the pen.

"Let him." she had told them. "He is the law. He will crush you." Her parents did not know D.C. Stephenson, but she did. He was a man who could give a word to Clyde Worley and secure safe passage through police-patrolled roads, who knew the governor did his bidding, whose money could buy almost any politician. "Without federal authorities," she had said, what hope could there be for help from a local legal system Stephenson controlled?

George Oberholtzer went to one Indianapolis official Stephenson did not control: the Marion County prosecutor, William H. Remy.

Bill Remy was neither paralyzed nor hypnotized by Stephenson and the Ku Klux Klan. Young as he was—"the boy prosecutor"— he had earned his stripes. Remy served several years as deputy prosecutor before the embattled Governor McCray named him prosecutor in late 1923 over Steve's objections.

Remy was a consummate prosecutor. He came to the office from a cultured background, with a superb education and sound skills. He developed cases in maddeningly meticulous detail; he presented them with dispassionate but disarming sincerity.

He was a thoroughbred, a steel greyhound of a fellow, all bone and sinew, without a trace of flab. He had a direct, arresting gaze that livened his lean, schoolboy face beneath the short hair parted down the middle and plastered against his skull.

The Indianapolis Times' reporter, John Niblack, grew to know Remy very well. "Once he had taken hold of a case, he pursued it through thick and thin, like a bloodhound on a warm trail. He had a keen, logical mind, a world of determination.... He hated organized or premeditated crime like the devil hates holy water. He had high ideals for public office, and for crooked politicians and cheating public officials he had only the highest disdain. He was a masterful trial lawyer before a jury. There was none better in the State of Indiana."

Would Bill Remy take on the Grand Dragon? No question. George Oberholtzer filed a sworn criminal complaint against D.C. Stephenson, Earl Gentry, and Earl Klinck. The charges: assault, battery, kidnapping.

The next day, Remy put Madge Oberholtzer's case before a Marion County grand jury.

April 2 a warrant was issued for Stephenson's arrest.

The arresting officers knocked on the Washington Hotel room door and asked the man answering it, "Is Mr. Stephenson in?"

"No," the man answered, "but I am his secretary, Mr. Butler." After some insistent questions, however, "Mr. Butler" admitted, "Yes, I am Mr. Stephenson, what is the racket?"

They said they had a warrant.

"Very well, read it," Steve said. And after they read it: "I am armed; do you want me to disarm?" They did, so he took a 45-caliber automatic from his pocket. He also removed his badge of the Horse Thief Detective Association. Then he said, "Well, I'm used to being framed; this is another frame up."

When he came to the Marion County Courthouse to surrender—
briefly, since he immediately posted his $25,000 bond and the
$5,000 bonds for Klinck and Gentry—Stephenson was met by
reporters.

"[We] finally cornered him in the office of the County
Commissioners, where he was waiting to meet his attorney," Niblack
remembered. They asked if he had any statement.

"I refuse to discuss such trivial matters," Stephenson said—
"airily," as Niblack recalled. "How would you boys like to be fishing
right now and watch a red darter spinning in front of a bass?"

"Yeah, it would be nice," Niblack said. "But what about this charge,
Mr. Stephenson?"

"Nothing to it! Nothing to it! I'll never be indicted."

But Remy's grand jury promptly returned indictments against
all three for assault and battery with intent to commit a criminal
attack, malicious mayhem, kidnapping, and conspiracy to kidnap.

What now, Mr. Stephenson? Niblack asked. "I'll never be tried,"
Stephenson said.

Newspapers across Indiana issued bulletins on Madge's
condition. Some days she seemed to improve, and the papers
reported she was rallying.

Then, on April 14, 1925, thirty days after she went to Stephenson's
house, her temperature shot up to 106. Ten minutes later, Madge
Oberholtzer was dead.

George Oberholtzer filed a new criminal complaint charging
Stephenson, Gentry, and Klinck with murder.

This was no suicide, prosecutor Bill Remy concluded. As he
saw it, Madge had been kidnapped, assaulted so viciously that she

was driven to take poison, and then denied medical remedy by Stephenson. Legal precedent or no, Remy believed Stephenson was responsible for Madge's death. And, Grand Dragon or no, Remy intended to push the case through trial.

But first he had to convince the grand jury. He immediately placed the case before them. His arguments raised some lawyers' eyebrows, but the grand jury agreed. On April 18, the Marion County grand jury indicted Earl Klinck, Earl Gentry, and David Curtis Stephenson for murder.

With Stephenson's indictment in early April 1925, newspapers could finally print the rumors they had been tracking—at least part of them, since libel-cautious editors still held back most of the story. They referred only to possible abduction, poison, and assault.

His indictment was impossible, incredible, one reporter wrote 20 years later. It could not be true. "By a wonderful irony, the leader of organizations sworn to uphold virtue and smite immorality was brought to trial for a crime involving gross moral turpitude; and his victim was described as an innocent girl helpless in his powerful clutches, one who could be regarded as symbolic of Indiana's electorate during Stephenson's reign."

If the newspapers were cautious in telling the more lurid details of the story, the rumor spreaders—including Stephenson's jubilant enemies in the Evans/Bossert Klan—were not.

One of Steve's most effective political tools, The Whispers, took wings, recalled *Indianapolis News* reporter Harold Feightner. "People who first heard them were incredulous. Grown women could not be lured away and attacked in such a fashion. Sadism could not be practiced by the man who stood at the right hand of the Governor. The story must be a fabrication....

"Soon the whole state, which had watched the rise of David

Curtis Stephenson from mysterious obscurity to the head of the Ku
Klux Klan and then to a post of influence in political circles, stood
aghast."

Now the Klan invoked silence lifted from Indiana, in a buzz of
rumors. The only one stony silent was The Old Man.

In late April, warrants were issued to arrest Stephenson, Gentry,
Klinck. This time there would be no option to buy their way out of
the county jail on bail bonds. But this time arresting Stephenson
was not so easy.

First, the embattled Old Man's Irvington mansion caught fire—a
mysterious fire that nearly gutted the place in mid night on April
16, only hours after Madge was buried. Stephenson had fortuitously
taken up residence in the downtown Washington Hotel. Someone
had spread generous amounts of gasoline around before striking the
match to the house Steve said he had just sold.

The fire was the work of his enemies, The Old Man said.

Second, a major problem arose in picking up Stephenson for
his arrest. The Old Man was out of town, reported Sheriff Omer
Hawkins, who was also Stephenson's close associate. It seemed
the trio had left town only moments before the grand jury issued
the indictments; they were fishing on a lake in northern Indiana,
perhaps watching a red darter spinning in front of a bass.

The delay aroused public outcry, particularly in Irvington
among neighbors of both Stephenson and the Oberholtzers. Five
hundred Irvington neighbors held a mass meeting and demanded
immediate prosecution and punishment, "swift and adequate
justice." Feeling was no less high at Butler College, where women
students and teachers passed a resolution of grief at Madge's death.
She was, they said, "a young woman who was highly esteemed and
beloved," and they urged community support for prosecutor Remy

"in his endeavor to bring to justice those who are responsible for the tragedy...."

The three fishermen returned shortly and were arrested at Stephenson's room in Indianapolis' Washington Hotel. Some say he hid in a closet when the four officers arrived.

The Grand Dragon took up a new residence in the Marion County Jail.

Now the case—and Stephenson's future—belonged to the lawyers. He hired the best. They filibustered and maneuvered for five months, all throughout the hot Indiana summer, when—perhaps by sheer coincidence—two burlap bags of Klan records and correspondence were found floating in Indianapolis' White River.

The legal footwork commenced, as one national writer said, "one of the longest and bitterest contests in the history of criminal prosecutions," with knotty issues still debated among attorneys.

Stephenson's lawyers snared the case in delaying tactics, using "every technical procedure known to Indiana practice," first, to prevent or delay the trial; second, to tie prosecutor Remy's hands in every possible way; and third, to move the trial outside Marion County because, they argued, citizens there were too excited and prejudiced to allow an impartial trial.

They filed a summer blizzard of pleas and motions to free the defendants on bail: to impugn the grand jury evidence as, among other things, "ambiguous, duplicitous, indefinite, and vague;" and to quash the indictments. All failed.

Stephenson won, however, on his request for a change of venue. The trial was moved north of Indianapolis, beyond Marion County, to the little town of Noblesville, Indiana, in Hamilton County.

The change of venue moved Stephenson's temporary abode from the Marion County Jail to a small block building behind the handsome Hamilton County Court House. There, in the tiny Noblesville jail, Stephenson languished throughout the months.

Actually, by some reports, he lived rather well there. "Stephenson and his buddies lived in style in the old jail," contended Indianapolis Times' reporter John Niblack, as "guests of a kindly old sheriff who became so attached to Stephenson that he shed tears" when Steve left. Sheriff Charles Gooding "was firmly convinced Stephenson was innocent, believing wholeheartedly D.C.'s vociferous charges, long and loudly repeated, that the whole thing was a gigantic frame-up" by Evans and Bossert. Court Asher later recounted that the sheriff gave Steve the run of the jail, and that Steve had returned the affection by giving Gooding enough money to pay off his home mortgage.

Niblack said Steve had company every night, "sometimes a lovely lady whom he entertained in private." He was showered with gifts—money, books, food, liquor—from his numerous friends, including Klansmen and politicians. The liquor was said to be particularly fine whiskey that had been confiscated by U.S. prohibition agents and stored for safekeeping in Indianapolis' federal building basement.

"The three defendants were never in irons or hand cuffs," Niblack said. "They would amble over every morning for trial, half of the time unaccompanied by any deputy, and sit all day at the defense table unguarded. On adjournment, they would fool around a while and finally go back to jail for supper and the night."

Stephenson wrote furiously in the Noblesville jail. The newspapers reported he was completing a book on "Home Economics." The former Klansman Edgar A. Booth believed The Old Man was writing a kind of memoir: "the most intimate details of his entire political activities in Indiana and elsewhere," so that, in the unlikely event that Steve was not freed, "the manuscript will make its appearance in the shape of a most sensational book, and innumerable persons will curse the day they met David Curtis

Stephenson."

Steve managed to keep his political pots boiling from jail, too. Indiana Senator Sam Ralston was failing fast, and Steve wanted the job either for himself or his friend Arthur Robinson. Of particular interest to Steve was the Indianapolis mayor's contest in the November 1925 elections. The Old Man's favorite was Republican John Duvall, president of the Marion County State Bank and the incumbent Marion County treasurer.

Stephenson may or may not have had the high time in jail that Niblack recalled, but his residency there certainly brought joy to some: specifically, Imperial Wizard Evans and Walter Bossert. They couldn't have had a more fortunate turn of events if they had arranged it themselves—which Steve always contended they did.

If Steve thought he could find a sympathetic community in Noblesville, however, he was dead wrong.

Noblesville: Twenty miles north of Indianapolis, a pleasant town of about 5,000, set amidst bucolic Hamilton County farmlands, centered by the town square and its Civil War red brick courthouse generously iced with milky Indiana limestone.

Noblesville was the veritable heart of Hoosier Klankdom. From the time of the first rumor, the Evans/Bossert Klan worked "day and night" to spread their own poison against Stephenson; their "scandal department" spent at least $100,000 on the venom, Booth wrote later. Their campaign was centered in Noblesville and Hamilton County, from whose citizens the jury would be selected.

"Whispering campaigns were started in which the age of the young woman shrank from twenty eight to fifteen; she had been kept prisoner in Stephenson's house for two weeks; she had undergone daily torture; and in fact, many of the tales were too horrible to hint at here," Booth wrote delicately.

"Seldom a day passed on which some organization of women did not pass a resolution condemning Stephenson," some directly inspired by Evans' poison squads. Public sentiment did not subside; in fact, it grew daily, more and more bitter. After papers printed Madge's declaration, when it was aired at a bail bond hearing in midsummer, public anger exploded.

In August of 1923, shortly after his triumphant Kokomo coronation, Stephenson had made a grand speech near the Noblesville jail. A crowd estimated by some newsmen at 200,000 listened, then cheered for twenty minutes without stopping, while his name—"Steve"—burned against the sky in fiery letters twenty feet tall.

Then his followers did not know his full name. But now, in 1925, they were growing to know it well. And on August 9, 1925, almost two years to the day later, Imperial Wizard Hiram Wesley Evans himself visited Noblesville. Evans held his own rally, outside Steve's cell window, drumming up moral hysteria before a crowd of thousands. In a different time and place, Steve might have been lynched.

In the midst of it all, there appeared from nowhere—or more precisely, Oklahoma—a mysterious woman from Steve's past: his first wife, she who had once been voted the prettiest girl in Oklahoma. Whether Nettie Stephenson was brought by nationwide publicity naming Stephenson or, as Booth contended, by Evans' money, the former Mrs. Stephenson set up headquarters in one of Indianapolis' fine hotels. She demanded support for the child he had abandoned a decade earlier.

As the weeks wore on through a simmering summer and mellow fall, Stephenson's lawyers maneuvered with first one and then another delaying tactic. Their final card was a challenge to the judge. The elected judge of the Hamilton County Circuit Court was Fred E. Hines, "a fair minded man of unimpeachable integrity," as one observer wrote later. But Steve's lawyers filed again for a change of venue, arguing that Hines was prejudiced against the defendants. Judge Hines, following Indiana practice, included in his defense a list of three alternate judges. Prosecuting attorney Bill Remy struck one name; Steve's lawyers struck another. The remaining name was the Honorable Will M. Sparks, the elected circuit judge of Indiana's Rush County.

Judge Sparks was "a jurist above reproach, and an able lawyer," Niblack wrote later.

Sparks was in many ways an interesting choice. Born in 1872, the son of a physician, Sparks was from Rushville, where he was a close friend and political ally of Rushville's Senator James E. Watson. Sparks practiced law with Watson's former law partner—until 1901, when Sparks entered into Republican politics, serving in the Indiana legislature until 1910. He was first elected circuit judge in 1914.

In part because of Judge Sparks' ties with Watson, Steve forever claimed that Judge Sparks was a Klansman, aligned with Hiram Wesley Evans to destroy The Old Man. But Sparks' peers gave him high marks and said he always opposed the Klan.

Now Stephenson's lawyers had played out their hand in delaying tactics, as the fall days faded into what looked like an early winter.

On Monday, October 12, 1925, the trial was scheduled to begin.

What now, Mr. Stephenson? Niblack asked.

"I'll never be convicted," The Old Man said.

PART III

17
TWELVE TALISMEN

Monday, October 12, 1925
Noblesville, Indiana

Came now the lawyers and the press, through the cold and misty Monday morning, marching up the courthouse steps. They came in little packs and coveys: watched and watchers, preening, posing, tense or teasing; playing roles in such a drama as for most came only once in their lives.

As the trial opened, Indianans watched with high expectations. Notwithstanding studied grimness, many watched for pure entertainment, of a kind that was rarely available in Noblesville or elsewhere, in an age when court trials, religious revivals, basketball games—and for some, Klan doings—offered the height of excitement.

The Stephenson case dominated front pages of Hoosier and

American newspapers for months. For reporters, the trial was a bonanza, a chance to make a name, a roller coaster of adrenaline highs and bootleg whiskey lows.

Local and national, the cream of the news-writing crop came to Noblesville for the big event—some fresh from another reporters' heaven in the tiny town of Dayton, Tennessee. There, only weeks before, Clarence Darrow had made a monkey of the famed fundamentalist orator William Jennings Bryan, who died, heartbroken, only six days after the Scopes evolution trial. It was a tough summer for fundamentalists: first David Curtis Stephenson's indictment for murder, then Darrow's indictment of the literal Genesis.

Indianapolis Times' reporter John Niblack drove up to Noblesville every day for Stephenson's trial, in his little 1919 Model T Ford coupe with a hand crank starter and no windshield wiper. He brought his co-assigned reporter, Tubby Toms. In they came, the spare "Nibby" Niblack and the rotund "Tubby" Toms, up the classic marble staircase of the old Noblesville courthouse with its darkened baroque wood railings, across the boot-scuffed floors of black and white checkerboard marble blocks, to the upstairs circuit courtroom.

Together, Niblack and Toms produced sensational copy on the trial. Nearly every day for a month, they churned out story after story, sometimes entire newsprint pages of stories, under conditions that were marginal to impossible.

Since the *Times* was an afternoon newspaper, they had to leave the court at somewhere before noon each day to file their stories, which they had no time to write. They had to dictate them off the tops of their heads, to rewriters clanking out each word on manual typewriters, thence to linotypes and hot-type and clanging presses, and to the streets within hours. After dictating, the reporters would dash back to the court to pick up the rest of the day's events; sometimes to run back and dictate more pieces or dramatic bulletins, in a day when newspapers printed extra editions to flash the most current news to readers who had few or no other sources of news.

"We would dictate," Niblack remembered later, "via telephone, from two to fourteen columns a day from the press room behind the courtroom." He was charitable to call it a press room. It was a converted public toilet, perhaps 10-by-20-feet in size, a teeming pit of cutthroat competitive news hounds.

Niblack had an edge in court reporting because he had just graduated from night law school. He and the other reporters set down in "hot history" a record of the trial that would mold Indiana and American opinion about Stephenson and the Ku Klux Klan. Their record would become even more valuable in later years, after significant court records disappeared.

Niblack and Toms were certainly not the big press guns there. They were no more than gnats to the big guys: Horace M. Coats with the *Indianapolis Star*; Walter "Wally" Watson from the *Indianapolis News*; and, among many other heavyweights, two *Chicago Hearst* newspaper reporters named Rueful and Bensinger whose antics were immortalized later in the classic play, "The Front Page."

And the lawyers: each side had a battery of them. Stephenson had at least seven; the number seemed to change daily. The State of Indiana had five. They were a colorful crew, lining up behind the ornate carved rail in the imposing circuit court with its dark aged wood paneling, time worn seats, and ornamental bookcases.

The clear standout of the group was Steve's star attorney, the Honorable Ephraim Inman of Indianapolis. "Eph" Inman had a mane of silver hair and a tongue to match. He stood well over six feet tall, with an air of invulnerable assurance. Eph was more than handsome; he was beautiful; he could have played the star lawyer in any movie. But he was also a shrewd judge of human nature and endlessly resourceful, with captivating flair. He had gained fame in the Gay Nineties because he could sway the most recalcitrant jury; now in his golden years, he was a patrician orator who was the most formidable of Hoosier attorneys.

Nearly matching Eph Inman in ability, if not in style, was Floyd Christian of Noblesville. Inman and Christian were backed up in the defense corner by a clever attorney, Ira W. Holmes, and four supporting lawyers: Ralph Waltz, Alfred F. Corwin, Ralph E. Johnson, and John Kiplinger. Other bit part attorneys floated in and out of Steve's defense lineup, but the Stephenson show was clearly dominated by The Old Man's old man, Eph Inman.

The cast on the state's side was unquestionably more modest, at least in number and dazzle. Heading up the list were young Bill Remy and Justin A. Roberts, prosecuting attorneys for Marion and Hamilton Counties, respectively. They were assisted by Charles E. Cox, Ralph Kane, and Thomas Kane.

Judge Cox was 65, a former chief justice of the state Supreme Court and president of the Indianapolis Bar; more a legal scholar than a showman; painstakingly thorough; a skilled examiner of witnesses. George Oberholtzer had persuaded Cox to leave retirement and act as a special prosecuting assistant to Remy. Madge's father had pledged what fortune he had to pay Cox, who would take the lead for the prosecution in cross examination and presentation of the key medical evidence.

Ralph Kane also had an important role: to speak directly to the jury chosen from Hamilton County, where he grew up on a farm. Kane was a bright but unpretentious lawyer, honest, likable, hot tempered, articulate in common language.

Asa Smith worked behind the scenes, because he would be called to testify about the dying declaration. He bore scars of World War service, and his demeanor was uneven—now brilliant, now suspicious. He was devoted to the case.

Madge's father entered alone and sat down silently behind the state's attorneys. The reporters watched George Oberholtzer closely. "Oberholtzer," Niblack reported, "had no vengeful look in his face..., only the sad, worn expression." Later, after Stephenson said the entire affair was an Evans/Bossert frump, reporters asked Oberholtzer if the Klan wars figured in his case. "Neither faction of the Klan is mixed up in this," Oberholtzer said. "I am going through with this uphill fight for the sake of humanity—for the sake of other fathers and their daughters."

The opening day crowd, if crowd it could be called, was remarkably small for such a notorious case. Spectators were mostly a few Indianapolis people and a few Noblesville natives.

There were noticeable absences behind the rail. Matilda Oberholtzer was at home, where a reporter found her for an agonizing interview, betraying raw pain. Another noteworthy absentee was Stephenson's faithful secretary, Fred Butler, who had always had a cheerful word in the tightest situation. When Stephenson was arrested the first time, Butler refused to panic. "We've always landed on our feet, haven't we?" Butler said cheerfully. But when the charge was changed to murder, Butler apparently decided to land on his own two feet and use them to leave the state. It was rumored that he had entered the real estate business in Florida. Joseph "Shorty" De Friese, Steve's driver, and Marian Darr, his former personal secretary, had similarly vanished.

The most glaring absence was Stephenson's. He was among the missing until just before 9 a.m. when he strolled in, fashionably late and jovial, with Sheriff Charles Gooding and the two Earls, Klinck and Gentry. In high spirits, The Old Man posed for newspaper photographers but refused comment when asked what he thought about the proceedings: "I have nothing whatsoever to say."

One of the photos lined up Steve with the Earls on either side. They looked like three smiling brothers in their similar snap brimmed hats, fresh starched shirts, dark ties, bankers' dark suits, and conservative vests buttoned up chest high. Only Gentry's omnipresent cigar stood out to distinguish individuals among the trio, who from all appearances might have been pictured just after they heard they had made a killing on Wall Street.

Steve seemed to have put on a bit of weight in jail. Sheriff Gooding's wife was reputed to be a fine and generous cook. With an air of studied indifference that he seldom abandoned throughout the trial, Steve moved up the aisle to a chair behind his attorneys, midway between the witness stand and jury box. He nodded at whispered comments from his attorneys, made an airy wisecrack, cupped his chin in his hand, and settled in to listen with a fair degree of patience, considering that he clearly had more important things to do. From his air, he might have been presiding, rather than on trial. At center stage, he nonetheless appeared to be watching his drama from some far distance.

On one wall of the courtroom was a great clock, of the darkest fine wood, as tall as a man. In moments of courtroom silence, the clock punctuated the stillness with a somber tock that a fanciful listener could hear ticking away the seconds of life. Precisely at the instant that the stately clock's hand reached 9 a.m., the bailiff barked: "All rise!" And with the entrance of the Honorable Will M. Sparks—fifty-ish, bespectacled, with a thoughtful face—the Hamilton County Circuit Court was now in session.

Thus the trial began, the State of Indiana versus David Curtis Stephenson, in the matter of the death of Madge Oberholtzer, the young woman from Irvington whose prematurely graying chestnut hair had been tied back with a simple black ribbon, who had left home late on a Sunday night six months before, without a hat.

Jury selection was the first critical hurdle for each side. Each
had to wrest its best possible mix of mentalities from among the
Hamilton County candidates. Steve's fate literally would be up to
those twelve men—and only men, since no women had ever served
on a jury in the Hamilton County Court House which lacked "proper
accommodations" for women jurors. The trial began with a fight
between the lawyers over who should begin questioning potential
jurors. On each point, it was important to both sides to strive for
advantage, such as the right to have the ultimate final question. Judge
Sparks ruled that the state should open.

The process was like an intricate game of table top war, with
hundreds of human pieces and life or death odds. Eph Inman
conducted the interrogations for Stephenson; the folksy Hamilton
County lawyer Ralph Kane, for the state. They worked at a fever pitch
of intellectual combat, day after day.

The jury selection opened with twelve men—"talismen," potential
jurors—seated in the jury box and another 100 standing by. They ran
through the first 100 talisman, and Judge Sparks convened another
100, then another, then another; but still the jury selection process
was deadlocked on the horns of the two sparring attorneys.

The game of wits had precise rules: first Kane questioned each
individual talisman, discarded most, questioned another, until the
state tentatively accepted a full jury box of twelve. The ball then
passed to Inman, who questioned and discarded until the defense
tentatively accepted its full jury box of twelve. Then the ball went
back to the state, then back to the defense. Only when twelve had
been accepted and thus passed through four rounds could the jury be
considered final. But even then, if the defense—in the role of the last
player—challenged even one talisman, the game opened up again.
Each side began the game with a maximum of twenty "preemptory
challenges" to draw down and an unlimited number of challenges
for cause, so long as Judge Sparks agreed. In addition, Sparks could

excuse jurors who convinced him service was an undue burden, such as family illness in the smallpox epidemic that swept through Hamilton County during the trial.

Thus it went for days: question, challenge, question, challenge; and men of Hamilton County—predominately farmers—were discarded by both sides like chaff. Niblack and the other reporters eagerly logged each question, searching for clues to the strategies each side would follow in the game. They also watched for other clues: to the personalities of the attorneys, the judges, the jurors, and the defendants.

The morning of the first day gave Niblack his first important clue.

Kane, for the state: "The fact that one of the defendants might be a man of social or political influence and a man of some wealth or reputed wealth would not have any influence on your decision, would it?"

Talisman: "If a man violates the law, he ought to be punished, regardless of his former political or social prominence or wealth." It was the right answer, from Kane's point of view. On that question, the talisman tentatively passed the state's scrutiny.

Answered another: "I believe in the laws, all alike, but I don't believe in all the laws, quite." A curious answer. Kane pressed for clarification. "Well," said the talisman, "I don't believe in capital punishment."

Kane: "You believe the crime of murder should be prohibited by law?"

Talisman: "Yes."

Kane: "If the man is guilty of murder he ought to be punished, you believe?"

Talisman: "Yes, but I never believed in capital punishment."

Kane: "Your honor, we move to excuse this man for cause."

Stephenson suddenly sat up straight, losing momentarily his pose of boredom. Could it be?

Yes. As the day wore on, the state interrogated every talisman on the death penalty and challenged those who said they didn't believe in it. Before the first day was out, it was obvious: Remy intended to seek the death penalty. He was aiming to put David Curtis Stephenson to death in the electric chair.

Judge Sparks was obviously growing weary of what he called the "cross word puzzles" of jury non-selection.

Were they Klan members? Would they be guided by the principle of reasonable doubt?—a point that gave many talismen trouble until one explained it succinctly: "Well, now, if the witness up there proves them guilty, they're guilty, but if the witnesses don't prove them guilty, they hain't guilty." Did they have any ties to anybody involved in the case? The questions went on and on, veering into allegations from both sides that various persons had tried to tamper with the jury and influence potential jurors.

As the tedious days of jury selection wore on, fatigue and frustration began to fray the salvages of some temperaments. Fist fights nearly broke out twice between the attorneys, but they were quickly squelched by Judge Sparks, who ruled his court with a firm hand. The only person showing no sign of wear was the one working hardest, Miss Maude T. Dale, official reporter of the Hamilton County Circuit Court, who had already filled four 500-page books with her methodical shorthand record of the case.

For a trial centered on human bites, there was a remarkable amount of chewing going on in the courtroom. Stephenson, Klinck, and Gentry chewed gum, "their jaws moving up and down in unison," Niblack wrote. George Oberholtzer sat alone, either in a far corner or behind the state attorneys, chewing his fingernails. And jurors whiled away the days by chewing tobacco, in the company of that indispensable courthouse artifact, the brass spittoon.

Stephenson appeared every day in a different suit, flawlessly tailored and freshly pressed. Sometimes he received and dispatched mysterious messages by couriers to the outside world. The world beyond the courtroom continued to spin, as candidates battled toward the November 3 election that was critical to Steve's political strategies. The Indiana Supreme Court outlawed vigilante searches for suspected liquor without search warrants—a disappointing setback for Steve's Horse Thief Detective Association, severely curtailing reformers' midnight raids.

Senator Ralston died, opening up the vacancy Steve had hoped to fill.

But The Old Man's ladder to the White House was lost in the Noblesville jail. Governor Jackson could hardly appoint Steve while he had a murder charge hanging over him. So Jackson did the next best thing: he named Steve's choice, a callow fellow named Arthur Robinson. A Klan attorney, Robinson was the butt of jokes in the nation's press because of his known KKK ties.

But no news was bigger than the continuing drama in the Noblesville courthouse. In jury selection, the hardest problem for the defense was that most talismen had already formed an opinion on the case, usually from news stories written after the summer hearing when Steve tried to get freed on bail bond. The talismen who indicated their opinion said they had already decided the defendants were guilty, after reading Madge's dying declaration in the newspapers.

Inman, for the defense: "Have you talked about this case?"

Talisman: "Oh, yes, so much I've sort of gotten disgusted with it."

Inman: "Have you formed an opinion on whether the defendants are guilty or not guilty?"

Talisman: "No man, I don't believe, with a normal mentality, but would form some sort of an opinion from reading this case in the newspapers."

Before long, the talismen, listening to questions put to those before them, grew canny. When Kane neglected to ask one about capital punishment, he volunteered: "What about this capital punishment thing? I'm opposed to it."

Soon an amazing number of fundamentalist farmers from Hamilton County, Indiana, expressed vehement opposition to capital punishment; and even more had formed adamant opinions on the case. It became apparent, Niblack wrote, that they had learned which answers would get them thrown off the jury, and they were eager to volunteer those answers.

"A man would be a fool to sit on that jury," one talisman told Niblack after he succeeded in getting himself rejected for jury duty. "Between Stephenson's friends and the rest of the community, he would have a _____ of a time, no matter what the verdict might be."

"We are spending too much time here, gentlemen," Judge Sparks announced abruptly on Monday, October 26, after every conceivable delay from smallpox to winter wheat. "After this, there'll be no gun fire, no cross questioning after the court rules on a challenge."

On Wednesday, October 28—the twelfth day of the interminable poker game of jury selection—both sides abruptly agreed on a jury of 10 farmers, one truck driver, and one businessman.

Observers could not discern that the twelve selected were manifestly different from the 268 others who had been called and excused or discarded.

Before jurors could be sworn in, Steve's attorneys moved quickly to try to tie Prosecutor Remy's hands. The court should rule, the defense said, that prosecutors must choose which of the four counts of the indictment would go to trial. Judge Sparks overruled the defense question without comment, giving Steve his first major setback of the trial. Now the jury could return any one of four verdicts: not guilty;

or, if guilty, a 2- to 21-year prison term, life imprisonment, or death.

The jury was swiftly sworn in by Judge Sparks, who lectured jurors before adjourning for the night.

"I know there are men on this jury who are hardly in a position to serve," Sparks said. "I know some of you would like to be relieved of the duty, but it just can't be done. I don't want to be here any more than you do. But it is a sense of duty. I have sickness at home and am in as bad condition as you are. But the courts have to go on. I am not asking one of you to do any thing that I am not doing myself."

Ten farmers, a businessman, a truck driver. The newly formed jurors lined up for newspaper photographers on the courthouse steps, each in his bulky winter topcoat, each holding his hat in his left hand; and in the jury box, each in his dark Sunday-go-to-meeting suit, each with his hands folded demurely on crossed knees.

They were a somber crew, betraying not a wisp of a smile, as if they took soberly Judge Sparks' delegation to them of the burden of determining Justice, on behalf of the State of Indiana and the human race. It would be greatest adventure of their lives.

They were family men, by and large; men close to the soil, but those faces were not those of yokels. They could have been a men's church choir or an investment klatch at the Indianapolis Exchange Club, awaiting cigarettes and scotch. In a day when prosperity was rising for most—except the farmer—their faces betrayed more quiet concern than agrarian anger.

By name, they were:

Ben F. Clark, 52, farmer, married, no children.

L.H. Linsmyer, 37, manager of Indiana Gas Company in Noblesville, married, with a son, 2, and a daughter, 7.

Harley Huffman, 30, Clarksville truck driver, married, with a son, 6.

Clyde Clark, 45, farmer, married; son, 11.

William Lehr, 51, farmer, married with a daughter, 16.

Zeno E. Mundy, 35, farmer, married with five children.

William A. Johnson, 57, farmer.

W. O. Inman, 50, farmer.

Leotis Neese, 50, farmer, married, two sons, one daughter.

Ralph Finley, 34, farmer, married, no children.

Samuel Gerrard, 49, farmer, married, five children.

Cash Applegate, 46, farmer, married, son and daughter.

Were they Klansmen? Who could say? Only another member of the Klan, someone such as The Old Man. Attorneys queried most about membership in any "secret society." But Klan ethics allowed a member to "resign" at the moment he was swearing he did not belong, then be instantly reinstated after the word "no" had fallen from his lips.

Klansmen or no, most were shaped by strong Indiana fundamentalism, including faith in temperance and the sanctity of womanhood. Before them was the man who epitomized such fundamentals, the man who had pledged not only to clean up those lawless towns but to clean up the very Klan itself.

Twelve Indiana men, of solid stock. With their swearing in, the trial's 13th day ended, and the heart of the trial began.

The following day would begin with an opening statement by Charles Cox, for the state, followed by the first witness. The defense held its opening statement until the state completed its case, thereby continuing to withhold any clue of the defense strategy—whether Steve's lawyers would try to offer some alibi or confront the murder charge head on.

Now the preliminaries were finally over. Now the courtroom could fill and overflow, and the trial could begin in earnest on Thursday, October 29, 1925, as temperatures plunged to record lows, snow dusted across Indianapolis, and the roads to Noblesville were covered by glare ice. It looked like an early winter was closing in on

Indiana, as a northern cold front blew across the Midwest and edged, prematurely, far into the South.

18
JEKYLL AND HYDE

Thursday, October 29, 1925
Noblesville, Indiana

When state's attorney Charles Cox—"Judge Cox," as the reporters called him respectfully—walked forward to begin his opening statement, he was cut short by a fiery objection from defense attorney Ira A. Holmes.

"Each of the defendants objects to the opening statement being made by anyone but the prosecutor," Holmes said.

"Overruled," said presiding Judge Sparks.

"Exception," said Holmes.

Another defense attorney, Floyd Christian, interrupted again, asking that Miss Maude Dale, the court reporter, take notes on Cox's opening statement.

"I really see no need for this," said Judge Sparks. "She's been working pretty hard. However, if there be any objection, we shall call her and it will be taken," Judge Sparks said.

Judge Cox began his opening statement by asking for a copy of the indictment. The bailiff produced it while Cox read, slowly and deliberately, from the Indiana statutes defining murder and homicide. He heavily accented the word "death," while Stephenson busied himself taking notes.

The prosecution's case did not rest on a new definition of murder, but merely "a crystallization of the law for all time," Cox said.

Cox read the April 18 indictment, charging that the three murdered Madge Oberholtzer by kidnapping her, assaulting her so viciously that she was driven to take poison, and denying her medical care for the wounds and poison that caused her death.

"Each count of this indictment constitutes a good lawful charge of murder," Cox said. "To each of these counts, the defendants have pleaded not guilty. The state must prove the material element of some one of these counts beyond a reasonable doubt."

"Objection," interrupted Holmes, for the defense. Cox was "making an argument of the case in the opening statement," Holmes said.

"Of course, the gentleman is only stating a theory of his," Judge Sparks said. "If he begins to argue, we'll stop him."

"Exception," said Holmes.

"The principal witness for the state," said Cox, "will be Madge Oberholtzer, the dead victim of the foulest murder that ever stained the history of our state. Madge Oberholtzer, clean of soul, but with her bruised, mangled, poisoned and ravaged body, standing by her grave's edge with the shadowy wings of the dark angel over her, will tell you, so far as possible in the circumstances, the story of her entrapment, of her being drugged, kidnapped, assaulted, beaten, lacerated with beastly fangs, ravished, and finally, as the culmination of indignities and brutalities unheard of in a civilized community before, how she was forced, by the loss of all a good woman holds most dear, to take the deadly poison which contributed to her untimely and cruel death."

Women spectators gasped, and Sheriff Charles Gooding for the first time placed himself behind the defendants, apparently not to control them but rather to protect them.

"She will tell you," Cox continued, "as nearly as, with a tortured soul, a pain wracked body, and a distracted mind, she could, of the horrors of a night drive in an automobile from Hammond, 190 miles; of help refused her; of her imprisonment, not in Stephenson's palatial home, but in his garage; and finally of being carried to her home at a time when her distracted father and mother were away hunting for some trace of her, by one of the defendants, and laid broken and dying down on her own bed."

George Oberholtzer lowered his head and wiped away tears with a closed fist.

"Gentlemen of the jury, the evidence will show that Madge Oberholtzer sprung from the soil of Indiana. Here she first saw the light of day. Here her childhood was passed; and here she grew to womanhood; here she was educated; here she lived an ambitious, a useful and courageous life.... 'None knew her but to love her. None named her but to praise.'"

Cox turned his attention to Stephenson, whose eyes were fixed upon the notepad on his knee, where his pen moved rapidly.

"The evidence will show, gentlemen of the jury, that the defendant Stephenson was born in the State of Texas; that he has drifted to many parts of the country and undergone many and varied experiences; that he drifted into Indiana some four years ago and took up his abode at Evansville; that quickly he rose to a position of great affluence, and social and political power.

"The evidence will show that Stephenson has a double personality," said Cox, tossing his iron gray hair and gazing toward Stephenson within his circle of attorneys. "That on one side of him was the magnetic, sympathetic, cultured, attractive man of the world. He was an impassioned orator. Something about him enabled him to attract and to dominate better men and good women.

"The evidence will show that there was another side of him, and that side shows him to be a violator of the law, to be a drunkard, a persistent seducer and destroyer of women's chastity."

"Objection," shouted Holmes for the defense, jumping to his feet. "The defendant objects to any statement about whether he is a drunkard or whether he came to Indiana and rose to great affluence and political power...."

Mr. Cox could proceed with his theories, Judge Sparks said gently.

Now Eph Inman rose to his feet, arguing the defense case with Judge Sparks. "We have reached a very important point in this case, your honor," Inman said. Cox was using his opening statement to make wild charges without proof, Inman said. Cox could not prove any of his allegations about dual personalities or other personal attacks, Inman said.

"Do you want the jury out of the room?"

"Yes," said Inman.

But Sparks yielded. "I think you'd better leave that out of your statement," he told Cox. "I can't control your statement of your theories, if you make it in good faith, but I can control the admission of evidence."

"Our evidence will show," Cox continued, "that this palatial house of Stephenson had a double character—"

"Objection," cried Holmes.

"Overruled," said Judge Sparks. "Such evidence may explain why Miss Oberholtzer went there."

"Exception."

David Curtis Stephenson was a classic case of a double personality, a "Dr. Jekyll and Mr. Hyde," Cox said, growing more impassioned.

"The evidence will show, gentlemen, that Stephenson installed himself, more than a year ago, in a palatial home in Irvington; that this house—it was not a home—had a double character like its master.

"There, on occasions, were gathered as his guests, people of character and high repute and all was propriety and decorum; and on other occasions others who were different were gathered there, and all was drinking and lascivious debauch. To this house upon occasion virgin girls and good women were lured to be entrapped and debauched."

The Irvington mansion of David Curtis Stephenson was like a spider's web, Cox cried in ringing tones, and Stephenson was the preying, poisonous, murdering spider.

"This is a case of vast importance," in which more than the defendants were on trial, Cox said. Also on trial was the law itself—and justice. The outcome of the case would determine whether the law "is sufficient to protect the sanctity of the home and of womanhood," and whether the law could be applied equally to one of the most powerful men in the state, "a man who said over and over again, 'I am the law in Indiana,'" Judge Cox said.

He paused and took a deep breath that could be heard through the hushed courtroom. In the tense, listening silence, the tick-tock of the stately wall clock was loud and somber.

"It will appear from the evidence, gentlemen of the jury, that on the night of the Sabbath of March the 15th of this year, the defendants, all of them, with minds inflamed to lustful passion by strong drink, planned in that house the entrapment and soul destruction of Madge Oberholtzer."

Madge's story alone, said Cox, was enough to "demand the black brand 'Guilty' on the foreheads of these defendants, but the state will give you more, far more, than her story. She will be supported and corroborated by creditable witnesses, unassailable facts, and inescapable inferences, until there can rest in no one's mind the reasonable doubt of the guilt of these defendants."

A muffled shuffle, as spectators shifted and craned their necks to watch the defendants.

"Her statement will show that she was taken to the Washington Hotel where railroad tickets were procured, and it will be corroborated by an employee of the Washington Hotel.

"She tells you that she was taken to the Union Station, and it will be shown to you that Stephenson and Gentry sat on either side of her with guns in their hand. She will tell you that she was taken to the drawing room of a Monon pullman car and that this man Stephenson said to the porter, 'You don't seem to like us very well.'

"This man, Gentry—" At the mention of his name, Gentry started and sat up rigidly. Cox pointed a finger at Gentry, who locked his eyes on Cox. "This man, Gentry, remained in that compartment all the time until Hammond was reached. She will tell you that they threw her in the lower berth and undressed her. She will tell you that they took her off the train at Hammond and took her to a hotel room."

Stephenson's eyes never left his notes, and his expression did not change. The courtroom was absolutely silent, with every inhabitant listening intently.

Cox waved his arm toward Stephenson. "We will show that these fiends, shut up in that drawing room with Madge Oberholtzer, wounded her from her cheeks to her ankles until her very blood flowed.

"That this man, Gentry! Gentry!—When this girl lay on her bed in the hotel at Hammond, instead of calling a woman, this man Gentry—Gentry! mind you—laved her wounds with witch hazel the next morning, because of the shame and disgrace of it.

"They took her to Indianapolis, kept her in Stephenson's garage, begging for help, until Tuesday morning about 11 o'clock when this man, this man Klinck..." Cox advanced on the defense table and thrust his arm toward Klinck, who did not blink. "This Klinck took her home in Stephenson's automobile and carried her into the house....

"The story will be corroborated by people from the Indiana hotels where this man Stephenson wrote on the register, 'W.D. Morgan and wife, Franklin, Ind.,' and this man Gentry wrote 'Earl Gentry, Indianapolis.'"

Now Cox threw aside his notes and stalked to the front of the jury box. "There is one thing I have not said that I want to say now," he said. "The evidence will prove incontrovertibly that part of these marks inflicted on Madge Oberholtzer by these fiends—by teeth, gentlemen, by teeth—became infected and caused blood poison in their victim."

Tears were now running in uncontrolled rivulets down George Oberholtzer's face. Steve had turned pale and was staring down with a worried air, as if he had just realized that this was a real murder trial and that he was the defendant.

Cox paced deliberately before the jury box. "The evidence will show that parts of the body of Madge Oberholtzer were lacerated, bruised in such a condition to leave an imprint; that these two defendants, Stephenson and Gentry, attacked her, both of them!" He cast his arm toward the pair.

After a lengthy pause to let his ringing rhetoric sink home, Cox spoke gently of Asa Smith, the Oberholtzers' attorney who wrote down Madge's dying declaration. Smith was young, a veteran afflicted by shellshock. He had broken down and become confused at the bail bond hearing, and Cox apparently wanted to bolster Smith's credibility in advance, anticipating attack on the man who should be the state's star witness.

"Asa Smith," said Cox, "was bred from the blood of Hamilton County. He volunteered as a Marine and fought as a private at the battle of Belleau Woods. He was wounded. He was burned with mustard gas. He bears the marks today. He was in the hospital three months blind. I tell you this because he will be a witness. He cannot be discredited unless you discredit the American flag."

In all, Cox spoke 85 minutes, closing by speaking softly to jurors. "I haven't told you details. I have just given you a brief outline of what the state expects to prove. I have tried to be fair."

Then center stage was occupied by Prosecutor Bill Remy, who began the process of introducing evidence and calling witnesses. The first on the stand was Madge's mother, Matilda Oberholtzer.

Matilda Oberholtzer came to the witness stand haltingly, with her head bowed, reluctantly leaving her seat beside her husband George and their son Marshall.

She was dressed in deep mourning: black dress, hat, shoes. But beyond the clothes, she wore the distracted air of a woman nearly crazed by grief, frazzled, worn.

Prosecutor Bill Remy gently helped her to the witness chair. "You may state your name," he said.

"Mrs. George Oberholtzer," she said, in a voice too low to be heard beyond the bench.

"Where do you live?"

"5802 University Avenue." The clock was louder than her words.

"How long have you lived there?"

Judge Sparks asked her to speak a little louder so she could be heard by the jury.

She tried to muster more force. "About 23 years."

"What relation did you sustain to Madge Oberholtzer during her life?"

Now the voice was gone entirely. She opened her mouth, but no words would come. She twisted a handkerchief, tried again and again. Finally in a shaky voice: "I'm her mother."

"Was she married or unmarried?"

"Unmarried."

"Do you recall an evening in March, about the fifteenth of March, when she left home—where were you?"

"I was at home. I had been sick."

"State whether or not Madge had been away during that afternoon?"

"Yes."

"What time did she arrive at home that evening?"

"Between 9 and 10."

Each answer was preceded by the agonizing search for her voice, the twisted handkerchief. Somewhere in the room, a moving chair squeaked periodically, in a kind of rhythm, out of sync with the wall clock.

"Was there a telephone message for her?"

"Objection!" boomed Floyd Christian, for the defense.

"Overruled."

"Exception."

The testimony established its own rhythm: a crisp question from Remy. The struggle for a fragment of an answer. The interrupting staccato objection. The judge's response, like a door slamming: "Overruled." The defense rejoinder, like a kick at the door: "Exception." The pattern continued throughout the day like a refrain.

"When she left home, did she have a hat on?"

"No, just a coat."

"After you related to her upstairs the contents of the message, what did she do?"

"She went downstairs to the front door." A single tear traced slowly down Matilda's right cheek.

"Tell what you heard or saw."

"I heard the voice at the front door—it was a man's voice. I heard the door close, and she left. I went to the window and looked out, and I felt that I should "

"Objection!"

"Don't tell what you felt," Judge Sparks said.

"I looked out of the window and saw her and a man—a large man—cross the street to the other sidewalk."

"When did you next see her?

Now the tears had became a flood, and Prosecutor Remy involuntarily reached out a hand to steady her, for it appeared she might fall from the witness chair. She could not answer for some time, and the sound of her weeping was louder than any answer she had given thus far.

"...Tuesday afternoon...."

"Who was present in the house with you the next morning?"

"Mrs. Shultz and Dr. Kingsbury and Nurse Spratley."

"Where was Madge when you saw her?"

Matilda folded and unfolded the handkerchief against her knee. "Upstairs, in her room, on the bed."

"Mrs. Oberholtzer, just what was your daughter's condition and appearance when you saw her?"

"Oh—"

She bowed her head, and it appeared she would fall forward.

"Just take your time," Judge Sparks said softly.

Matilda covered her eyes with her handkerchief and mumbled, "She was torn and bruised and—and her breasts had open wounds all over."

"Describe the wounds as you saw them."

"Round bruises on her cheeks and both sides of her face."

Judge Sparks, no more than two yards from Matilda, could not hear her, and asked the court reporter to read her answer back. The reporter read: "Her face on both sides was bruised—on this side was a round bruise, kind of jagged like." She pointed to her right cheek.

"Describe the bruise itself."

"A bruise on the right side of the face with an imprint around it."

"Where else were there bruises?"

"All up and down her body to her ankles."

Remy tried to shift the questioning to a more neutral territory, apparently sensing that Matilda was near collapse. "Do you recall that telephone number you gave her that evening when she returned?"

"Irvington 0492."

"Do you know whose number it was?"

"Where Madge went."

Floyd Christian, for the defense, leaped to his feet and lunged forward. "Objection!"

"Oh, no," said Judge Sparks. "If you looked in the telephone book and found the number and name, it would be admissible."

"But it wasn't in the book—but one of the men—"

Five defense attorneys interrupted her with objections.

"Sustained."

Remy passed the witness to the defense. Eph Inman proceeded gingerly, in what the reporter John Niblack described as a "suave and grilling cross examination." Mrs. Oberholtzer had won the obvious sympathy of the jury and the court, and they would resent any mishandling on the part of the defense. Inman tried to lure Matilda into admissions about Madge's past, but he was sternly overruled at each turn by Judge Sparks, who said her past life had nothing to do with the case at hand.

Inman did succeed in bringing out that Madge had been out with a young man, George Watson, the afternoon and evening of Sunday, March 15.

"Who is George Watson?" Inman asked.

"That's about all I know," Matilda Oberholtzer said. "I met him in the parlor that night, and then I went upstairs to bed."

"Did he come in the house?"

"Yes. He stayed a short time. I met him and excused myself and went upstairs. A short time later, Madge came up. She took off her hat."

"When your daughter came home was she wearing this same velvet dress, same hat and same clothes?"

"She was."

"What sort of hat was that?"

"A little black silk hat." Now the sobs began again. She was stuttering.

"How long before they came home did you get those telephone calls?"

"She got two early in the afternoon and two about 7 o'clock." Matilda tried to dry her eyes with the drenched handkerchief, stabbing at them absently.

"You gave her the telephone number when she and Mr. Watson came in the room?"

"Yes, and then I went upstairs." Madge took off her hat and gloves, her mother recalled, and then heard the doorbell ring and went downstairs to answer. "I never saw her anymore. I watched her walk away with a large man. They went across the corner of University and Dewey Avenues and went on west."

"Your daughter didn't have a hat on?"

"No."

"Was there a light before your house, Mrs. Oberholtzer?"

"Yes, a street lamp, right on the corner, and another on down." Matilda recalled that she had awakened the next morning about 6 o'clock to find that Madge had never returned.

"Your daughter never came back until Tuesday?"

"No—no—she didn't." Matilda was stuttering again.

"Did your daughter at one time work for the Modern Finance Corporation in Indianapolis?" It was a clever question, since the corporation was owned by Will H. Adams, a former state Supreme Court reporter whose name kept cropping up during jury selection, in defense allegations of jury tampering.

"Yes."

Prosecutor Remy jumped to his feet. "I object, Your Honor. The question is not competent."

"Sustained."

"Did she have something to do around the session of the Legislature last winter?"

"Not to my knowledge."

"Do you know when your daughter began to work for the Reading Circle?"

"I don't remember."

"Was it in the fall of 1924?"

"I—I don't remember—or I can't remember at this time somehow. I have had so much on my mind."

"That's all," said Inman.

Mrs. Eunice Shultz, a motherly woman who was the Oberholtzer's roomer, testified next. She came to the stand from outside the courtroom, since Judge Sparks had banished all the witnesses except the Oberholtzers and their son Marshall.

"I was in the kitchen preparing lunch and heard a terrible groaning at the front door," she said in a strong, soft voice. She recalled how a very large man had carried Madge through the door and up the stairs.

"What did he say?" Remy asked.

"We object, Your Honor. The defendants each separately and severally object."

"Overruled."

She recounted the conversation, how she had asked whether Madge was hurt and the man said she had been hurt in an automobile accident, and how he had identified himself as "Johnson—from Kokomo."

"What was his manner?"

"He hardly had time to tell me," Mrs. Shultz said, while the chorus of defense attorneys objected.

"Overruled."

"He went rapidly and kept his face toward the door. He said he must hurry on, but I got a good look at his face as he came downstairs."

Is that man in this courtroom? Remy asked.

"Yes," she said, in a strong voice, unperturbed by the chaos of objections. "I see him, in the back row, on the end." She pointed to Klinck, who stared at her with fixed, unblinking eyes. "Behind Mr. Stephenson. That's him, the man with the dark hair." Mrs. Schultz said that later she learned "Mr. Johnson" was Earl Klinck.

"Now, Mrs. Shultz, now when this gentleman left the house, this Mr. Johnson or Mr. Klinck, what did you do?"

"We object! We object! That would be out of the defendants' presence, therefore not competent."

"Overruled. Mrs. Shultz may have gone up to see Miss Oberholtzer."

"I went upstairs and knocked on Madge's door, and asked her—"

"We object to what she said," shouted Floyd Christian for the defense.

"Yes, yes, Mrs. Shultz, you mustn't tell what you said because the defendants weren't there, just tell what you did," said Judge Sparks, patiently.

Mrs. Shultz described going into Madge's room, finding her disheveled, battered, bruised, bleeding, and groaning. Over a storm of objections, the woman said, "'Oh, I'm dying, Mrs. Shultz,' Madge told me."

"When Mr. Klinck left the house, did he walk, drive, or how?"

"I saw the auto. It was a dark one, and very large. I would call it a closed car.

"Madge told me to call Dr. Kingsbury, and he arrived in less than an hour."

19
Her Virtue or Her Life?

Thursday, October 29, 1925
Noblesville, Indiana

The strategy of Prosecutor Bill Remy began to unfold before
the press and public, witness by witness, meticulous question by
question. John Niblack, night school lawyer, tracked the minute
revelations of the strategy; and the same John Niblack, *Indianapolis
Times* reporter, transmitted them in news accounts. As the strategy
took shape, Niblack saw it as a phantom: Madge Oberholtzer, on the
witness stand, summoned by Remy from her grave.

The entire case rested on Madge's story of her trip with
Stephenson, as she had told it to others. Somehow Remy had to get
that story told and into the record—no small challenge, since the law
normally would not allow so called "hearsay" testimony. But there

was a small crack of an open window in the law, an exception for "dying declarations" in a trial for murder, on the apparent theory that a person who was about to die would tell the truth.

But in this case, the declaration had been written down by another, Asa Smith, and was subject to challenge. It must be shored up and corroborated. Remy had to prove that the story actually came from Madge, that it was consistent and true, that her death was not a mere suicide, and that she knew she was dying when she told her story.

It was Bill Remy's most important fight of the trial, and the defense lawyers knew it.

Remy's first major move was to try to get the story recounted independently by others, beginning with Madge's doctor, John Kingsbury. He was called to the witness stand after Mrs. Shultz, just after noon on Thursday, October 29.

The doctor recalled, under Remy's questions, how he had arrived at the Oberholtzers' on March 17, anticipating that Madge had been hurt in an automobile accident.

"When you got there, what did you find?" Remy asked.

"I went upstairs and saw Madge Oberholtzer lying on a bed in the northwest bedroom. She was in a state of shock.... Her body was cold. Her dress lay open at the breast, exposing bruised areas... and lacerations...."

"After that examination, did you have a conversation with her?"

"We object."

"That's all right, go right on," said Sparks.

"I'll ask you if there was anything said about dying," Remy repeated.

Floyd Christian rose to his feet. "The defense objects, Your Honor," he said. "The corpus delicti of homicide has not been proven. The conversation was outside the presence of the defendants. It is not shown that death was then impending. It has not been shown that she was then in extremis, or recognized she was about to die. Such conversation would not be part of the res gestae of a homicide case. It has not been qualified as a dying declaration. It is incompetent, irrelevant, and does not tend to prove any charge in the indictment."

Judge Sparks looked Christian over blandly. "That all?"

"Yes, Your Honor," said Christian.

"Overruled."

"I asked her how it happened," the doctor continued, "and she said, 'When I get better I'll tell you the whole thing.' I pressed her for an answer, not knowing her condition. And she told me."

"Objection," cried Inman. "She said she'd get better." Thus, he argued, her statement was no "dying declaration" and was inadmissible hearsay.

"Overruled."

Dr. Kingsbury said he had to learn from her what had happened to cause such injuries before he could hope to treat her. "I had no idea; she might have died in five minutes, I could not tell; she was so tremendously ill.... She said she did not expect, or want, to get well—that she wanted to die."

Dr. Kingsbury related the story she told him—abduction, assault, poison. She told the doctor that Stephenson was very drunk and that "he bit her, chewed her, pummeled her—that she didn't remember all that happened." Kingsbury detailed her wounds and physical suffering, all over a continual chorus of objections from defense attorneys, who fought every word of the way. And objection by objection, Judge Sparks overruled them; inch by inch, word by word, Remy was getting the story before the jurors and into the record.

"From the appearance of the lacerations," Remy asked, "would you say they were such as might have been the result of bites by human teeth?"

"In my opinion, they were.... Some of them were," Dr. Kingsbury said.

"Which in your opinion were inflicted by teeth?"

"Those on the left breast and the right cheek."

"Did any of the wounds later become inflected?"

"Yes."

"Which?"

"The lacerations on the left breast and the right cheek."

"Was the infection one that might have resulted from a bite?"

"Objection," said Christian, arguing that Kingsbury was not qualified to answer that question.

"Overruled. The man said he graduated from Indiana Medical College," Judge Sparks said evenly.

"In your opinion, what would have been the prospects for recovery if she had had medical aid four or five hours after she took the poison?"

"Objection!" The defense objection filled page after page of the recording clerk's minute book.

"Overruled."

"The chances both for prolonging her life and for her getting well would have been better had she had treatment earlier or within four or five hours after she had taken the poison," the doctor said.

"In your opinion as a physician, state whether the delay caused by the auto ride from Hammond to Indianapolis and her detention in the garage lessened the chances for recovery or for saving her life."

Objection, again consuming pages of the minutes. Overruled. "You may answer the question, doctor," Sparks said.

"Most certainly it did."

Success! But then, Eph Inman, on cross examination, accused Dr. Kingsbury of changing stories. The doctor's testimony was different from the stories he told at the coroner's inquest and the bail hearing, Inman contended.

"The reasons I have testified to are the only reasons I can recall having given her as to why I thought she could not recover," Kingsbury responded. "I don't know whether I testified to the same reasons on the bail hearing or not, but that is what I told her."

But, said Inman, was it not true that Dr. Kingsbury's testimony had been discussed since the bail hearing with the prosecutor?

"I have talked twice, I think, with attorneys representing the prosecution. I didn't discuss the thing I have discussed today. It has been in my memory all the time that I said to Madge Oberholtzer that from the shock and the things that had happened to her, and from her lack of food and lack of medical attention, she could not recover. (Those reasons) were all true, and I gave them to her as such."

Inman probed, parried, and maneuvered, but Kingsbury's story remained firm.

As Dr. Kingsbury left the witness stand, Floyd Christian rose to his feet for the defense: Dr. Kingsbury's entire testimony was improper and should be stricken, "for all the reasons they had previously stated and several others besides," Niblack wrote.

"The death was not the proximate result of any act of the defendant," Christian argued. "All the parts prior to the taking of the poison are irrelevant, incompetent, and not germane. She took the poison secretly in the absence of the defendant, and not with any connivance of any of the defendants. It is not a dying declaration, it is hearsay evidence."

The point was central to the case. But Judge Sparks did not hesitate. "Overruled," he said.

The case was moving along rapidly now, perhaps too rapidly for Prosecutor Remy. Ideally, he would now fight to introduce Madge's dying declaration; but it was locked in a safe back in Indianapolis, and the Thursday afternoon hours were waning. It as too late to procure the statement that day. So the prosecutor moved next to bring Madge's father to the stand, for further corroboration of the story and to fill an important gap in logic in the dying declaration. Why, people asked, did Madge not bolt from her captors at Union Station, at the hotel, on the auto ride back from Hammond? Was she truly abducted or a willing participant on the trip to Hammond? Remy's best hope for an answer was to have George Oberholtzer recount into the record the reasons his daughter gave him—but the defense would again argue it was mere hearsay testimony.

For the prosecution, Judge Cox began the questioning of George Oberholtzer, who told of spending much of March 17 at Union Station watching the trains, then returning home to find Madge there.

"I sat on the edge of the bed and she told me to hold her hand. 'Oh, Daddy,' she said, 'that was the longest trip from Hammond to Indianapolis. I was so sick I thought I would die every minute.'"

Objection: Hearsay.

Sustained. The sentences were struck from the record.

"She said, 'And I begged and begged them to get me a doctor and they refused that, and I begged them to throw me out at the side of the road that somebody might pick me up.' And I asked her then why she had not cried out for help "

Objection. Sustained. The latter sentence was struck. Remy's strategy was floundering.

"'Shorty, the chauffeur, called Claude Worley from the Washington Hotel and told him to fix it up to protect them on the trip at Stephenson's direction,' she told me. And I said, 'Why didn't you make an outcry? Why didn't you jump out?' "

Objection, as a shiver ran through the spectators at the mention of Claude Worley, Prosecutor Remy's own special investigator. Judge Sparks directed that the latter two sentences be struck.

"She said, 'Why, Daddy, I had no show. Stephenson on one side of me and Gentry on the other, with guns in my sides threatening to shoot me through if I made an outcry.' She said, 'I had no show, he told me his word was law.' And she said, 'Daddy, if you can't get the federal authorities, I don't...'"   A storm of objections from the defense attorneys, who contended nothing more than a suicide had been shown. Thus, they argued vehemently, Oberholtzer could not legally recount a conversation with Madge before her death.

But Judge Sparks countered with remarkable logic that would frame the balance of the trial and memorialize the case in legal text books. The jury must decide, said Sparks, whether George Oberholtzer's story was true and whether the case was one of suicide or murder.

"Suppose," said Judge Sparks, "suppose her virtue were dearer to her than her life—then death would be her alternative. Whether a virtuous woman holds her virtue dearer than her life or her life dearer than her virtue, if attacked by superior forces, and whether those superior forces were bound to take that into consideration, is a matter for the jury to decide."

He struck the words "I had no show," both times in the testimony but allowed the balance—the critical explanation of fear for her life— to remain in the record.

Defense attorneys took strenuous exception to Sparks' comments. "Such remarks are more damaging to the defendants than any testimony that could be introduced," Christian shouted. "This is a case of suicide, not homicide. We ask that the submission of evidence be stopped and the jury be discharged, so we can start all over in this case with clean hands. This is a very clear case, and the defendants are entitled to a fair trial."

"Oh, no," said Judge Sparks. "We'll not lose any time now on arguments."

"Here we have a statement made by the court in all good faith, but we think the court has committed a very grievous error," Christian argued. "What the court states to a jury bears great weight."

Inman joined the chorus of shouted objections. "We have enough errors in the record now to reverse this case on appeal," Inman said with great force. The defense again demanded that the trial be halted immediately.

There was a perceptible change in the expressions of the three defendants now. Their faces were marked with worry, and Steve sat forward with both fists poked intently against his rosy cherub face. And now the attorneys' agitation soared beyond mere courtroom histrionics. Ralph Kane, for the state, began a high-pitched debate with Eph Inman, prompting Judge Sparks to intervene. "Gentlemen," the judge said firmly. "We are not here to try your personalities, but to try a lawsuit. You're too big for that."

The judge agreed that the defense could submit arguments the following day on whether his statements on "her virtue or her life" had so prejudiced the jury that the trial must be aborted.

Before he adjourned the Thursday session, Judge Sparks considered a request from defense attorney Ira Holmes for a recess the following Tuesday, November 3, to allow participants to vote in Indiana's general election.

Sparks said he sympathized with the problem confronted by Mr. Holmes, who was not only Stephenson's attorney but also chairman of the board of election commissioners in Indianapolis.

But, said Sparks, "I don't feel it would be right to hold these jurymen here without holding court." Anyone who wanted to vote the following Tuesday had better do so by absentee ballot, Sparks said, because there would be no recess. In fact, court would continue through Saturday.

If the intensity of the trial had made the courtroom seem its own world, the larger world beyond nonetheless was being touched by the trial.

Side by side with newspaper trial accounts were stories on election campaigns that seemed extensions of the trial itself. Democrats were jubilant. The troubles of Stephenson and the Republicans had breathed new life into Democratic hopes. Tom Taggart, the grand old man of Indiana's Democratic Party, was on the job, pushing to elect Walter Myers as the new Indianapolis Mayor, over the strong Republican candidate, John L. Duvall—Stephenson's man.

The election's chief issue, said Myers, was whether Indiana wanted to be ruled by "self appointed masters."

"D.C. Stephenson is done in Indiana," said a speaker at a Democratic rally at Indianapolis' Odd Fellows Hall. "But the machinery which made Stephenson one of the most powerful figures in our current history is ready for use of another. He is George V. Coffin, head of the Duvall forces, soldier of fortune, political strategist, and Hoosier czar."

Just before the election, Duvall was scheduled to address a mass rally at Cadle Tabernacle, called by George V. Elliot, head of Indianapolis' Marion County Ku Klux Klan. Stephenson trial or no, Duvall was running ahead. A case in point was the straw poll conducted by *Indianapolis Times* reporters at local clubs and watering holes such as the male-only Chamber of Commerce Smoking Room. The poll showed Duvall leading, plus two strong trends: voter disgust with political corruption, and "indecision of colored persons." Since the Civil War, black voters had been solidly in Republican ranks, but now there were strong signs that the Klan was costing the GOP the support among Indianapolis' 45,000 registered black voters.

With Steve's pick of governors, Ed Jackson, in the State House; his pick for senator, Arthur Robinson, on his way to Washington; and his pick for mayor, John Duvall, leading the City Hall pack—it appeared that David Curtis Stephenson's political fortunes were continuing to rise, even in his Noblesville jail cell.

As the second day of the state's testimony closed Thursday night, the principal problem shaping up for Stephenson was not so much the man on the street as it was the man on the bench, in the person of Judge Will M. Sparks—the unassuming circuit judge from Rushville, who was turning out not to be to The Old Man's liking at all.

Stephenson's motion to stop the trial went before Judge Sparks early on Friday, keyed on the defense contention that Madge was a victim of suicide, not murder.

The jury was sent from the courtroom, and Floyd Christian read the defense motion: Judge Sparks had prejudiced the jury with his Thursday statements that suicide could be murder if caused by another's action.

"If this was suicide," Christian bellowed, "it can't be homicide, for the two are diametrically opposite." No, not homicide; Madge took poison by her own hand, as her own free agent. Now the defense could never match the influence of the judge upon the jury, and the same judge who prejudiced the jury could not undue the damage, Christian argued. "It is impossible for the court to determine the effect of his statement on the jury, and we ask that submission of evidence be halted and the jury discharged," said Christian.

Judge Sparks allowed a pause to fill the room, adjusted himself easily in his chair, and began his response.

"Gentlemen," he said, "the situation as I see it is just this: Of course, I wouldn't say anything to the jury that would jeopardize the defendants. That I have not done. This is one court, I think, that has done less to influence the jury than any I know. To say they (the jury) would follow my instructions, instead of yours, is in conflict with my experience. Of course, you are all in earnest in the case, but I think you are taking yourselves a little too seriously."

Judge Sparks allowed for another brief silence, so that point could sink in. And then another: "All yesterday you had the privilege of asking the jury to step outside and make your remarks. It's not my duty to suggest those things to you. You didn't ask the court to discuss that matter Thursday. You asked for a ruling."

Another pause. "It seems to me, gentlemen, that the fundamental conditions in this case are well established."

Sparks peered over his glasses at the defense table.

"I don't say the jury shall consider the suicide as a natural consequence of the act. If they don't consider it so, then it isn't murder. When a person commits a felony he is bound to assume the natural consequence of the act. Now whether the act in this case was the natural consequence of the defendant's actions is a matter for the jury to decide and I so informed them. I'm following the indictment and going according to its theory....

"I think," Sparks continued, "a murder can be committed indirectly, and so the decisions say. Here's a case: Three men took an old man from his home and loaded him into a carriage. They carried ropes and clubs, not with the purpose in mind of killing him, but to beat and frighten him. He jumps from the carriage, falls into the river, and is drowned. The three are convicted of murder "

"But," interrupted one of the defense attorneys, "but suppose he shot himself instead—would that be murder?"

"No, you're misquoting me," Sparks said.

"This jury is bound to understand here from your remarks, Your Honor, that this woman took her life to save her virtue," Christian argued. "There is no issue here like that. At least I don't think so."

"Well, I do," Sparks said. "And that's where we differ. The motion is overruled, with 30 days in which to file a bill of exception. Call the jury in."

Judge Sparks looked weary. It was years later before he explained why.

He preferred to drive home every night—until the night he

narrowly averted wrecking his car on a barricade someone had stretched across the black road before him, just south of Noblesville.

Perhaps it was a coincidence that earlier that day Stephenson was riled by one of Sparks' rulings and glared at the judge, mouthing soundlessly with his lips: "You bastard!"

No one could have fixed blame precisely, amidst the currents and cross currents of Klan and anti Klan hysteria.

Far later, Asa Smith and Prosecutor Remy revealed that they received death treats throughout the period of the trial.

More than once, in the crowded halls, Niblack and his partner Tubby Toms had bumped against cold steel beneath waistcoats. During one break a farmer, fumbling for a match, dropped a revolver, which he pocketed again quickly with a hoarse explanation: "We're here to see that Steve gets a fair trial." And did that mean—? Who could say which side anyone was on?

Niblack and Toms puzzled over the complex threads of the case, as they drove back and forth between Indianapolis and Noblesville—by the billboard-sized signs someone erected along the roadside during the trial: "AYAK?"—Are You a Klansman? and "YIAAK!"—Yes, I am a Klansman.

20
"HE'LL CRUSH YOU"

Friday, October 30, 1925
Noblesville, Indiana

Another blanket of snow covered Indianapolis and Noblesville Friday, the second day of Remy's offensive—hinging on his most critical and vulnerable witness, Asa Smith.

It was, said the newspapers, more like the heart of winter than autumn. Cold: temperatures in the 20s. Unseasonably cold, while the world outside Steve's courtroom was heating up for Indiana's hard-fought November 3 elections. It would be recorded as one of the state's hottest elections, in the coldest fall in Indiana history.

Snow began sifting down at midnight and continued through the early morning hours. But optimists predicted it would warm for the weekend, as Indianapolis celebrated Halloween with its own "Mardi

Gras"—street festivals, dancing, parades, a Midwesternly moderated, madcap affair with thousands of masked and costumed revelers.

The slick road to Noblesville, a challenging pre-dawn maneuver for John Niblack and other reporters, did not deter festive spectators in the courthouse. By the time court opened at 9 a.m., the audience had become a human sea, filling every available seat and standing space, lining the walls, spilling through every aisle, surging against the jury rail. Crowd energy did not diminish through the first hour while defense lawyers argued, in vain, that Judge Sparks stop the trial.

The chill must have invaded the Noblesville jail, where Steve appeared more engrossed in controlling the election than his own trial. He surely knew that the early days of testimony belonged to the prosecution. His defense strategy of silent detachment was a puzzle to observers. But The Old Man had a surprise of his own ready to spring Friday, during Asa Smith's testimony.

Asa Smith's credibility was the linchpin of the prosecution's case, but his believability could not ride on either his emotional stability or his appearance. He moved to the witness box hesitantly, uncertainly: slight, looking more like a boy who might deliver groceries than a lawyer who could deliver a compelling case. It was reasonable, looking at him, that Madge would have compared Asa Smith to Stephenson and said, "He'll crush you—he'll crush you." If this was the best they could pit against the Grand Dragon, a boy prosecutor and this wounded lad, it hardly seemed a fair fight.

There was something vaguely asymmetrical about Asa Smith's face, something poorly hidden that had twisted him slightly askew, something raw and haunting within the dark and unyielding eyes. Was it shellshock? Or—?

Asa Smith's introduction, two days earlier by Judge Cox, had placed him as a courageous Marine volunteer at the battle of Stephenson's own fantasies, Belleau Woods, had seared Asa Smith with mustard gas, three months blind, and wrapped him in an American flag. But Cox's words had faded from the courtroom now, and what remained was this unimpressive lad, walking wounded, who had fallen apart at the bailbond hearing, whose eyes now sought the floor rather than the jury's faces.

Asa Smith. 3850 Winthrop Avenue. Office, 613 Fletcher Savings and Trust Building. Have lived in Indianapolis four years. Before that, private secretary to Senator New, in Washington and Wabash, 1919 to 1921. Served one year in the state legislature, 1923. Practiced law since 1917. In the World War, yes—

Objection! "I had a son who did the same thing, served in the war," said Eph Inman.

"Yes, it's not material," said Judge Sparks.

Prosecutor Remy stepped back, hesitated, and left the matter of shellshock understated. "Do you know the Oberholtzer family?"

"Yes."

"During last March when Madge Oberholtzer disappeared from home, did you receive notice of it?"

"Yes. They talked to me on the phone before she was found."

"Before she was brought back, state whether you went to Stephenson's home in Irvington."

"Yes. Miss Ermina Moore—Madge's best chum—and Mrs. Oberholtzer went with me."

"What time did you go to the Stephenson home?"

"Monday evening, March 16. We must have reached the house about 11 p.m. When we got there, I stayed in the machine while the two women went to the front door."

"While you were in the car, did you see anything?"

"I saw a closed car, a sedan, drive into the Stephenson yard and drive back to the garage. The car, when it reached the garage, the lights snapped out, and I could hear barking of dogs from that garage.

Then some lights were made in the garage, the car went in, and the lights went out."

"Did you see or learn anything of Madge Oberholtzer that night?"

"No, sir. Mr. Remy, there is something I forgot. The dogs quit barking. A short young man came from the garage and went up on the porch."

"Do you know who he was?"

The courtroom crowd, leaning forward to hear every word, turned their eyes toward Stephenson, who busied himself with some serious business with his pencil.

"No, sir," said Smith. "Mrs. Oberholtzer and Miss Moore were on the porch, talking to some man in a dressing gown, who had answered the door, and the man from the garage talked to them. I was at the curb. Miss Moore and Mrs. Oberholtzer came back, and I took them home."

"At whose suggestion did you go to Stephenson's home?"

"At my suggestion." Asa Smith was getting nervous. His answers were slower now, and he corrected himself several times on minor details.

"Had you been hunting Madge Oberholtzer?"

"Yes, sir, ever since her mother called me."

"Did you see Madge Oberholtzer the next day."

"Yes, she was at home, in bed. It was Tuesday. Yes, it was Tuesday, I am sure.

"Who else was present?"

"Mrs. Oberholtzer took me up, and she was present all the time. Oh, she may have gone out of the room a few minutes once or twice, or something like that."

"Did you have any conversation with Madge?"

"Yes, She said, 'I'm done for.'"

Her mother showed him Madge's chest, Smith recalled. "It is almost impossible to describe. It was a solid mass of bruises, black and blue and purple. No spots but just solid masses. I could not swear to lacerations because I did not look so closely. Yes, black and blue and purple. Bloody appearing."

The haunted eyes were clouded now, "as if looking at a mental picture," the reporter John Niblack wrote in his notebook, "while a slight shudder ran through his frame."

Remy: "What did she say to you and you to her?"

Mr. Christian, whom Niblack called "the safety man of the defense, whose duty it is to scent damaging testimony," leaped to his feet. "We object, your honor!" Christian turned to the witness: "Were these remarks afterward reduced to writing, Mr. Smith?"

"The substance was."

"We object. The writing should be the best evidence."

"Overruled," said Sparks. "Anyone who hears a statement, later reduced to writing, can testify about it."

"I wrote down the substance myself, from memory, of her entire story as she told it to me at different times," said Smith.

"We further object," chorused the defense, led by John Kiplinger of Rushville, "because it is not part of the 'res gestae.'"

"Res gestae," wrote Niblack. "The gist of the affair."

"That's overruled, too," said Sparks.

Now Mr. Christian rose. "We further object because the defendants were not present. It calls for hearsay. It has not been shown she was in extremis"—dying.

"Objections sustained on those theories."

Prosecutor Remy stepped back, narrowed his eyes in thought, and tried another angle. He was aiming carefully for the narrow sliver of open window in the law through which he intended to thrust the dying declaration. If Madge knew she was dying, "hearsay" could become testimony.

"What was her condition?" Remy asked.

"We object," said the defense lawyers, wearily.

"Overruled."

"She was apparently in great distress, physically and mentally," said Smith, who mirrored that distress.

"After that, from time to time, did you have any conversation with her as to the manner of her death?"

"Yes, the first time was Tuesday. I took Miss Ermina Moore with me."

Ermina Moore. Smith recalled that when she walked into the bedroom and saw her friend Madge, Miss Moore tumbled to the floor in a dead faint.

Objection. And elated defense attorneys succeeded in striking the incident from the record after they brought out that Smith was downstairs when Ermina fainted, that he heard but did not see her fall.

Remy returned to building the foundation for the dying declaration, brick by cautious brick, every one a fight.

"When was the next time she mentioned her condition?"

"About a week after this Tuesday. It was about 6 o'clock in the evening. I think her mother was in the room. She was in great agony. I said 'Good-bye,' and she said 'Good-bye' to me, seeming in great anguish. The next day she said to me, 'When I said good-bye to you last night, I thought it was 'good-bye.' She always said she would not get well."

Back at his office, Smith had prepared the manuscript, piece by piece, from his notes and his memory. "I first drafted out everything she had said to me that I could remember and in the words she used, as nearly as I could remember.

"On Thursday, March 26, at about 9:30 or 10 o'clock in the morning, I called Miss Ermina Moore to my office and she brought her own notes. I took my draft and Miss Moore's notes and read them out loud, using Miss Moore's notes, and those I had written in consecutive order relating Miss Oberholtzer's experience. I corrected any grammatical errors that might have existed, called a stenographer, and dictated the entire statement. Then Saturday, March 28, two days later, I called Miss Moore and we corrected the typed matter.

"The last two pages had a number of breaks, and I rewrote it again on yellow paper. As I recollect, I redictated the entire statement except one change I had made to the page I had rewritten."

"Was the statement as prepared by you substantially the same as she had related to you?"

"Yes."

"And then you went to the Oberholtzer home?"

"Yes."

"Who was present in Miss Oberholtzer's room besides yourself?"

"Dr. John K. Kingsbury, Miss Moore, and my law partner, Griffith D. Dean. When we got in the room, Dr. Kingsbury had a conversation with Madge Oberholtzer in our presence relating to her condition. She said that she understood and believed that she was not going to get well. She was going to die."

Prosecutor Remy now procured the dying statement and carefully unfolded it. Throughout the courtroom crowd, heads stretched upward to see it.

"Did you show her the statement?"

"Yes."

"Did you read it to her?"

"Yes."

"What was her position?"

"She was lying in bed, and I was near the head."

"Did you read it as you wrote it?"

"Yes, I read it very slowly and distinctly. Every word. Every sentence. Every page. Slowly and distinctly." Asa Smith was speaking firmly now, slowly and distinctly, and his eyes were fixed on

Remy's. "Every sentence, I stopped and asked her if it was true. She interrupted me several times in the midst of sentences to say, 'Yes, that's right.'"

"Did she request any corrections?"

"Yes, three or four times, she interrupted me. While I read to her, I made corrections with a fountain pen at the suggestion of Miss Madge Oberholtzer. I made the corrections in her language. She would stop me and say, 'No, that is not right,' if I said a certain person had done this, 'No, he didn't,' and she would name who did, and I made the changes."

"After reading her the statement, did she sign it?"

"Yes."

"Where was she when she signed it?"

"Still in bed. Dr. Kingsbury and I propped her up, and I think, possibly, that Miss Moore assisted him. We took a magazine, and laid it on a pillow, held it before her, and I placed the pen in her hand. I said, in essence, 'Madge, here is the place to sign what I have read to you, and the place for the signature is below that which I have read. If it is true, you may sign it, if you desire to do so, and if it is not true, you will not sign it. She said, 'I will sign it,' and I placed the pen in her hand and she signed it. No one guided her hand or helped her in any way at all."

With the manuscript in his hands, his eyes never leaving Smith's, Prosecutor Remy strode forward to the witness box and thrust the declaration into Smith's hand. "I hand you state's exhibit number one and ask you to say whether, or not, this is the statement."

Smith examined it meticulously, page by page, paragraph by paragraph, to Madge's signature, to the last line. And then he said evenly, "Yes, sir."

Now he faced the toughest test: cross examination, a rapid fire,

exhaustive grilling by the silver-haired Eph Inman. Inman's clear
first goal was to criss-cross back and forth through a maze of minor
and major issues, to rattle Asa Smith in the process, to crack his poise
and, thereby, his credibility. There was nothing gentle about it.

No, the notary was not present when the statement was signed.
She was called in later and affirmed an affidavit that Madge signed
then. What fountain pen? What time that Miss Moore or Dr.
Kingsbury entered the room? What moment when Smith added the
date, "March 28, 1925," to the statement? What motive and hints of
meaning in any additions by Griffith Dean? On and on the questions
went, implying in sum that Asa Smith had dreamed up the statement,
had forged Madge's signature, for some purpose, to some end that
could not be discerned.

Inman: "You selected the words and phrases to give it the proper
color, did you?"

Asa Smith: "That is not true."

"From March 17 to March 24 or 25, you simply carried in your
memory the things she had said without making notes of them?"

"That is a correct statement of the facts."

"Were you familiar with Madge Oberholtzer's signature before you
wrote this statement?"

"No, sir."

"Have you familiarized yourself with her signature since then?"

"I have not."

Inman handed Smith a photograph of a signature. "I hand
you Defendants' Exhibit Number One and ask you to look at her
signature."

"I object," said Remy. "They assume it is her signature. There has
been no proof on that point."

"Sustained."

"I just wanted to ask if it looks like her signature," said Inman, a bit
lamely.

"That would not be cross examination," said Sparks. "He's not a handwriting expert."

Undeterred, Inman tried another route, snaking through reams of testimony from the bail bond hearing, trying to shake Smith over minor discrepancies, boring harder and harder wherever Smith began to show nervousness. And then, suddenly:

"Now, Mr. Smith, are you sure, sir, that Madge Oberholtzer wrote that name?" Inman glared at Smith.

"Yes, sir, she did," Smith declared firmly, glaring back.

"Ah—weren't you employed as an attorney by the Oberholtzer family to sue Mr. Stephenson?"

"Object," cried the state's attorneys.

"Overruled," said Sparks. "The answer will tend to show his interest."

"Mr. Oberholtzer employed me to sue, or to do anything I thought proper," Smith said.

And then Inman detonated his bombshell, leaning forward from his graceful waist, with one slim finger lifted in the air. "I'll ask you, Mr. Smith," he said, his voice rising, "if you didn't go to Mr. Stephenson's office to extract money from him, and that he said, 'I've had experts try to blackmail me and fail, and amateurs can't get away with it.'"

"Objection!" cried Bill Remy and Ralph Kane, springing to their feet.

"That's not fair!" said Remy.

"That's nothing but pettifogging," said Kane.

Overruled. "That may go in," said Judge Sparks.

"No," said Asa Smith. "No. I did not."

"Did you go to the office of D.C. Stephenson and demand $100,000?"

"No, sir, I did not."

"Then you went back and asked $50,000, then $25,000, and finally got down to $10,00, did you not?"

"I did not," said Smith, leaning to the judge's bench, resting his elbow on the bench, crossing his legs.

"You didn't collect anything, though, did you?"

"No, sir."

Then, asked Eph Inman, was the demand ever transmitted through others—through specifically Robert L. Marsh—the man who had been Stephenson's attorney, the former law partner of Governor Ed Jackson?

"No."

"I will ask you, if you did not go to the office of Mr. Stephenson in the Kresge building and demand that he pay you $100,000 to settle the case?"

"I did not."

The hands on the courtroom clock were nearing noon before Smith's ordeal was over. "Smith," wrote John Niblack, "refused to be shaken in his testimony by the veteran attorney, despite question after grilling question."

Before the day closed, jurors heard from Asa's law partner, Griffith Dean, and from Madge's chum Ermina Moore—in her best cloche hat and little black dress, touched off with a fur stole whose small fox faces nuzzled, with perpetually pleading eyes, around her slender shoulders.

But the day belonged to frail Asa Smith, who set the state's case on firm footing.

Now, with that solid foundation, Prosecutor Remy could set the cornerstone of his case: State Exhibit Number One, the Dying Declaration of Madge Oberholtzer.

21
THE CLOTHESPIN SLATE

Saturday, October 31, 1925
Indianapolis, Indiana

Halloween.

Over on Meridian and Market, the Indianapolis cops were
readying for the mammoth Saturday night parade. Miss Olive
McGriff, Mardi Gras queen, had been lavishly outfitted for the parade
by her sponsors, the Pennsylvania Street businessmen. Downtown
would be filled with masked marchers and merrymakers. Police
warned townsfolk to secure privy doors and leave nothing lying
around that might be used for mischief.

It was shaping up as a lively weekend. Of particular interest were
the new 1926 Hupmobiles, just coming into Indiana. A favorite was
the six cylinder Hupp, a four-door sedan in ocean green with darker

green stripes.

After a real estate dispute, the city's mules and horse teams, as well as their related public works equipment, were being moved to an undisputed city barn. In their wake, the city was launching a fall street cleaning blitz.

Major excitement was building over the coming week's election. Steve's army spent Saturday completing preparations for their Sunday morning delivery of their "clothespin slate"—mock ballots, marked with the Klan favorites such as John Duvall, Republican candidate for Indianapolis Mayor. They included a scandal sheet on Duvall's Democratic opponent Walter Myers. The knights were jamming sheets into the jaws of clothespins, to be thrown from passing cars on to porches before the election.

Meanwhile, up at Noblesville, the courtroom was packed, and few would relinquish their space even for a lunch break. Hawkers had moved into the courthouse, selling foodstuffs in the halls from a table spread with a snow white cloth. Many spectators ate lunch in their sitting or standing spaces in the courtroom. Others, afraid to leave for even a minute, contented themselves by chewing gum.

Bill Remy was playing his trump card: Madge's dying declaration. Methodically, without melodrama, in what John Niblack called Remy's "free and easy manner," the prosecutor had read the statement into the record just before noon Friday. Defense objections followed nearly every sentence, like punctuation marks.

Remy's move to place the statement into evidence was met by an impassioned two-hour objection by Ira Holmes, for the defense. The corpus delicti—the essential fact of the crime—had not been proved, nor had the allegation that Madge knew she was dying; this was suicide, not homicide, Holmes argued. He set a record for an objection in a criminal case, wrote the *Indianapolis Star*, adding that the defense wanted everything struck from the statement except that Madge procured and took poison by her own hand. The result would have been no more than a declaration of suicide.

Another hour of arguments among the attorneys.

Judge Sparks chided the defense. Steve's attorneys were saying, in effect, that the corpus delicti couldn't be proved until the statement was introduced, but the statement couldn't be introduced until the corpus delicti was proved, Sparks said.

"I realize that there is enthusiasm on the part of counsel on both sides on the parts of their clients, and it is right that there should be," Sparks said. "But the court is wrapped up in the cause of the State of Indiana.

"Here's a case that's very peculiar in some of its characters. Some questions presented in this case perhaps have not been passed on by any court in the United States and possibly the world." Without precedent to guide him, Sparks said he could be guided only by his own opinion "as I honestly believe it....

"This thing has been so appalling to everybody that we all have to share the burden of getting this thing settled."

It was late in the day, and weariness had settled down over the courtroom, when Judge Sparks said softly, "There's no question that the statement should go in"—with some cuts that he would announce Saturday.

The judge's Saturday morning decision was the most severe blow thus far for Steve. Judge Sparks cut neither bone nor muscle from the statement. He merely trimmed minor portions relating to events before Madge went to Steve's on March 15.

Grim resignation marked the faces on Stephenson's side of the aisle. Despite the severe setback, "we are still going to make a real case out of this," one of The Old Man's lawyers muttered to Niblack.

The prosecutor, on the other hand, was clearly jubilant. Remy momentarily cast aside his understated air, indulged himself in a deep breath, and then rose to face his next challenge: to corroborate the details of Madge's statement through a series of witnesses from the hotel and the Monon train.

"'POISON ROOM' IN HOTEL PICTURED," read the headlines in Saturday night's *Indianapolis Times*, above pictures of Remy's corroborating witnesses: the hotel elevator operator, desk clerks, and chambermaid; the Monon train's conductor and porter. "Chambermaid at Hammond Hotel, Where Miss Oberholtzer Is Said to Have Taken Potion, Tells of Finding Blood and Liquor," the headlines read across the page. "Identifies Stephenson As Man Who Paced Corridor. State Tightens Evidence by Presenting Actual Bottle of Witch Hazel Used, It Is Alleged, to Bathe Girl's Wounds."

Link by link, Remy was welding a chain of evidence, Niblack wrote.

Who was pacing the corridor by room 417? Remy asked the chambermaid, Mrs. Lillian Reed.

"That man—there," she said, pointing to Stephenson, who laughed grimly.

"Did you see anyone else around there?"

"Yessir, that big fellow over there," she said, pointing to Ralph Waltz, one of Stephenson's attorneys—a mistaken identification that gave the defense a fleeting hope of discrediting the witness. But their spirits lifted only momentarily Saturday, as one by one Remy's barrage of witnesses corroborated the details of Madge's dying declaration.

Lew Ayres and Ted Wilson, Hammond hotel clerks, said Stephenson was the same man who arrived at 6:30 a.m. March 16 with a woman—"pale, with no make up on and no hat"—and registered as "Mr. and Mrs. W. B. Morgan." Gentry was the same man who registered as "Earl Gentry." They were assigned rooms 416 and 417. In the afternoon, after arrival of a man they called Shorty, the two men and a staggering woman left in "a big, closed car."

James Hollins, Hammond hotel bellhop, identified Stephenson and Gentry as the men who left supporting a woman who "looked awful bad" and had "a red place on her cheek."

W.S. Porter, the Pullman conductor, identified Stephenson and Gentry as the men who, in company of a woman with no hat, gave him tickets for and occupied one of the cars on the Monon train that left Indianapolis' Union Station at 1 a.m. March 16, bound for Chicago.

"Levi Thomas, colored, porter of the Pullman car 'Herkemer' which the party is alleged to have occupied on the trip to Hammond, was the last witness of the day," reported the *Indianapolis Star*.

In response to Remy's questions, Thomas said two men and one woman boarded his car on the night of March 15, in Indianapolis' Union Station. One man was short, the other tall. The woman, he said, wore no hat.

When Thomas entered the compartment to make up the beds, the tall man was removing the lady's shoes and stockings. While Thomas made up the beds, he heard the lady vomiting in the compartment toilet. And the short man showed Thomas a revolver.

Remy: "Did you hear the lady say anything about a revolver?"

Thomas: "She asked him to put it away. She said she was afraid of it. She said, 'Oh, dear, put the gun up. I am afraid of it.'"

Remy: "Do you see those men in the courtroom now?"

Thomas nodded toward Stephenson: "That fellow sitting in the corner." Remy asked him to walk over and make a more precise identification. Thomas walked directly to Stephenson, laid his hand on the defendant's shoulder, and said, "This man."

Was the other man present? Thomas said he couldn't be sure, perhaps—and he pointed to Klinck. Another fleeting hope rose for the defense, since he was surely wrong; no story had placed Klinck on the train. But Remy convinced Judge Sparks to ask defense attorneys to shift to one side, so Gentry became visible to the witness. Ah, exclaimed Thomas, pointing to Gentry: "That's the man right there."

The courtroom burst into spontaneous applause, silenced quickly by Judge Sparks' gavel.

On cross-examination, defense attorneys tried to show that the statement, "Oh, dear, put the gun up," showed that Madge had affection for Stephenson. Not necessarily, said Judge Sparks. She might have used the expression out of fear.

When Sparks failed to rule for the defense, Stephenson's attorneys demanded, for a second time, that the trial be halted. The judge again had prejudiced the jury by his remarks, they argued.

Not so, said Sparks. There is no requirement that the Court rule in favor of the defense on every question, he said. "That, gentlemen, is not fair."

Sunday off. The jurors went, in mass, to Noblesville's First Christian Church to hear a sermon titled "Love in Tears." They ate dinner at the Houston Hotel and then, for exercise, walked a mile west of town to see a recently collapsed bridge over Cicero Creek.

Nearby, 300 Chicago policemen were charged with being on a bootlegger's payroll. It was the height of the Roaring Twenties. Meanwhile, Indianapolis police quelled several near riots, including one shooting, that erupted as Steve's army forces tossed clothespin-bound campaign literature on to porches throughout the city.

Defense prospects brightened again Monday, November 2, when Stephenson's attorneys elicited from Madge's nurse, the thoroughly British Miss Beatrice Spratley, that Dr. Kingsbury had given the girl morphine just before she signed the dying declaration. "STEPHENSON SCORES ON TESTIMONY," the *Times'* headline read. The headline was fortuitous. It was not only the first report of the trial that gave life to the defense; it also gave young John Niblack an opportunity he had been waiting for.

Rumor had it that Stephenson was a bit chummy with some of the boys of the press, liberal with gifts of good whiskey and money to those who would deal with him.

"Tubby and I had discussed what we would do if offered money to touch up the news or slant it," Niblack recalled later. "Tubby had an inspiration: 'We'll take the dough, expose the attempted bribe, and give the money to charity,' he suggested."

They talked over the idea with their city editor, Volney Fowler. "Swell idea," Fowler said. They were ready; they could hardly wait to be bribed.

The morning after the *Times*' "Defense Scores" headline, Niblack was in the little press room when a Chicago reporter approached him with a $100 bill and a statement: "Here's a little present from Steve for you, and I have one for Tubby, too."

"What's this for? What's this all about," Niblack asked.

"It's for that good story you had in the *Times* yesterday. Keep it up! Get Tubby here, will you?"

"I was excited," Niblack recalled later. "Our trap had sprung. I raced out and plucked Tubby by the arm as he was interviewing the prosecutor, just before court convened.

"'Come here, Tubby, at once. Come with me.'"

Tubby Toms was preoccupied. "In a minute. Leave me alone now. I'm getting a story."

But Niblack would not be dissuaded. "I dragged him away anyhow, which was a mistake because he got hot under the collar. Steve's reporter friend shoved the $100 bill into Tubby's hand."

"What's that for?" Tubby demanded, with a blank look.

"Why, that's from Steve for you, for that good story."

"Well, for God's sake!" Tubby exploded in rage. "I don't want his dirty money. Just tell him to stick it up his backbone!" And with that, Tubby threw the money on the floor and stomped back to the courtroom.

"Well," Niblack recalled, "there stood Ole Honest John, red faced and foolish. The Chicago reporter picked up the bill. I pulled out my pocketbook and handed him back my $100 bill. 'I guess I don't want mine either,' I told him, looking silly."

On their way back to Indianapolis that night, Niblack reminded Tubby of their plan. "Tubby, don't you remember you and Fowler and I made it up if Steve gave us money we would take it and expose him?"

"Well, for goodness sakes! I sure do. I forgot all about it, I was so mad," Tubby said. "I forgot. Excuse me, Nibby."

"Well, you sure made me look like and feel like an ass," Niblack said.

Courtroom crowds were harder and harder to control. The crush of humanity grew each day, as did hostility toward the defendants. The crowd included young women from Butler College and a remarkable number of young mothers who sat, throughout the long trial days, holding their babies.

The crowds included "gray-haired farmers and their wives—honest folk," reported one newspaper man who said their faces hardened in anger as Matilda Oberholtzer wept. Her sobs still echoed, and now the crowd's faces were harsh toward the defendants. "In the courtroom, on the streets of Noblesville, one hears nothing in defense of the prisoners. 'They're good lawyers—they may fight free, but we hope the state will win,' is the usual comment," the reporter wrote.

"Stephenson, casually observed, seems nonchalant, but tell tale signs are showing through," the *Times* reported. "There are nervous little twitchings at the corners of his eyes and he can't control those plump, smooth hands of his. Idle they may be, but a censorious intimation from the state, and those fingers fly to a pencil and he writes rapidly, anxiously."

The somber parade of state witnesses moved quickly now, while spectators shuffled, pressing forward for better views, occasionally breaking into laughter at some peculiar testimony. Outbreaks were sternly silenced by Judge Sparks' gavel.

Jess Culbertson, Hotel Washington night clerk, testified that he received a call the night of March 15 to reserve a drawing room for Stephenson on the Monon night train bound for Chicago.

Andrew A. Brown, Indianapolis' Western Union superintendent, identified a telegram received at 8 a.m. March 18: "We are driving through to Chicago. Will take train back tonight. Madge."

Mrs. Lelia Hadley, Stephenson's neighbor, testified that Shorty washed Steve's big closed car about 6 a.m. March 17 and laid the cushions out to dry.

Mrs. Josephine Lowes, another neighbor, said she was awakened sometime after midnight March 17 by a "terrible scream" coming from Stephenson's garage. When Remy asked her to describe it, Mrs. Lowes said, "Oh, it would be impossible, it was so terrible."

Perhaps the cry came from Butler College, Eph Inman said to her on cross examination. "How do you know it was the 16th?"

"It was the 16th, because the next day was the 17th," Mrs. Lowes said.

"How do you know the next day was the 17th?"

"Well, it was the 17th because—because the day before was the 16th, that's why."

Now Matilda Oberholtzer had broken down. Her weeping echoed through the courtroom as Prosecutor Remy, having succeeded in corroborating most of the details of the dying declaration, moved on swiftly to the final chapter of his prosecution case: his carefully crafted medical testimony.

Remy's first medical expert was Dr. Virgil A. Moon. He was
a pathologist from the Indiana University School of Medicine; a
physician, surgeon, toxicologist. He had performed more than 900
autopsies.

Dr. Moon conducted a microscopic examination of the vital organs
of Madge Oberholtzer after her death, as part of his post mortem
examination made at the request of the Marion County coroner and
in the presence of Dr. Kingsbury and three other physicians.

What he found was a puzzle: Madge's death was at variance with
every other mercury poisoning case in recorded medical history.

Death from mercury poisoning usually occurs within five to 12
days because of kidney destruction, said Dr. Moon, who testified
that he had conducted extensive study of mercuric poisoning. If the
patient lives 14 to 25 days, the corroded tissue repairs itself.

In all the available history, there was not a single case recorded
when the patient lived more than 25 days after taking the poison and
then died. But Madge had lived 29 days.

What could be the explanation? asked Charles E. Cox, the
Oberholtzer's special prosecutor.

"I would say some other factor entered other than the mercuric
poisoning," Dr. Moon replied. His microscopic examination
determined that the damage to Madge's kidneys had nearly healed—
but an abscess in one lung remained actively infected.

Cox: "Did the post mortem examination disclose any injury to her
body that might have caused the infection which you discovered in
her lungs?"

Dr. Moon: "I found only one area which might have caused it."

"Tell what it was."

"It was a lacerated and recently healed infection in the skin over
one breast from which it probably could have resulted."

"Could such injury have been infected by human teeth?"

"It could have been, yes.... In my opinion, the infection in the lung came from the skin on the chest." And, Dr. Moon said, he found evidence that the infection had spread to Madge's kidneys.

"Do you believe Madge Oberholtzer would have recovered from the effect of the mercurial poisoning had she not been subjected to the disease germs in the manner you have described?"

"I believe she would have recovered, for the kidneys had begun the repair work sufficient to recover their functioning."

The defense challenged Dr. Moon's testimony with spirited cross examination. Eph Inman, for the defense, had the doctor dissolve a bichloride of mercury tablet in a glass of water to show how quickly it would disappear.

"That's not our drinking glass you're using, is it?" asked Judge Sparks. "If it is, you can throw it away afterwards."

Inman accused Dr. Moon of not shaking the glass hard enough to dissolve the tablet quickly. The attorney took the glass, poured about one third of the liquid into a spittoon so the doctor could shake it vigorously without spilling. The tablet disappeared.

"It took just a few seconds now, didn't it, Doctor?" Inman said with triumph.

"I think the jury is supposed to be the judge of how long it took," Dr. Moon replied.

Cross-examination lapsed deeply into medical jargon; Niblack reported that Inman and Dr. Moon "buried themselves in a maze of sesquipedalian medical terms which no one but the doctor understood."

The howl of a baby broke the stillness.

"I like children awfully well," Sparks remarked. "But when they cry, they should be taken from the room. I think that last term the doctor used must have frightened the child." A hearty laugh momentarily broke the tension.

Despite their spirited challenge, defense attorneys could not shake Dr. Moon's testimony. The implication was clear: Madge died not merely of mercuric poisoning but also of infection introduced into her body by a human bite.

Prosecutor Remy's second medical expert came to the stand Tuesday morning, November 3: Dr. J.A. MacDonald, one of the specialists Dr. Kingsbury called to Madge's bedside in her final days.

Yes, Dr. MacDonald said, 25 days is the record case for anyone to live, then die, from mercuric poisoning. But in Madge's case, curiously, she died with a 106-degree temperature, he said.

"Does bichloride of mercury poisoning usually produce high fever?" asked Judge Cox.

"There is no reason why such poisoning should produce such temperature," Dr. MacDonald said.

"Is the temperature of such patients usually normal or subnormal instead of high?"

"That's my observation."

"State whether, if a wound had been received by Madge Oberholtzer March 16 and had become infected and septurated and if the infection had continued several days, what is the fact as to whether it might have been the cause of her high temperature."

"It might have been."

Dr. MacDonald said he had examined Madge on April 6 and 10, before her death April 14.

"Describe her condition to the jury," Cox said.

"On the first occasion, this patient was very ill. She was semi-unconscious and showed evidence of critical illness."

"What did you see, if anything, of physical injuries?"

"Over the front chest were one or two small abrasions, practically healed. Over the left hip was a large bruise. Those were the only evidences of external injuries I saw."

"What was her condition when you saw her the other time?"

"She was worse. Her temperature had ascended to 105.4. She was profoundly unconscious."

Then, asked Cox, in a 15-minute recap of the chain of events described in Madge's dying declaration, how would the patient be affected if medical care were denied for 24 to 26 hours?

"We object!" cried defense attorney Floyd Christian. "It was admitted by Madge Oberholtzer that she was given one of the prescribed antidotes, milk."

"Overruled," said Sparks.

"Adversely," answered Dr. MacDonald.

"In my opinion, death was caused by toxic nephritis inflammation of the kidneys due to mercuric chloride ingestion, with a terminal or super added infection," he said.

"What do you mean by terminal infection?"

"Bichloride poisoning is a chemical poisoning which is removable. In addition, there was pus nephritis of the kidney."

Now Stephenson had lost all buoyancy. His confidence had collapsed like a deflated balloon. No more frenetic notetaking. He was leaning back in his chair, staring at the doctor through glazed eyes.

Cross-examination did not shake Dr. MacDonald's firm testimony that infection was the mystery element that killed Madge's rally from poison.

Then a clean-up witness: James Carver, manager of Indiana Bell's Irvington area office: Yes, in March of 1925 the telephone number Irvington 0492 was assigned to D. C. Stephenson, 5432 University Avenue.

Click, click, click. As methodically as the ticking of the courtroom wall clock, Remy was fitting the pieces of the state's case into place.

The first two physicians' testimonies were ratified again by Dr. R.

N. Harger, a chemistry professor from the Indiana University Medical School. He found some evidence of mercury in Madge's kidneys after her death, he said—but less than any he had ever examined in a patient who died of that poison.

Eph Inman, who had been spending his nights boning up on medicine, "swept down on Dr. Harger like a March hurricane," Niblack reported. But his showmanship and bluster yielded little.

Remy's next witness was Dr. J. H. Warvel, a young assistant professor of pathology from Indianapolis' Methodist Hospital, a chemist who drew out the bully in the defense attorneys. They laughed loudly each time he spoke during examination by Judge Cox and grueling cross examination by Eph Inman.

"In my opinion," Dr. Warvel said, "death was caused by some secondary infection superimposed on nephritis."

"If there was a delay of 24 to 26 hours in giving the approved medical aid to a person who had taken bichloride of mercury, what would be the effects?" asked Judge Cox.

"It would increase the chances of fatality."

"But for the infection which you described, what is the possibility of the patient's recovery from the bichloride of mercury if the infection had not intervened?"

"I believe she would have recovered."

Wednesday afternoon, November 4, state's witness Dr. H. O. Mertz presented substantially the same medical testimony. Madge would have recovered from the poison, but for the infection, he said.

The prosecution's train was barreling down the track now. At 4:15 p.m. Wednesday, Remy concluded his case with dramatic abruptness.

"The state rests, Your Honor," Remy said simply.

"Wait! Wait!" cried Inman, leaping to his feet. "Before the state closes, we wish to renew our request that some of the state witnesses be recalled from Hammond for further cross examination."

"I am ruling the defense had their chance at the time the witnesses were on the stand, as I said then," said Judge Sparks evenly.

Stephenson had spent Wednesday reading returns of Tuesday's election, assiduously, Niblack reported. "Although his double chin is prominent after seven months in jail on a good diet, the ex Klan leader these days is wearing as haggard a look as it is possible for a well fed, fat man to register," Niblack reported.

"Gentry sits all day with his hands fixed or holding his knee. Gentry pays more attention to the proceedings than the other two defendants. He wears a serious air at all times.

"Klinck weighs 215 pounds after his seven months in prison. He towers over six feet in height. Klinck is an ex deputy sheriff of Marion County, once a preliminary prize fighter in the stable of the 'Frisco K,' who sits at the press table, spending his time reading, now and then picking his teeth. He is the least worried of the three, from appearances," Niblack wrote.

The young reporter's clever turn of descriptive phrases did not go unnoticed by the defendants. Wednesday afternoon, after Remy rested the state's case, Stephenson "suffered an attack of nerves," as Niblack dutifully reported the following day.

As court adjourned, Stephenson came up to the press table. "Niblack," he said, "I think I'm going to punch your nose!"

Niblack was taken aback. "What for?"

Stephenson said nothing, just glared.

"Go ahead," said Niblack. "Try it. You're too yellow."

Into the standoff silence came Earl Klinck, "doubling up his fist as big as a ham," Niblack remembered.

"Let me hit him, boss!" Klinck said. "I'll knock him out that window!"

"Hold on, that's a little different," Niblack said, heading without ceremony for the nearest door.

The crowd was a little smaller as the state wrapped up its case, but reporters predicted "monstrous throngs" would overflow the court if Stephenson took the stand. The defense strategy remained as much a mystery as Stephenson himself.

Whatever the defense strategy, Remy intended to be ready.

Just before the state rested, Remy sent a message to Stephenson through the press: If the defense made any move to attack Madge Oberholtzer's character, the state would call as many as 100 witnesses in rebuttal.

22
KLanapolis Kaiser

Thursday, November 5, 1925
Noblesville, Indiana

Steve's timing was right on target.

Moving from defense to offense, while his attorneys were opening his case Thursday, November 5, The Old Man was riding the crest of victory in an unprecedented statewide election sweep.

Tuesday's election returns were electrifying. The Klan slate—Steve's slate, Republicans, what the press called "the clothespin slate"—had zipped up the state:

Indianapolis' City Hall was clearly in Steve's pocket, including Mayor John Duvall and six of nine members of the City Council—six being the maximum available by law to Steve's Republican Party in that election.

All five school board winners were members of the "United Protestant" party, all openly supported by the Klan.

Steve's sweep was even more dramatic statewide. Except for South Bend and Marion, his slate had sewed up the state, from the State House to the farmhouse.

Stephenson's Klan/Republican/Protestant coup left the Indiana press breathless. The *Indianapolis Star* was sputtering, nearly speechless. The election proved, the *Star* wrote in a sour front page editorial, that most people voting had no idea what they were voting for, and "a majority will be disappointed."

Republicans pronounced "a moral victory."

Now the questions in Indianapolis turned to spoils: Whom would Mayor Duvall appoint for major City Hall jobs, beginning with the prized plum of police chief? The *Times* speculated that Clyde Worley, Remy's special investigator, was the front runner but now was jeopardized by his close ties to Stephenson.

As he closed out his city treasurer's office and moved into the mayor's chair, Duvall was becoming a center of explosive political pressure. Bug-eyed and shifty, Duvall was nonetheless a pet of the press because of his penchant for deliberate bad grammar. In the dullest interview on city finances, Duvall would suddenly feed the color-hungry reporters a line like this: "If I'd aknowed I coulda rode, I would've went, but if I hadda went I wouldn't of et nuthin."

Duvall climbed to the Indianapolis mayor's office on a web of patronage promises, which he had spun in every direction. He promised the same jobs to as many as three groups. Stephenson, for example, had secured from Duvall a written "contract" pledging that Steve could approve appointments in advance, including the police chief, the Board of Public Safety that controlled the police force, the Park Board, and the Board of Works. Now elected, Mayor Duvall began to spin in his own web. Floundering and quickly ensnared, he did the only honorable thing: the mayor simply disappeared, playing an extended game of hide and seek with both reporters and the spoils-starved holders of his patronage promissory notes.

"To the ox which pulls the load goes the fodder," said Republican boss George V. Coffin. But others were disgusted with the spoils system. The *Indianapolis Times* and 1,400 Indianapolis citizens launched a reform movement to change the city's government to a manager/council form.

Buoyed by the election victory—and accurately predicting that a Catholic would seek the U.S. Presidency in 1928—Indiana Grand Dragon Walter Bossert divulged a plan to unite the Klan with "friends of negroes and Jews" to fight the dreaded Roman menace.

While Steve's white-robed Fascists were marching across Indiana, with an eye toward Washington, The Old Man was also keeping an eager watch on another march, in Rome: the black-shirted forces of Benito Mussolini, Premier of Italy. On Wednesday, as Remy was resting the state's case, Mussolini capitalized on rumors of an assassination plot, arrested his enemies, seized control of Italy's Masonic lodges, and dissolved the Socialist and Unitarian parties.

Meanwhile, Stephenson's defense opened a little late on a fine and clear morning in Noblesville Thursday, November 5. The court waited for the delayed arrival of Steve's attorney Ira M. Holmes, who had missed two days of the trial while attending to his duties as chairman of the Indianapolis board of election commissioners.

It was 9:15 a.m. when Floyd Christian rose, for the defense, before the biggest crowd yet assembled. Excitement was high, wrote reporter John Niblack; the crowd hoped the day would reveal Stephenson's mysterious defense strategy and perhaps even a glimpse of The Old Man himself on the witness stand.

"The defense moves," Mr. Christian said in ringing tones, "for the judge to issue peremptory instructions to the jury to return a verdict for the defendant on the indictment and each separate count thereof." The state had failed to make its case, he said, so the jury should find the defendants not guilty and acquit them, forthwith.

Judge Sparks cleared his throat. "Gentlemen," he said, "in regard to these motions, I want to be entirely courteous in the matter. But I'll say frankly, gentlemen, that I am not going to hear arguments on these motions. I have my opinions about these matters, and so have you, but I'm not going to sustain these motions."

"But, Your Honor," interrupted Christian, "I think there are some legal points in this case that have not been presented."

"Arguments at this time would merely attack the validity of the indictment or points in it," Sparks said. "I'm willing to take the risk of making the error. I know we all make mistakes. I have my own notions about it. That I should have these notions, of course, is not wrong."

Mr. Christian suggested that the judge did not know all the points of the law.

"I am not so sure about that," Sparks retorted. "We all have access to the same books." Indeed, he said, he had allowed the case to be unduly prolonged because he did not want to trample on the defendants' rights. But now, Sparks said, it was time to move along. "Gentlemen, I don't care to hear any arguments on these motions. Frankly, this is a case for the jury to decide."

A dark cloud settled over Steve's face, and the defendants and their lawyers huddled for a twenty minute, whispered strategy session. Then the silver-haired Eph Inman, chief defense attorney, rose and announced, "Your Honor, the defense waives its opening statement."

"All right," replied the judge, while spectators buzzed. Why would Stephenson waive his chance to lead off strongly by laying out his defense case, all in one forceful piece? His only advantage, surely, lay in prolonging the element of mystery, keeping his strategy secret from Remy and the crowd for longer tantalizing hours.

Eph Inman called the first defense witness, Dr. Orvall Smiley, 143 West 35th St., Indianapolis physician, whose testimony consumed the morning and extended beyond the noon break.

It soon became clear that Dr. Smiley was Steve's key medical witness, whose role was to fix Madge's death as a mercury suicide, undermining Remy's medical experts.

"SUICIDE, STEPHENSON'S OPENING GUN," said the *Times* headline Thursday afternoon. "Dr. Smiley Testifies Girl Was Beyond All Medical Aid If She Kept Secret for Six Hours Fact She Had Taken Poison."

Dr. Smiley told the court he was a surgeon with offices in the Bankers Trust building, a 12-year resident of Indianapolis, and an expert in mercurial poisoning who had treated 100 cases, including three in the past six months.

"Are there different ways mercuric poison may be taken into the human system?" Eph Inman asked.

"Yes. By breathing or through the mouth and other body openings," Dr. Smiley said.

"What is a fatal dose?"

"From three grains up, depending on the circumstances."

"Now, doctor, suppose six tablets of this size, seven and three tenths grains each, were dissolved in a glass of water, and the solution drank into the stomach, would absorption take place faster than if they were taken in solid form?"

"Yes, somewhat."

"As to the rapidity with which the system takes up the poison, would that depend on whether the stomach had food in it or was empty?"

"Yes, very much."

"Suppose...the stomach was empty, and that six of these tables,

...dissolved in water, were dropped into the stomach. What would be the effect on absorption?"

"It would start at once. It would start spasmodic action of the walls of the stomach."

"Suppose that the patient hadn't taken any solid food for twelve or fifteen hours, and that at 9 a.m. she drank one cup of coffee, would her stomach then be empty one hour after drinking the coffee?"

"Ordinarily, yes, in a normal stomach."

Was it not possible, Inman asked, in a long hypothetical question, that Madge had used bichloride of mercury to prevent or abort pregnancy, causing vomiting that had seared and burned her lips, her tongue, her mouth, her chest, and other body openings?

"Yes," Dr. Smiley said. Use of bichloride of mercury as a prophylactic can and often does cause death, he said.

"Suppose," said Inman, in a second hypothetical question covering 30 minutes, "suppose a young woman, about 28, in good health, has the flu and apparently recovers. On an empty stomach about 10 a.m., she dissolves six tablets of bichloride of mercury in a glass of water, swallowing the solution...and for six hours, at least, keeps the fact an absolute secret. She soon becomes ill, vomits..., faints, and knows nothing that goes on."

A person who discovers her "tells her she is a fool" and forces her to drink milk to counteract the poison, then drives her to Indianapolis and puts her to bed, Inman continued. A doctor discovers evidence of mercuric poisoning, including abrasions on her chest and lower body, and begins treatment for the poison. She begins to improve but develops anemia, and a blood transfusion is administered. "After the transfusion, she becomes markedly worse...and dies. An autopsy shows there was no abscess in or about the kidneys, but portions of the liver and kidneys show the presence of mercury." What then would be the cause of death? Inman asked.

"Bichloride of mercury," said Dr. Smiley.

"Suppose," said Inman, in a new hypothetical question that
stretched over an hour, repeating much of the same story, that
the patient was thrown into the lower berth of a Pullman car, was
attacked and beaten, and took poison, with the same chain of events
thereafter. "Would those things change your opinion as to what
caused her death?"

"No, sir," said Dr. Smiley. Death in either case would have been
caused by bichloride of mercury, he said firmly.

Would it be possible, Inman asked, for a case of influenza to
reassert itself disastrously in the patient's vital organs?

"Yes." Influenza is often followed by "a bad heart, bad kidneys, or
bad lungs," the doctor said.

"Is it possible to inject germs by blood transfusion, or by
catheterization?"

"Yes, sir." Yes, said the doctor to a series of questions, faulty
techniques in blood transfusions or catheterization could well
result in germs getting into the kidneys. Both procedures had been
administered to Madge.

"Now, doctor," said Inman, "keeping in mind the history of the
case I have assumed, after concealment of the fact that she had taken
poison for six hours or more, in your judgment would medical aid
have saved her life?"

"After six hours, a lethal quantity would have been absorbed and
the patient would have been beyond the aid of medical science."

"Is milk a recognized antidote?"

"Yes."

"Is pouring a quantity of milk into the stomach the proper thing to
do?"

"Yes."

"But after six hours had elapsed, could even that have saved her
life?"

"No, sir," said Dr. Smiley, emphatically.

Dr. Virgil A. Moon, the pathologist who had testified earlier for the state, sat at Remy's elbow while Judge Cox conducted an exhaustive cross examination. Making an occasional note, Dr. Moon puffed on a pipe, his eyes never leaving Smiley.

"You never saw Madge Oberholtzer, did you?" Judge Cox asked the defense witness, Dr. Smiley.

"No, sir," the doctor said.

"Do you know any of the defendants?"

"I've seen Mr. Stephenson a few times."

"Have you ever been in his house?"

"Why, yes."

"Whom did you treat there?"

"I don't remember now. It was 18 months ago."

"How many cases of bichloride of mercury poisoning have you treated yourself?"

"About 30."

"How many of your 30 cases got well?"

"I can't say definitely. Of the mouth cases, I'd say less than 10 percent. Most [were] vaginal cases [in attempted abortions]. Nearly all cases will get well if you get them early, before absorption takes place."

"How many took the poison by mouth?"

"At least twenty."

"Only two or three of them got well?" Cox whispered with Dr. Moon, who leaned forward in his chair with the omnipresent pipe clenched in his teeth. "Do you know of the record of a Cincinnati hospital where out of 131 cases, only 6 percent of them died?"

"Yes, but most of them took the poison on a full stomach," Dr. Smiley insisted. "On an empty stomach, immediate vomiting would leave a fatal, or lethal, dose sticking on the walls of the stomach, absolutely."

"Why, doctor, don't you know that there have been recoveries after 40 or 50 grains of bichloride of mercury have been swallowed?"

"Yes, sir, I know that, but their stomach was full."

"How do you know their stomachs were full?"

"From my own experience, and I read it." Dr. Smiley detailed a list of medical journals and authors.

"You read most of those in the last few weeks, didn't you?"

"I've read some of them in the last few weeks."

"Now, doctor, what is the longest reported interval in recognized medical literature, between taking the poison and death?"

"In Blair's Toxicology—Blair, a great English authority—"

Ralph Kane, state's attorney, interrupted, saying the witness was not answering the question. Judge Sparks agreed.

"Forty one days," answered Dr. Smiley, with obvious irritation.

"I wish you would just describe what Blair says," said Cox.

An attorney's fight ensued, but after considerable wrangling, Dr. Smiley was allowed to answer. "Blair says that 41 days such patients can live."

With prompting from Dr. Moon, Judge Cox asked Smiley a rapid fire series of questions about specific Indianapolis cases of mercury poisoning.

Smiley had not heard of them. "There are about 350,000 people in Indianapolis," Dr. Smiley said, "and I can't keep track of them all."

"You've read nothing of their recoveries, then?" Cox said. "And after admitting that 90 percent of your patients died, you call yourself an expert?"

Spectators laughed, and Judge Sparks rapped for order.

Cox pointed his finger at Dr. Smiley. "I'll ask you, doctor, if it is not possible for one person to bite another person and thereby infect the bitten person with staphylococci germs?"

"Yes, possibly."

"Are you then absolutely sure that the death of this girl was due to mercurial poisoning?"

"Absolutely."

More wrangling, as the doctor took Judge Cox on a journey though a typical patient's alimentary canal with a dose of poison, with or without water or food. The trip produced nothing. Dr. Smiley was excused.

From Remy's side, Dr. Moon stirred his pipe ashes thoughtfully, watching Smiley as he left the stand. Then abruptly Dr. Moon smiled and whispered something to Remy, who made a quick note, with a sober nod.

Next up was Dr. Paul F. Robinson, Marion County coroner (and active Indianapolis Klansman) who presided at Madge's autopsy and conducted the inquest into her death. He was followed by Dr. John W. Williams and Dr. J.D. Moschelle, Indianapolis physicians. All were adamant in their belief that bichloride of mercury poisoning killed Madge Oberholtzer.

Judge Cox, for all his vigorous questioning, had failed to shake Steve's medical testimony. Now, finally, Stephenson's case was moving out.

Reporters, who earlier thought young Remy had his case sewed up, were treating Mr. Stephenson with new deference. They looked forward eagerly to the following days of defense testimony, when the defendants were expected to take the stand.

The speculators shifted the odds to at least even, and there was no certainty at all about the outcome of Steve's trial.

Suddenly everything heated up on Friday morning, November 6.

Remy's case began to dip and wobble under a barrage of defense testimony. John Niblack got to drag out words he was longing to use: "bombshell" and "sensational."

The trial lawyers finally moved beyond the medical witnesses—to the delight of spectators bored with the technical testimony.

The defense set out to undermine the credibility of Madge's dying declaration in two ways. First, they sought to establish that Earl Klinck could not possibly have done anything Madge described, since he was preoccupied elsewhere at the time. Second, they tried to raise clouds of doubt about her "virtue" and her previous relationship with Steve. If Madge was a loose woman having a long-term affair with Steve, he would not be a kidnapper, they reasoned.

First the matter of the Klinck alibi: Defense attorney Ira M. Holmes assumed the lead in examining four defense witnesses, all deputy sheriffs in Marion County. Like Klinck, also a deputy sheriff, all four served under Sheriff Omer Hawkins in March of 1925.

James Carter, who had been Klinck's partner, said Klinck was around the county jail Sunday morning, March 15, then left saying he was going to Terre Haute. Carter also sharply recalled Klinck's doings on Monday and Tuesday—especially around noon Tuesday, when the state contended he was bringing Madge home.

"I saw him in the jail at about 8:15 Tuesday morning," Carter told Ira Holmes. "I saw him take more prisoners from the jail and leave for the Indiana State Farm with them."

Holmes: "When did you next see him?"

Carter: "About 11 or 11:30 in the forenoon. He came back to the table where the officers eat. I was with him the rest of the day."

Niblack noted that Klinck put in a busy day Tuesday. Starting with the trip to the farm, near Greencastle, Klinck ate lunch. Then the two deputies went out on the National Road near Memorial Park Cemetery and made an arrest, Carter said. They made three other arrests that afternoon. "Then we took a colored girl, Frankie Knight, to the Indiana Woman's Prison. I left him after 6 o'clock that day," Carter testified.

Prosecutor Remy cross examined Deputy Carter. "Did you make

an arrest on March 12, you and Klinck?" Remy asked.

"Wait till I look up my notes," Carter said, pulling out a notebook.

"May I see your notes?" said Remy. Defense attorneys objected, and Remy handed them back, smiling, after reading them.

"Now, Mr. Carter, were you a deputy sheriff in March..."

"We can't hear you, Mr. Remy," called Attorney Holmes.

"You'll hear me in a minute."

"Well, I want to hear you now," retorted Holmes.

"You were a deputy sheriff when Mr. Stephenson was indicted?" Remy shouted, so loudly that defense attorneys objected again.

"Yes."

"And it took you three days to arrest Mr. Stephenson?"

The defense objection was overruled.

"No, sir."

"Well, how long did it take?"

"Well, the indictment was Saturday morning and he was arrested on Monday afternoon. We didn't know anything about the indictment until we read it in the newspapers."

Virtually the same alibi came from the other three deputy sheriffs: Leonard "Red" Koffel, Sheriff Hawkins' driver; Frank Kempf; and William Anderson. Holmes introduced into evidence Klinck's prisoner receipts from Ralph Howard, prison farm superintendent, and from the Women's Prison, to verify that Klinck had delivered those prisoners. He made the trips in the sheriff's Hudson machine, they said.

Remy cross examined each deputy, and each had photo-clear memories of actions on Tuesday but less specific memories of the other days.

Carter began to flounder under Remy's barrage of questions. The witness nervously fumbled with his pocket keys and, before each answer, looked desperately toward the defense table.

"Don't look at the defendants—just look at me," Remy said.

Judge Sparks remonstrated Remy from further discussion with the witness, directing the young prosecutor to address his remarks to the court.

Deputy Kempf said he remembered clearly what happened on Tuesday, March 17, because it was St. Patrick's Day.

Deputy Anderson remembered that day for the same reason, but he could not remember details about July 4, Christmas, or Thanksgiving,

"What were you doing on George Washington's Birthday?" Remy asked him.

Deputy Anderson scratched his head and smiled at Remy.

"That was on a Sunday," Anderson said. "You taught a Sunday School class that day, and I was in the class, Mr. Remy, don't you remember that?"

Remy pulled out a pocket calendar, leafed through the pages, stared into space, and then grinned. "You're right," he said.

"You're both exonerated," Judge Sparks said.

Rather than trying to undermine Klinck's alibi at present, Remy pulled out a bombshell. Judge Charles Cox abruptly moved to recall the leadoff defense witness, Dr. Orvall Smiley, Friday afternoon.

Throughout the questioning, the pipe-puffing Dr. Virgil Moon sat by Remy. Occasionally they whispered, and Remy would slip a note to Judge Cox.

Cox began questioning Dr. Smiley's self-asserted expertise in mercury poison cases. That toxicology authority he had quoted in Thursday's testimony—"Blair"—"Where was this Blair book published?"

"In London," said Smiley.

"Now, as a matter of fact, it's Blythe, not Blair, isn't it?" Cox demanded.

Dr. Smiley blushed. "Yes, that's right." He became obviously nervous, twisting his hands.

"Where did you get it?"

"From another doctor." The defense attorneys were leaning forward, glaring at Dr. Smiley, adding to his discomfort.

"When did you see it?"

"Last night."

"Did you attend a veterinary's school?" Cox asked, gleaming with delight when the witness started and squirmed at Cox's second line of questioning.

"No, sir," answered Dr. Smiley, "but I taught in the Indiana Veterinary College last year."

"You have some veterinary remedies, do you not?"

"No, I'm not entirely a horse doctor."

"Answer the question, answer the question," Cox shouted.

"What do you mean by that?"

"Have you ever had any connection with the Standard Veterinary Remedy Company?"

"Yes, but it was eight or ten years ago."

Satisfied, Cox moved to his third line of questioning: "What is the fact as to whether you ever treated D.C. Stephenson for delirium tremens?"

"No."

"Ever treat him for alcoholism?"

"Not alcoholism alone."

"Well, partly then?"

"Well, one time he was a little nervous, and when I treated him, he might have had a little alcohol," Dr. Smiley admitted reluctantly.

Eph Inman took over the questioning. When and where did the treatment occur?

In February, in a room on North Meridian Street, Smiley said.

Niblack noted that the spectators were sitting on the edges of their seats, craning their necks to hear every word; but Stephenson was reading a magazine, paying no attention at all to the testimony.

"Mr. Stephenson was very nervous, possibly from overwork because of his activities in the Legislature?" Inman asked.

"Yes," Dr. Smiley answered.

As Smiley left the stand, Dr. Moon watched him squarely.

Dr. Smiley's testimony had stunned the courtroom. Steve's star medical expert had been shattered, by his own admissions that he was in fact a veterinary specialist, whose knowledge of mercury poisoning in humans was limited to a few days' boning up—reading the wrong books by non-experts whose names he could not recall correctly. It was the most electrifying testimony of the trial thus far.

Dr. Moon cupped the bowl of his pipe in his hand and nodded curtly to Smiley. Then, rising to shake Remy's hand, Dr. Moon gave the young prosecutor a pat on the shoulder and a deadpan wink.

23
A SHADY LADY

Friday, November 6, 1925
Noblesville, Indiana

Friday afternoon was full of surprises for Prosecutor Remy and the state attorneys, as the defense put Madge's character on trial.

First, a woman of mid-age with a plush hat, pursed lips, and sagging jowls came reluctantly to the witness stand for the defense in midafternoon.

She was Mrs. Cora H. Householder, 5850 Beechwood Avenue, Irvington, three blocks from the Oberholtzer home.

Her husband of 20 years, Charles Householder, was well acquainted with Madge, she said. In fact, he boarded with the Oberholtzers for a while. The Householders separated on Christmas Day, 1924.

How well did he know Madge? defense attorneys asked her.

Objection from Remy. The jury was sent from the room while defense attorneys explained to Judge Sparks why they felt it necessary to attack Madge's reputation. They alleged that Charles Householder, a policeman, and Madge were very, very close friends.

Well, the judge said, you'll have to find another way to introduce this witness. And Mrs. Householder was dismissed, much to her relief. My sympathies are with the Oberholtzers, she told the press.

Next up was Dr. Vallery Ailstock, dentist from Columbus, Indiana, one of Steve's KKK field men. Dr. Ailstock said he talked to Stephenson and Madge early in January in Columbus and that Madge wanted alcohol.

An argument arose between state's attorney Ralph Kane and Dr. Ailstock: Had the dentist resigned from the Klan, or had he been kicked out for drunkenness?

"How many times have you been out to Porter's Camp (near Columbus) drunk?" Kane shouted. "I'll ask you if on many occasions you haven't been out there on drunks? Is that the reason they kicked you out of the Klan?"

"No!" Dr. Ailstock shouted back.

Spectators clapped and cheered. Judge Sparks rapped for order and threatened to clear the courtroom.

Kane: "Are you still Klan organizer in Bartholomew County?"

Dr. Ailstock: "No, sir, I resigned."

"When was that?"

"The first quarter of this year, when my dues ran out."

"You were a member of the Stephenson branch of the Klan, weren't you?"

"Not exactly."

"And that's another reason they put you out, isn't it?"

"They didn't put him out," yelled Eph Inman. "He's told you a dozen times."

Judge Sparks pounded for order. "Gentlemen, I won't have this. If you want to continue in this case, direct your conversation to the court. If not, someone else can handle it. Such performances are undignified and beneath both of you."

Another snow storm Saturday morning. Ralph Kane took another swing at Dr. Ailstock, who said one Dr. Chester L. Clawson, Columbus chiropractor, was also present during the conversation with Madge and Steve.

Kane tried to show that the entire story was fabricated by the defense. Who first asked about the incident? Kane asked.

"Some gentleman representing Mr. Holmes," Dr. Clawson said.

"When was that?"

"Three or four months ago."

"And you went over the whole story with him?"

"Not entirely."

"And when did you tell all of this for the first time?"

"To Mr. Holmes a week ago in his office. I was called there by long distance phone. I talked to Mr. Holmes about 20 minutes."

"Was anybody else present?"

"Dr. Clawson."

"That is, you, Dr. Clawson, and Mr. Holmes got together in Mr. Holmes' office and talked this case over?"

No reply.

"I insist on an answer," thundered Kane, pounding the table with his fist and glaring wildly at the witness.

"Yes."

"How much did they agree to pay you?"

"Not a thing, not one dime."

The defense called Dr. Clawson, the Columbus chiropractor, who said he first met Madge at Columbus in January.

"We were standing at the corner of Fifth and Washington Streets, and a machine drew up to the curb. A man called out 'How are you, Doc?' And it was Stephenson, and Miss Oberholtzer was with him. Well, I talked to Miss Oberholtzer most of the time, and we talked about a little bit of everything. Then she asked me if it was a very live town, and I said it was about the general run. She asked, 'Can you get hold of good liquor or booze down here?' And I told her there were several places. She asked me why I couldn't get some alcohol, and I told her Doc Ailstock was a dentist and that he ought to get it, thinking to turn the joke on Doc." Dr. Clawson said Stephenson intervened, saying to Madge, "That's enough of that."

Prosecutor Remy took over cross examination of Dr. Clawson and determined that the doctor worked with Steve on an unsuccessful bill to license chiropractors. Remy tested Clawson's memory on numerous events and found it sharp on the meeting with Madge but otherwise hazy. "You have a sort of moonshine memory, haven't you, Doctor?" Remy asked—but objections cut him short.

Remy's case for kidnapping was unraveling, and the worst was yet to come.

Next up was a comely couple, Mr. and Mrs. Edward E. Schultze of Laurel, Indiana. Mrs. Schultze, a young women in her mid 20s with snapping black eyes, testified first, saying Steve and Madge had visited the Schultze home the previous November.

"I remember it well," she said. "Mr. Stephenson got down on the floor and played with the baby.... It was in the evening.... Mr. Stephenson got down on the floor and played with our 2-year-old-baby, and he played with the baby a long time...."

Ira Holmes, for the defense: "Did Miss Oberholtzer say anything to Mr. Stephenson just before they left?"

Mrs. Schultze: "Just before they left, she said, 'Hadn't we better leave, dear?'" And, she said, Madge also said, "The baby wants you to play with him again, Stevie." Mr. Stephenson made a great hit with the baby, Mrs. Schultze said.

Her husband, Ed Schultze, corroborated the story. "As I remember, she said, 'Don't you think we'd better start back, dear? We have a long way to go.'"

On Prosecutor Remy's cross examination, Schultze said he met Stephenson in the early days of the Ku Klux Klan, in September of 1922. "I later worked for him as an organizer," Schultze said, adding that he had been to Steve's office since the assault charge was filed but had not visited him in the Noblesville jail.

"Have you ever been to the Stephenson home?"

"Yes, a few times."

Remy caught Schultze off guard with a series of questions about his subpoena, served by one Carl Losey, a shadowy figure of controversy, who had been dropped from the state motor police force about six weeks earlier—one of Steve's key men.

"Was that the Carl Losey who used to be a state policeman?"

"Yes."

"Where did you meet Carl Losey?"

"In Rushville."

"What was he doing?"

"Taking part in a liquor investigation."

"What were you doing there?"

"I was organizing the Klan in Rushville."

Judge Sparks, who was from Rushville, sat up straight and listened intently.

"Did Losey tell you at that time that 'We all must stick by Steve and help him out?'"

"He did not!"

"You didn't receive any money from Stephenson, did you?"

"No, sir."...

If Remy was losing ground on the kidnapping question, now the ground was about to fall out from under him, with the next witness,

James H. Lambert, 1018 1/2 North New Jersey, Indianapolis—chief clerk of Indianapolis' Washington Hotel.

"SAW MADGE ALONE IN AUTO ON FATAL NIGHT, HOTEL MAN STATES," read Niblack's headline in Saturday night's *Times*. "Witness Attacks Dying Statement in Which Alleged Victim Said She Was Held Captive En Route to Union Station."

The haunting question would not go away: If Madge had been kidnapped, why didn't she break and run? Her answer had been that she was never alone, that she was always guarded by men with guns. But defense witness Lambert said he had often seen Miss Oberholtzer around the hotel, asking for Mr. Stephenson.

"At the Hotel Washington, Miss Oberholtzer introduced herself about January or February one evening. She came up to the hotel. Miss Oberholtzer inquired for Mr. Stephenson. I asked the lady to wait a minute until I rang his room. He was not in. She said she would wait on the mezzanine floor while I tried to locate him. I couldn't find him."

Defense attorney Ira Holmes: "Did you see her on other occasions?"

Yes, in the Top O' Town Cafe. I daresay two weeks after that."

"That is in the top of the hotel?"

"Yes. I saw her twice in the hotel and once out in front."

"Who was she with when you saw her in the hotel?"

"D.C. Stephenson and others."

"When she was out in front—where was she?"

"In an automobile."

"When was that?"

"March 15, very late at night."

"What part of the automobile was she in?"

"The front seat."

"Was anyone in the car with her?"

"No one."

A buzz ran through the crowd, for Madge's statement said she was in the back seat, under armed guard.

"You may cross examine," Holmes said, turning his witness over to Remy.

"You have been promoted in the last two weeks, you say? Did D.C. Stephenson have a financial interest in the hotel?"

"Not to the best of my knowledge."

"He maintained headquarters there, didn't he?"

"He had a room there a short time, on different occasions."

"To whom did you first tell this tale?"

"To whom did I first tell this tale? Why, to the jury."

"No one ever heard it before?"

"No."

"And you knew the authorities of the city of Indianapolis were trying to find out all they could about this case, and yet you told not a one?"

"Yes, that's right."

"You never told Klinck, or Stephenson, or Gentry?"

"Not a one of the three."

"Then, do you know how it comes about these men subpoenaed you to come up here and testify about this, if you had never told a living soul?"

"No, but I can guess."

"This is a trial," said Remy sternly, "and we can't guess about these matters... And when you did learn of this case, you never said a word to a living soul?"

"Don't misconstrue me. I never mentioned my part."

"Then if Mr. Holmes a few minutes ago asked you to state when you went out there if anything happened, he didn't know either."

"No, he didn't know."

"Say, who subpoenaed you?"

"A deputy, I suppose."

"Describe him."

"A short man, black hair—in fact, his name was Losey," Lambert said.

"Ye ah, Losey," shouted Remy. "Eh heh! Losey! Do you know that Losey is one of Stephenson's henchmen?"

"We object, Your Honor!" shouted Eph Inman. "We object to the word henchmen."

"Henchmen has a perfectly good legal meaning," Judge Sparks said evenly. "If he knows, he may answer."

"No, I don't know," Lambert said, but he added that he had seen Losey around the hotel with Stephenson.

It was noon Saturday, November 7. Judge Sparks declared that court would be in recess Saturday afternoon, to allow attorneys to prepare their jury instructions, and would reconvene Monday at 9 a.m.

Remy had fought every inch of the way, but there was no doubt that Stephenson was gaining ground fast, on several fronts:

Implying, or more, that Stephenson and Madge had a close, long standing relationship, and questioning her character

—Establishing an alibi for Klinck.

—Arguing that Madge died from poison, administered by her own hand.

Jurors could follow, if they chose, the logic path Remy was trying to trace: that the defense, acting through Steve's Carl Losey and others, had fabricated stories told by these witnesses, giving Klinck a false alibi and clouding Madge's good name. But Remy had yet to undermine their stories.

Over the weekend, news began to trickle into Indianapolis from the city's lost mayor-elect, John Duvall. From wherever he was hiding, Duvall began to dispatch names for key jobs in his new administration. Each brought its own explosion from those spurned among the three factions he had promised the same jobs.

Two of the factions, led by George V. Coffin and William H. Armitage, were disappointed. "It's a mighty dangerous thing to promise a man something and not give it to him," said the incumbent, Mayor Lew Shank.

The big winner in the spoils game was David Curtis Stephenson.

The parks, police board, much of the police and fire leadership, streets, public works, and public purchasing were securely in the KKK corner. Many appointees were Horse Thief Detectives. Clyde Worley, Remy's special investigator who was also Steve's special crony, was placed in charge of traffic control. Judge Chuck Orbison, national counsel for the Klan, was named corporation counsel. Duvall's brother in law, also a Klansman, was named controller.

The biggest headlines were still reserved, however, for the happenings in the dark paneled courtroom in Hamilton County, where the fifth week of the trial got underway Monday morning.

Stephenson opened the week with two newspaper reporters, the *Indianapolis Star*'s Herbert Eiler and the *Times*' Eugene J. Cadou, who testified they had viewed Miss Oberholtzer's body in the morgue and saw no bruises or lacerations.

Two workers at Union Station—David Giblin, ticket gateman, and Fred Kemper, night manager—said no one cried out or made any unusual display the night of March 15 when Madge and Steve had boarded the train for Hammond.

Miss Maxine Elliott, 18, Steve's stenographer, told of seeing Miss Oberholtzer at Steve's office four or five times. The visits began in January 1925—not earlier, as other witnesses had hinted, she said. Miss Elliott said that Madge always went into Steve's private office when she called, and that on several occasions they left together.

Ralph Rigdon, whom Niblack identified as "one of Stephenson's politicians," said he had seen Madge in Steve's Washington Hotel room when gin was being served.

Rigdon, a former solicitor for the Indiana Republican State Committee, said he went to Stephenson's rooms in the Hotel Washington one afternoon during the Legislative session and found Madge there.

"A bottle of gin was on the table," Rigdon said. "Mr. Stephenson poured it out in three glasses. We only had one apiece. I was there about five minutes, I judge."

Rigdon also said he saw the Oberholtzer's attorneys, Asa Smith and another man Rigdon did not know, in Stephenson's office shortly before the news of the case broke into the press. Defense attorneys, in their questions, hinted that Smith was trying to blackmail Stephenson at the time.

State's attorney Ralph Kane cross examined Rigdon, in a series of the most explosive exchanges of the trial. Rigdon was a giant of a man, and he spent most of the cross-examination period with his feet on the railing, looking as if he were ready to pounce on Kane at any moment.

Kane started by rapid-fire questions about Rigdon's family and political connections. Rigdon said State Representative Joshua D. Carney of Morristown, Indiana, was his wife's cousin.

Kane: "Who are you working for now?"

Rigdon: "Clyde A. Walb," chairman of the Republican State Committee. Before that, Rigdon said, he sold oil securities.

Rigdon said he met Steve three years earlier at the home of Mr. and Mrs. Edward E. Schultze, the Laurel, Indiana, couple who testified Saturday.

"I was joining the Knights of the Ku Klux Klan when I met him," Rigdon said, laughing. He looked over toward Stephenson and shook his fist at him.

"When did you begin to work politics with him?"

"During the last campaign, the primary."

"How often did you visit him?"

"Three or four times a week, some weeks."

"Have you ever been employed by Stephenson to do political work?"

"Not in any capacity." Rigdon's answer was drowned out by a chorus of defense objections and an argument at the state's table.

"Overruled," said Sparks, banging down his gavel for order.

"What were your political schemes with Stephenson?"

"We were trying to elect our friends."

"Who were your friends?"

"Most every one that was elected." A mingled murmur among the crowd soon swelled into laughter.

Judge Sparks warned the witness: "I wish you'd refrain from laughing. If you laugh, these people here will laugh."

"I beg your pardon, judge," Rigdon said.

Kane: "Are you on Stephenson's payroll now?"

Rigdon: "Only that I wish I was."

"What particular thing brought you to the Legislature every day?"

"I'd say the things that brought hundreds of others. I enjoyed seeing the manipulation."

"What manipulations?"

"Your friends and my friends."

"Oh, I don't care about my friends," Kane interjected; and he and Rigdon lapsed into an argument that was cut short by Judge Sparks' gavel.

"I don't want to be hard, gentlemen, because this relates to my home folks, the Republican Party, but I don't want to cover anything up," Sparks said. Kane began to argue with the judge, in heated anger, and Sparks had to remind him the ruling had already gone in the state's favor before Kane quieted down.

"Manipulation!" Kane repeated. "Manipulation? What did you see manipulated? Answer yes or no."

Rigdon tried to argue that the question couldn't be answered by yes or no, but Kane would not be appeased. "I saw bills introduced, passed, and defeated," Rigdon said, laughing again.

"You think this is a joke, don't you?" Kane said.

"Objection!" cried defense attorneys, and Kane's question was stricken from the record.

"Did you ever see Stephenson at the Legislature?"

"I don't remember a single occasion."

"Well, then, did you ever see any members of the Legislature in Stephenson's office?"

"Yes."

"Who?"

"Give me a roster, and I'll name them off." Laughter exploded throughout the room at the sweeping admission of Steve's legislative influence. Even Judge Sparks could not resist a hearty laugh.

"Did you ever talk with Foster Strader about this case?" Strader was one of Steve's secretaries.

"Only in a general way."

"How many times?"

"Oh, I couldn't begin to tell you."

"He had a good deal to do with framing up the defense, didn't he?"

Every attorney at the defense table shouted objections, and Judge Sparks struck the word, "framing."

"Do you know Carl Losey?" Again, the mystery name, the former state policeman, said to be a Stephenson agent, Niblack wrote.

"Yes."

"Did you ever talk with him about this case?"

"Only in a general way."

"He helped organize this defense, didn't he?" Defense attorneys objected again.

"There's nothing inferential in the word, 'organize,'" Sparks said. "It is to be assumed that the defense would be organized."

Rigdon said he didn't know about Losey's role in the defense. To another series of questions, Rigdon said he had visited Stephenson the day he was brought to Hamilton County jail.

"Oh, you got him on the first, eh?" Kane said. "How many more visits since?"

"I have no idea."

Kane switched to another line of questions, pressuring Rigdon for specific dates, times, and details about the day he said he had seen Madge in Stephenson's room. Kane was firing questions faster than Rigdon could answer. And then Kane shouted, "You came here to help this little thing through, didn't you?"

Eph Inman jumped to his feet. "Your Honor," he said, pointing to Kane, "can't this man be held at all?"

"When was the second time you met Stephenson?" Kane asked Rigdon.

"I can't tell."

"When was the third time?"

"To be honest with you, I don't remember."

"How many times did you see Miss Oberholtzer in Stephenson's office?"

"Frequently. I wouldn't say daily, but three or four times a week."

"And all this time you were in Indianapolis you were just loafing— just a common hanger on?"

Rigdon started forward, stopped himself, and parried. Kane thrust his finger toward the witness and cried, "Answer it! Answer it!"

"Just phrase it to suit yourself."

"Will you tell the jury why you were hanging around the Legislature, loafing around Stephenson's office doing nothing at all?"

Rigdon lunged forward again, with one foot over the rail, then stopped again, clenched and unclenched his fist, and glared at Kane.

"I don't know whether I should say this, Judge, but if you were—if you were—" Judge Sparks stopped him with his gavel.

Far from pulling back, Kane jabbed harder: "Haven't you been in this courtroom during this trial?" The judge had prohibited most witnesses from attending.

No!" Rigdon shouted. "No!"

"Didn't you talk with Strader and Losey about what you were going to testify?"

"Positively no!"

"That's like most of your answers," Kane said.

Inman was on his feet. "You Honor, I think this man ought to be admonished."

"I think the court can handle itself without any suggestions from the counsel," Sparks said. "It's about six of one and half a dozen of the other."

Kane asked Rigdon what time it was that he and Stephenson and Madge supposedly drank gin at the Washington Hotel. "Was it 1-o'clock, 2, 3, 4, or what time was it?"

"I told you I didn't know," Rigdon roared.

"Don't you know that this is a lie," screamed Kane, with a wild look in his eye, "that there is not a word of truth in what you have said here! And that you came here for the express purpose of committing perjury."

Suddenly the courtroom was dead still. The word echoed.

Rigdon stood up and raised a clenched fist. "You're not big enough to tell me that on the street," he shouted at Kane.

"Yes," cried Kane. "I'll meet you on the street or anywhere—"

Judge Sparks interrupted. "This is not a justice of the peace court, and we'll not have any dog fights in here! Now you keep still," he said, shaking his gavel right under the nose of the witness, who was about to scream another threat at Kane.

"I'm running this court," Sparks said, and he continued to

admonish both men to keep still until he was certain they had backed off from their impending fist fight.

"You're a pretty good friend of Stephenson's, eh?" said Kane, still baiting Rigdon. "You're here to help him out, eh?"

"If my testimony will do him some good, he's welcome to it," Rigdon said.

When court reconvened Tuesday morning, November 10, state's attorney Ralph Kane appeared with a battered jaw and black eye. His peers teased him that Ralph Rigdon must have "met him on the street," but Kane sheepishly claimed that he bumped into a cellar door.

Testimony opened with two Noblesville doctors, J. D. Sturdevant and L. R. Lingeman, testifying for the defense. The theory among observers, wrote John Niblack, was that Stephenson's lawyers wanted to make an impression on the jurors by getting hometown doctors to say the same things the Indianapolis doctors have said for the defense: that Madge died of bichloride of mercury poisoning.

Perhaps the only new information was that Cox accused one of the defense doctors of receiving $1,000 from Steve for his testimony—in contrast to the $100 a day the other defense physicians had admitted receiving. A hundred dollars was no small potatoes, in a day when a car could be bought for $65. In fact, as the trial rounded into its fifth week, the total jury costs, including the 228 men examined for jury service, had climbed above $2000—the biggest jury service bill that Marion County had ever received, but still dwarfed by the money Steve was pouring into his defense.

The morning of dry medical testimony, retracing old defense ground, did not diminish a feeling of high expectation among the crowd. From the moment the state rested its case the previous week, defense attorneys had been promising a bombshell. The bomb would be in the form of a sensational disclosure that would take the state totally by surprise, and it would come two hours or less before the defense rested, Steve's attorneys said.

Surely the time was drawing near, when the defendants would take the stand, perhaps to reveal the surprise disclosures then. Niblack's deadline was drawing near—he didn't want to be in second place on this story. But no matter how he pressed, he could not pry information from defense attorneys.

After the Noblesville doctors left the court, Steve, Klinck, Gentry, and their attorneys held a five-minute, whispered conference in an adjoining room.

Niblack checked his pocket watch: It was 11:30 a.m.—only minutes before deadline.

The defense group returned, beaming broadly, and all but Eph Inman sat down.

"Your Honor," Inman announced, speaking slowly and deliberately, emphasizing every word, "the defense now rests."

Prosecutor Remy blinked, then turned to Inman and smiled. "Your Honor," Remy said, "we have been taken somewhat by surprise. We can have our rebuttal witnesses here by 2-o'clock."

"Very well," said Judge Sparks. "We'll adjourn until 1:15 and indulge the state at that time with whatever reasonable additional time they may need to assemble their witnesses."

And thus, the defense rested. The promised bombshell had fizzled, leaving unanswered the puzzling question: Why had none of the defendants testified on his own behalf?

24
In Defense Of Her Honor

Tuesday, November 10, 1925
Noblesville, Indiana

Rain. Cold rain, moving in from the northwest, the kind that dampens the spirit, even before the rain arrives, with a chill no wool or wrap can dispel.

The icy wind gathered dead leaves and stray papers outside the courthouse and swirled them high, slamming them against cobwebbed courtroom windows as if demanding entrance. Surely, on such a day, something significant would happen.

Within, the court was tense and packed with the largest crowd yet, wrote reporter John Niblack. Prosecutor Remy had 75 witnesses lined up to rebut Steve's defense testimony. His rebuttal strategy was to challenge the credibility of Steve's witnesses, to attack Klinck's alibi, and most of all to refute the insinuations that Madge was a loose woman with a long-standing relationship with Steve.

It was a tall order for the young prosecutor.

At 1:15 p.m. Tuesday, November 10, Remy called his first rebuttal witness: Dr. R. N. Harger, the toxicologist from Indiana University's School of Medicine who had testified for Remy earlier.

Judge Cox questioned the witness for the state. He splintered the testimony of Steve's medical witnesses.

Madge could have recovered from the poison, Dr. Harger asserted. Medical literature contained at least 11 cases of patients who recovered after large doses of bichloride of mercury, even when no medical aid was given for as long as two days.

How did Dr. Harger explain the difference between his testimony on medical literature and that of Steve's medical witnesses? Ah, said the doctor, it is important to read the work of true authorities on the subject.

Judge Cox named over the books cited by Steve's medical witnesses.

Most of those writers were not authorities, Dr. Harger said. The U.S. surgeon general kept a list of the best expert books on toxicology, Dr. Harger said. Steve's doctors cited people who were nowhere on the list.

Eph Inman tried to rattle Dr. Harger through a rough cross examination, but the doctor's testimony held firm.

Remy's next witness was Dr. Cleon A. Nafe, superintendent of the Indianapolis city hospital, called by Remy to refute the defense charge that Madge died of mercury poisoning. But defense attorneys objected that Remy's use of medical experts did not constitute rebuttal testimony. Judge Sparks agreed and ruled out Dr. Nafe's testimony.

It was a setback for Remy, but less dramatic than the one that followed.

Remy's upcoming witness lineup included fifty prominent Indianapolis citizens, who had agreed to speak as Madge's character witnesses, including three who were in the court Tuesday afternoon: State Librarian Demarchus C. Brown; a prominent doctor, E.E. Wishard; and a matron named Jennie H. Brown.

Remy called Mrs. Brown to the stand: "State your name."

"Jennie H. Brown."

"Are you married?"

"Yes," she answered, "I'm the wife of Hilton U. Brown."

The name swept across the spectators like the sharp wind beyond the windows. Hilton U. Brown was managing editor of the *Indianapolis News*, the most powerful newspaper in the state and among the most powerful in the country. The *News*, as Asa Smith recalled years later, "was God—you mentioned the *News* anywhere in Indiana and you trembled, you know, in those days." Mrs. Hilton U. Brown was the state's reigning social goddess, recalled Smith, who said he convinced her to testify and drove her to court in his little coupe.

Mrs. Brown said she lived at 5087 East Washington Street and had lived in Irvington 32 years.

Did she have any children?

"Nine living, one dead, killed in France."

Did she know Madge? Remy asked.

"Why, I certainly did," said Mrs. Brown, who added she had known Madge for 20 years. "She spent the night as our guest in our home two nights before this awful thing happened."

"Were you acquainted with the general reputation of Madge Oberholtzer in the neighborhood where she lived, as regards chastity and morality?"

"I certainly am."

"Well, state what that reputation was."

Floyd Christian leaped to his feet. "The defense objects," he shouted. "We haven't challenged the reputation and character of this girl. We object, Your Honor." Character witnesses cannot be used unless the defense has attacked her character, he argued.

Remy was stonefaced. "It is our theory that the defense has attacked the character of Madge Oberholtzer," he retorted. "The defense has brought witnesses here who have testified that Madge Oberholtzer was addicted to the use of liquor and ran around with questionable people"—Remy turned and stared purposefully at Stephenson to underscore the word "questionable."

Judge Sparks arranged a stack of papers, took a deep breath, and responded. "I've put a good deal of time on that proposition, Gentlemen," Sparks said. "In case of murder, the deceased's character is never to be brought out as an issue except when the person's character has been attacked by a defending party. I find no authority to support a theory to the contrary, and if you have any to support it, I shall be mighty glad to hear it."

"But," said Remy, "there has been an attempted attack by innuendo against the character of Madge Oberholtzer. When the defense goes so far as to put a girl in a room with a man, and to allege that the two are drinking, I regard that as an assault against a person's character. It is a principle of the law that a person can do indirectly what he can't do directly."

"I'm not telling you what ought to be the law," Sparks said. I'm just telling you what I think is the law. I'm a preacher of the higher courts, and I must follow them. The Supreme Court says it can't be done, that's all. If you can cite one case, I'd be glad to have it. I couldn't find one."

It was a significant loss to the state's case, wrote Niblack, arraying as a backdrop the silhouettes of fifty character witnesses Remy could not now call to testify. But Remy had anticipated the ruling, and he had a backup ace in Mrs. Brown's pocket.

"You may go now, Mrs. Brown," Remy said, yielding to the defense objection.

"Oh. I don't have any more testifying to do?"

"No, Mrs. Brown."

As she rose from the witness stand, Mrs. Brown shook her head in disappointment. Then she hesitated, raised her patrician chin, and stared squarely at the jury. "I'm so sorry I didn't get to testify," she declared. "I had so many wonderful things I wanted to say about Madge. She was such a lovely girl, and I loved her so."

It was the next morning, Wednesday, before Remy regrouped and fetched his next witnesses. The rain had settled in now, a steady downpour that was swelling the White River to flood stage in Hamilton County.

Court resumed with a statement by Judge Sparks. There would be no more smoking in the court, he said. Newsmen, defendants, and attorneys sighed. "The air gets so foul, it's awful," Sparks said sternly. "Please just step out to some side room. And that applies to women as well as men."

In the packed courtroom, the audience of mostly women included few non-whites. There was some stir, then, when Remy's next panel of witnesses included four in prison garb, including two young black men.

First up, as Niblack wrote, was "Pete Majors, colored, ...a prisoner at the Indiana State Farm."

"When did you go there?" Remy asked.

"On March 17."

"Where did you go from?"

"The Marion County Jail, in the sheriff's Hudson."

"Who went with you?"

"Three prisoners, excusing myself, and a deputy sheriff."

"Who was the deputy?" Remy asked slowly.

"Koffel—Red Koffel."

"Any one else?"

"Yes—a trusty—you know, Mr. Remy, one of them prisoners what they trusty around the jail."

"When did you start?"

"About 1-o'clock." A buzz rose from the spectators, since the defense witnesses had testified that Klinck was on that trip and returned to Indianapolis by 11:30 a.m.

"Do you know a deputy named Earl Klinck?"

"No, sir."

Stephenson and Klinck, who had feigned boredom over recent days, were watching the witness intently. Steve had a haggard, haunted look.

"Did a man named Klinck go with you?"

"No, sir."

"You may cross examine," Remy said to defense attorney Ira Holmes.

"When were you sentenced to the farm?" Holmes asked.

"March 13—Friday the 13th—'hoodoo Friday,'" the witness said, with a broad, white toothed grin and laugh that was echoed by spectators.

"Who drove the car?"

"Red drove it."

"Who guarded you?"

"Didn't need no guardin'. Was handcuffed on the back seat by both hands."

"What are you doing time for on the farm?"

"Whiskey. Violatin' liquor law."

"Had you been arrested before and convicted before?"

"Yes, sir, twice."

"What for?"

"Whiskey."

"Who first asked you about this trip?"

"One of the officers out at the penal farm yesterday. He asked me did I remember what deputy brought me out and I says yes."

"How tall was this deputy?"

"Well— " The witness gazed around the courtroom. "Well, he's lower than I am." Like Klinck, the witness stood over 6 feet tall.

"Who brought you here?"

"Mr. Howard, the superintendent."

"Who came to the farm to see you?"

"Two men. I don't know who they were. Last night."

When Remy resumed questioning, he pointed to two men. "This is Mr. Judson Sparks, chief deputy prosecutor of Marion County, and Mr. William Shaeffer, grand jury deputy," Remy said. "Are these the two men who came over to see you?"

"Yes, sir, that's them," the witness said, with another broad, white grin of recognition.

Next up was, as Niblack reported, "Thomas Tuggie, 18, colored," another State Farm prisoner who had been on the same ride and verified the previous prisoner's story.

"Do you know who took you?" Remy asked.

"I don't know who he was, but they called him Red. He had red hair and a red mustache."

The description was a dead ringer for Deputy Koffel. In contrast, Klinck had graying brown hair and was smooth shaven.

Stories from both the black prisoners matched perfectly with those of the other two prisoners on the ride, Harry Mescall and Louis Brunner, both 19, both white.

Who asked him to be a witness? Remy asked Brunner.

"One of the screws," he answered, explaining that a "screw" was an assistant prison superintendent.

Following the four prisoners were two white prison clerks, Oren D. Williams and Orville Collins.

"Now, Mr. Collins," Remy said, strutting up and down in front of the jury with unusual pomp, "I hand you State's Exhibit No. Twelve." It was a page from the prison record. State's Exhibit No. Five followed, a receipt for the prisoners.

"That's my record, and I made it out," the witness said. The stub showed the prisoners were delivered at 3 p.m., not in the morning as contended by those who testified to Klinck's alibi.

For the first time in days, Prosecutor Remy turned to Stephenson and gave him a blissful smile.

"REBUTTAL BOLSTERS DYING STORY," Niblack's Wednesday afternoon headline read. "Prisoners at Indiana State Farm Attack Klinck's Alibi, Testifying He Did Not Go With Them on Trip March 17."

But the larger headlines were captured by the witness who followed the prison workers and prisoners: a businessman, age 38, slightly balding, a widower whose quietly assertive air caught the immediate interest of the crowd. His name was Stanley C. Hill.

Hill said he lived at 3312 Ruckle Street in Indianapolis, with his three children and mother-in-law.

"Were you acquainted with Miss Oberholtzer?" asked state's attorney Ralph Kane.

"Yes, since October 1923."

"Were you at the Governor's banquet at the Indianapolis Athletic Club the night of January 12?"

"Yes. I was secretary of the inaugural committee. It was my duty to make arrangements for the banquet, and to arrange the seating order."

"Was Madge Oberholtzer there?"

"Yes. She was there as my guest." The room buzzed again. "She helped me arrange the seating."

"Were you seated near the defendant, Stephenson?"

"Yes. Mr. Stephenson sat directly across the table from us."

"Was Stephenson introduced to Madge Oberholtzer that evening?"

"She was."

"Who by?"

"By me."

The whispered buzzing became a roar, rising to the ceiling until Judge Sparks' gavel cut it short.

"Now, do you know whether Madge Oberholtzer had ever met D. C. Stephenson before that night?"

"I am positive she had not," Hill said, over the shout of defense attorneys' objections.

"Sustained," said Sparks, who ordered the remarks struck from the record.

Eph Inman swooped down on the witness. "Mr. Hill, were you on every day and night consistently in the presence of Madge Oberholtzer?"

"I was in communication with her or saw her sometime every day with few exceptions," Hill said, swinging around in the witness chair to glare at Stephenson.

"Yes, but when you didn't call her on the phone, you didn't know where she was?"

"I had a pretty good idea."

"But you didn't know, did you?"

"Of course not," Hill snapped.

"You say you are in the real estate business. Where do you operate?"

"St. Petersburg, Florida."

"Weren't you connected with Mr. Stephenson, in an affair down there?"

"Yes, but it was not an affair, Mr. Inman."

"What was it?"

"It was in business."

"Now, I'll ask you if it isn't a fact that you severed your connection with that business in February?"

"I most assuredly did."

"And is it not a fact that you are short $200 in your account?"

"I was not," the witness yelled, rising from his chair. "I was not!"

"Do you remember the campaign of 1924?"

"I do."

"Were you in Mr. Stephenson's office then?"

"Yes, it was not over two times. It was in October 1924."

"Is it not a fact, Mr. Witness, that you were in Mr.Stephenson's office with Madge Oberholtzer in 1924?"

"I was not! Never!"

"I'll ask you, weren't you in that office with Madge Oberholtzer, discussing arrangements for the Governor's inauguration?"

Stephenson whispered to Inman, who then continued, "I'll ask you if you weren't in room 1001 in the Severin Hotel with Madge Oberholtzer during the 1924 campaign."

Hill denied it.

"I'll ask you, Mr. Witness," Inman thundered, "if you weren't seen in a theater party which was given at Mr. Stephenson's expense, with Mr. Stephenson and in Madge Oberholtzer's company, after a drinking party at the Severin Hotel in October 1924?"

"I was not!" Hill replied, with great certainty. "It is not true." His right hand tightened into a fist that he captured in his left hand, massaging intently, while he glared at Stephenson.

Remy's next witness was Ralph Roudebush, who contended neither Madge nor Dr. Chester L. Clawson was present when Steve met Dr. Vallery Ailstock in Columbus. Roudebush said he saw Stephenson on the street that January night with the Columbus dentist, but there was no woman in the automobile.

"Well," Roudebush testified, "I asked Mr. Stephenson about some

stock I'd bought in the Cavalier Motion Picture Company. He said he
guessed the company had fallen through and he said, 'It's no use to
complain. You know I'm the law in Indiana, and I've got the money to
back me up—so what can you do?'"

As Roudebush left the witness stand at 3:30 p.m., Remy suddenly,
without ceremony, closed the state's rebuttal.

Defense attorneys were jubilant. They had blocked Remy's dozens
of character witnesses.

But reporters, assessing the trial over cigars and white mule that
night, chalked up some points for the state's rebuttal. Steve's medical
witnesses had been largely discredited, and Mrs. Hilton U. Brown
had found a way to stand up for Madge's character. Stanley Hill had
lent an air of clean-cut freshness to the proceedings, in contrast to
most of the defense witnesses. Most triumphant was Remy's rebuttal
trump card: shattering Klinck's alibi by none other than two Negro
prisoners.

As the night wore on and the rum flowed, the irony of it all became
richer and richer. The reporters watched in wonder as Watty Watson,
star reporter of the *Indianapolis News*, slipped slowly under the table,
into a happily drunken heap on the press room floor.

The next act in the drama was defense surrebuttal, set to begin
at 9 o'clock Thursday morning. But rather than dramatic rebuttal
testimony, only minor actors appeared; and the morning produced
nothing for the defense.

With the final testimony of Dr. Roscoe Carpenter, Indianapolis—
head of Cavalier Motion Pictures, who denied Stephenson owned any
stock in his company—the defense ended its surrebuttal, and the last
of the witnesses passed from the scene.

Defense attorneys offered Sparks their draft instructions to the
jurors—161 items—which the judge agreed to take under advisement

with those from Remy.

Now, ordered Judge Sparks, attorneys for both sides should present their final arguments, no more than 8 hours for each side. After a brief recess, it would be up to Remy to begin.

25
A Plain Case of Suicide

Thursday, November 12, 1925
Noblesville, Indiana

Bill Remy marched to the fore of the courtroom. Like a pitcher staring down a first-base runner, he turned to glare intently at D.C. Stephenson, then folded his hands over his dark wool vestcoat. The boy and man still wrestled in him for dominance: Prosecutor Remy looked like a boy, but he spoke and moved like a man.

He took a deep breath, bestowed a congenial smile on the jury and, without further preliminaries, began. It was 10 a.m. Thursday, November 12.

"Gentlemen of the jury, we've had some rather trying days.

"I'm going to speak to you briefly. The state has done its duty in this case to the best of its ability. It is now for the jury to determine whether the evidence against D.C. Stephenson, Earl Klinck, and Earl Gentry has removed beyond a reasonable doubt the question of their guilt."

Remy paused, took one step toward the three defendants, glared at them, then turned back to the jurymen.

"I don't know of any case in the history of Indiana, in the entire history of jurisprudence, where the defense has had a fairer trial, a fairer judge. I know the state is satisfied."

Klinck and Gentry were listening intently, while Stephenson was writing furiously, with a touch of a sneer on his face.

Remy read the definition of first degree murder, then thrust the book aside and again faced the jury.

"Gentlemen, Madge Oberholtzer is dead. She would be alive today were it not for the unlawful act of D.C. Stephenson, Earl Klinck, and Earl Gentry. They destroyed her body and tried to destroy her soul. And in the last few days they have tried to dishonor her morals....

"Oh! They didn't attack her character directly—they didn't dare to do that. They knew if they tried it, they would open the very flood gate of evidence. So they tried it by innuendo. All the means they had at their command, however few, they tried," he shouted fervently.

Waving the dying declaration, Remy cried out: "Madge Oberholtzer's story still stands unfinished! Her dying declaration is before you again, with corroborating and supporting evidence from witness after witness, creditable witnesses. It stands not only with the solemnity of the declaration of a person who faces certain death, it still stands, most of it not even denied. They didn't dare deny it."

Remy was casting aside his typical, colorless precision and becoming animated, moving to and fro with atypical verve.

"He said he was the law in Indiana," Remy said. "That's what he told Madge Oberholtzer, and circumstances surrounding this case must lead every thinking man in the state to think that he was the law. And sometimes I, myself, think he was the law—that is, in some places.

"I don't believe D.C. Stephenson is, was, or ever will be the law in Hamilton County! Even he must know it by this time....

"He bit her, he attacked her, he ravished her, he chewed her all over her body. And it isn't denied by any evidence in the case, gentlemen of the jury."

Stephenson flushed, then turned pale, his pencil frozen in midair.

Step by careful step, Remy traced through Madge's statement, turning to the time Madge said she was returned home.

"Not knowing about Mrs. Schultz being at home, Klinck brought her there. Didn't knock. Just opened the door. But Mrs. Schultz was there—Providence—

"And Klinck—caught—turned his head one way and then the other to avoid recognition. Told her, 'I'm Mr. Johnson of Kokomo. She'd got hurt in an automobile accident!'

"...Why, the evidence shows that Earl Klinck was a deputy sheriff, but the prisoners didn't even know him. That's because he was a deputy sheriff assigned to the particular service of D.C. Stephenson— the man who said he was the law in Indiana. And Marion County paid the bill....

"And Klinck wants you to believe he took prisoners to the Indiana State Farm and got back by 11 o'clock the same morning. Oh, if the Marion County sheriff's office had shown such speed when D.C. Stephenson was under indictment, and was being sought— and Stephenson on a fishing frolic—and they later found him conveniently waiting in his office—armed...."

From the exhibits table, Remy picked up the telegram, held it high, then walked over and flicked it in Inman's face. The prosecutor leaned over and stared dead center into Inman's eyes.

"She begged Stephenson to wire her mother. The first thing she thought of was her mother."

He returned to reading from Madge's statement."'Stephenson said he was sorry, but that he was three degrees less than a brute,'" Remy read. "'I said he was worse than that.'

"I guess there's no controversy over that....

"She had lost everything that a good woman had. When she got her hat, she knew just what she was going to do."

Remy paced in silence, and the tension rose unbearably in the packed courtroom. The ticking of the clock rose louder and louder, in sync with a muffled creaking of a chair as Matilda Oberholtzer methodically rocked forward and back.

"Dr. Virgil A. Moon, professor of pathology at the Indiana University School of Medicine, the school where half the defense's medical witnesses graduated. Dr. Moon—recognized officially by the county officer whose duty it was to arrange the autopsy—said that wound, that wound on her breast, that abscess on her lung, was brought on by the fang of D. C. Stephenson!"

Involuntarily, someone in the room clapped twice. Judge Sparks jerked up his gavel, then gently laid it aside.

"Stephenson's own personal physician, who had treated him for alcoholism—that 'expert'—he tried to tell you that it didn't hurt her to ride from Hammond to Indianapolis, in an automobile, that it didn't hurt her to spend the night in a garage, because nothing could have helped her. That's what they want you to believe....

"Then they started in to write the blackest page in this case. It was the last resort.... The best toxicologists in Indianapolis had testified for the state, so the defense grew desperate. They had to do something. So they tried to blacken that girl's character, and they used some mighty foul blackening."

After another pause, as Remy glared at Inman.

"Then there was Rigdon, another defense witness. Anything nobody else would testify to, he would. Loafing around the Legislature every day in Stephenson's office with Klinck, a deputy sheriff of Marion County paid by the people. Yeah, 'I am the law in

Indiana.' No wonder he said it."

Like a refrain, again and again: "I am the law in Indiana" and "I have been in a worse mess than this and got out."

At times, the prosecutor dropped his voice into a whisper so low that only the jury could hear what he said. Other times he shrieked until the courtroom echoed.

"My goodness, what an array.... Why, they didn't produce anybody but the gang to testify against this girl—and only when all else had been blown to the winds...."

Noon recess, with vendors hawking food and the crowd swirling in and out of the courtroom, in clouds of smoke from hallway cigars and cigarettes.

Remy started again softly, slowly, with the law.

"This case is as complete a case as has ever been made in this state. The statement of this girl is completely corroborated—unless you want to take the word, the unsupported word, of men like Rigdon, who have been up here visiting Stephenson in jail—the old strong-armed gang Stephenson relied on when he said, 'I am the law,' to come up here and swear him out, any way, any how...."

Remy walked over to one of the jurymen, and said, "I shoot you in the lung. Every doctor in Noblesville says you have only five hours to live." Remy turned to another juryman.

"And you shoot him in the heart. He dies instantly. You are a murderer."

The three defendants, Remy shrieked, "are guilty—of psychological murder—and actual murder!"

Stephenson leaned back in his chair, brushed his tousled hair with his hands, and yawned.

The defense case was a web of lies told by paid liars, Remy shouted.

He seized the record book of the Indiana State Farm, containing official notations on the dates prisoners were received—"Regular records made by regular men in their regular line of duty, and they made regular fools out of D.C. Stephenson!"

The young prosecutor, gasping for breath, slapped the jury rail.

"'I'm the law in Indiana. I've been in tighter fixes before and gotten out.' Wouldn't it be interesting to hear what that tight place was? I'd like to know if he has ever been in a tighter place than now," Remy screamed, his face inches from Stephenson's.

"If there is a defense in this case, it has not yet been disclosed. That statement of Madge Oberholtzer stands uncontradicted and undenied, because they knew better than to attack it. There was no defense and they knew it."

Remy took a deep breath and let the words sink in.

"They say, 'Why did she go to his house?' Say, gentlemen, this man fooled some of the best people in Indianapolis and in the State of Indiana. It isn't the first time he's fooled anybody.

"Why didn't she use the telephone in the hotel? A poison far more virulent than bichloride of mercury had entered her soul. She had lost everything she had to live for."

Another pause. Remy was circling toward his conclusion.

"Madge Oberholtzer is dead. She would be alive today were it not for the unlawful act of three men. They destroyed her body, they tried to destroy her soul, and in the last few days they have tried to dishonor her character...with this gang of witnesses, this gang who helped D.C. Stephenson believe his word was the law in Indiana.

"Well, his word may be law in Marion County—but not in Hamilton County!

"We're going to see if the law of the State of Indiana has any majesty left. We are going to see which is the bigger, one man or Indiana. We're going to see if a man can get by with murder in this state.

"I don't believe D.C. Stephenson is the law in Indiana—and I believe your verdict will prove it!"

At a break in the arguments, Stephenson sauntered over to a booth, established by the Noblesville Red Cross in the courthouse to get contributions from the large crowds attending the trial. Steve airily picked up a Red Cross button, pinned it on his crisp tailored suit, and handed one of the women $5.

Next up was Ira Holmes, assuming center stage with the first closing argument for the defense.

"It is a plain case of suicide, just as Coroner Paul F. Robinson held," Holmes declared. "I say to you, gentlemen of the jury, there is no evidence in this case at all."

A faction of the crowd muttered darkly each time Holmes uttered the word "suicide."

Suicide! Nothing more! Despite the flimsy testimony of the state's medical witnesses.

Suicide! Nothing more! And not of a stranger. "Did Madge Oberholtzer meet D.C. Stephenson for the first time at the Governor's ball? No!" Holmes cried, reviewing the defense testimony that Madge knew Stephenson well before the January 12 inaugural.

"To say this woman was abducted, kidnapped, and forced to go away from home, is absolutely absurd," screamed Holmes, waving the dying declaration under the noses of the jurors.

As for the "dying declaration": "Madge Oberholtzer didn't made that statement. It originated in the mind of Asa Smith—it was made by Asa Smith to get money from Mr. Stephenson."

The charges were concocted to entrap Steve politically, Holmes said.

"It has cropped out in this trial that Mr. Stephenson was once connected with an organization, and that he quit for some reason. It has been shown Mr. Stephenson had some influence in the organization after he left it, and I wonder, yes, indeed, I wonder if there can be any influence coming from that organization behind this case."

The entire trial was a plot by the Klan, the anti Klan, or the newspapers—or all three, Holmes hinted.

Niblack could hardly suppress a sarcastic grin at the thought—until he remembered, with an involuntary shiver, the barricade across the judge's roadway, the thump of a revolver against the courthouse marble floor, and signs that blazed along the roadside: AKAY? YIAAK!

The third speaker was Judge Charles E. Cox, the Oberholtzer's special prosecutor. "The slime of the serpent of perjury is over them all," cried the old warrior in his closing arguments for the state.

Cox marched before the jury for hours, wearing himself to exhaustion, wrote John Niblack, "in a flow of eloquence said never to have been displayed before in this courtroom. Shaking his mane of iron gray hair, Cox waved his arms and..., time and again he advanced to the defendants' table, where the trio sat unmoved by the epithets, and shook his fist in Stephenson's face, his own countenance purple with passion."

"There is a man and a woman in this courtroom now," Cox said, "a broken father and mother, who brought Madge Oberholtzer into this world, who rejoiced in her coming, who brought her from her infancy into childhood and young womanhood, and who—" but Cox was so filled with emotion that he could not finish the sentence.

"The law must be reinstated on its throne. Madge Oberholtzer's brutal murder must be avenged by the law.

"In the name of the law, in the name of virtuous girls, and in the name of justice, I ask you to write your verdict in a way to stop what has been going on."

He decried Madge's "imprisonment in Stephenson's garage without the ministration of a woman, in the hands of a gorilla."

Cox whirled on Klinck. "Look at the sardonic grin on his face. You can't get him— The man is made of stone—concrete!"

Inman leaped to his feet and shouted an objection, and Judge Sparks said, "You must not refer to the look or demeanor of any person unless he's on the stand."

Klinck continued to laugh.

Cox glared at the defendants. "They will, by insinuation and innuendo, try to lead you to believe Madge Oberholtzer was a bad woman. If she had been bad she would have been alive today."

Striding over to Eph Inman, Cox cried out: "Are you going to permit this unparalleled, this unequaled painter of words, this man of stately bearing and melodious voice—are you going to allow him to take the brush of scandal and write the scarlet letter on Madge Oberholtzer's tomb?"

Inman leaned forward with his elbow on the arm of his chair. His face betrayed no emotion.

Pausing, appraising the jurymen one by one, Cox whispered, "I think I know what is in every good man's heart regarding this case." The room fell silent.

"I told you at the beginning of this case that Madge Oberholtzer would be the principal witness." Cox painted a word picture of Klinck dressing Madge before he took her home, and contrasted it with her mother dressing her when she was a little girl. Tears welled in the eyes of two of the jurors.

And as for the defense contention that Asa Smith concocted the dying statement?

"Attorney Holmes told you, though he was not sworn as a witness, that Asa J. Smith fabricated this statement. What about

Dr. Kingsbury's testimony, told to him by Madge the morning of her return? It is the same in substance....

"How do they defend against the impregnable wall of corroborative evidence raised by the state, these chevaliers, these knights pledged to defend the sanctity of the home and the sanctity of womanhood?" he said sarcastically. "By slandering the dead they have killed."

Stephenson sat erect, watching Cox with a faint smile.

"If a sheep-killing cur got into your barn and killed your ewe lamb, would you spare him?" Cox demanded, in stentorian tones, of the ten farmers on the jury.

"No, you would kill him!

"And when these defendants—Stephenson, the degenerate; Klinck, the gorilla; and Gentry, the iron man—got into the Oberholtzer fold and destroyed the one ewe lamb of George and Matilda Oberholtzer, the law should kill them!

"All three of these men must pay the extreme penalty of the law for this crime, else the law confesses a self subordinate to D.C. Stephenson, a beastly chieftain of the middle ages.

"Are you going to have that reproach cast on the good county of Hamilton?

"I was born in Hamilton, and God forbid such an outcome," shouted the old man.

Suddenly silent, he sank to his chair in exhaustion.

Friday belonged to the defendants, with powerful closing arguments for acquittal from defense attorneys Floyd Christian and Eph Holmes.

The issue was reasonable doubt, Christian said. "Let's leave this tirade of oratory and get down to this lawsuit. Let's find out whether Madge Oberholtzer was murdered or committed suicide."

From a far back corner of the room, someone whistled through his teeth, a low-scathing hiss.

Christian ignored it and focused on the jury. "I have the deepest and the greatest sympathy for Madge Oberholtzer and her parents. But, gentlemen, are we going to try this case on sympathy and sentiment, or are we going to try it on evidence—on reason and fact?

"The first question is 'Was she murdered?'"

More hissing, now joined by others.

"This is not the story of Madge Oberholtzer, but of that little fellow with his finger pushed up to his nose," Christian cried out, whirling around to point to Asa Smith. "What is on trial here? The so-called 'dying declaration,' hashed up by Asa Smith and his vulture of a law partner, Griffith Dean!" Christian shook the document in his hand.

"This old man, Dean, who looks like a vulture, and his gosling, Asa Smith—they didn't take the girl's good father and mother into the room when the statement was signed. Why? They wanted money, the root of all evil. They wanted to shake Stephenson down. It was you, Asa Smith, who concocted this whole ugly morass."

The concerted hissing rose from the back half of the room, followed by a laugh of derision; and Judge Sparks rapped sharply with his gavel.

"Why aren't they down in Indianapolis enforcing the laws down there?" Christian asked. "There wouldn't be so much notoriety down there. I guess they're afraid to—some politician down there might jump on their backs."

No, said Christian, the state's attorneys would rather serve the evil forces that were "out to get D.C. Stephenson."

Christian's argument was interrupted while four men carried out an 81-year-old spectator, Mrs. D.J. McMath, after she swooned in her front row seat. She was the second woman to faint during the morning, overcome by the crush of the crowd and the excitement of the closing hours of the trial.

"How did this girl happen to know about bichloride of mercury?

What's that stuff generally used for? You know the answer," Christian said, hinting that Madge used the drug for an abortion.

The hissing had died away, swept aside by the force of Christian's arguments. Madge's death was a clean case of suicide, he argued, saying the state's medical experts were perjurers and quacks.

But the defense brought in hometown doctors from Noblesville, people who could be trusted to tell the truth, Christian said.

"Well, there is Doc Joe Sturdevant, the Noblesville doctor who appeared for the defense. Even Ralph Kane—the big thunderbolt they're saving until the last of the closing arguments—won't dare call Doc Joe a liar. Why, Doc Joe said the wound on her breast could not have caused her death." Christian leaned close to his fellow countymen on the jury, speaking in a congenial, neighbor to neighbor tone.

Christian argued that to be guilty of murder, it must be done purposely.

"The state's theory that Stephenson was the cause of the cause is far-fetched. Under that theory, the man who mined the iron to make the steel to make the dagger would be guilty. If you raised rye that makes whiskey that makes the wife of a drunkard so despondent she kills herself, under their theory of the cause of the cause of the cause, you're guilty of murder—and that's all there is to the state's case."

The last word of the defense was reserved for Eph Inman, the dean of Indiana criminal lawyers, who moved slowly from his seat to the open space before the jury box. There he stood silent, with his silver, patrician head bowed, as if in prayer.

When he spoke, his voice flowed like honey, sad and soft, almost caressing his listeners.

"Gentlemen of the jury, in all my connection with this remarkable case, I have been conscious of the weight of responsibility which rested upon us all," Inman began.

Inman said he feared for his clients because the case was tainted by "the transient spirit of the mob, the spirit of the lynching party, stirred by forces of hatred and prejudice, unreasonably demanding the lives of three men for purely the suicide—the tragic suicide—of a girl."

His hope, he said, was in the law.

"The law has been man's safeguard down the ages," Inman said, his voice rising as he brushed a lock of hair over his temple. "Shall it be brushed aside to meet the cry of revenge?

"The sole question presented here is: Can suicide be murder? Can suicide be homicide? No man has ever said so or ever will say so unless he says it in contradiction of the law."

Another silence, punctuated by the ticking clock. He paced slowly before the jury box, engaging with his eyes the eyes of each juror.

"A jury of intelligent men, of sensible-thinking men, have accepted to pass upon the question. A jury which we have a right to feel will not be stampeded into doing violence to common sense and law.

"That these men should ever have been indicted for murder is a shame to the jurisprudence of Indiana, and to the law of this land, and I sincerely believe that such an indictment would never have been returned except that the state's attorney and those privately employed to reap the vengeance of hate, determined to respond to the wishes of the unreasoning element of hostility, which wished to hurry Mr. Stephenson to destruction.

"There is not a lawyer in Indiana, not a lawyer in the nation, freed from prejudice and interest, who wouldn't say that this prosecution for murder is entirely without precedence in the jurisprudence of the country. Not only that, but every cool-headed, every fair-minded, reasoning man you may meet upon the street feels and will say they might be guilty of something, even assuming the theory of the state and the story of its witnesses to be true—we don't know—but they are not guilty and could not be guilty, of murder, or guilty of homicide in any degree.

"This case has brought us all to the point where we are to settle the question whether the law, which has been the safeguard of human liberty in the new world for 150 years, shall continue to prevail or whether orderly procedure in court shall break completely down, and we shall be compelled to try our cases before a portion of an intolerant populace, depending for the outcome upon who can present in advance of a trial the longest petitions and resolutions, irrespective of the facts."

The melody of his words seemed to mesmerize the crowd. Even Judge Sparks laid aside his pencil for a time, looking up from his instructions to watch Inman with a far away gaze.

After another pause, Inman stepped up the tempo:

"In this so-called dying declaration—this lawyer-made declaration, designed as poisonous propaganda to be used in the effort to get money—if it declares anything, it is a dying declaration of suicide and not homicide. Why, she only told of how she committed suicide....

"She—by her own concealment of taking the poison, for six hours—made medical aid of no avail. She—by her own willful act of conduct—made it impossible for these men to save her life."

Inman shook his head, sorrowfully. He laid his hands against his lips, linking his long fingers into a cathedral shape, as if in prayer.

"Has everybody lost his head? Pray! Are we all insane?" he cried. "Must prejudice and passion submerge the world for the purpose of some particular case, leaving us, when it is over, in a wild, disorderly state, in mental bewilderment, anarchy in the heart's regret, and the soul's darkness of remorse?"

He let the words' echo die away.

"Such a conclusion is impossible to my own vision in this land where the law is supreme, running on and on forever, arching as the sky above the contingencies of an isolated case. Such a termination, gentlemen, is inconceivable to me.

"The muddy waters of prejudice and hatred, the fierce elements of hostility, and the devoted elements of friendly support may clash—may lash wildly around your feet.

"But—thank God!—this jury is standing fearlessly and solely for justice and supremacy of law, sacredly sworn and conscience bound, breathing clear and pure atmosphere and judgment and reason, far removed from the foul, murky air that lurks and poisons the regions below. Thank God this jury will never suffer sanity and sense to be borne from their minds to outrage and disgrace the civilization of this great state, merely to vent the vengeance of certain forces of hatred and persecution.

"Thank God! we can have juries in this great country who will stand, at all hazards, as a pillar of safety against swirling elements of the mere madness of men—and women."

A fleeting smile crossed Judge Sparks' face, and he began again to busy his pencil on his instructions.

Returning to Stephenson—sitting quietly with his legs crossed at the ankles, his eyes on the floor—Inman placed a hand lightly on The Old Man's shoulder.

"These men have been made helpless for seven long months by fate, unwarranted and cruel. They have been forced to languish in their dungeons, for all this time, upon a charge which every man has known from the beginning could never be sustained, unless violence and outrage be committed upon the law. Unfriendly interests on the outside of jail, unhampered and free, have operated and designed, in savage glee, to compass the destruction of these three men."

He moved to Gentry, who was rocking gently to and fro. "And during all these terrible months, they have sat in their cells, through the sweltering summer days from the dawn of morning to the shadows of evening, unable to meet and cope with forces of hate that clamored round them from without."

And to Klinck. Inman touched Klinck as a father touches a newborn son.

"There has been a tinge of sadness in my soul as I have seen the injustice of it all, while these men, of as fine sensibilities as were ever possessed by any man, have had to sit for all these months, staring at stone walls and bars by day, lying upon prison cots within bars of steel by night."

He paced back before the jury.

"And yet, gentlemen, in this sore distress, under the weight of this great calamity to them, they have friends, many friends." He turned and smiled benignly toward the spectators. "Through the bars of the prison, the best people in this country have come to grasp their hands. They have come with their hearts beating with sympathy in so sad surroundings. And this is consolation after all.

"My being is not so that I wish to hate. My heart is not the home of ill will. I want to give men the benefit of doubt. If one wrongs me, for the moment I may resent; the next moment I want to forgive....

"Maybe, someone feels that I say these things because I am engaged in the defense of these men. It is true I am so engaged. But after a life of service in the great profession of the law—and, I pray, an honorable one—my heart gives utterance to this: that I have not in all my professional life defended one for murder where I felt in my soul there was as complete absence of justification for such a charge as there is in this case."

Leaning over the jury rail, Inman held out his hands, cupped together and outstretched as if they held a most precious gift.

"Gentlemen, I have done. I give this great issue—the safety of my clients—to you.

"By the law of reason, courage, right, I feel that your consciences will not allow any harm to come to these men. They have already suffered much. Too much, far too much. I am grateful to heaven in the confidence that they are now approaching the end of it all."

Dropping his hands to his sides, Inman closed his eyes, with his face lifted upward toward the heavens. Then his chin dropped sharply to his chest, in a gesture of humble supplication.

26
GUILTY OR NOT GUILTY?

Saturday, November 14, 1925
Noblesville, Indiana

Now it remained for the final word to come from the state.
Saturday morning Ralph Kane, the plainspoken farmer lawyer, son of
Hamilton County, rose to close for the prosecution.

Every seat in the court was full; and jurymen, who had listened to
14 hours of previous closing arguments, looked glassy eyed and weary
as Kane moved to the center of the courtroom.

"Gentlemen," he said softly, "we'll all be glad when this trial is over.
We then can go our separate ways and follow our own chosen tasks.

"I'm not going to try to throw a smoke screen over the facts in this
case. I'm going to try to show them in their nakedness for the purpose
of dispelling the screen that others have thrown.

"Something has been said by defense counsel about the gigantic conspiracy that has been framed to destroy their precious clients. Something has been said about the gold that jingles in our pockets. As far as I am concerned, I am here without a penny of compensation for my efforts, without looking to one person for a single dollar." His voice began to rise.

"From the day I was asked to assist in this case, I have done everything in my power to bring about the conviction of the men who have committed the most heinous crime that has ever plagued the fair State of Indiana.

"This is the case of the State of Indiana versus D.C. Stephenson and others, and the state demands their punishment for offending not only the laws of their state but their Creator." Rising still, his voice reached a shriek, and then dropped back to a hissing whisper.

"The theory of the law maintained by the state in this case has been the law of England more than 500 years, and it has been the law of this country ever since the English common law was brought to this country," Kane said.

And the defense medical testimony, doctor after doctor—a fraud and smoke screen, full of conflicts and deceptions.

"I don't care anything about germs!" Kane shouted. "When these defendants unlawfully abducted her, and dragged her to Hammond, they made themselves criminals, and by that very act drove that pure girl—honored and respected in her community, loved by all—drove her to the position where she had lost all, where she was bereft of all she cherished, forced her to take that potion of death, and D.C. Stephenson and his cohorts became murderers just the same as if they had plunged a dagger into her throbbing heart.

"Every case cited to you by the defense in this argument was one where the woman went willingly. If that were true in this case, I wouldn't be taking your time. I'd be back at my office trying to draw together some of the loose ends of my business, making some money for my own family."

A pause, while Kane backed away from the jury box. Niblack looked up from his notes to assess the mood of jurors. "Although Kane's argument was not the pyrotechnical display of some others who had preceded him, his pleading was based on plain logic, and it was having a tremendous effect on the jury," Niblack wrote.

Kane slid both hands into his pockets and leaned over the jury rail. "I'll say to you frankly." he said, "if she went there willingly, there's no case. It's written here on the undeniable book of evidence that Madge Oberholtzer was the unwilling companion of this desperate triumvirate.

"What's the story, gentlemen? Why, it's the most scurrilous in the history of the ages. Trapped in a garage loft, two blocks from her home—dying!

"Don't let the defense befuddle you about this story. Madge Oberholtzer told you a coherent story.... We didn't have to call a hand writing expert, as Mr. Inman suggested, to identify the writer of 'W.B. Morgan and wife.' We had the man who held the pen, and there he is," Kane cried, stabbing his right forefinger toward Stephenson.

Beside Steve, Inman stretched his legs, looking calm and complacent, a little bored. Kane could not resist:

"And Eph Inman, sullen as a boiled owl, looked like an affidavit as he stood before you."

Kane whirled back before the jury and dropped his voice into a conversational whisper. "Now, let's take another step in the history of this outrage.

"These gentlemen don't like Asa Smith. How happy they would be if they had his character.... He's no Stephenson. He's no Klinck. He's no Gentry....

"When the dread news came from the sick room, that this poor girl couldn't recover, and that any evidence would have to be as a dying declaration, Smith wrote it down. God bless him. He brought the evidence in the court which cinches this case, and will send those men to the place where they belong. That's why they don't like Asa Smith.

"These men raped Madge Oberholtzer, attacked her, kidnapped her. But the state can't use the dying declaration in those cases, under the law. It can only be used in homicide cases. Yet these hired and paid criminal lawyers—who wouldn't be here unless for the filthy dollars of the men who manipulated the Legislature—had the effrontery to attack Smith."

Kane painted the scene of Madge's dying, pacing back and forth before the jury, waving his arms aloft for a full five minutes.

"No, they sped on and on, through the night, and instead of taking this poor girl to a doctor, they locked her up in a garage, while her own mother stood helplessly outside.

"Oh, my God! When he got her this bottle of milk, that was altruistic of him, wasn't it? That measly little bottle of milk. Wanted to marry her—coward!

"There's some things you and I know. If Madge Oberholtzer had gone willingly with Stephenson that night, she would have done it by pre arrangement—she would have worn a hat.

"On that fateful Sunday, Madge was out with her friend. She was a happy, joyous girl, and little dreamed of the fate that awaited her....

"If she was going to make a trip with him, wouldn't she have made some preparations at least? Wouldn't she have worn a hat? If I understand women, they usually take some cosmetics. Some lingerie and other things. Especially when they start on a 250-mile Pullman ride."

Lifting both hands, with a question on his face, Kane turned to the audience for affirmation. More than half the spectators were women, and many nodded confirmation of his theory.

"Kane's arguments were going over with a bang," Niblack wrote in his shorthand notebook.

"Do you think she would have had a big, pug-nosed Gentry in the same compartment, if she had been conscious of what was happening? If she was a willing companion, why did they bring her home looking as if she's been in a fight?"

Again he turned to the audience, threw his hands in the air, and accepted affirming nods.

And the newsmen witnesses for the defense! Kane, who had been at loggerheads with the press throughout the trial, shook his head in disgust. "Newspaper men had no business at the autopsy, gazing on the nude form of this poor girl. Humiliation even in death!"

Marching to the prosecution table, Kane seized a copy of the testimony of Miss Beatrice Spratley, Madge's nurse, and read:

"'Her left cheek was bruised. Her left breast was bruised. The lower half of her abdomen—the inside of her thighs, and her legs, down to her ankles—all were bruised.'

"A willing companion, eh? Oh, gentlemen, she wasn't hurt. She just went along with this Stephenson because she loved him," Kane hissed.

Gazing at Inman, Kane said, "And that able, touted, newspaper-boomed criminal attorney, Inman—if he had half as much sense as any one of you jurymen, he wouldn't have had the nerve to make such flimsy arguments.

"I want to demonstrate to Klinck, to Gentry, to Inman, to Stephenson, and to Christian, if it can be done, that in Indiana the law is supreme. Put them away, so others will be safe."

Kane launched a fierce attack against the four Marion County deputy sheriffs who testified regarding Klinck's alibi:

"If the prosecutor of Hamilton County has the nerve, and I think he has, and the judge does his duty, the grand jury will be called to prosecute Red Koffel and those other deputy sheriffs and all others who had a hand in it, for perjury. Men testified who should be in jail—instead of taking good money to lock others in jail. Are you going to believe their word against that of the good mother Mrs. Schultz, who saw Klinck with her very eyes?" Kane hooted.

"These fellows are guilty of murder, staphylococci or no staphylococci!"

He thrust his left hand, stiff palmed, toward Steve. "That wound was placed on that girl's body by the fangs of this serpent. The infection which followed caused her death."

Stephenson watched the attorney with a fixed gaze, unmoving, without visible emotion—except for the nearly imperceptible twitching of a muscle in his jaw.

"Has Indiana no law that will protect her daughters from conduct of this kind?" Kane said softly. He bowed his head briefly, then sprang against the jury rail and gazed for a long moment into the faces of the twelve men.

"You're going to write in your verdict whether your daughter, my daughter, or other reputable citizens' daughters are to be protected from vandalism. The eyes not only of Indiana but of the whole country are on you.

"Gentlemen, I stand on hallowed ground as I stand before you. It is from the heart.

"Gentlemen, it wasn't suicide, it was murder. They drove her to her death—it was murder!"

Kane's words ricocheted off the walls. Before he had reached his seat, Judge Sparks began reading his instructions to the jury.

It was 11 a.m. Saturday. John Niblack was working himself up to a fair twit over the timing. His deadline was noon—absolutely no later than 1 p.m., if the paper was to hit the streets that afternoon. And except when the most sensational of stories warranted an extra edition, the *Times* didn't publish on Sunday—but his competitors did. Niblack wanted the case to go to the jury on his time. Even more importantly, he wanted the verdict on his time. Was there anything he wouldn't do to get this story first?

The judge's instructions droned on and on, as Niblack and his partner Tubby Toms recorded them in shorthand, almost automatically, barely listening, wanting them to end.

But then Niblack jabbed Toms with his elbow. The instructions to the jury began to take shape, and they were remarkable— unprecedented in Niblack's experience and perhaps in Indiana.

"If you find from the evidence in this case," Sparks read in a monotone, "that the death of the deceased resulted directly or indirectly from a bite inflicted upon her person by one of the defendants, then I instruct you that he could be criminally responsible for such death, even though other causes may have contributed to her death, provided that all the other material allegations of either the first or third counts in said indictments have been proven beyond a reasonable doubt."

Huh? If Steve's bite caused Madge's death, even indirectly, even if there were other causes, he could be criminally liable for her death.

If they forced Madge on the trip and denied her medical care, they were guilty of homicide, he said.

If they forced her on the trip and she became ill for any reason, "it was their duty under the law to care for her without wicked negligence," the judge said. If her death resulted, "I instruct you to find the defendants guilty of manslaughter, if you find said omission to act was mere negligence.

"But if you find that such omission or failure to act was done willfully, with a reckless disregard of the consequences, then I instruct you they would be guilty of murder."

The jury had four options, the judge said.

"If you think the evidence warrants it, you may find the defendants guilty of murder either in first or second degree, or of manslaughter, or you may find them, or either of them, not guilty...."

"The death penalty or life imprisonment may be given to whoever purposely and with premeditated malice, or in the perpetration or attempt to perpetrate a rape, arson, robbery, or burglary or by administering poison or causing the same to be administered, kills any human being."

Where there is no premeditation, but the killing is done purposely and maliciously, the penalty of second degree murder may be inflicted—life imprisonment, he said.

"The presumption of innocence remains with the defendants throughout the trial, and they are entitled to its benefits unless the evidence convinces you beyond a reasonable doubt of their guilt.

"But in clothing those charged with crimes with the presumption of innocence, the law does not contemplate that the guilty shall be shielded from merited punishment. Its object is to protect the innocent, as far as human agencies can, from the effects of unjust verdicts."

Judge Sparks reviewed the four counts of the indictment: criminal attack, malicious mayhem, kidnapping and conspiracy to kidnap, and murder.

"If any one of the material allegations has not been so proved, it would be your duty to acquit. If all the material allegations of the indictment have been proved, it is your duty to convict...."

As the judge read on and on, a toddler became separated from her mother among the spectators, wandered to the front of the courtroom, and crawled under the defense table, nuzzling up to Stephenson's shoes. Steve bent down, patted the child, lifted her up, and handed her to her mother.

"You are the exclusive judges of the weight of the evidence and the credibility of the witnesses," Judge Sparks read. "It is your duty to consider all the evidence..., and any other fact or circumstance, shown by the evidence, which from your experience and observation, you believe will aid you in arriving at the truth...."

"When you retire to your jury room to deliberate on your verdict, appoint one of your members as foreman. It will be his duty to sign your verdict, when agreed upon. When your verdict shall have been signed, return it to open court."

So saying, Judge Sparks swore in Bailiff Ingram Mallory, who took the jury out to their deliberations room, where they immediately had lunch.

Niblack zipped out to the press room phone. It was 11:46 a.m. He had made his first deadline. But the larger question remained for him: Would the jury report back at a time when Niblack could beat his competition to the streets with the verdict?

After calling in his morning story—"STEPHENSON CASE WITH JURY"—John Niblack leaned back in the press room for a cigarette. But he did not relax.

The converted public toilet they called a press room soon became a smoke-filled pit of roaming, fuming, cigar-puffing newsmen, as the moments of waiting stretched into hours.

Outside the 10-foot by 20-foot room, it was a gray November day. Within, reporters were as edgy as caged cats. The tension was broken when Watty Watson, the jovial City Hall reporter for the *Indianapolis News*, reappeared after a brief absence, carrying a box of thirteen newspaper-wrapped half-pints of white mule whiskey. Watson was the king of Indianapolis reporters, the one Niblack most hoped to beat on any given story—especially this one.

Newsmen swooped down on Watson's box, but he held them at bay. "A dollar a half-pint," he said. After spirited grousing, the parched reporters forked over the cash, which Watson pocketed eagerly. Contentedly, he perched his feet on the box and, in concert with his fellows, began to down the four half-pints he hadn't sold.

As the afternoon light began to dim, Watty Watson began to hum softly as he slumped slowly, slowly, beneath the nearest table, into a happy heap on the cigar-littered, black and white checkered, marble floor.

The news came abruptly, somewhere after 5 o'clock Saturday afternoon. The defendants were summoned hastily from the jail next door and brought into the courtroom. Stephenson and Gentry were smoking cigars.

"Gentlemen, have you reached a verdict?" asked Judge Sparks.

"We have, your honor," said Foreman W.A. Johnson, a Hamilton County farmer, rising from his seat number 7 in the jury box.

"Please pass it to the bailiff."

The foreman handed the paper to Bailiff Ingram Mallory, in a dead silent courtroom. Stephenson watched intently, his legs crossed at the ankle, his teeth set. No juror even glanced toward the defense table, where the three sat with only one of their attorneys present, Floyd Christian. Klinck and Gentry were leaning forward.

The bailiff gave the verdict to the judge, while the old wall clock punctuated the silence with its somber ticking. Unfolding the paper, Judge Sparks adjusted his spectacles and read:

"We, the jury, find the defendant, D.C. Stephenson, guilty of second degree murder, as charged in the first count of the indictment, and assess his punishment as life imprisonment.

"We, the jury, find the defendants, Earl Klinck and Earl Gentry, not guilty."

The blood drained from Stephenson's face. Stunned, he opened his mouth, then closed it while his eyes sought the floor.

"They can't—!" he whispered. "They can't...."

In ten seconds, Steve had regained his composure. He congratulated the two Earls and shook Christian's hand, almost jauntily. But blood had returned to his cherub face, now flushed fiery red.

Pandemonium broke loose. Reporters tore out for the press room telephones. Women spectators crowded around to congratulate Remy, while Sheriff Gooding escorted Stephenson back to his cell. Gentry and Klinck dragged along behind him, without Steve summoning them with his usual imperious fingersnap.

"I don't understand how they let me go and convicted Steve," Gentry told reporters. "If he was guilty, so was I."

"It's the most ridiculous verdict I ever heard of," stormed Klinck. "It...is not a vindication of any law but persecution of the best man that ever lived!"

"We are astounded, and we have no understanding of how the jury could have freed Klinck and Gentry," Madge's mother said.

"The life sentence for Stephenson—well, that's all right if it means what it says, but so often such a sentence means only a comparatively few years. For Stephenson to go free in time—menace to society as he is—it should not be, that's all.

"Judge Sparks was entirely fair, and the state lawyers worked awfully hard," Matilda Oberholtzer said, touching her cheek under one eye. "We have no criticism, only we can't understand about Klinck and Gentry.... When they tried to intimidate against our dear girl's character " She turned away.

The last word of the scene came from Steve, who told reporters: "In the words of the famous general: 'Surrender? Hell, I've just begun to fight!'"

Niblack ran so fast that he could scarcely breathe as he gasped out the story to his rewrite man. Before the early winter moon rose over Indianapolis, the *Times* extra would be on the street, in the hands of eager newsboys who would be shouting, "Stephenson Guilty of Murder!"

As Niblack dictated his story, he heard a moan from the floor.
Watty Watson rolled his way, mumbling. "Whash goin' on, Nibby?" he
groaned. "Wherrish jury?"

The *Indianapolis News'* telephone rang, and Niblack answered.
Micky McCarty, Watson's city editor, was on the other end of the line.
McCarty asked for Watty Watson.

"He's under the table," Niblack said.

McCarty groaned. Was the jury out? he asked Niblack.

"Yes," Niblack said.

"What's the verdict, Nibby?" McCarty asked.

"I'll tell you, Micky, just as soon as we get on the street with our
extra."

After ten minutes of pleading, the *News* city editor convinced
Niblack to tell him that the jury found Stephenson guilty. With
brotherly love, reporters doused Watson with cold water and told him
the high points of the story.

Niblack propped him up to the candlestick phone.

"What did Steve say, Watty?" the city editor asked.

"Ole Steve sez, 'Fight hell—I've just begun to Shurrender!'" Watty
yelled toward the phone, as he slipped slowly back to the floor.

Shortly after noon Monday, November 16, Sheriff Gooding escorted
Steve back into the courtroom for sentencing.

Judge Sparks asked Stephenson if he had anything to say.

The Old Man walked slowly to the center of the courtroom, before
the judge's bench. He stood with his head bowed briefly, then lifted
his dimpled chin and looked into Judge Sparks' eyes.

Steve's voice quivered as he said, in little more than a whisper, "I'm
not guilty of murder or any lesser degree of murder, or manslaughter.
It has always been my impression that no man should ever be
deprived of his liberty without due process of law. I believe it is

universal opinion that this procedure was not due process of law."

His voice rose. "Three hundred people out of the three and a half million people in Indiana, with outbursts of applause and hissing, rendered it impossible for the jury to return a fair verdict."

He turned slightly and stared at Remy, then looked back to the judge. "Time will unfold the cold, white light of truth that D.C. Stephenson is not guilty of murder in any degree, or of nay degree of homicide."

As Stephenson stood silently, Judge Sparks read the sentence, as directed by the jury: "I find you guilty of second degree murder and sentence you to the Indiana State Prison during life."

Indianapolis Mayor Duvall was still in hiding from the KKK, and disgruntled Klansmen, angered at their mistreatment by a Republican Party now eager to shun them, were thinking about shifting their loyalties to the Democrats, reported the *Indianapolis Times* the same day. Democrats shuddered at the thought.

In the aftermath, the *Times* carried not just one but two editorials about Steve's conviction.

The first editorial was headlined, "The Man Who Would Be King":

"David C. Stephenson a year ago today was at the height of his career," the *Times* said. "He had just succeeded in placing himself in a position of more influence than any one man ever possessed in the free State of Indiana. He had won an election. Men whom he had supported had been elected to office. A Legislature over which he knew he had almost absolute control was about to convene. He had set up a kingdom and he proposed to rule.

"David C. Stephenson today sits in a cell in the little jail in the public square at Noblesville. He has been found guilty of the crime of taking a human life and he faces the prospect of spending the remainder of his days behind prison walls. His influence, which continued even after he was behind iron bars, is gone.

"The man who would be king is dethroned and imprisoned, as a result of his own acts.

"'I am the law in Indiana,' this man once said, according to the girl whose life he has been convicted of taking. He acted on the theory that a king can do no wrong. He was centuries behind his time. He attempted to set himself up as a medieval ruler and to act as one. He attempted to rule ruthlessly and according to his own desires. But he went too far. The people of Indiana during the last few years have calmly sat by and watched strange occurrences—but in Indiana not even a king can get away with murder.

"The jury had before it only the evidence surrounding the death of Madge Oberholtzer. It acted according to the views of the law and the evidence. Stephenson says he has just begun to fight and that probably is true. He will carry his case to a higher tribunal, but all that court can do will be to order a new trial.

"Regardless of the outcome of the fight he will make, a higher tribunal than the Supreme Court of the state, a tribunal that comprises the population of Indiana, should hold that David C. Stephenson, nor any other man, ever again will be permitted to mount a throne."

The second editorial was by *Times* columnist Gaylord Nelson.

The verdict did much to settle the question of whether Steve was the law in Indiana, Nelson wrote:

"He is not.... Even Stephenson—the Hoosier Warwick before whom legislators and high state officials hastened to 'bend the pregnant hinges of the knees,' who dictated policies and dominated the politics of a great state—can't get away with murder...."

"The man himself may be 'the best man that ever lived,' as his henchman and co-defendant Earl Klinck says—a victim of unholy persecution.... But whatever the character of the man himself, the greatest disgrace to Indiana comes from Stephensonism, not from the last notorious outrage that caused the arrest, trial and conviction of Stephenson.

"The same forces of hate and bigotry that elevated Stephenson to the imperial purple and dictatorship in the political affairs of the democratic state of Indiana are still at work, ready to be harnessed by other adventurers thirsting for power.

"It will take more than the verdict of a Hamilton County jury to vindicate the fair name of the state. The dozen farmers who returned that verdict merely lightened the spot on our body politic, instead of eradicating it. The spirit of 'I am the law' marches on."

Handcuffed, David Curtis Stephenson walked slowly down the worn stone steps of the Noblesville courthouse, bound for prison.

"What now, Mr. Stephenson?" asked John Niblack, tagging after the little party.

"I'll never serve," The Old Man said.

EPILOGUE

The story of the Knights of the Ku Klux Klan began in 1915, with the death of a young girl—in the case of Mary Phagan and Leo Frank. And now, with the death of a young girl—in the case of Madge Oberholtzer and David Curtis Stephenson—the story closed, surely if not swiftly.

On November 21, 1925, he who would "never serve" was transported to the Indiana State Prison at Michigan City.

He came, jauntily carrying his reading lamp, secure in the knowledge that his best friend, Governor Ed Jackson, would parole him shortly.

The first shock came when they took his reading lamp away; the second, when the days stretched into weeks without a parole.

Then months. Then years.

The Old Man, imprisoned at 34, would not see the light of freedom again for longer than he dared imagine.

Had he been a common murderer who served time meekly, he could have been paroled with little fanfare. But Steve was neither common nor meek.

When Governor Jackson declined to grant a parole, Stephenson raged like a caged lion—to no avail. Politicians saw quickly that the fiery Grand Dragon was too hot for them to touch. The safest course was to keep him silent, behind bars. He became, in truth, a political prisoner.

The Times reporter John Niblack, meanwhile, joined Marion County Prosecutor Bill Remy's staff on January 1, 1926, as deputy prosecutor. Remy and Niblack were determined to unlock the secrets of the Klan's Indiana supergovernment. Others shared their determination. Among them were a new Indianapolis Times' editor, Boyd Gurley, and the crusty old publisher of the Vincennes Commercial, Tom Adams. They launched separate crusades.

In time, as Steve's impotent fury mounted in prison, he threatened to help them. If he didn't win parole, he would open Pandora's box of political blackmail secrets. He could tell, he whispered, a tale of "an amazing intrigue… such as you have never listened to." But Ed Jackson kept his prize prisoner incommunicado.

By some accounts, Steve became a broken man, wasting away on bread and water, standing handcuffed to his cell bars in solitary confinement for as long as eight days at a time.

Others reported being ushered into Steve's private quarters by his Japanese servant, where they found The Old Man pink and fat, chatting pleasantly, dressed not in prison gray but rather in a natty, pin striped business suit, crisp white shirt, and pearl gray tie.

Governor Jackson's most coveted convict was visited monthly by his lawyer: a slender young woman, no more than 60 inches tall, long of face, with a cloud of dark hair and keen hazel eyes. Some of Steve's few intimates suspected that for some time she had been the chief stabilizing force in his life, perhaps the only constant, the woman to whom he turned for counsel and support.

She was "a highly respected married woman," whose "domestic relations are happy and pleasant," said a friend at the time. "Her home life is ideal."

She was Mrs. Martha Loretz Dickinson, the wife of Klansman

W. T. Dickinson of Seymour, Indiana. They were among Steve's staunchest supporters, in prison or out. W.T. launched the Liberty Foundation to raise money for Steve's release and served as its vice president until W.T. died in 1953.

Who knows what began their alliance. This much is known: Martha was devoted to Steve. Why? "Because," she once cried out in a fund raising meeting, "he is the logical and wonderful leader of the 'Great Cause!'" And then, an acquaintance remembered, she flushed and fell silent, nervously picking imaginary threads from her skirt, no less intense in silence than in exclamation.

Mrs. Dickinson visited Stephenson every month throughout his prison years, regular as a metronome, elusive as a shadow. Newspapers described her as a mystery woman in black. She smuggled mail and documents in and out under her dress. In time, bribed guards provided them with a private room, complete with a fainting couch and candle lighted dinners; and Martha and Steve became very close indeed.

The times were stimulating, Martha remembered later: "exciting and very passionate. There was always something going on."

Thus separated by fate and prison bars but joined in spirit, Martha and Steve survived on love and shared dreams—and money The Old Man hid under false names in Hoosier banks.

Stephenson's trial and conviction stunned Americans, especially Klansmen in Indiana and elsewhere who had believed that The Old Man epitomized love for purity and womanly virtue.

Was this the brilliant young man who had promised to clean up not only lawless towns but also the Klan itself? Guilty? Of a crime so foul it could be reported only in whispers?

Public outrage raged.

Madge's death and Steve's conviction delivered a mortal blow to the Ku Klux Klan. The KKK's name was irrevocably blackened.

For mainstream America, Steve had unmasked the Klan.. For
several years thereafter, the KKK writhed like a wounded snake,
periodically seeming to spring back to life, then stilled.

Just when reporters pronounced the Klan dead, it burst alive
in Washington, with an awesome march of scores of thousands
of hoodless knights in August of 1925. Washington watched in
curiosity that turned to grudging admiration at what one journalist
called the largest parade in the capital's history. To what purpose
did the Klan march? the reporters asked. Perhaps, one speculated,
to convince itself—more than spectators—that the Invisible Empire
still reigned.

They marched through the capital city for hours, 16 to 20
abreast, with arms folded across their chests; slowly, silently, or to
the beat of "Onward Christian Soldiers;" with masks folded back
upon hoods. From time to time they thrust arms upward, in the
stiff elbowed, palms down salute of Fascists. Amongst the crowds,
scattered arms rose to mirror the salute.

Through rising waves of August heat made even more stifling
by an approaching thunderstorm, they marched with wondrous
discipline to the Washington Monument where host Kleagle L.A.
Mueller led a raft of speakers.

"Don't leave!" Mueller told the crowd. "Don't leave. It will not
rain. God won't let it." And then, as if on that cue, the heavens
opened and drenched the Kleagle and the crowd.

As the political campaigns of 1926 drew to a close, the imprisoned
Stephenson was growing more and more frantic. Through Martha
and his old pilot, Court Asher, Steve smuggled information
to Hoosier newspapermen Tom Adams and Boyd Gurley, who
pressured for the right to interview Steve.

He had evidence. Attorney D.F. Christian reported that on
one visit he saw Steve's prison cot entirely covered with stacks of

checks and documents that he was threatening to release. Adams had organized an investigation committee of fifteen Republican editors—whose work was disavowed and blocked by the majority of Indiana Republican editors, once it appeared Adams intended to air dirty party linen.

"I have been railroaded to prison to protect others," Steve wrote in a letter smuggled out to newsmen Adams and Gurley. "I am cooped up where I cannot talk. I am simply buried alive by men who owe me a fortune. Certain individuals framed me, and others want me out of the way."

"What the public wants," thundered Boyd Gurley in the Indianapolis Times, "is a thorough inquiry, and if Stephenson is ready to talk, the people want to hear what he has to say." Adams and six state senators demanded to interview Steve, but Warden Walter H. Daly refused.

Daly was a tough warden, installed by Governor Ed Jackson after the abrupt resignation of Warden Edward Fogarty, just before Steve arrived at Michigan City. There was little doubt that Jackson asked Fogarty, an eminent penologist and a Catholic, to resign. Jackson thereby kept his promise to the Klan to remove Catholics from high state offices.

But if Steve thus had selected his own warden, he had thereby sealed his own lips. Fogarty's policy had been to grant requested interviews with prisoners. Whether Jackson shifted wardens to silence Steve cannot be known, because Fogarty passed quickly from the scene, inexplicably dying at his own hand in 1929.

Denied his interviews, the enraged Boyd Gurley launched a barrage of daily stories and editorials in the Indianapolis Times. "These charges of graft, corruption, and infamy in state affairs are too grave to be... smothered. The Times, in the name of the people and of decency, demands that you act and act at once," he wrote in an open letter to the state's political leaders.

Then, in October 1926, the Times printed a front page copy of a letter purportedly written by Indianapolis Mayor Duvall on February 12, 1925, while Duvall was campaigning for office. "In return for the political support of D.C. Stephenson, in the event I am elected Mayor of Indianapolis, I promise not to appoint any person as a member of the Board of Public Works without they first have the endorsement of D.C. Stephenson. I fully agree (sic) and promise to appoint Claude Worley as Chief of Police and Earl Klinck as a Captain."

It was Steve's first volley. It would not be his last.

"There are some empty seats up here by me in the chair factory," Steve said, "and I am sending for some of my friends to occupy them."

The master of tantalizing suspense hinted at great revelations to come, then withdrew into silence. His promises flared and dissipated like smoke, then rose again. Stephenson leaked word that his damning evidence against Indiana's political leaders was hidden in mysterious "little black boxes" throughout the state. It was irresistible stuff for front page editors.

Now Marion County Prosecutor Remy, who had been quietly amassing evidence, convened a grand jury to investigate corruption related to the Indiana Klan. After hearing 200 witnesses—including Stephenson, who appeared for questioning but was mysteriously silent—the jury adjourned with no indictments but a recommendation that a subsequent grand jury take up the investigation.

The second grand jury investigated during 1927—a year marked by Charles Lindberg's flight from New York to Paris; and, in Indiana, the impeachment of one of the Klan's best orators, Delaware Circuit Court Judge Clarence W. Dearth—he who had threatened to jail boys for hawking the Muncie Post Democrat edited by anti Klan newsman George Dale.

Finally, on July 1, 1927, Stephenson opened up during a long conference with Prosecutor Remy. Beneath the smoke of Steve's on again, off again teasing promises, Remy found fire.

Later that month, Deputy Prosecutor John Niblack donned his linen duster and drove southwest from Indianapolis, toward Vincennes and the farmlands of his birth, in search of Steve's black boxes.

"Mr. Remy delegated me and Emsley W. Johnson, Sr., a prominent attorney retained as Special Deputy, to get the boxes," Niblack recalled later. "Accordingly, on a warm sunny Thursday, July 24, 1927, Mr. Johnson and I and his fourteen year old son, in knickerbocker, Emsley, Jr.,—later a Hoosier Superior Court Judge— motored down to Lick Skillet, Indiana, a little town just south of Washington. Amidst great secrecy, Steve's partner in the Coal Company met us in a round barn on a farm belonging to Johnson's wife's cousin.

"After a few wig wags, yoo hoos, and other preliminary signals, previously agreed upon, he gave us the two black boxes and their keys. His name was L.G. Julian, and he had driven up from Evansville in an ancient jalopy to meet us.

"Mr. Johnson and his son stayed over for a little visit and well earned vacation, and they exhibited the famous boxes at a dinner and family reunion given in their honor the next Sunday, where they showed them to wondering relatives, though refusing to let them see the contents. I went on over to Wheatland, in the next township, where I was born, and did a little feasting in my father's home in my own right."

Who knows how many other black boxes Steve hid around the state? At least one other was found in later years, in an attic, but burned without being opened.

Niblack was present, later, when the Lick Skillet boxes were opened. And, cynical newsman to the core, he was disappointed.

They contained "contracts"—pledges that Steve could control patronage appointments—with two state politicians, Indianapolis' Representative Ralph E. Updike, and Congressman Harry Rowbottom of Evansville. There was also a large ring that belonged to Stephenson but, like the fireworks Niblack wanted, the diamond was missing.

Nonetheless, Remy found pay dirt aplenty in the boxes, including copies of 31 checks and numerous letters. Among them: a copy of a $2,500 check from Steve to Ed Jackson, with a note on the back dated September 12, 1923: "This check is the first one fourth of $10,000 given Jackson personally for primary expenses."

Steve saw to it that Boyd Gurley received—and published—a copy of the check. After a long silence, Governor Jackson said Steve had bought "The Senator," Jackson's horse, for $2,500. The unfortunate beast could not now be found because he had choked to death on a corn cob, Jackson said.

The check "was given to Jackson sitting on my back porch at 5432 University Avenue," Stephenson told the grand jury. He was a willing witness at last.

"The later payments were made, $5,000 in cash, no check, delivered to Mr. Jackson on December 24, 1923, at his home in Irvington in the presence of Mr. Fred Butler, my secretary. I took the money out of my safe in the library, counted it, and we drove over to Ed Jackson's home. There I gave Mr. Jackson an envelope containing $5,000 in currency. Jackson gave me a second hand Marlin shotgun that night for a Christmas present. I don't know whether he considers I bought a second hand shotgun from him for $5,000 or not.

"The remaining $2,500 was delivered in a sealed envelope at his office in the State House, as he then was Secretary of State. He telephoned and said he had just received it, and he thanked me."

"Was this campaign contribution ever reported?" Remy asked.

"No! I knew he was not going to report it, and I joked him about it. He laughed and said a man was justified in perjuring himself on his own behalf and he asked me if I didn't think so. I evaded him. Anything I hate is a liar and a perjurer."

Stephenson also testified that he delivered $23,000 in utilities' money, intended for the Republican State Committee. "He (Jackson) never delivered a dime of it to the Committee," Steve said. "He bought a farm over in Hancock County with part, paid off a note, and stuck the rest in his sock. It never was used in the campaign."

All told, Steve said he spent $227,000 on Jackson's campaign. "I had a written contract with him that I was to get it back by getting the coal contract from the state, by control of the Highway Commission and of the State Purchasing Department," he said.

In July 1927, the Times carried its most serious accusation: that in 1923 Jackson and Stephenson tried to bribe then Governor McCray to block Remy's appointment as Marion County prosecutor.

For six weeks, Jackson refused to confirm or deny the report, while Gurley kept up a daily barrage in the Times. Finally, in September, Jackson wrote Gurley that he was innocent of any wrong doing. Then, Gurley shot back, Jackson should volunteer to waive the statute of limitations and testify under oath before the third grand jury, convened by Remy in July. "There has been guilt," Gurley wrote. "If your statement be correct, not only myself but those who furnished me with the evidence should not be at liberty."

Remy's third grand jury, a blue ribbon panel, indicted Mayor Duvall, who was fined and forced to resign; and Governor Jackson, who won acquittal because of the statute of limitations but was discredited and forced to retire from politics.

Before Steve was through, six of the Indianapolis alderman resigned over charges they accepted bribes, and a horde of other Indiana politicians suffered political damage beyond repair.

"Oh, the moon is fair tonight along the Wabash,
From the fields there comes the breath of new mown hay:
Through the sycamores the candle lights are gleaming...."

But now it was not candle lights gleaming through the sycamores—nor even the glimm'ring twinkle of fiery crosses. What burned most brightly in Indiana were faces, as hundreds of thousands blushed with embarrassment at being duped.

The Old Man's testimony had turned Indiana wrong side out.

"Indiana is on trial before the nation," wrote the Literary Digest.

"The history of the rise and fall of The Old Man is the history of the metamorphosis of Indiana"—from "tolerance (to a) post war wave of Pecksniffery and prejudice," wrote The Nation. "He became a white robed Warwick... with his eyes on the Presidency...."

And he led the way up and down with "as crude a lot of adventurers as ever sunk a ship of state," wrote another.

The Old Man's rise and fall was also mirrored in the rise and fall of the Klan, journalists noted. As he intended to be President, so the Klan intended to take over the American government. Instead, the Klan was discredited; and The Old Man was in state prison, dragging the names of Hoosierdom's political leaders into the mire with his own.

By the close of 1927, the Indiana landscape was littered with political bodies. Indianapolis Times' Boyd Gurley copped the 1928 Pulitzer Prize for his Klan fight.

In the same year, Stephenson dealt the death blow to the remnants of the Klan, in blunt testimony about "its shoddy, money grubbing, and violent practices." In a Pennsylvania court battle between Evans and rival Klansmen, Steve testified that the KKK's membership "was once composed of the best manhood of America, representing the best traditions of the Republic, but its sinister leadership is the most corrupt thing that has ever been thrust upon the American people; and Evans himself, if he had been born in Perdition and sired by Satan, would disgrace his parents and dishonor his country."

His testimony, Steve said, represented "the real unmasking of the Klan...."

Like Sampson, D.C. Stephenson brought down the house.

It remained for Arthur Gilliom, the Indiana Attorney General from South Bend—with Remy, one of only two of Steve's political enemies to survive his Klan sweep of the 1924 elections—to file suit in Marion County Circuit Court in 1928 to revoke the Klan's charter to do business in Indiana. The suit was never tried, but publicity veered public opinion still further away from the Ku Klux Klan.

By 1928 the Klan had no more than 4,000 members in Indiana.

"On Monday night," reported a town newspaper, "the Women of the Ku Klux Klan entertained the Knights of the Ku Klux Klan. Refreshments were served and short talks were made by members of both organizations. After the entertainment at the hall, they all went to the rink and enjoyed a couple of hours roller skating."

In the wake of the Stephenson case, Klansmen had been resigning around the country, with varying blasts of disgust. "No organization can exist in this country whose principle of government is un American," declared a resigning Indianan.

"Real Americans must awaken (to learn) that the Klan is America's greatest menace," said six hundred "real men" resigning in New Haven.

In its short life, the Knights of the Ku Klux Klan had kicked up a powerful cloud of dust. By the trailing years of the roaring twenties, the fallout from exploding illusions was sifting down upon the idealistic among the flock. For many at the grassroots, even faith based on sham, fear, and hate was better than no ennobling cause, and they had vigorously tended the Klan's meager ideological crop. Now they were left with little harvest but the acrid dust of bitterness.

For others at the grassroots, whose chief aim was fraternity, a new Klan was emerging. And how did these mellowing members spend their evenings? Burning crosses and churches?

No, they were more apt to be burning candles and fatted calves: setting the table with a "100 percent roast beef supper," dining on box suppers where the women donated home canned jellies, or listening to "Mrs. Roy Hess on the piano and Miss Martha Shick on the violin."

By 1927, the Invisible Empire probably had no more than several hundred thousand dues paying members nationally, forcing leaders to consider the unthinkable—an austerity program.

Above the grassroots, Evans and the Klan leaders still fomented revolution, and for a time exerted Washington leadership out of all proportion to the KKK's dwindling membership. Disillusioned members might have abandoned the Klan in name, but the old spirit still marched in the land.

"With all our devices for communication and information," wrote The New Republic about America in 1927, "our 23 million automobiles, 6 million radio sets, 10 million daily attendance at motion picture theaters, 35 million newspapers, and 800,000 college students, we seem to have made hardly any inroads at all on the parochial mindedness which has made the Klan once and may do it again."

It was such a spirit, prodded by the remnants of the Klan, that defeated a popular New York Catholic Democrat in his bid for President. D.C. Stephenson didn't move into the White House in 1928—but neither did Al Smith.

1929: the stock market crashed, while the Klan cuddled up to the rising Nazi party throughout the '30s. Curiously, Adolf Hitler hated the Klan and himself killed the German Order of the Fiery Cross—the remnant of the German Klan sparked in the early 1920s by Edward Young Clarke. Secret societies, by their very nature, could not discipline members and could only have illegal ends, Hitler reasoned.

On July 4, 1929, Imperial Wizard Hiram Wesley Evans convened a klonklave in Kokomo, but hardly a thousand came.

The lean years of the depression took their toll on the Wizard. Evans had to look for supplemental employment, selling asphalt by means that netted him a $15,000 fine for price fixing. Even worse, he had to liquidate most of the Klan's real estate. By 1939, the Imperial Palace had been cleared and the site redeveloped—into a new Catholic church.

The Catholic bishop, perhaps with tongue in cheek, invited Evans to attend the dedication of the new Cathedral of Christ the King. Perhaps in retaliatory whimsy, Evans came.

After Evans settled into richly earned retirement in 1939, one of Stephenson's Evansville boys, James A. Colescott, took the KKK helm. Colescott, 42, a Terre Haute veterinarian, presided over the remnants of the Klan until 1944, when the U.S. Internal Revenue Service filed a lien for $685,000 in back taxes on profits the Invisible Empire had earned in the 1920s.

"It was that nigger lover Roosevelt and that Jew Morgenthau who was his Secretary of the Treasury who did it!" Colescott said later.

"I was sitting in my office in the Imperial Palace in Atlanta one day, just as pretty as you please," Colescott said, "when the Revenuers knocked on my door.... We had to sell our assets and hand over the proceeds to the Government and go out of business. Maybe the Government can make something out of the Klan—I never could!"

Colescott called a special klonvokation April 23, 1944, when members revoked charters of all established klaverns and formally disbanded the Knights of the Ku Klux Klan.

The Knights of the Ku Klux Klan "is dead," Colescott told reporters. "The whole thing is washed up. After Reconstruction when the Klan disbanded, the Klansmen continued to function in clubs and on their own, and it will likely be that way from now on."

No longer could one speak of the Klan in the singular. What survived were Klans—splintered hit and run squads who gave themselves various names such as Independent Klans of America, many but not all centered in the South and in pockets such as the prairie cornfields around Indianapolis.

More enduring was the spirit of the Klan. Like the tides, the disembodied ghosts of Klans quickened and died with the years, swelling after World War II, again with the 1950s around the time of the Korean War and after Brown vs. Board of Education ordered integration of the nation's public schools with "all deliberate speed."

(The embers of Klan-style hatred were destined to burst into flames again during the 1960s, the years of Vietnam and civil rights advances; again in the 1990s, when camouflaged militias cavorted in backwoodlands and built fertilizer bombs; and in the early twenty-first century, in consternation over Mexican immigrants and Muslims, as well as backlash to the election of America's first non-white President. Demographers prophesied that nativist whites would soon become an American minority; who could say whether the nation would accept such change peaceably?)

Ebb and flow, while D.C. Stephenson grew old in the Indiana State Prison, making chairs.

D.C. Stephenson filed more than forty appeals—each with a different set of attorneys—and nearly as many versions of why he was innocent. He variously claimed that he wasn't with Madge; that the woman on the train was really the wife of Lt. Gov. Harold

Van Orman; and that Madge was pregnant by the husband of Cora Householder and he was helping her get an abortion.

Why had he remained silent during the trial? He was either trying to protect others or living in fear that he would be killed at the instant he began to testify.

His most persuasive argument was that he was under death threat by the Klan. To prove his case, he pleaded for investigation into the case of a young woman, Edith Irene Dean, secretary of the Indianapolis Young Women's Republican Club. Steve said she came to visit him in the Noblesville jail on July 2, telling him she had been offered $50,000 by two Klan officials, Robert McNay and Robert Lyons, to testify that Steve kidnapped and raped her. Instead. she went straight to tell Steve. She was found the next day, beaten and dying, near a White River bridge near Noblesville. Her murderer was never found, and the state never investigated Steve's story.

All Steve's appeals were denied, including his bitterest disappointment in 1932, when the Indiana Supreme Court refused to grant a new trial.

"When suicide follows a wound inflicted by a defendant, his act is homicidal, if deceased was rendered irresponsible by the wound and as the natural result of it," the court ruled.

Stephenson was properly found guilty of murder while engaged in the crime of attempted rape, the Supreme Court majority held, because his unlawful acts drove Madge to a state of such distraction and mental anguish that suicide was the natural and probable consequence.

But the jurists' vote was split, as was Indiana public opinion, on whether The Old Man was guilty of murder. "There is no evidence to indicate that at any time the mind of the deceased was not clear and sound," wrote a dissenting justice; thus, argued this minority opinion, Madge merely committed suicide, and Steve should be granted a new trial.

Many in Indiana agreed.

"I should have been put in jail for my political activities but I am not guilty of murder," Steve told a reporter.

"D.C. Stephenson was sentenced to life in prison for the only crime he didn't commit," someone said later.

Perhaps.

John Niblack once asked Prosecutor Bill Remy if he believed Steve was really guilty.

"Well," Remy replied, "a jury and seventeen courts, both federal and state, have said he was guilty. That's good enough for me."

Stephenson's prison years were not uneventful. At various times Steve was rumored to be plotting escape or, in at least one instance, an assassination attempt on Governor Ed Jackson.

At one point Martha found a perfect double for Steve and convinced the man to allow himself to play Stephenson's substitute. Even more bizarre was the plot to smuggle Steve an experimental drug that would throw him into a pseudo dead, cataleptic rigor. Then a substitute prison "doctor" would declare Stephenson "dead," allowing his friends to claim the body and revive him outside the prison walls.

The schemes were foiled by news leaks.

During the depression, Martha worried about banks closing where she and Steve had hidden money under false names. "What about the $2 million we put in those two banks in Columbus, Ohio, back in March of 1925?" she asked Steve. He was certain the money was secure, in four safety deposit boxes of two sound banks.

"I wonder what the bankers of those two banks did," Martha wondered later, "when the banks went broke, and later found $1 million in two safety deposit boxes left unclaimed because of a false name and address."

At some point, according to legend, a governor finally agreed to parole Steve, but he was tricked by love. The governor's secretary, smitten by another prisoner, substituted his clemency papers for Stephenson's. When the governor discovered he had signed the wrong papers, he was too embarrassed to admit the mistake.

Steve wrote more than appeal briefs in prison. He wrote a novel, entitled "Dust On the Levee," apparently never published. He sold the manuscript to a southern Illinois businessman—a Negro, according to a news account. Steve chose as his protagonist a young, ambitious black man who was befriended by a political boss. The politician worked to win his protege "as high a political office as any white man could attain." Of the liberal political boss, a friend said: "Steve wanted to be that man."

The years wrought changes in the lives of other actors in Steve's drama.

Gentry, for one, bobbed in and out of trouble until the mid 1930s, when he was shot to death in Wisconsin by a jealous rival in a love triangle. His murderer never denied guilt: "I am not the least sorry for the act I committed," Gentry's killer said, "as I feel I did a good deed for society when I killed Earl Gentry!"

Earl Klinck simply disappeared.

John Niblack practiced law; and he served in the Indiana Senate from 1928 through 1932. In 1931 he married an Indiana girl, and the couple reared two daughters. Niblack served as a Hoosier judge for 31 years, until shortly before his death on December 31, 1974.

Judge Will Sparks earned quite a reputation in Indiana for his work in Steve's murder trial. In 1929 Sparks was named to the U. S. Circuit Court of Appeals for the Seventh Circuit; the appointment came from Sparks' old friend Senator Jim Watson and the man who was once called Steve's senator, Arthur Robinson. Sparks served on the court "with great distinction," according to one legal observer. He died quietly at home November 4, 1941.

Asa Smith practiced law with growing distinction and won great community affection, also serving in World War II as a lieutenant

colonel in the U.S. Marine Corps. Smith was Marion County deputy
prosecutor in the 1950s, helping expose highway scandals that led
to convictions among the state's politicians. He spent his last years
blind, still a victim of mustard gas. He died Feb. 12, 1973.

The number one idealist of the Knights of the Ku Klux Klan,
Colonel William Simmons, finally accepted that he had been
duped by Evans. Simmons took his $90,000 settlement to Florida,
plunging into a scheme to create a rival fraternity, the Knights of
the Flaming Sword. Ever a romantic, Simmons invested his new
knights with his old dreams of religion, ritual, and racism. But the
dreamer was denied the spoils. Broke and disillusioned, Simmons
wandered through Georgia and his native Alabama—ending his
days in 1945, in the company of strong drink and other down and
out, forlorn and forgotten fellows.

Finally, in 1950, Stephenson was paroled. It was on St. Patrick's
Day, 25 years to the day from that Tuesday that Madge returned
home.

"I am stripped of property, position, and all but my inner
strength," Steve told a news conference as he left prison. "With this
single asset, I shall be secure.

"I am leaving Indiana for good and cogent reasons.... I wish
to avoid being involved in politics, and I wish to choose my own
associates.... I ask nothing of my fellow man except an opportunity
to walk in peace with God."

He went to live with the daughter he had denied, Katherine, in
Tulsa, Oklahoma. She had kept in touch with him all through his
prison years. Katherine was a secretary, and they lived modestly in
a simple white frame house east of downtown.

Stephenson promptly became so unruly that she despaired of
managing him. "He still lived back in 1924," said Katherine, "when

he was a man of wealth and power. He just couldn't adjust himself to the new way of living."

Stephenson disappeared. Months later, on November 15, 1950, he was found working as a printer in Robbinsdale, Minnesota.

"I did not violate parole," he said. Rather, he was evading underworld criminals who wanted him dead. "If released from underworld control, I shall spend the remainder of my life quietly. I shall engage in legitimate business, refrain from political activity, and ask only an opportunity to walk at peace with God."

He was shipped back to prison for violating parole.

Five years later, at Christmas 1956, he was paroled again. He emerged a paunchy old man, 65, bespectacled. He had lived nearly half his life in prison. Ironically, if Stephenson had been a run of the mill murderer, he could have been paroled in 15 years. But because he was who he was, he served 31 years.

The Old Man won parole on his promise to leave Indiana forever. But in 1958, newsmen discovered Stephenson in Seymour, Indiana, where he had married a wealthy widow, Mrs. Martha Loretz Dickinson—his long time confidant, attorney, and prison playmate.

The newly weds lived in a new home she built for him: a huge white house, furnished in lavish neo Valentino style, draped in fringed shawls, with Oriental rugs and lamps swathed in beads and tassels.

At last Martha could nourish her romantic side. Specifically, she took up painting.

Steve traveled. He peddled a type cleaning machine he had invented. Specifically, he sold franchises: for $10,000, a franchise holder could obtain his machine, a new station wagon, and a sales territory.

He was a loner, his neighbors reported, a nice looking man,

polite, quiet, and highly intelligent—a dreamer.

In November of 1961, Stephenson was convicted of attempted assault in Independence, Missouri, where a judge upheld the charge that Steve tried to abduct a 16 year old girl on the street. Not so, Steve protested; he had merely asked her for directions. The sentence was suspended on condition he leave Missouri forever.

"My goodness," said Martha, when reporters told her of the conviction. "It's simply amazing. Everyone has their faults, but I can hardly grasp that."

Shortly thereafter, Martha and Steve separated. But Martha— nothing if not faithful—waited nearly ten years to obtain a divorce.

A reporter visited her in 1971, when the divorce was granted. Townspeople in Seymour considered her odd, a recluse. The reporter found her in the white house she had built for Steve, now nearly hidden behind overgrow trees and shrubs. Inside, the curtains were pinned together to keep out the light; and the Oriental rugs were completely carpeted in layers of newspapers.

"I have three cats and a dog," Martha explained.

It was a large house for the tiny woman, barely 5 feet tall, slightly stooped with the weight of her 76 years. She threw back her head and laughed. "I like space to move around in. I even bought six cemetery lots so I'd have room to kick."

She leaned forward. "Steve did not kill that girl. He's not guilty. He was a political prisoner. I know this to be true because the man who did commit the crime confessed to me.

"And I have written proof, many papers and letters that I've saved....

"It was all a political move. I was given power of attorney by Steve and handled his business. But my main purpose in regular visiting was because I feared someone would try to kill him."

The reporter asked her opinion of the Ku Klux Klan.

"I don't know any more about the Klan than a rabbit," Martha snapped. She straightened a layer of newspaper covering a card table and peered intently at the reporter. "You have a very kind face, my dear. I paint, and I can tell. I've always studied faces."

She laughed again, a low rasp. "That's been quite a day or two ago, my dear! We were married when he was released from prison.... No one would give him a job. People snubbed him. And, although I gave him money to begin several businesses, they all failed because no one would have anything to do with him."

A cloud passed over her face.

"I like it here," she said, darkly. "I prefer to be alone. I just want to be with my animals and to paint. I'm a good painter." She rose, left the room abruptly, and returned with an irregular wooden plaque on which she had painted sprays of lilacs in delicately muted shades of lavender.

"It's best that everything be forgotten," she said. "Including myself.

"Steve's mind is sick. And no wonder. But he's been hurt enough and shouldn't be hurt any more."

She was never to see him again. Martha Loretz Dickinson Stephenson died January 7, 1976.

From the day he left Martha in 1962, Stephenson lived free of public notice for several years.

As time passed, the curious case of D.C. Stephenson lapsed deeper into mystery. Researchers discovered in 1963 that nearly all records of the case had disappeared, including Madge Oberholtzer's dying declaration and both the shorthand and typed transcripts of Steve's trial.

The next news stories appeared in 1978. Newsmen had traced Stephenson to 1963, when he fell into ill health. Suffering from a heart condition and spinal arthrosis—joint degeneration—the old soldier was admitted to a veterans' hospital, then went to work for the weekly Jonesboro, Tennessee, Herald & Tribune as a printer and writer.

The editor suggested that he board in the home of Mrs. Martha Murray Sutton, a comely widow and schoolteacher. A year later, on May 25, 1964, they wed. Steve was 73; his second Martha was 55. Legally, he was still married to Martha Dickinson.

"He just swept Mrs. Sutton off her feet," a neighbor recalled.

He had a special way with children, she said later. Sometimes he would take the neighborhood children—both black and white—to a local swimming hole.

They lived quietly. She knew nothing of his past until reporters traced the man of mercury, the Grandest Dragon of them all, to Jonesboro in 1978. But they found him dead.

David Curtis Stephenson had died a dozen years before, on June 28, 1966, in obscurity.

"I loved him very, very much," Mrs. Sutton told the reporter who found his grave.

"My heart was broken when he died in my arms, at home.

"I am sure he is in heaven."

Many people contributed to this book, and I wish I could thank each by name. I will take space to name only a few, but I hope all you others know that I remember and treasure your contributions.

There would be no book without the late Neal McNeill Jr., who first told me about this story and suggested I write a book about it. As I recall, his father had been a justice on the Oklahoma State Supreme Court (1919 to 1925) and was targeted by the Klan. Neal had a brilliant intellect and never forgot anything he ever knew. He helped focus my research, contributed many insights, and walked with me along every step of the writing. We often remarked about how relevant the story is in modern times. Regrettably, Neal died in 2014 and so never witnessed the phenomenon of Donald Trump, who echoes a reincarnated David Curtis Stephenson in political message and method. This book is dedicated to Neal.

My friend Jerrie Townsend, who was studying for her PhD in library science, spent untold hours helping me find and retrieve research materials. And my husband Bob Patton spent many more hours photocopying the materials so I could take them to a writers retreat. I wrote most of the book in a few months alone in a cottage in the Texas woods, in the company of the nefarious characters in the story. Among the many people who encouraged me along the way were Juanise Stockdale, Jay Dew, and the late J. D. Metcalfe and Ken Jackson, *Tulsa World* book editor.

If it took a village to write this book, it took a focused little team to publish it. I am particularly grateful to Carlos Moreno, who served as book coach and designer, and William Franklin, a talented Tulsa artist who designed the cover.

My goal was to write a documented, factual story using the techniques of fiction and journalism. I am particularly indebted for all I learned from the late Tulsa historian, Danney Goble. And I am most grateful for the researchers and writers who came before me; I have tried to be faithful to their knowledge and insights.

This story has many lessons for us today, and I am delighted to have an opportunity to share it.

— Ann Patton

Notes

The Ku Klux Klan and David Curtis Stephenson did everything possible to obscure or skew their histories. Key records have disappeared, and principals have passed from the scene. The story now can be pieced together only from remaining shards. We are in debt to previous recorders, researchers, and scholars who have set out portions of the story. We hope future students will find some benefit in the following notes on our sources. Full data on each is contained in the Selected Bibliography.

In deference to lay readers, we have included in our text an occasional interpretative link. In deference to students of history, we identify those "interpretations" in these notes.

Part I

Chapter 1   The Kokomo Klonklave

Fact can hardly be separated from myth surrounding Stephenson's triumphant Kokomo Klonklave. There are clear conflicts between the legend and reporter John Niblack's eyewitness version, written years later. Niblack places Steve in a business suit, without any shower of trinkets in contrast to the purple robe legend repeated by Coughlin and Harrison, neither of whom was present at the ceremony. Niblack's first person account is cynical and remarkable, as is his entire autobiography. Niblack estimated the crowd at 10,000; legend, at 200,000.

Other sources include Cates; Chalmers; Merritt's *"Klan and Anti Klan in Indiana;"* Shepherd's *"Mystery Man;"* Wade; and Weaver.

Lutholtz contends that Steve's "greetings" speech did not take place at Kokomo.

The full text of Stephenson's speech, "Back to the Constitution," was printed in the Fiery Cross July 6, 1923. It has the ring of a man planning to run for national office, a serious politician; in time, many of the things he advocated would become reality. Niblack, however, concluded that the speech "didn't amount to two whoops."

Our account of Niblack's conversation with his editor is interpretative and includes information from Niblack's autobiography.

CHAPTER 2   A NEW RUGGED CROSS

The story of the Mary Phagan murder and Leo Frank lynching is told in detail by Harry Golden and in summary by Busch.

Sources for information on the gestation, birth, and youth of the 1920s Ku Klux Klan include Alexander, The Ku Klux Klan in the Southwest; Chalmers; de Silver; Dixon, The Clansman; Duffus, "How Salesmen Sold Packages of Hate at Ten Dollars Each;" Frost, "The Business of Kluxing;" "Imperial Wizard and His Klan;" Katz; Mecklin; Randel; Rice; Shepherd, "How I Put Over the Klan; and Wade.

CHAPTER 3 – BIRTH OF A SALESMAN

D.C. Stephenson's early years remain largely a mystery, and some of the information in this chapter is interpretative, based on what may be speculative information by various sources. Steve gave various stories of his beginnings, including conflicting birth dates, birth places, and family names. In the mid 1920s, at the height of the Klan wars, a KKK investigator developed a Stephenson history, clearly adversarial, which is largely in line with data in the first Stephenson "biography," a rambling and fairly incoherent book by a former Klansman who adopted the pseudonym of "Edgar A. Booth."

The Klan investigator's findings are summarized in a current anthology, by an Indianian who uses the pseudonym of "H.R.Greenapple." Additional data was compiled by Cates; he did not footnote some of this information, which was perhaps speculative.

A good summary, with some new findings, is in a 1991 history by Lutholtz, who believes Steve's father was named Andrew Monroe Stephenson. Stephenson's story of his rearing by parents he called "Blanche Bennett and Howard Stephenson" is contained in a psychiatric survey dated Sept. 10, 1942, while he was in Indiana State Prison, available in the Indiana State Archives. Lutholtz notes that Blanche and Howard Bennett were Steve's housekeeper and bodyguard in his Irvington mansion.

A copy of Steve's 1915 marriage license (Nettie Hamilton and D. C. Stephenson, March 26, 1915; Tishomingo [Johnston County], Oklahoma) shows ages of both as 22   one of many conflicts in data, since most sources believe Steve was born in 1891.

Useful articles on this period include Rascoe and Shepherd's "Indiana's Mystery Man."

Other sources include:

On Oklahoma Socialists: Ameringer and Scales/Goble.

On Oklahoma history: Debo and Scales/Goble; Franks and Gregory on early Oklahoma oil; histories of Cushing, Madill, Sulphur, Garvin County, Marshall County, McClain County, and Johnston County. Morris, et al, published useful historical maps of early Oklahoma development.

On early Oklahoma newspapers: Edward L. Carter's comprehensive story of the Sooner press development.

Perhaps the clearest picture of the emerging Stephenson is contained in the remaining fragments of Oklahoma newspapers where he worked, at Madill, Cushing, and elsewhere. The best sources we found were *Madill's Marshall County News Democrat* (later the *Madill Record*), April September 1915; and the *Cushing Independent*, June July 1916. The account of the 1911 Purcell lynching is from two articles in the *Vinita Weekly Chieftain*, Sept. 1, 1911. These and other newspapers are available on microfilm at the Oklahoma Historical Society and are cited in the bibliography.

We reviewed a number of Oklahoma newspapers for this period, trying to confirm the versions of Steve's beginnings that were traced by the Klan investigator and Booth. We confirmed Steve's presence at the locations and times cited in our text, establishing enough of a pattern to conclude that the Klan and Booth stories were at least partly correct or at least correlated by newspaper accounts.

It was particularly instructive to compare Stephenson's early writing and activities to his peers in "Little Dixie;" by comparison, his early editorials were moderate and lively. For a student, Steve's early patterns clearly foreshadow his later political activities.

We combined some information from Steve's Madill editorials in his speech to the Madill Woodmen of the World.

Chapter 4 "Jus' Sailin' 'Long, Doin' the Best We Can"

In addition those cited for Chapter 2, sources on Steve's early years include the following:

Steve's war service: David Curtis Stephenson's military records.

Data on Steve's marriage to and divorce from Violet Mary Carroll: Booth; Stephenson's obituary in the Sept. 17, 1978, *Louisville Courier Journal*; and Lutholtz's review of divorce documents from the Indiana Historical Society.

The account of Steve's adoption of "The Old Man": an *Indianapolis News* article by Tubby Toms, Oct. 9, 1950.

Several excellent dissertations discuss the early Indiana years of Stephenson and the KKK, including Cates, John Augustus Davis, Leonard Joseph Moore, and Weaver. Stephenson told his own version in Butler's pamphlet, *So They Framed Stephenson*. Booth, Greenapple, and Wade contain summaries. Lutholtz surveyed Evansville newspapers of the period, producing useful data.

Bigham has additional information on early Evansville, from a black perspective.

CHaPter 5 – THe Texas TOOCHPULLer

The rich story of Colonel Simmons' struggles with his fledgling KKK is scattered amidst a lively series of contemporary magazine articles. Among the best: "Imperial Wizard and His Klan;" Walter F. White; Frank Stockbridge; de Silver; "The K.K.K.;" "Ku Klux Klan Again;" "Imperial Lawlessness;" "For and Against the Ku Klux Klan;" "Ku Klux Condemned by the Religious Press;" "The 'Invisible Empire' in the Spotlight;" and Shepherd's "How I Put Over the Klan," "Ku Klux Koin" and "The Fiery Double Cross."

Information on the formation of the Klan in Texas, including formative years of Hiram Wesley Evans, is less abundant. Some information is contained in Frost's 1924 series, including "Old Evils in the New Klan;" and Duffus' thoughtful series.

Among outstanding summaries of this period: Alexander's *The Ku Klux Klan in the Southwest*; Chalmers; John Augustus Davis; Katz; Randel; and Wade. Also recommended: John Moffat Mecklin's 1924 book, *The Ku Klux Klan, A Study of the American Mind*. Mecklin's tone is established by his beginning quote from Spinoza: "Human actions are not to be ridiculed, feared or hated, but rather to be understood." (Our translation.)

The *New York World* series ran in September 1921 and is available on microfilm.

CHAPTER 6 ONWARD, CHRISTIAN KLANSMEN

Information on the Klan's salad days in Indiana has been combined from several academic papers, including Cates, John Augustus Davis, Leonard Joseph Moore, Warren, and Weaver.

Also useful were Booth; Greenapple; Mecklin; Niblack; Wade; and Wilson's *Indiana, A History.*

Pertinent articles include Dreiser; Samuel Taylor Moore, "How the Kleagles Collected the Cash;" Elmer Davis; Harrison; and Nicholson.

CHAPTER 7 – FIERY DOUBLE CROSS

This chapter title is taken from an article of the same name by William G. Shepherd in Colliers, July 28, 1928—telling of the 1923 Klan coup from Colonel Simmons' point of view. All Shepherd's articles are useful. Conflicting with Colonel Simmons' story is the alternate scenario—that Stephenson blackmailed Simmons with compromising photos—which is outlined by Loucks and Monteval.

Other useful information on this period is from Booth, Cates, Chalmers, Duffus, "Great Bigotry Merger," Randel, and Wade.

CHAPTER 8 – GENTLEMAN FROM INDIANA

The story of Steve's fake phone conversations is described in Shepherd's "Indiana's Mystery Man," and Samuel Taylor Moore's "How the Kleagles Collected the Cash." Their probable source was Court Asher.

Other useful articles on Stephenson's Indiana power play include Frost's 1924 series, "When the Klan Rules;" and Johnson's "The Ku Kluxer." Frost and Johnson generally wrote with more sympathy for Klansmen than most of their acid contemporary journalists. One theory is that Frost worked closely with *Indiana Fiery Cross* editor Milton Elrod. Johnson worked closely enough with Gutzon Borglum to complete a favorable book, *The Undefeated*, about Borglum.

Other sources include: *The Fiery Cross*, April 2 and 13, 1923; *Indianapolis Times* April 13, 1923; Booth; Cates; Chalmers; John Augustus Davis; Greenapple; Randel; and Wade.

Lutholtz' research leads him to conclude that Violet Mary Carroll went with Steve to Evansville and Indianapolis, where she lived with him there until she left him in August of 1922.

The estimate of 300-400,000 Indiana Klansmen is from John Augustus Davis. Leonard Joseph Moore's more recent research into membership rolls leads to his estimate that membership was around 250,000, about 30 percent of Indiana's eligible white, native born men. Other estimates range upwards of 500,000. Given the secret and ephemeral nature of membership, a student can take his pick.

Part II

Chapter 9   Press Oppression

Although their record was far from perfect, we found individual Hoosier newsmen to be among the more courageous actors in the KKK drama. We believe they are exemplified by the *Indianapolis Times'* John Niblack. Another view is that the *Times'* coverage was self serving and sensationalized; and that other Indianapolis newspapers were more responsible (see Lutholtz for information on this point of view). In their academic reviews, Warren and Scharlatt are critical of newspapers' overall performance. In general, it is a delight to re-read 1920s newspapers, with their colorful language and passionate coverage.

Additional sources on this issue include Niblack's autobiography, Cates, Booth, and several contemporary articles: Aikman's "The Home Town Mind;" Harrison; Nicholson; and Hoover.

Stephenson quoted the journalists' call in the *Marshall County News Democrat* Aug. 19, 1915. Warren compared it to the Klan call.

CHAPTER 10   KKK Bar B Q

Stephenson's free form revolutionary plans, and his various conspiracy talks with Gutzon Borglum, are reported by Booth, who also reports on the Valpariso University take over attempt. A more coherent version of the Valpariso University story is told by Trusty. National journalists' reaction is cited in our text.

In addition to data about Borglum in his papers, three lesser known sources are worth noting: a favorable portrait about his work on Stone Mountain, in Johnson's *The Undefeated*; Heard; and Shaff.

Stephenson's Indiana promotions for the Klan had a striking likeness to the good ole boy, family funfests promoted in Oklahoma the Socialists, Woodmen of the World, and Democrats. In full page ads for any of the events, including the KKK, he could use virtually the same format and text. His foray into fraternalism in the north, for political purposes, followed a natural continuum that can be traced from Madil to his own promotions and accounts in the Fiery Cross.

Other sources include Batten; Shepherd's "Mystery Man;" "Alma Mater, K.K.K.;" "The Klan Backs a College;" Wade; Fiery Cross Dec. 19, 1922, and Apr. 13, 1923.

Among sources on the Klan in Oklahoma and elsewhere: Alexander; Chalmers; Clark; Cronley; and The Tulsa Tribune June 2, 1920.

CHAPTER 11   Uncivil War

Steve's actions as he departed the Klan are among the most confusing and conflicting of his story. Few of the escalating declarations of war were public during the initial months. Useful sources include Booth and depositions taken later in lawsuits involving various Klan wars, cited in Cates, John Augustus Davis, Chalmers, Greenapple, Lutholtz, Niblack, Wade.

One of the more interesting articles on the '20s Klan was written by KKK scholar Alexander, "Kleagles and Cash, The Ku Klux Klan As a Business Organization." Also useful are Trusty's 1986 article on the Valpariso

University incident, "All Talk and No Kash;" and Shepherd's "Fiery Double Cross."

CHAPTER 12   WARWICK ON THE WABASH

Accounts of this period's political triumphs and tragedies vary among sources including Booth, Cates, Chalmers, John Augustus Davis, Niblack, and Wade. Greenapple's summary is not footnoted but appears to have been taken from the Feightner papers at Franklin College. Of particular interest is the account of William E. Wilson Jr. about Evansville politics in the summer of 1924, summarized here from his article "Long, Hot Summer in Indiana."

Among other sources: Frost's "The Klan Shows Its Hand in Indiana;" Harrison; Nicholson; and Elmer Davis' "Have Faith in Indiana." (Note: Davis' article was satirized in a followup article by the same name by Lawrence Abbott, also cited in our Bibliography.)

Sources on the South Bend riot include the *South Bend Tribune*, May 20, 1924; the *Indiana Jewish Chronicle*, May 23, 1924; and Wade. Sources on Gutzon Borglum include Shaff, Heard, and Lutholtz.

CHAPTER 13   DAVID BECOMES GOLIATH

 Stephenson's Klan trial is documented in transcripts and tribunal documents which are summarized in Greenapple, apparently from the Feightner papers. Whether legend or truth, speculations about his sadism and paranoia have been carried in sources such as Booth and Niblack; a frequently cited source is Court Asher.

Information on the Klan in Texas and elsewhere is drawn from sources including Chalmers and Alexander. Information on the Little Egypt fringe of Illinois comes largely from Angle, Chalmers, and O'Brien.

The Indianapolis Times anti-Klan election editorials were printed Oct. 31, Nov. 3, and Nov. 5, 1924. The *New York Times'* last rites editorial was printed October 16, 1924.

Other political information is drawn from Shepherd's "Mystery Man;" Cates, John Augustus Davis, and Weaver.

The account of Bill Remy's post election dinner is from Remy's unpublished memoirs, cited in Lutholtz.

Chapter 14   The Dragon Meets a Lady

The story of Stephenson's tour de force in the 1925 Indiana legislative session comes from multiple sources, including Walsh; Booth; Chalmers; Greenapple; Wade; Niblack; Shepherd's "Mystery Man;" Leibowitz; and the Feightner papers, Franklin College. Leibowitz and Feightner were both journalists.

Information on Madge Oberholtzer's life and her Stephenson comes from The Drift, Butler University's 1917 yearbook, cited in Greenapple; depositions of Matilda Oberholtzer and Asa Smith; testimony of Stanley Hill; and an oral interview of Asa Smith on file with the Indiana State Library.

Data on the public fall out of Madge's assault comes from the Feightner papers; oral interviews of Feightner and Asa Smith, on file at the Indiana State Library; Niblack; Busch's summary of the trial and surrounding events; a summary in the Indiana State Supreme Court's findings on Stephenson's appeal of case 25310; and a document named "Stephenson's Undelivered Speech," available in Indiana State Archives.

Chapter 15   Irvington 0492

Original copies of Madge Oberholtzer's dying declaration have long since disappeared, but the version admitted to evidence was reprinted in Leibowitz' *My Indiana*, pp 195 203. The Oct. 31, 1925, *Indianapolis Times* identified the excerpts stricken from the statement. We combined both to recreate the original statement.

CHAPTER 16   From Mayhem to Murder

Sources on Madge's last days of life include excerpts transcribed from trial testimony for several witnesses, including Matilda and George Oberholtzer, Dr. John Kingsbury, Asa Smith, and Eunice Shultz, on file at the Indiana State Archives. Other sources included Smith's oral interview; Busch; Leibowitz; Lutholtz; Niblack; and the *Indianapolis Times* Nov. 2, 1925.

The quote comparing Madge's abduction to Steve's hold on Indiana comes from Martin's article, "Beauty and the Beast, The Downfall of D.C. Stephenson, Grand Dragon of the Indiana K.K.K." This article later became a chapter in Martin's book, *Indiana, An Interpretation.*

Other sources include Booth; Cornelius; Shepherd's "Mystery Man;" and Court Asher testimony before the Marion County (Indiana) Grand Jury Oct. 13, 1926, cited in Lutholtz.

Newspaper sources include the *Indianapolis Times*, Oct 5, 1925; the Indianapolis Star Oct. 6, 1925; and the Indianapolis News Aug. 20, 1925.

Part III

CHAPTERS 17-26

The transcript of Stephenson's trial disappeared 30 years ago. For us to trace the events of the trial in summary, it thus became necessary to reconstruct the trial from remaining accounts. Our principal sources were newspaper accounts of the trial, supplemented by some fragmented accounts in legal textbooks. Once transcribed from these sources and arranged in chronological order, the events of the trial were summarized for our account.

The newspaper accounts were nothing less than stunning. Under deadline pressure and without today's sophisticated techniques, the reporters had traced the high points of the trial with amazing clarity and detail. The trial covered more than a month, so our primary sources were newspaper accounts for the period between Oct. 12 and Nov. 16, 1925. We relied most heavily on accounts by John Niblack and Tubby Toms in the *Indianapolis Times* and by Horace M. Coats in the *Indianapolis Star*. Additional information came from the *Indianapolis News* and the *Noblesville Ledger* for the same period.

For simplicity's sake, we attributed most of the *Times*' articles to Niblack; but most carried a joint Niblack-Toms byline, making it impossible to determine who wrote which articles. By this time, Niblack had completed night law school, which must have given him an edge in covering the trial; but Toms (No. 25310) later referred to Niblack as a "cub reporter" at the time of the trial.

Supplementing the newspaper accounts was information from Niblack's autobiography; Busch, who wrote a lawyers' summary of the trial; personal visits; and a portion of the transcript reprinted in Cornelius' legal textbook on cross examination, which contains useful snapshots of the critical medical testimonies. We also used transcribed excerpts, on file in the Indiana State Archives, of testimony by Asa Smith, Dr. John Kingsbury, George and Matilda Oberholtzer, Eunice Shultz, Griffith Dean, Ermina Moore, Ted Wilson, Lee R. Ayres, and Lillian Reed.

Useful color items, such as the incident when Stephenson threatened to punch Niblack, came from a series of retrospective articles about the trial written by Tubby Toms for the *Indianapolis News* in October of 1950.

These sources, while more difficult to use than a transcript, gave us added information such as the *Times*' description of a single chair creaking in the silence of the courtroom or the remarkably diverse sorts of chewing that were going on during the trial—that the precise, cold pages of transcript could not.

EPILOGUE

Sources on Stephenson's post trial years and the slow demise of the Klan include Niblack; Booth; Busch; Greenapple; Leibowitz; John Augustus Davis; Martin's Indiana, An Interpretation; and Weaver. Chalmers and Wade trace the Klans into the 1960s and 1970s.

Useful court documents include the remaining fragments of depositions and trial documents from Stephenson's 40 appeals, various Klan lawsuits, the Supreme Court 1932 findings in Stephenson's appeal; and court proceedings such as Atty. Gen. Gilliom's suit against the KKK.

Most interesting was Stephenson's testimony against the Klan in the "Strayer" case (Knights of the Ku Klux Klan v. Rev. John F. Strayer, et al, April 1928, No. 1897 in Equity District Court of the U.S. for the Western District of Pennsylvania). Key documents are cited in the bibliography.

Useful articles include Budenz; Merritt's "The Klan on Parade;" Harrison; Martin's "Beauty and the Beast;" "What the Klan Did in Indiana;" "Indiana's Political Scandal;" and Merz; "The Rise and Fall of the K.K.K."

On the Pulitzer prize award to the *Indianapolis Times*: George E. Stevens; and "Pulitzer Medal Won by Indianapolis Times."

Additional information about Asa Smith came from Farmer. Descriptions of Smith vary widely among sources, some painting him as a shell shocked young veteran, others as a respected and influential statesman. Like most of our descriptions, Smith's was based on a photo (Smith photo in Indianapolis Times Oct. 31, 1925).

Supplemental data about Judge Will Sparks came from Solomon's History of the Seventh Circuit, 1981 1941.

Helpful newspaper articles on this period include:

Indianapolis News Sept. 9, 1958, Oct. 14, 1926; March 22 and Nov. 24, 1950; and Aug. 17, 1971 (interview with Martha Dickinson Stephenson).

Indianapolis Times May 11 and Sept. 27, 1927; Dec. 30, 1956.

Indianapolis Star Nov. 11, 1950, and Nov. 17, 1961.

Louisville Courier Journal, Sept. 17, 1978 (Stephenson obituary).

Selected Bibliography

Books

Abbott, Lawrence F. "'Have Faith in Indiana.'" *Outlook* 144, Oct. 6, 1926, pp 170-171.

Aikman, Duncan. "Prairie Fire." *American Mercury* VI, October 1925, pp 209-214.

Aikman, Duncan. "The Home-Town Mind." *Harper's* CLI, November 1925, pp 663-669.

Aldrich, Gene. *Black Heritage of Oklahoma*. Edmond: Thompson Book and Supply Co., 1973.

Alexander, Charles C. *The Ku Klux Klan in the Southwest*. Lexington: University of Kentucky Press, 1965.

Alexander, Charles C. "Kleagles and Cash: The Ku Klux Klan As a Business Organization, 1915-1930." *Business History Review* XXXIX, 1965, pp 348-367.

Allen, Frederick L. *Only Yesterday: An Informal History of the Nineteen Twenties*. New York: Blue Ribbon Books, Inc., 1931.

"Alma Mater. K.K.K." *The New Republic*, Sept. 5, 1923, pp 35-36.

"Anarchy in Oklahoma." *The Nation* 117, 3040, Oct. 10, 1923, p 369.

Angle, Paul M. *Bloody Williamson: A Chapter in American Lawlessness*. New York: Knopf, 1966.

Barrett, Maj. Gen. Charles F. "An Outline of Oklahoma National Guard History," Chapter XVI, and "Our Progress Under State Government," Chapter XXIX, in *Oklahoma After Fifty Years, A History of The Sooner State and Its People, 1889-1939*. Hopkinsville, Kentucky: The Historical Record Association, 1941.

Batten, Neil. "Nativism and the Klan in Town and City: Valpariso and Gary, Indiana." *Studies in History and Sociology* 1973 4 (2), pp 3-16.

"The Beast in a New Form." *The New Republic* 41, Dec. 24, 1924, p 121.

Benedict, Michael Lee. "Ku Klux Klan." *Academic American Encyclopedia*. Grolier Inc., 1968.

Bigham, Darrell. *We Ask Only A Fair Trial, A History of the Black Community in Evansville, Indiana*. Indiana University Press, 1987.

Blake, Aldrich. "Oklahoma's Klan-Fighting Governor." *The Nation* 117, Oct. 3, 1923, p 353.

Blake, Aldrich. "The Strength of the KKK." *The New Republic* 46, Apr. 7, 1926, p 201.

Blee, Kathleen M. *Women of the Klan, Racism and Gender in the 1920s*. University of California Press, 1991.

Blum, John M., et al. *The National Experience, A History of the United States since 1865*. Part Two, 4th ed. New York: Harcourt Brace Jovanovich, Inc., 1977.

Bohn, Frank. "The Ku Klux Klan Interpreted." *The American Journal of Sociology* XXX, January 1925, pp 385-407.

Booth, Edgar A. *The Mad Mullah of America*. Columbus, OH: (Boyd) Ellison, 1927.

Boorstin, Daniel J. *The Americans: The National Experience*. New York: Random House, 1966.

Boyd, Thomas. "Defying the Klan." *Forum* 76, July 1926, pp 48-56.

Brown, George Alfred. *Harold the Klansman*. Kansas City: Western Baptist Publishing Company, 1923.

Budenz, Louis Francis. "There's Mud on Indiana's White Robes." *The Nation* 125, July 27, 1927, pp 81-82.

Budenz, Louis Francis. "Indiana's Anti-Saloon League Goes to Jail." *The Nation* 125, Aug. 24, 1927, pp 177-178.

Budenz, Louis Francis. "Scandals of 1927, Indiana." *The Nation* 125, Oct. 5, 1927, pp 332-333.

Busch, Francis X. *Guilty or Not Guilty* (includes "The Leo Frank Case," pp 16-74, and "The D. C. Stephenson Case," pp 77-124). Indianapolis: Bobbs-Merrill, 1951.

Butler, Robert A. *So They Framed Stephenson*. Huntington, Ind. 1940.

Callahan, Rick. "Great American Neighborhoods." *City, The Magazine for New Indianapolis*, 27:6, June 1989, pp 44-53.

Carter, L. Edward. "Rise and Fall of the Invisible Empire: Knights of the Ku Klux Klan." *Great Plains Journal* 16, Spring 1977, pp 82-106.

Carter, L. Edward. *The Story of Oklahoma Newspapers, 1844 to 1984*. Muskogee, OK: Western Heritage books, Inc., for Oklahoma Heritage Association, 1984.

Cates, Mark. *The Ku Klux Klan in Indiana Politics: 1920-1930*. Ph.D diss., Indiana University, November 1970.

Catton, Bruce. "The Restless Decade." *American Heritage* 16, August 1965, pp 5-6, 18.

Chalmers, David Mark. *Hooded Americanism*. New York: New Viewpoints, a division of Franklin Watts, 1981. Chapman, Charles H. "Oregon: A Sighted Beauty." *The Nation* 116, Feb. 7, 1923, pp 141-143.

Clark, Carter Blue. *A History of the Ku Klux Klan in Oklahoma*. Ph.D diss., University of Oklahoma, 1976.

Coale, Burton V. "Mount Rushmore National Memorial." *Encyclopedia Americana*, p 568.

Coleman, McAlister. "When the Troops Took Tulsa." *The Nation* 117, Sept. 5, 1923, pp 239-240.

"Constitution Week in Oklahoma." *Literary Digest* LXXIX, Oct. 13, 1923, pp 12-13.

"The Conviction of Governor Walton." *Outlook*, Nov. 28, 1923, pp 519-520.

Cook, Fred J. *The Ku Klux Klan, America's Recurring Nightmare*. New York: Simon and Schuster, 1980.

Coughlan, Robert. "Klonklave in Kokomo" in *The Aspirin Age, 1919-1941*, ed. Isabel Leighton. New York: Simon and Schuster, 1949.

Cronley, Connie. "At The Doleful Hour of The White Night of The Melancholy Moon." *Oklahoma Monthly*, 1976, pp 30-39.

"D.C. Stephenson: Shadow of the '20s." *Newsweek* 45, Jan. 3, 1955, p 20.

Davis, Elmer. "Have Faith in Indiana." *Harper's* 153, October 1926, pp 615-625.

Davis, John Augustus. *The Ku Klux Klan in Indiana, 1920-1930: An Historical Study*. Ph.D diss., Northwestern University, June 1966.

Davis, Rod. "Free Speech for the Klan is a Fraud, Not a Right." *Progressive*, July 1983, pp 22-26.

de Silver, Albert. "The Ku Klux Klan: The Soul of Chivalry." *The Nation* 113, September 14, 1921, pp 285-286.

Debo, Angie. *And Still the Waters Run, The Betrayal of the Five Civilized Tribes.* Norman, OK: University of Oklahoma, 1972

Debo, Angie. *Oklahoma, Foot-loose and Fancy-free.* Norman, OK: University of Oklahoma, 1949.

Debo, Angie. *Prairie City, The Story of an American Community.* Tulsa: Council Oak Books, Ltd., 1985

Dixon, Thomas. *The Clansman, An Historical Romance of the Ku Klux Klan.* New York: Grosset & Dunlap, 1905.

Dixon, Thomas. *The Leopard's Spots: A Romance of the White Man's Burden.* New York: A. Wessels Company, 1906.

Dreiser, Theodore. "Indiana: Her Soil and Light." *The Nation* 117, 3039, Oct. 3, 1923, pp 348-350.

Duffus, Robert L. "Salesmen of Hate: The Ku Klux Klan." Five-part series in *The World's Work* 46:

-- "How the Klan Was Built Up by Traveling Salesmen," May 1923, pp 31-38.

-- "How the Ku Klux Klan Sells Hate: How Salesmen Sold Packages of Hate at Ten Dollars Each," June 1923, pp 174-183.

-- "Counter-Mining The Ku Klux Klan: The Reasons for and Work of the Commission for Inter-Racial Cooperation," July 1923, pp 275-284.

-- "The Ku Klux Klan in the Middle West: The Growth of the Invisible Empire Above the Mason-Dixon Line," Aug. 1923, pp 363-372.

-- "Ancestry and End of the Ku Klux Klan: Its Forebears and Its Probable Course and End," Sept. 1923, pp 527-536.

Ellsworth, Scott. *Death in a Promised Land, The Tulsa Race Riot of 1921.* Baton Rouge: Louisiana State University Press, 1982.

Evans, Hiram Wesley. *Is The Ku Klux Klan Constructive or Destructive?* Little Blue Book No. 652. Girard, KS: Haldeman-Julius Company, circa 1923.

Evans, Hiram Wesley. "The Klan: Defender of Americanism." *Forum* LXXIV, December 1925, pp 800-814.

Evans, H.W. "The Catholic Question as Viewed by the Ku Klux Klan." *Current History* 26, July 1927, pp 563-568.

Evans, Hiram Wesley. "The Ballots Behind the Ku Klux Klan, An Article on the Political Aims and Purposes of the Order." *The World's Work* LV, January 1928, pp 243-252.

Farmer, James E., ed. *Asa Jessup Smith, Lawyer, Patriot, Wit.* Indianapolis: Central Publishing Company, November 1988.

Fecher, Charles A. *Mencken: A Study of His Thought.* New York: Knopf, 1978.

Finch, Phillip. "The Never-Never Land of Racial Politics: Can the Klan Ride Again?" *The New Republic*, September 1983, pp 18-21.

Fischer, Leroy H., editor. *Oklahoma's Governors, 1907-1929: Turbulent Politics.* Oklahoma City: Oklahoma Historical Society, 1981.

"For and Against the Ku Klux Klan." *Literary Digest* 70, Sept. 24, 1921, pp 34-40.

Frank, Glenn. "Christianity and Racialism: Has the Ku Klux Klan the Right to Celebrate Christmas?" *Century* 109, Dec. 1924, pp 277-284.

Franks, Kenny A., et al. *Early Oklahoma Oil, A Photographic History, 1859-1936.* College Station, TX: Texas A & M University Press, 1981.

"From the Oklahoma Front." *The New Republic* XXXVI, Oct. 17, 1923, pp 202-205.

Frost, Stanley. "The Regeneration of Oklahoma," Four-part series in *Outlook*:

-- "The Oklahoma Regicides Act," Nov. 7, 1923, pp 395-396.

- "Night-Riding Reformers," Nov. 14, 1923, pp 438-440.

--"Behind the White Hoods," Nov. 21, 1923, pp 492-495.

-- "The Klan, the King, and a Revolution," Nov. 28, 1923.

Frost, Stanley. "When the Klan Rules," series in *Outlook* 136:

-- Old Evils in the New Klan." Jan. 2, 1924, pp 20-24.

-- "The Crusade of the Fiery Cross." Jan. 9, 1924, pp 64-66.

-- "The Business of Kluxing." Jan. 23, 1924, pp 144-147.

-- "The Lure of White Masks." Jan. 30, 1924, pp 183-186.

Frost, Stanley. "The Klan Shows Its Hand in Indiana." *Outlook* 137, June 4, 1924, pp 187-190.

Frost, Stanley. "The Klan's 1/2 of 1 per cent Victory." *Outlook* 137, July 9, 1924, pp 384-387.

Frost, Stanley. "The Masked Politics of the Klan and How the Candidacy of Smith May Be Affected." *The World's Work* LV, March 1928, pp 399-407.

Fuermann, George. *Houston, The Once and Future City* Garden City: NY: Doubleday & Co., Inc., 1971.

Fuller, Edgar I. *The Visible of the Invisible Empire: The Maelstrom.* George LaDura, ed. Denver: Maelstrom, 1925.

Gannett, Lewis S. "Is America Anti-Semitic?" *The Nation* 116, Mar. 12, 1923, pp 330-332.

Griffin, William W. "The Political Realignment of Black Voters in Indianapolis, 1924." *Indiana Magazine of History* LXXIX #2, June 1983, pp 133-166.

Gist, Noel P. *Secret Societies: A Cultural Study of Fraternalism in the United States.*

Ph.D. diss., University of Missouri Studies, XV, Oct. 1, 1940.

Golden, Harry. *A Little Girl Is Dead*. Cleveland: The World Publishing Company, 1965.

"Governor Behind Bars." *Literary Digest* LXXXI, May 17, 1924, p 15.

"The Great Bigotry Merger." *The Nation* 115, July 15, 1922, pp 8-10.

Green, James R. *Grass Roots Socialism: Radical Movements in the Southwest, 1895-1943*. Baton Rouge: Louisiana State University Press, 1978.

Greenapple, H.R., compiler and editor. *D.C. Stephenson, Irvington 0492: The Demise of the Grand Dragon of the Indiana Ku Klux Klan*. Plainfield, IN: SGS Publications, 1989.

Greene, Ward. "Notes for a History of the Klan." *American Mercury* 5, June 1925, pp 240-243.

Gregory, Robert. *Oil in Oklahoma*. Muskogee: Leake Industries, 1976.

Harrison, Morton. "Gentlemen from Indiana." *Atlantic Monthly* 141, May 1928, pp. 676-686.

Haskell, H.J. "Martial Law in Oklahoma." *The Outlook* 135, Sept. 26, 1923, pp 132-133.

Hausknecht, Murry. *The Joiners: A Sociological Description of Voluntary Association Membership in the United States*. New York: Bedminster Press, 1962.

Heard, Alex. "Mount Rushmore: The Real Story." *The New Republic*, July 15-22, 1991, pp 16-18.

Hodsden, Harry, ed. *The Stephenson Case: Stephenson Was Framed in a Political Conspiracy*. Valpariso, Indiana: Hodsden, 1936.

Hohenberg, John, editor. *The Pulitzer Prize Story*, volumes I and II. New York: Columbia University Press, 1971.

Hoover, Dwight W. "To Be a Jew in Middletown: A Muncie Oral History Project." *Indiana Magazine of History* LXXXI #2, June 1985, pp 131-158.

"Imperial Lawlessness." *Outlook* 129, Sept. 13, 1921, p 46.

"Imperial Wizard and His Klan." *Literary Digest* 68, Feb. 5, 1921, pp 40-46.

"Indiana's Political Scandal." *Literary Digest* XCIV, Aug. 13, 1927, p 10.

"Indiana's Political Housecleaning." *Literary Digest* XCV, Oct. 1, 1927, p 14.

"The 'Invisible Empire' in the Spotlight." *Current Opinion* 71, Nov. 1921, pp 561-564.

"'Jack, the Klan-Fighter' in Oklahoma." *Literary Digest*, Oct. 20, 1923, pp 39-44.

Jackson, Kenneth. *The Ku Klux Klan in the City, 1915-1930*. New York: Oxford University Press, 1967.

Jarboe, Betty. *Studies on Indiana: A Bibliography of Theses and Dissertations submitted to Indiana...1902-1977*. Indianapolis: Indiana Historical Bureau, 1980.

Jenkins, Alan. *The Twenties.* New York: Universe Books, 1974.

Johnson, Gerald W. "The Ku-Kluxer." *American Mercury* I, January 1924, pp 207-211.

Johnson, Gerald W. *The Undefeated*. New York: Milton, Balh, and Co. 1927.

"The K.K.K." *New Republic* 28, September 21, 1921, pp 88-89.

Katz, William Loren. *The Invisible Empire, Ku Klux Klan Impact on History*. Washington: Open Hand Publishing Inc., 1986.

"The Klan and the Candidates." *Literary Digest* 82, Sept. 6, 1924, pp 10-11.

"The Klan as a National Problem." *Literary Digest* 75, Dec. 2, 1922, pp12-13.

"The Klan 'Backs' a College." *Literary Digest,* Sept. 15, 1923, pp 43-46.

"The Klan Issue" in "The March of Events." *The World's Work* XLVIII, Oct. 1924, pp 573-581.

"Klan Senator from Indiana." *Literary Digest* 87, Nov. 14, 1925, pp 16-17.

"The Klan Sheds Its Hood." *New Republic* 45, Feb. 10, 1926, pp 310-311.

"A Klan Shock in Indiana." *Literary Digest* LXXXI, May 24, 1924, p 14.

"Klan Victories and Defeats." *Literary Digest* LXXXIII, Nov. 22, 1924, p 16.

"The Klan Walks in Washington." *Literary Digest* 86, Aug. 22, 1925, pp 7-8.

"The Klan's Challenge and the Reply." *Literary Digest* 79, Nov. 17, 1923, pp 32-34.

"The Klan's Political Role." *Literary Digest* 79, Nov. 24, 1923, pp 13-14.

"The Ku Klux and the Next Election." *The World's Work* 46, Oct. 1923, pp 573-75.

"Ku Klux Condemned by the Religious Press." *Literary Digest* 71, Oct. 1, 1921, pp 30-31.

"Ku Klux Klan." *Colliers Encyclopedia.* MacMillan, 1986.

"Ku Klux Klan." *New Catholic Encyclopedia.* New York: McGraw Hill Book Co., 1967.

"Ku Klux Klan Again." *Outlook* 129, September 21, 1921, p 79.

"The Klux Klan is Suffering a Decline." *The New Republic* 42, Apr. 22, 1925, p 224.

"Ku Klux Klan Symposium," five articles in the *North American Review* 223, March-June 1926:

-- Evans, Hiram Wesley. "The Klan's Fight for Americanism. March, pp 32-63.

-- Scott, Martin J. "Catholics and the Ku Klux Klan." June, pp 269-281.

-- Silverman, Rev. Dr. Joseph. "The Ku Klux Klan A Paradox." June, pp 282-291.

-- Du Bois, W.E. Burghardt. "The Shape of Fear." June, pp 291-304.

-- Myers, William Starr. "The Ku Klux Klan of Today." June, pp 304-309.

"The Ku Klux Klan Viewed from Moscow." *The Nation* 118, 3069, Apr. 30, 1924, p 507.

"The Ku Klux Victory in Texas," and "Quaint Customs and Methods of the Ku Klux Klan." *Literary Digest*, Aug. 5, 1922. pp 14, 47-52.

Leary, Edward A. *Indianapolis: The Story of A City*. Indianapolis: The Bobbs-Merrill Company, Inc., 1970.

Leibowitz, Irving. *My Indiana*. Englewood Cliffs, NJ: Prentice-Hall, Inc., 1964.

Lindsey, Ben B. "My Fight with the Ku Klux Klan." *Survey* LIV, June 1, 1925, pp 271-274, 319-321.

Loucks, Emerson. *The Ku Klux Klan in Pennsylvania, A Study in Nativism*. Harrisburg, PA: The Telegraph Press, 1936.

Lutholtz, M. William. *Grand Dragon: D.C. Stephenson and the Ku Klux Klan in Indiana*. West Lafayette, IN: Purdue University Press, 1991.

The Madill (Oklahoma) Record, Historical Edition, Sept. 11, 1952.

Markey, Morris. "Why Did Indiana Free the Klan Killer?" *Coronet* 28, October 1950, pp 94-100.

Martin, John Barlow. *Indiana, An Interpretation.* NY: Knopf, 1947.

Martin, John Bartlow. "Beauty and the Beast: The Downfall of D.C. Stephenson, Grand Dragon on the Indiana K.K.K." *Harper's Magazine* 189, September 1944, pp 319-329.

"The Masked Floggers of Tulsa." *Literary Digest*, Sept. 23, 1923, p 17.

McWilliams, Wilson Carey. *The Idea of Fraternity in America.* Los Angeles: University of California, 1973.

Mecklin, John Moffat. *The Ku Klux Klan: A Study of the American Mind.* New York: Harcourt, Brace, 1924.

Mellett, Lowell. "Klan and Church." *Atlantic Monthly* 132, Nov. 1923, pp 586-592.

Memories of Marshall County, Oklahoma, Then and Now. Madill, OK: Curtis Media Corporation for Madill City Library, 1988.

Mencken, H.L. Malcolm, Moos, ed. *A Carnival of Buncombe.* Baltimore: Johns Hopkins Press, 1956.

Merritt, Dixon. "The Klan on Parade." *Outlook* 140, Aug. 19, 1925, pp 553-554.

Merritt, Dixon. "Klan and Anti-Klan in Indiana." *Outlook* 144, Dec. 8, 1926, pp 465-469.

Merz, Charles. "The New Ku-Klux Klan." *Independent*, Feb. 12, 1927, pp 179-180, 196.

Mindeman, George Andrew. *The Ku Klux Klan in Oklahoma During the Early 1920s: Threat to Constitutional Government?* Wheaton College, 19 March 1976.

Monteval, Marion. (pseudonym for Edgar I. Fuller?) *The Klan Inside Out.* Claremore, Oklahoma: Monarch Publishing Company, 1924.

Moore, Leonard Joseph. *White Protestant Nationalism in the 1920's: The Ku*

Klux Klan in Indiana. Ph.D diss., University of California, 1985.

Moore, Samuel Taylor. "A Klan Kingdom Collapses: Behind the Scenes in the City that Once Was Known as Klanopolis." *Independent* 113, Dec. 6, 1924, pp 473-475.

Moore, Samuel Taylor. "How the Kleagles Collected the Cash, The Story of the Hoosier Sales Campaign -- and Its Director." *The Independent* 113, Dec. 13, 1924, pp 517-519.

Moore, Samuel Taylor. "Consequences of the Klan: Results of the Hoosier Experiment in Invisible Monarchical Government." *Independent* 113, Dec. 20, 1924, pp 534-536.

Morris, John W., et al. *Historical Atlas of Oklahoma*, 3rd Ed. Norman, OK: University of Oklahoma Press, 1986.

Mosser, George H. "The State of Indiana." *Journal of National Education Association* 14, January 1925, pp 151-152.

Mowry, George E., ed. *The Twenties: Fords, Flappers & Fanatics.* Englewood Cliffs, New Jersey: Prentice-Hall Inc. 1963.

"Mutiny in the Invisible Empire." *Independent* 116, Jan. 16, 1926, pp 58-59.

"Mr. White Challenges the Klan." *Outlook* 138, Sept. 24, 1924, p 154.

Neuringer, Sheldon. "Governor Walton's War on the Ku Klux Klan: An Episode in Oklahoma History, 1923-1924." *The Chronicles of Oklahoma* XLV - 2. Oklahoma City: The Oklahoma Historical Society, Summer 1967.

Newsome, D. Earl. *Drumright.* Perkins, OK: Evans, 1985.

Niblack, John Lewis. *The Life and Times of a Hoosier Judge.* Washington, IN: Self-published, 1973.

Nicholson, Meredith. "Hoosier Letters and the Ku Klux." *Bookman* 76, March 1928, pp 7-11.

O'Brien, Darcy. *Murder in Little Egypt*. New York: William Morrow and Company, Inc., 1989.

"Oklahoma Kingless, Not Klanless." *Literary Digest*, Dec. 8, 1923, p 9.

"Oklahoma's Uncivil Civil War." *Literary Digest*, Sept. 29, 1923, pp 10-11.

"Oregon's Outlawing of Church Schools." *Literary Digest* 76, Jan. 6, 1923, pp 34-35.

Pattangall, William Robinson. "Is the Ku Klux Un-American?" *Forum* LXXIV, September 1925, pp 321-332.

Patton, R.A. "A Ku Klux Klan Reign of Terror." *Current History* XXVIII, April 1928, pp 51-55.

Pauls Valley (Oklahoma) Historical Society. *From Blue Stem to Golden Trend: A Pictorial History of Garvin County* (Oklahoma). Fort Worth: University Suply & Equipment Company, Publishers, 1957, 1980.

"Pink Ballots for the Ku Klux Klan." Outlook 137, July 25, 1924, pp 306-309.

"Probe a Rebirth of Hoosier Klan: Indianapolis 'Star' Reporter Secures an Admission by 'King Kleagle' that State-wide Action is Planned." *Christian Century* 63, Nov. 27, 1946, p 1446.

"A Protestant View of the Catholic Forward Movement." *Literary Digest* 63, Dec. 13, 1919.

"Pulitizer Medal Won By Indianapolis Times." *Editor and Publisher* LX, May 12, 1928, p 16.

Pulliam, Russell. *Publisher: Gene Pulliam, Last of the Newspaper Titans.* Ottawa, Illinois: Jameson Books, 1984.

Quillen, Isaac James. *Industrial City: A History of Gary, Indiana, to 1929.* Ph.D diss., Yale, 1942. New York: Garland Publishing, Inc., 1986.

Randel, William P. *The Ku Klux Klan: A Century of Infamy.* Philadelphia: Chilton Company, 1965.

Rascoe, Burton. "Oklahoma: Low Jacks and the Crooked Game." *The Nation* 117, July 11, 1923, pp 34-37.

Rex, Joyce A., ed. *McClain County, Oklahoma, History and Heritage.* Purcell, OK: McClain County Historical & Genealogical Society, 1986.

Rice, Arnold S. *The Ku Klux Klan in American Politics.* New York: Haskell House Publishers Ltd., 1962.

"The Rise and Fall of the K.K.K." *The New Republic* 53, Nov. 30, 1927, pp 33-34.

Roberts, Waldo. "The Ku-Kluxing of Oregon." *Outlook* 133, Mar. 14, 1923, pp 490-491.

Rosen, E. I. *Peasant Socialism in America? The Socialist Party in Oklahoma Before The First World War.* Ph.D diss., The City University of New York, 1976.

Sann, Paul. *The Lawless Decade.* New York: Bonanza Books, 1957.

Scales, James R., and Danney Goble. *Oklahoma Politics: A History.* Norman: University of Oklahoma Press, 1982.

Scharlatt, Bradford. *Hoosier Newsmen and the Hooded Order.* MA Thesis, Indiana U, 1978.

Schlesinger, Arthur M. *Paths to the Present.* New York: The MacMillan Company, 1949. (Chapter II, "Biography of a Nation of Joiners, pp 23-50.)

Schuyler, George S. "Keeping the Negro in His Place." *American Mercury* 17, August 1929, pp 469-476.

"Senate to Query Klan Scandal," in "What the World Is Doing." *Independent* CXVII, Oct. 23, 1926, pp 481-483.

Shaff, Howard and Audrey Karl. *Six Wars at a Time.* Sioux Falls, SD: The Center for Western Studies, Augustana College (in cooperation with Permelia Publishing, Darien Connecticut), 1985.

Shepherd, William G. "Indiana's Mystery Man." *Colliers* 79, Jan. 8, 1927, pp 9-10.

Shepherd, William G. "The Whip Hand." *Colliers*, LXXXI, Jan. 7, 1928, pp 8-9, 44-45.

Shepherd, William G. "The Whip Wins." *Colliers* LXXXI, Jan. 14, 1928, pp 10-11, 30-32.

Shepherd, William G. "How I Put Over the Klan." *Colliers* 82, July 14, 1928, pp 5-7, 32-35.

Shepherd, William G. "Ku Klux Koin." *Colliers* 82, July 21, 1928, pp 8-9, 38-39.

Shepherd, William G. "The Fiery Double-Cross." *Colliers* 28, July 28, 1928, pp 8-9, 47-49.

Smith, Robert B. "Klan Spooks in Congress." *Independent* 116, June 19, 1926, pp 718-719, 726.

"Solemn But Undignified Penguins." *The Nation* 116, Jan. 3, 1923, p 6.

Solomon, Rayman L. *History of the Seventh Circuit, 1891-1941*. Published under the auspices of The BiCentennial Committee of the Judicial Conference of the United States, U.S. Government Printing Office, 1981.

Speranza, Gino. "The Immigration Peril v. The National Issue of the American Public School." *The World's Work* 47, Feb. 1924, pp 479-490.

"A State Divided Against Itself." *Outlook* 135, Oct. 10, 1923, p 210.

Stephens, Harold W. "Mask and Lash in Crenshaw." *North American Review* 225, April 1928, pp 435-442.

Stevens, George E. "Winning the Pulitzer Prize: The Indianapolis Times Battles Political Corruption, 1926-27." *Journalism History* 2, 1975, pp 80-83.

Stockbridge, Frank. "The KuKlux Klan Revival." *Current History* XIV, April-September, 1921, pp 19-25.

Sullivan, Mark. <u>The Twenties</u>. Vol. VI of *Our Times*. New York: Charles Scribner's Sons, 1935.

Tait, Samuel W. Jr. «Indiana.» *American Mercury* 7, April 1926, pp 440-447.

Thornbrough, Emma Lou. "Segregation in Indiana during the Klan Era of the 1920's." *The Mississippi Valley Historical Review* XLVII, No. 4, March 1961, pp 594-618.

Trelease, Allen W. "Ku Klux Klan." *Encyclopedia Americana.* Grolier Inc., 1988.

Trusty, Lance. "All Talk and No 'Kash': Valpariso University and the Ku Klux Klan." *Indiana Magazine of History* LXXXII #1, March 1986, pp 1-36.

"The University of Oklahoma and the Ku Klux Klan." *School and Society* XVI, Oct. 7, 1922, pp 412-413.

Untitled article on the Klan. *The Nation* 118, Mar. 12, 1924.

"The Various Shady Lives of the Ku Klux Klan." *Time* 85, Apr. 9, 1965, pp 24-25.

"WBOX and the KKK." *Newsweek* 66, August 16, 1965, p 75.

Wade, Wyn Craig. *The Fiery Cross, The Ku Klux Klan in America.* New York: Simon and Schuster, Touchstone Books, 1981.

Walsh, Justin E. *The Centennial History of the Indiana General Assembly, 1816-1978.* Indianapolis: Indiana Historical Bureau, 1987.

Warren, Carl N. *The Influence of the Press Upon the Ku Klux Klan.* Unpublished Master's thesis, Northwestern University, 1922.

Weaver, Norman Fredric. *The Knights of the Ku Klux Klan in Wisconsin, Indiana, Ohio, and Michigan.* Ph.D dissertation, University of Wisconsin, 1954.

"What the Klan Did in Indiana." *The New Republic*, Nov. 16, 1927, pp 330-332.

"What Is Wrong with the Klan?" *The Nation* 118, 3076, June 18, 1924, p 698.

Wheeler, Ed. "Profile of a Race Riot." *Impact* 1, June-July 1971, pp 14-30.

White, Arthur Corning. "An American Fascismo." *The Forum* LXXII, Nov. 1924, pp 636-642.

White, Hoseph Michael. *The Ku Klux Klan in Indiana in the 1920s as Viewed by the Indiana Catholic and Record*. Master's thesis, Butler University, December 1974.

White, Walter F. "Reviving the Ku Klux Klan." *Forum* 65, April 1921, pp 426-434.

White, William Allen. "Annihilate the Klan!" *The Nation* 120, Jan. 7, 1925, p 7.

"Why They Join the Klan." *The New Republic*, Nov. 21, 1923, pp 321-322.

"William Allen White's War on the Klan." *Literary Digest* LXXXIII, Oct. 11, 1924, p 16.

Williams, Lee E, and Williams, Lee E. II. *Anatomy of Four Race Riots, Racial Conflict in Knoxville, Elaine (Arkansas), Tulsa and Chicago, 1919-1921*. Jackson, Mississippi: The University and College Press of Mississippi, 1972.

Wilson, William E. "Long, Hot Summer in Indiana." *American Heritage* 16, August 1965, pp 56-64.

Wilson, William E. *Indiana: A History.* Bloomington: Indiana University Press, 1977.

Wilson, William E. *The Wabash.* New York: Farrar & Rinehart, 1940.

Writers Program. *Indiana: A Guide to the Hoosier State.* New York: Oxford University Press, 1941 and 1973.

II. Newspapers

a. Indiana Newspapers

Evansville Courier

Evansville Journal-News

Fiery Cross

Indiana Catholic and Record

Indiana Jewish Chronicle

Indiana Times

Indianapolis News

Indianapolis Star

Indianapolis Times

Muncie Post-Democrat

Noblesville Ledger

South Bend Tribune

Tolerance

Vincennes Commercial

b. Oklahoma Newspapers (including Indian Territory)

Ada Star Democrat

Ada Weekly News

The (Maysville) Booster

The Byars Banner

The Byars Enterprise

The Byars News and Advertiser

The Choctaw Herald

Cushing Citizen

The Cushing Democrat

Cushing Independent

Garvin County Herald

Huyo Choctaw County Chronicles

Hugo Husonian

Madill News-Democrat

Madill Record

Marshall County New-Democrat

Maysville Friend

Maysville News

The Maysville Register

McClain County Democrat

McClain County News

Miami Herald

Daily Oklahoman

Pauls Valley Enterprise

Pauls Valley Republican

The Purcell Register

The Purcell Republic

The Shawnee News-Star

Surphur Democrat

The Tulsa Tribune

Tulsa World

The Vinita Daily Chieftain

The Vinita Weekly Chieftain

Washington Democrat

Washington Press

Washington Progress

Wayne Gazette

Wayne Ignitor

c. Other Newspapers

Louisville Courier-Journal

New York Times

New York World

III. Records and other documents

Birth certificate, Florence Katherine Stephenson, May 12, 1916, Oklahoma City, OK.

Death certificate: Katherine Stephenson Thompson Wayland (Mrs. H. Russell Wayland III), May 12, 1978, Oklahoma City, OK.

Manuscript Collections:

Franklin College, Franklin, IN: Harold Feightner Papers in the Roger Branigin Collection.

Indiana State Archives: D.C. Stephenson and Ku Klux Klan collections.

Indiana State Library, Manuscripts Division: Harold

Feightner Papers, D.C. Stephenson Papers, Ku Klux Klan Papers; state newspaper collections on microfilm.

Indiana State Historical Society: D.C. Stephenson Collection.

Oklahoma Historical Society, Oklahoma City, OK: State newspapers collections on microfilm.

Marriage license, Nettie Hamilton and David Curtis Stephenson, March 26, 1915, at Tishomingo (Johnston County), OK.

Military records, David C. Stephenson, Iowa Department of Veterans Affairs, Boone County, Iowa.

Newspaper obituaries:

David Curtis Stephenson, *Louisville Courier-Journal*, Sept. 17, 1978.

Florence Katherine Stephenson Thompson Wayland, *The Shawnee (OK)*

News Star, May 14, 1978.

Oral interviews with Harold Feightner and Asa Smith, Indiana State Library, Manuscripts Division.

Prison records, David Curtis Stephenson, Indiana State Prison, Michigan City, IN.

Trial records:

Records of the Hamilton County, Indiana State Supreme Court, and Marion County courts.

Findings of the Indiana State Supreme Court in 'Stephenson v. State," Case No. 25310, January 19, 1932.

Knights of the Ku Klux Klan, Inc., v. the Independent Klan of America, Inc. No. 904 in Equity. In the District Court of the U.S. for the District of Indiana, March 1926.

Knights of the Ku Klux Klan v. Reverend John F. Strayer, et al. No. 1897 in Equity. In the District Court of the U.S. for the Western District of Pennsylvania, April 1928. (Decision reported in *The Federal Reporter*, 2nd Series, Vol. 26 (2d), June- August 1928, pp 727-729.

State of Indiana v. the Knights of the Ku Klux Klan, No. 41769 in the Marion Circuit Court of Marion County, IN, November 1928.

Videotapes:

"The Birth of a Nation," D.W. Griffith's 1914 movie, available on videotape.

"Cross of Fire," miniseries shown on NBC November 1989.